CATCHING SIN

J. SAMAN

ONE

ISABEL

I SHOULDN'T DO IT. I know I shouldn't. But that doesn't stop me. If anything, it pushes me forward. When I arrived at the club, Carla was standing there, waiting at the dressing room door, her features worn with agitation. I knew it wasn't going to be good news. Magic had called out sick. Again. Her son has asthma and without sufficient health insurance, the poor boy is sick a lot.

I feel for him. I feel for her. It's not easy being a single mother with no education and no help. And bringing the kid here, where cigarette and cigar smoke permeate the air, isn't the answer. Most times this happens, Carla pulls a waitress from the floor.

But tonight, she asked me.

"He's not going to like it, *mija*," Carla warns me, her sun-weathered hand clasping my shoulder as she stares intently into my eyes. "I know he's not. But we're desperate. I'm afraid to ask you to do this because I don't want you getting hurt. I just don't know what else to do."

Our profits are down. Big time. Things are always a bit slow in the winter, especially after the holidays. "I know. The girls could really use the boost in customers and tips," I agree. So can I, truth be told, which is why I'm saying yes when I shouldn't. "Maybe he won't find out," I suggest even though I know it's a lie. I'm trying to make her feel better for asking me the impossible request.

I don't wait for more of the useless back and forth on this. Instead, I walk to the dressing room to get ready. Finding a vacant spot, I park my ass in the chair and face my reflection in the lighted mirror. I wasn't going to argue with Carla. It's my ass on the line, not hers. I'll make sure of that. I understand what she is saying, and I know she's right, but desperate times are what they are.

It's been slow. Most of the girls who dance here have families relying on their money to get by. My life is not like theirs and it never will be. I'm alone and drowning.

So, screw it.

Consequences be damned.

The club has a routine. One girl does a set on the main stage, performing a choreographed dance to a specific song. Then, there's a twenty-minute intermission where girls dance on the peripheral stages—mostly just swinging and grinding on the poles—to whatever music our resident DJ feels like playing. At that point, the customers will request lap dances and buy their drinks, and even purchase time in the champagne rooms.

Then the process begins again.

Tonight, I'll be dancing in the middle of the night. Carla will spread the word like it's the coming of a tornado because I haven't danced here in over six months. Not since Anthony Conti discovered me on stage and physically dragged me off it by my hair in front of everyone. I was his best, most popular dancer—not that he knew it until he caught me. Since then, I've strictly been waitressing. I'm not even allowed to give lap dances, which means my tips, my earnings, aren't good enough.

I barely make ends meet now and that's because I refuse Conti's money.

He may own me, may control my entire fucking life, but I don't give him that. It's the one area I feel like I have a modicum of control. So, even though this will likely end badly for me, I can't help but crave the money I will earn. Five minutes on that stage can be a month's rent, utilities, and food. If Anthony doesn't hear about me dancing, I could make more with lap dances, and if I am really lucky, the champagne room.

Private dances bring in excellent money.

Even if I hate every single second of it.

Shaking out my hair, I flick my hands back and forth, my fingers spread, trying to work out my unease. The makeup I wear to wait tables is not the same as stage makeup. Honestly, I don't usually try all that hard. Typically, I just put on some mascara, blush, and lipstick and call it a night. No one really cares what the waitresses look like.

Flipping open one of the compacts, I attack my eyes first, lining them in thick kohl and adding on dark shadow for a smoky look. "Thank you," a voice says behind me. When I peek up in the mirror, I find Ariel's reflection smiling at me. "Carla said you're really good on the stage. I heard her talking with a few of the customers, advising them to call their friends to see your show. How come you don't dance if you're that good?"

Ariel is new. A pretty blonde thing with curves like a nineteen-fifties pinup. "I used to. But now I just waitress."

She gives me a knowing smile, like we have something in common. "I get'cha. My boyfriend doesn't like it either, but the money is too good. Just don't tell your guy." She gives me a conspiratorial wink, and I force a smile.

"Right. I'll see you out there."

"Sure thing."

She takes the hint and leaves me to my face. After I paint my lips red, I flip my head upside down and brush out my hair, spraying the hell out of it. Standing up straight, I brush it out again and now it's full, soft waves. Perfect. I borrow a fur coat from Whisper, slip on some thigh-highs with a lace border and leave on my killer heels.

All black, because that's all I wear.

"You're next, Star," Carla calls out to me, and that old familiar jolt of sickly butterflies takes over. I don't hate dancing. It's actually the more enjoyable part of this business. It's everything else that I hate. The stupid grinding. The pretending to fuck a pole or the floor or whatever prop I'm using. The taking off my clothes and baring myself to lust-drunk men.

That first time is the hardest to get through. That first moment you take your top off and reveal your breasts to the screaming hordes of drunken, horny men feels like the lowest moment of your life. The men make you feel dirty and trashy and cheap. They make you question yourself and who you are. Make your sense of self-worth plummet into the bowels of nothingness. No one spends their childhood striving to be a stripper. It's the sort of thing that happens mostly from a lack of options.

And, as Ariel said, the money is too good, especially at a club like this one. But I was never given the option to work here. Dancing was my act of rebellion and I took it. That didn't make me impervious to what I was doing. If anything, I was more aware.

That first time may be the hardest, but that doesn't mean the job gets any easier.

The DJ announces that I'm up next. Sucking in a deep breath, I wait until the stage goes dark and then I walk out, forgetting the rank stench of cigarettes, cigars, and dry ice. Finding the stool in the center of the stage, I straddle it backwards.

I close my eyes.

Clear my mind of the what I'm doing and focus on the why I have to.

And let the music take over.

I dance my heart out the way I was taught. My body twists and grinds, doing what it knows how to do. I flirt and tease the men who line the stage, mentally counting the money they've thrown at me. That's how this game is played. How the dance goes.

I coax and tantalize.

Smile and conquer.

This is the part of the show I hate. Where I'm bare and exposed and so wanting to be done I can hardly force myself to take the next step in the dance. Twisting around, my eyes collide with a strong steely gaze, my heart jumping up in my chest at the unexpectedness of it. I blink. Once. Twice.

The guy is hella hot. Even in this strange lighting I can tell that. He's beyond tall, with what I think is sandy-colored hair, clipped nearly into a buzz cut. His eyes are big and bright against the multi-colored strobes. His cheek bones are high, sloping perfectly into the most angled, chiseled jawline I've ever seen. Tall and imposing and ruggedly gorgeous. Intimidating. The man makes my hands tremble and my heart rate pick up with just a single look.

And that look . . .

I don't like it. It's unnerving. It's like he can see through to all the ugly parts of my soul.

Turning away from him, I finish the dance and collect all my money, blowing out a relieved breath as I go.

But the moment I step off the stage, Conti is waiting for me.

His fingers lace themselves around my biceps, a cruel smile turning his lips up as he speaks low and menacing.

"Come with me."

After he releases my arms, I slide on my faux-fur coat, but it does nothing to make me feel covered. I'm dragged into the office in the back and he shuts the door behind us with a deafening click.

I don't bother sitting. I stand, dull and despondent in the center of the room, tacky with sweat from my dance, yet uncomfortably chilled.

"What did I tell you about dancing, Isabel?"

I heave in a silent breath through my nose. "That you don't want me doing it."

His body slides in behind mine, not touching me. Not yet. He hums, practically in my ear. "And yet, you disobeyed me."

And yet, you still make me work here. Honestly, I think the man gets off on this. He doesn't like me working here, but he doesn't have me fired and doesn't give me other options. Wait, let me hit the refresh button on that. He doesn't *allow* me to have other options.

I twist around and meet his eyes head-on. Daring him. "Yes. I did. I needed the money, and so do the other girls."

His black gaze narrows infinitesimally, but other than that, there is no visible evidence that my words get to him. His hand wraps around my throat like a blanket. Gentle, warm, and soft. His fingers brush my pulse, toying with the *thump, thump, thump,* delighting in my body's reaction to him before he squeezes hard in warning. So hard, I lose my ability to breathe. The press of his fingers constricts the pulse he was thumbing. I choke and gasp involuntarily.

Giving him the satisfaction of my weakness angers me.

"You will come and sit beside me. Your shift here is done. You will keep your head down and your mouth shut, and I will consider how best to deal with you later." The squeeze around my throat intensifies, his face inches from mine. I reach up automatically, gripping his hands, a natural life-saving reaction that I'm trying to tamp down because it will only spur him on. Sparks dance behind my eyes, my lungs burning from starvation. "And if I ever hear of you on that stage again, it won't just be you that I punish. Understood?"

I hate you. I hate you. I hate you!

He loosens his grip and I gasp in a rush of oxygen. "Yes, sir," I push out past my constricted vocal cords.

Because that's all he has to say to get my ultimate, unquestionable capitulation. That is forever the price he holds over my head. He tortures me. Ransacks my privacy. Holds me captive. And yet, that one line is ultimately what holds me prisoner.

He purrs like a lion, pleased that he's put me back in my place.

"Now go and get dressed."

He releases me, and I walk out without running. My neck hurts and my throat aches, but it's not the first time and likely not the last. I change back into my waitressing uniform, and when I exit the back room, I find him sitting across the way. I hesitate. Desperate to make a run for it. But I pull myself together and sit beside him. I ignore the way he immediately begins speaking to his guests—some people from China that Conti is insistent on speaking Chinese to. It's just as well. I don't enjoy listening to the things he has to say. Not even when he mentions someone named Maddox Sinclair, asking Cami to make sure his drinks—and whatever else he wants—are on the house. Peeking up, I realize the man speaking to Brian in the far corner is the man I saw from the stage. The one who came off like he was seeking out my soul instead of my tits.

Of course it's him. Of course he knows Conti personally.

It makes me hate him on principle.

Though, I have to admit, for a fleeting second, I wish this Maddox would request me to sit beside him. To give him a lap dance. To tell Conti to fuck off.

He doesn't. He's not stupid, I'd guess. He can read a situation without fucking it up. Maddox doesn't linger. He finishes off his drink and conversation with Brian and leaves with another blatantly curious glance in my direction. Balls. The man has big balls, I'll give him that. I bet he even has the dick to match that impressive set.

And he's even better looking up close.

And bigger. He's a freaking linebacker. That doesn't make me hate him any less.

He's not a button. Conti doesn't buy drinks for his henchmen. No. This man is something else.

I'll admit it, I'm insanely jealous. I get the impression he has dealings with Anthony Conti and yet, retains his freedom. A freedom I'll never know.

TWO

MADDOX

THE RED, blue, and yellow lights of the club pulse across the stage as I enter. The bouncer, Chris, gives me a nod and doesn't bother to card me—they card everyone, from the new puppies all the way up to the old men—nor does he ask for a cover. I'm not here for the show and he knows that. I'm here for Brian, my chief of floor security for Turner Hotel casinos, who also happens to work as a bartender in this club three nights a week.

I've lived in this town for nearly four years, been the Chief Operating Officer for Turner Hotels for the last two. Chief of Security for the hotels goes with that job. But this is Vegas, a town known for pushing every envelope and limit ever conceived. Which means certain jobs fall well below my pay grade. Those tend to be my favorite jobs. The ones where I can get my hands dirty. But tonight, I'm not in the mood for the bullshit. For the strip-club vibe. Or the putrid stink of cigarette and cigar smoke that always cling to my clothes. And I'm definitely not in the mood for the horny old men upping their blood pressure pills as they pinch asses, or the bachelor party dude-bros hollering and trying to get the girls to fuck them for free. I'm not in the mood for the lights or the incessant pounding of house tick-hop music.

Honestly, the appeal of places like these was never there for me.

But tonight is not up to me. I would much rather be eating a great meal and drinking a fantastic glass of something while relaxing with my feet up and watching the Atlanta Hawks game. It's Friday and the week was nothing if not long and filled with endless crap. But, tonight somehow became about an asshole carrying a gun into one of my hotels and threatening his girlfriend—making a huge scene and scaring people—while two other shadows tried to cheat with loaded dice. It was a nice little operation. I'll give them that.

It was also a pro job.

Brian catches my eye, giving me a 'what's up' nod, as he pours a line of tequila into shot glasses without spilling a drop. I approach the bar, leaning against the polished wood.

"I need ten, mate," he says with his thick Australian accent. "Star is filling in for Magic tonight, and I have about fifty drink orders to finish for these drongoes before she goes on stage."

Whatever. Who cares? I shake my head. "I have no idea what anything you just said means, but do your thing. I'll wait." I slide onto one of the empty barstools, slipping out my phone just as everything, except the under-bar lights, goes black. "The fuck?" I hiss out.

"You should watch the show," Brian suggests from somewhere in the blackened abyss. "Star isn't allowed dance the stage, but she had to tonight. I swear, everyone from the gray hairs to the joeys barely off their mother's teats are out tonight to watch her. Somehow word got around fast." Does he have to speak like we're in the outback? I'm from Georgia; I get it, we have our own obscure way of speaking that most of the world doesn't understand, but come on. I have no idea what he's talking about. Which isn't all that uncommon for Brian, but at this moment, I'm not in the mood to tackle our language barrier. I check emails and respond to crap that doesn't really require my response when the cacophony of assholes whistling pierce my eardrums. "Strip clubs," I mutter under my breath.

I glance up reflexively toward the stage, but there's no way they could have seen the girl yet when everything—the club, the stage, the lights—is dark. A pounding *bump, bump, bump* starts, building up the anticipation. The lights flash on, pulsing with the beat, turning from black to purple as they swirl around the room before landing on an obscure form in the center of the long, phallic-shaped stage. I squint, attempting to decipher what my eyes are too slow to make out.

Fur coat.

Stockings.

Heels.

That's it. Whether or not there's a woman under all that is beyond me. If there is, I have no idea where her head is.

The symphony of swirling lights converges on her form in the center of the stage, upside down, sprawled across a bar stool. That pose tells me she's not new to the stage, despite what Brian just said. That *bump, bump, bump* continues, intensifying until she twists her body upright, straddling the back of the stool and dry humping it like it can actually get her off.

"Lord Baby Jesus," the man on my left groans. He's easily in his sixties, and judging from the band on his finger, has a wife. Probably a few kids and a string of grandkids, too. Yet here he is, watching her like he's on death row and she's his last meal. The man on my right doesn't even have words—his drool is too busy coating the floor.

Her body begins to undulate, grinding against the chair as her legs rise in the air, forming the most perfect V. Wider. Wider. She's practically doing a split before she stops spreading her legs. She throws her head back, her dark hair cascading down as she moans, her hips continuing to work their magic on that stool. *Damn.* What did Brian call them? Drongoes?

Evidently I'm no better because I can't pull my gaze away.

I'm watching with unadulterated lust as this woman with her

long black hair and curvy hips—because the rest is covered in her fur coat—dry humps a stool that is so annoyingly *there* it's ridiculous.

I am not this guy, I remind myself. But it's to no avail. I *am* this guy. I'm succumbing to my baser instincts. To caveman-quality brain function and Viagra-level blood flow.

It's just a show. Nothing wrong with watching the show.

Her arms reach behind her head, her palms planting onto the wood of the stage, arching her back and leaving her legs wide open and . . . *fuck.*

"Yeah, baby." That's Asshole One beside me. The one with the big-ass family. He crosses the room like a dog seeking a bone, tossing two hundred-dollar bills on the stage for her. She ignores them, like his offering isn't near her standards. More bills go flying. Hundreds, fifties, twenties. Thousands of dollars find their way up on that stage and all she does is dry fuck that stool with her legs in a V and her body completely upside down.

But then, she twists off it, flying backwards and landing on those crazy heels of hers. She rights herself, turns to the asshole who was beside me, and winks. Her hips sway, contorting this way and that. She locates the pole in the center and wraps her legs around it, spinning in so many circles, I'm dizzy. And enthralled. And hard.

She doesn't take off the fur coat.

It's an afterthought. This girl doesn't need to be naked or show any flesh to get hearts pumping. Her tease, her dance, is the ultimate weapon, and damn is it sexy. Then she flips her body upside down once more, fastening her body to the pole by knotting her legs around the metal and, yes, sweet baby Jesus, that fur coat slides up, revealing the creamy, toned flesh of her stomach. The room erupts into cheers and I inwardly twist that I am suddenly reduced to their level.

Men encroaching upon the stage in droves, each one vying to be just an inch closer than the other, desperate to be the one she notices. Only they don't dare touch that platform. They know once they do, they're out on their asses and their fantasy woman is lost to them.

She holds that position, arms extended out, until the music

changes once more. That *bump, bump, bump* eases, turns from pounding to drippingly slow and erotic. Her body slides down the pole with incredible precision until she lands on the floor in a graceful pool of flesh.

More cheers. More whistles.

But she ignores it. Ignores the chants and demands for her attention.

The music escalates once more, building suspense. She flips over, grinding across the floor of the stage, picking up bill after discarded bill and tucking them into her G-string. The girl offers her clamoring fans a seductive smile and an artful wink. Someone yells, "Show us your tits!"

She stands up, holding her coat tighter across her body, covering those perfect mounds with her arms like the crude request offends her.

"These?" she asks in a sultry voice that's all suggestion and temptation.

"Yes," the collective groan of men echoes through the room and she smiles, flipping around and shaking her glorious ass to the beat. The cries of the crowd grow inflamed, demanding. The dollars thrown increases and all she's done is give us a hint.

A peek.

A thrill.

I glance over at Brian, who is smiling a wide, toothy grin. "Told ya, mate," is all he says. I shake my head, like I'm trying to figure out the ruse, but I know I'm not fooling him for a second. He feels it, too —you'd have to be dead not to—and the bastard works here. The reality is, they don't make women like this in real life. All curves and muscle and softness and femininity, and pure, uncontained sex appeal. They don't make women with thick, ink-black hair, flowing in ribbons down her back. They don't make perfect asses like hers.

When she spins around, her coat somehow discarded during my exchange with Brian, I catch her full, real, unbelievable tits, and I know I'm just as screwed as every other guy in here. But it's not her perfect body that's holding my attention now. Or even the way she's moving.

It's her face.

It's those large, obsidian eyes. The arch of her black brow above them. The fan of what I think are real lashes around them. The high pitch of her cheekbones. The smooth, creamy slope of her cheeks, brushed in shimmer. The thin, narrow slope of her nose and the beautiful fullness of her red lips.

My breath stalls. She's fucking stunning.

Her eyes cast around the room and lock on mine. Something inside me burns, thrashing around violently. I hate the sensation of it. She doesn't smile for me. I don't even get a wink. Instead, she frowns like she doesn't like the way I'm making her feel, either.

Christ. *What the hell am I doing?*

Her eyes drop from mine and I turn around, moving back to the bar and taking a seat all the way at the end that has no clear vantage point of the stage. I don't want to watch her like that anymore. With all those men around her. I don't even know the woman, but that one look, that one secret exchange . . .

Brian comes over to find me, finally, sliding a glass of bourbon across the polished wood in my direction. "Thank you," I say, needing the liquor I rarely drink to clear my dry throat and muddled mind.

"Look at these blokes," Brian muses, wiping a glass with a clean towel. "Nothing fucks you up like a woman."

I raise my glass to that sentiment and take another pull. "Why isn't she allowed to dance if she does it that well and brings in the crowd?"

"Boss's orders. No one talks about Star much for that reason as well. She's quiet and keeps to herself, and I keep my nose out of her trouble. I'd advise you to do the same."

Huh. I don't like the way he says that. Her trouble.

Still, I clear the woman from my thoughts, focusing on the reason I came here. "Tell me what happened today at The Palace." That's what we call The Turner Palace. There's the Turner Grand, The

Turner Palace, and The Turner. Those are the three hotels and casinos we have on the Strip. Across the country, there are a dozen other hotels and resorts under the Turner name. My best friend, my brother in arms if not by blood, is Jake Harris Turner—the owner of the entire empire.

Brian launches into his account of today's events. He believes the couple with the gun and the guy with the loaded dice were working together and that they might be part of a sting, since we had a similar incident with a roulette ball and a man having a heart attack last week. I'm just hoping they aren't connected and part of a larger underground organization out to get us.

"We switched out the dice after their fourth seven in a row, but by that point, he'd already cleared over twenty-five grand."

I hum, taking another sip as I think this over. "And the dice looked just like ours?"

"Identical. There must have been something on it he knew about that we didn't notice because he continued to pick those two dice every time he was offered the six to choose from."

"Or he just felt the weight difference."

Brian nods, leaning forward and resting his elbows on the lip of the bar.

I run a frustrated hand through my short hair. Cheating is nothing new in this town. Some are your run-of-the-mill fools who think they can get away with it. Some are card counters who think they're smarter than everyone else. Some are well-funded, well-designed and well-executed. Like these people. And those are the ones you have to watch out for.

"Did we get him? I know we have the guy with the gun and the woman, but I didn't get an update on the loader."

"Yes. Marlin handled the initial conversation and then the bloke was handed over to police as required by law."

"Damn law." I laugh and Brian smiles, going to refill my drink before I wave him off. "I wish I had—"

"Brian," a woman's voice interrupts me. "Sorry."

I sit up and the blonde in a tiny black uniform gives me a contrite smile. I've seen her in here before on the few occasions I've come to speak to Brian. "Mister Conti is here and asked that we not only give Mister Sinclair another drink of our best bourbon, but that he is not to pay for anything while he is here. Also, he requested a bottle of Cristal be delivered to his table with three glasses. Star will be joining him, so we'll be down a waitress for the rest of the night."

Brian curses under his breath and I spin around, searching the room until I find Anthony Conti. His eyes are on mine, like he knew I'd seek him out the moment his name was dropped. I raise my glass in thanks and he nods. On his left is an older gentleman I've never seen before. Across from him is a woman whose back is to me, and on his right is the dancer, Star. Her eyes are cast to the floor, her posture rigid. She's no longer only wearing a thong or even a fur coat. She's dressed in a black tank top and mini skirt of sorts that covers her up enough.

It's the uniform of the other waitresses.

He's not touching her and she's not touching him, and I have no idea what her relationship is with her boss who also happens to own the Las Vegas underworld. I turn my back on Anthony Conti, and address the blonde waitress. "Please thank Mister Conti for me. His offer is extremely generous and much appreciated."

"Of course." But I hear the slight tremor in her voice and see the uneasiness in her posture. A pulse of tension now beats through the air. Brian loads up a tray of expensive champagne and crystal flutes that I imagine he keeps hidden somewhere else, and the blonde leaves us.

Finishing off the last of my drink, I slide the glass away. Brian gets back to work, our conversation done for now. My need to be here in this club over, I stand up, throw my jacket back over my shoulders and turn to face Conti. He's involved in a heavy discussion with his guests, my presence all but forgotten. But as I meander my way through the club, Star glances up and instantly finds me, like she was waiting for me all along. She follows me all the way to the exit, the smallest quirk of an eyebrow, the tiniest hint of a smirk playing on her lips.

She shakes her head at me, like I'm crazy for daring to peek in her direction considering who the man on her left is. But to hell with it. I smirk back.

Because if I was intrigued before, I'm downright enthralled now.

and appreciate the chiseled lines of his handsome face. My gaze rakes over the defined lines of his chest and abs beneath his plain gray t-shirt and the bulging of his biceps that appear as if they're teaching that t-shirt a lesson in dominance. I feel his body heat envelop me as he takes a step forward. I wish he would have maintained his distance. Now I'm forced to crane my neck and peer all the way up, seeking out his beautiful blue eyes.

I inhale a silent breath, berating myself for getting into this position with such a dangerous man. It's that long, smooth, angled jaw; those soft, full lips that are such a stark contrast to the raw interest in his eyes. I find myself leaning forward, drawn to his delicious magnetism like a moth to a flame. This is terrible. The bastard is silently killing my bitter resolve.

"I'm a waitress."

"I know."

"Then stop looking at me like I'm something else." I want to stomp my foot at him like a petulant child would. He's playing games he knows nothing about.

"Hard not to when I know you are."

And there it is. It's not even about the dancing or the fact that he pretty much knows what I look like naked. It's Conti he's after. Conti he's interested in. And I'm the eternal go-between. "I'm no help for you with him. Stalk someone else."

"You misjudge my intent, Starshine. I don't care about him."

I narrow my eyes, practically hissing at him in Parseltongue. "It's always about him. Especially with people like you."

His eyes devour me, dropping to my thrift-store blouse and jeans and worn-out boots before crawling so damn slowly back up. A fire I have no name for or experience with burns my skin, making my face flush in a way that angers me more than it turns me on.

"You don't have to tell me." He smirks. Smiles. Plays foolishly with my life and his. "I'll find out all on my own."

"Then you're even more daft than I pegged you to be."

Now he laughs. "Probably. Catch you later, Starshine. Let me know how those Depends work out for you."

Ha. Ha. *Bastard.*

I turn back to my cart. I don't watch as he walks away. I don't listen as his footfalls grow fainter. And I certainly don't care that he's feigning interest. No. Because he may play the game and know how to flirt up the caged girl, but at the end of the day, he's not a dumb man. He may not know the *how* of my life, but he knows the *who*.

It's all an act, I tell myself.

And I tell myself that it's just my protective instincts making me search for him out of the corner of my eye as I finish my shopping. Nothing else. I get into the checkout line and there he is, two lanes over from me. The girl checking him out shamelessly flirts, twirling her hair and giggling at something that cannot possibly be nearly as funny as she's making it out to be.

I sigh before I can stop myself. So lame. But I can't pull my eyes away, either. I watch voyeuristically in snarky mean-girl horror as she writes something on his receipt before handing it to him. He stares at the piece of paper, at her swirly handwriting that I can see from here, and then says something I can't hear. She gave him her number. After not even knowing the guy for two minutes.

He takes the receipt and tucks it into his pocket.

I scoff. Whatever. I don't care. Let him call Miss Perky Blonde Checkout Girl. Let them date and get married and have babies. "Whatever," I grumble under my breath and leave the store, ignoring the curious glances of my own checkout person.

I make my way outside, turn toward the street and watch as my bus pulls away from the stop, heading back out into traffic. *Crap!* Now I'm going to have to wait another fifteen minutes for the next one. God, I hate today. And today is supposed to be one of my good days.

"Missed the bus or can't find your car?"

I roll my eyes. Of course he's behind me.

"There'll be another bus soon."

FOUR

ISABEL

MADDOX UNLOCKS his car and opens my door for me. Gentle-man, indeed. And here I thought those were extinct along with the dodo bird and the western black rhinoceros.

I eye him curiously as he shuts my door with a triumphant smile and then goes about loading all the groceries in the back. He slides in and starts the car with the press of a button.

"Who are you?" The words are out of my mouth before I can stop them.

He laughs but doesn't answer my question. Not that I expected him to.

"What's your address?"

I tell him, and he punches it into his navigation screen, and off we go. His car is nice. Soft leather and a cool, sleek interior. The best part? It smells like him. But with an added something—like he took this Jeep off-roading through the wilderness and some of that clean, fresh air stuck to his seats.

"Will you tell me your real name now?" he asks as the sun slowly begins its descent on the western horizon. The orange ball of flames that accompanies this time of day and this time of year casts a warm glow, making his hair appear almost blond and his eyes colorless.

I take in his profile. He's just a bit too perfect. The sort of beautiful that is almost impossible to look at for any length of time. It's the type that affects you without permission, like a pleasure-filled pain you can't help but indulge in.

"No," I reply. I'm not sure why I'm holding onto it. It's stupid, really. He can just look up my address to figure it out.

"Are you always this stubborn?"

"Usually." I laugh, but it's humorless. "Where are you from, Maddox?" I make a point of saying his name, hoping he'll think my stubbornness and bitchy attitude are unappealing. He's the sort of guy a girl could develop a crush on without even breaking a sweat. And a crush is the last thing I need right now. "I know it's not Las Vegas."

He glances over at me for a brief moment, then turns back to the road. "No. It's not Las Vegas. I'm a Southern boy, but since you're being a brat and won't tell me your name, I won't tell you where I'm from."

"Fair enough. And before you go off and get ideas about me, I'm not fucking you."

He grins, his hand abandoning the wheel in favor of rubbing his jaw almost absentmindedly. "I didn't expect you would."

"Expect? Maybe not. But you shouldn't hope, either."

Now he laughs and it's big and hearty, the sound warm and so very unwelcome as it seeps into my pores. "I can't do much about that, but I promised I'd be good, and I will be. So, how about after we drop off your adult diapers, you let me buy you dinner?"

"A date? You're asking me out on a date?" I fold my arms and lean back against the leather. I'm smirking. But that's only because I'm doing my best to fight the smile threatening to break free.

He catches my eye. "Yeah. I think that's exactly what I'm doing."

"Can we go somewhere to talk?"

"I'm working." I don't bother glancing up when I answer him. I just carry my empty tray back over to the bar.

"I'm willing to pay for your time."

I laugh bitterly. "I don't do lap dances anymore, and I don't fuck patrons." Or anyone, for that matter. Getting involved with a man is as ridiculous a notion as escape. *Didn't I mention that to you already, Maddox? Oh, I left that part out? My bad.* I'm rocking my pity party hard tonight. "Go away, Maddox." I don't need more of an audience.

He sighs. It's heavy and hard and annoyed. Maybe a bit tired, too. Or maybe I'm projecting. "That's not what I'm here for. I promise. I just want to talk about a job proposition."

Is he fucking psychic?

"You don't know me well enough to offer me anything other than me spreading my legs."

Now he growls. "Stop it. Stop that shit now. It makes me fucking insane. You're not spreading your legs for anyone. Me included. So, go find us a quiet space where I can talk to you. I'll pay." He thrusts a handful of hundreds into my peripheral vision. "Is three thousand enough?"

More than enough. The champagne room is twelve hundred for an hour with a single girl. The club gets nine hundred, and the dancer gets the other three. It goes up by three hundred a girl. If he's paying me three thousand . . .

Who carries that kind of cash around unless they're like Conti?

"Fine," I grouse, like I'm just so done with him being here that his money is inconsequential. "Follow me."

I take his outstretched hand and tuck it back into his pocket before he gets jumped for the cash. Then I cackle. Out loud. No one in their right mind would jump Maddox. He's a mountain.

"Are you okay?"

No. I'm really not. I think I'm finally losing it. I'm stuck between rock bottom and the hardest place. "I'm fine." I shut my mouth and find Carla. "I'm taking room three for an hour."

She eyes Maddox for a long hard moment and then turns her gaze back to me. "No. You're absolutely not."

"He's a paying customer. Maddox, give Carla twelve-hundred dollars please. The rest you can give me in tips."

Carla's eyes widen, but she extends her hand and takes his money. Probably because my eyes plead with her. I need the money and she knows it and Maddox probably knows it. That's all there is to this moment. I'll dance for him for an hour and then I'll never have to see him again because I won't be working here anymore. I should have never let him drive me home. I most definitely should not have let him buy me dinner or kiss my neck or look into my eyes like he gave a shit.

He's a soldier and I'm a fool.

"Room three is yours. Give me five minutes and I'll have a bottle brought in."

"Save it," Maddox says coolly. "I'm not here for champagne."

Of course he's not. Carla doesn't even bat an eyelash. She just smiles warmly like it's all good and waves us on our way.

"He'll have an expensive bourbon on the rocks." I have no idea what make he likes, but I know Carla can improvise.

"I'll bring it straight away."

"No thanks. Again, I'm not here for that."

I shrug. "Suit yourself. It's your private show."

I picked room three for a reason. It's the smallest of our champagne rooms. Typically, men—usually in large groups given the cost —come into the champagne rooms requesting multiple women. They expect bar or bottle service. Maddox hasn't requested anything other than my presence and a conversation. We enter the room and I instantly turn on him, pushing him down onto the curved bench seat. His eyes lock on mine as he unzips his hoodie, removing it.

I shouldn't be excited by this. But I am.

It's the most alive I've felt since I was on that stage last week. In this private, intimate setting, I'm willing to play whatever game

Maddox is after—especially for that money and those heated looks he can't help but shower me in. I'll make him wish he never met me.

"What music would you like to me to play?" I ask, watching him as I turn on the small tablet affixed to the wall in the corner. "We have everything."

"Rachmaninoff?"

I laugh despite myself. Has Conti told him everything about me? Fucking bastard. "He doesn't do much for strippers. If classical is your thing, I'm sure we could rig up The Nutcracker and I can do the Dance of the Sugar Plum Fairy."

"What if I just want to talk?"

I glance up over my left shoulder, eyeing the cameras and microphones honed-in on us. "They'll pull your ass out of here. This room is for music, dancing, and stripping."

He holds up his remaining cash like a fan. It's an offering. A bribe. "They won't kick me out of here with this. Sit down. Let's talk."

"Didn't get what you were after the other night? Funny, I thought we talked plenty."

"Starshine." It's a warning. Probably for me to shut up and not mention our dinner when there are ears everywhere. Fortunately, that's not my name and I don't have to obey him. "What if I just want to talk without the dancing?"

"And what if I just want to dance without the talking?" I can't talk to him. I know he's here at Conti's bidding. And I hate all things Conti. Including Maddox. Instead, I queue up the iPad and put on *Porn Star Dancing*. If ever there was Vegas trash that women like me are forced to dance to, this is it. Maddox frowns, sitting back in his seat as I climb onto the stage in the center of the room. I'm wearing my waitress outfit—a tiny black skirt and tank top that stops just below my tits, leaving my belly completely exposed.

"I don't want this," he repeats, a bit more emphatically. "I just want to talk to you."

I don't care. There are no coincidences. The fact that he's here the same night Conti fires me . . . Nope. Not having it. The stupid beat and horrible lyrics begin, and I jump up, locking my legs around the brass pole, swinging around and around.

"Please stop."

"You paid for the room." He stares me down and I drop my feet to the platform, facing him before I spin around, my hands falling as I bend forward. I angle down, my back arched, almost into downward-facing dog so he catches the crest of my ass and my black thong as it rides up my ass. Peeking at him from between my spread legs, he narrows his eyes at my cheeky grin. "No? Not happy yet? I can fix that."

"Starshine—"

"That's not my name. In this club I'm known as Star." Righting myself, I spin around to face him, slowly slipping off the top of my half-assed tank and tossing it away. I'm left in only my black bra and skirt, which is still more than he saw me in last week, so what the hell is the difference at this point? Two things can happen in here. One, Conti finds out and loses his shit. Two, Maddox gets to the point faster and leaves. I'm banking on both.

"Fuck," he hisses, his fingers raking through his short hair. "I need to talk to you. Not watch you strip naked."

I turn around, bending over backward, my palms hitting the floor on either side of my face, my tits practically at my chin as they spill out of my bra. I curl my legs up, one by one, wrapping them around the pole. I roll my body once against the cold, metal meeting his eyes and savoring the flame I catch in them. My legs glide up, my hips undulating to the wretched beat of the music. Maddox licks his lips, and I lift my upper body, my hands grasping the top of the pole and swinging around it, sliding down slowly until my ass lands on the plastic platform.

"How did you learn how to dance like this?"

"I've been working here forever. The girls taught me a thing or two over the years."

"How old are you?"

I laugh, rolling my back and hips in his direction. "That's not a real question, Maddox. It's certainly not a job proposition. Try again."

He's a mess. All flushed cheeks, full lips, tousled hair and firm, hard body. Christ. The man is making me wet and he's not even doing anything other than looking pissed off.

"Fine. How's this then? I'd like to offer you a job as my executive assistant."

Bending forward, I set my palms on the red floor, showing him an obscene amount of cleavage. Straightening my legs, I hoist my ass in the air. My head raises, and our eyes meet. "I don't even know what that position entails. I've never been an assistant, let alone an executive assistant. I'm calling bullshit. What are you really doing here? And why tonight of all nights?"

I climb up the pole until I'm practically doing a handstand again, then swivel my hips against the pole in slow, hypnotic circles to whatever stupid, inane song comes on after the previous crap. I wish Maddox would leave. Just get up, toss me the money and go. Any high I was riding from dancing is starting to wane. I don't want him to see me like this anymore. I don't want to dance sexy. I just want to go home and be alone, lose myself for a bit in my misery before I pick myself up and start again.

"Did you graduate high school?"

I pause, peeking up to glare. "Yes. I graduated high school." *With honors, asshole.*

"Then you're qualified." I flip over and stand up, pressing my back into the pole to gaze down on him. He's so broad. So tall. So beautiful. All muscles and power and smiles that promise softness and devotion. Such crap. Everything about this man is a lie. I bet that whole grocery-store-slash-dinner thing was as planned out as everything else. And I fell for it. Men are the worst.

I quirk an eyebrow, tilting my head and folding my arms over my chest to try to cover some of myself up, while retaining the non-existent dignity I wish I had.

"Somehow I doubt a high school diploma is the only qualification needed. Let me clue you in on something. I'm not the hooker with the heart of gold. I already told you, I don't fuck men for money. If you think I'm a stripper working her way through college, you're wrong again. My higher education was earned here on this stage and it's the only one I'll ever be allowed to obtain. I'm not the cliché you're after. There's no saving me. I don't know what you're really doing here, Maddox, but I'm not the girl for your fake job. I have no experience. I have no education and no skills. Leave. Now. Please," I add before I can stop myself. This man. He cuts me down. Weakens me with bull-shit pretenses.

His expression softens. "Please talk to me. Come sit here with me and talk." He pats his thigh. It's not in a "come heel" way. It's in a "I want to feel you close" way. It's the same expression he had right before his mouth met my neck. I want to tell him to fuck off, but I suddenly need the contact more than my pride. I climb down off the stage and crawl over him. My legs spread, skirt hiking up, nudging over his firm, muscular thighs.

I sit back, and he smiles. His hand climbs steadily up and I shake my head. "You can't touch me, Mister Sinclair."

That hand drops just as quickly, and he nods, laughing lightly, before growling like the caveman he is. "God, you're so tempting."

"That's the point. What are you really doing here?"

"I already told you. I want you to come work for me as my executive assistant. The job includes a good salary and excellent benefits."

I smirk, sitting up straighter as I inch up his thighs. "And the catch?"

He half-groans, reaching up to stop me, but then seems to think better of it. He drops his hands. "You have to work for me."

I shake my head. None of this makes sense. "I won't fuck you."

He laughs, but it's slightly strangled. "I won't touch you, Starshine. I swear."

I meet his baby blues head-on. "Why me, Maddox? There are

hundreds of girls who could do the job better. Explain yourself. And don't you dare bullshit a bullshitter."

"You're the perfect person for the job. And before you start with that unqualified stuff, you've read more business textbooks than I have. I saw your bookshelf, remember? You're smart. You're street smart. You're honest and ruthless. You'll keep me in line with that naughty, naughty mouth of yours."

"Focus," I chastise with a barely contained grin. His gaze drops to my lips as his tongue darts out to wet his.

"I'm trying. It's not so easy with your tits spilling out of that black bra and your panty-covered pussy dangerously close to my cock. Your lips are right there." He licks his once more.

"You wanted me on your lap. This is on you."

"True. Not my best decision thus far." He laughs, dragging a hand across his cropped sandy-brown hair and down across his jaw.

"Not the best boss then, are you?"

He laughs—loud, sexy, and hoarse. "I will be. That's a promise. It's this moment of lust that's killing me. It's your scent and heat and the way you look so goddamn hot all over me."

I pick up his discarded hoodie and throw it over my shoulders. It's about ten sizes too big for me, but it's warm and smells like him and I think I like it. "Better?"

He frowns. "Much."

"What's the salary?" I ask, getting back to basics.

"Eighty-five grand to start plus full benefits."

My eyes widen before I can stop it. *Jesus.* His hands go for my hips, but I quickly smack them away. He smiles so wide I can see all his perfect, white teeth. God, he's so handsome. He could easily be the hero of my life if I let him. Or the destructor.

I lean forward, my lips hovering over his ear to keep the words from the microphones. "I'm the wrong girl for you in so many ways, Mister Sinclair," I whisper, rolling my hips. He groans, his hands clasping my waist under the large hoodie surrounding me, inching me closer to where he wants me most, yet holding me firm enough that I can't move. "I am entangled with the wrong man. You can't buy what someone else already owns. Don't do this. Walk away while you still can." I pull back and stare into his eyes, willing him to see my honesty there. He needs to know even if it kills me to say it. "I'm the girl you regret."

"Never," he hisses harshly, finally not giving a shit if we get caught because he grips my hips on the outside of the fabric of his hoodie. Mirroring my honesty, he sucks in a deep, resigned breath and says, "You're the girl I risk everything to save."

Christ.

How do I fight that?

"What do you say?" he asks, leaning back and speaking in a microphone-friendly tone. "Will you take the job?"

"Hmmm," I hum as if I'm actually mulling this over. It's the worst thing to say yes to. I have no idea what I'm agreeing to because there is no way this job is on the level. No way he came here tonight, the very night I get fired, out of the goodness of his heart to offer me something like this with no strings. I'm getting in way over my head, but I can't say no. I need this too much. "I guess you've just hired yourself a new assistant. I hope you know what you're doing." *And I hope I know what I'm doing.*

SEVEN

MADDOX

"MISTER SINCLAIR?" I drag my gaze away from the screen of my monitor over to find Mallory, Jake's assistant, standing in my doorway. "There's an Isabel Bogart here to see you."

My eyebrows draw together as I sit up straighter. "Who?"

"She claims she's your new assistant."

I stare at her for half a beat, then burst out laughing. Isabel Bogart. I guess that's her name. How disappointing that she didn't tell me herself. "Yes," I say, standing and rolling up the sleeves of my blue button-down shirt. "Thank you, Mallory. Isabel is my new assistant."

From the look on her face, Mallory clearly has a million questions for me. Honestly, that sentence felt weird coming from my lips, so I get her reservations. In all the time I've worked here, I've never had an assistant. I'm not really the type of guy to ask someone to do things for me. Truth be told, Jake only has Mallory because she's worked here forever and knows this business and this town better than anyone—including Jake. I glance around my office and realize I have no idea where to put her. "Is there a spare office somewhere we can stick her?"

Mallory raises a single eyebrow. "An empty office? You mean, like the one across the hall from your office? You know, the space set up for your *assistant*?"

Wow, it's not even nine yet, and I'm already messing this whole thing up.

I cross the room and slap a hand on Mallory's shoulder, surveying the space she was speaking of. "Is that where she's supposed to go?"

Mallory nods and rolls her eyes at me. She's entitled, and I've most definitely earned it.

"Okay. Then let's put her there. And get her a laptop or tablet or something. She's going to need an email account and a phone and whatever the hell else executive assistants typically get."

"Maddox." She pushes me back into my office with both her hands planted on my chest. "What are you doing with this girl?" she asks suspiciously, her voice a touch above a whisper. "Is she even qualified? I'm not trying to be a bitch and I'm certainly not judging. I mean, I'm a Vegas girl myself, but she's, um . . ." Mallory trails off and then nods her head over her shoulder, urging me to step into the hall.

"Dressed like a stripper," I finish for her on a groan when I catch sight of Starshine—er, I mean Isabel. I blow out a hot, heavy breath. She's wearing a short, tight, black, tank-top dress that barely conceals her ass and tits. At least she's wearing flats. Her long, black hair is tied back in a low ponytail, and to her credit, she's not wearing any makeup other than maybe some mascara. She's standing in the middle of the long corridor with people working all around her. Instead of slinking into herself, she's standing tall, with a confidence I doubt she feels. She's brave. I'll give her that.

"Thanks, Mallory. I'll take it from here."

I approach her slowly, watching her as she scrutinizes the office. It's bright over here, all tall windows and streaming sunlight. It makes her creamy, porcelain skin glow, giving her a sweet, angelic, and fucking young appearance, despite her attire, which is designed for catching sin. As if she senses me watching her, she swivels around, and her black eyes meet mine head-on. Out of all the times I've seen her, that afternoon in the grocery store is my favorite. She wasn't wearing a stitch of makeup. Her hair was down, but not done up in exaggerated waves. It was soft and natural. She wore a simple blouse that did nothing to accentuate her curves, and skinny jeans that were a size too big. Her simplicity was stunning. Staggeringly so.

That was the real Isabel.

The one standing here comes off as a caged lioness.

Scared. Vulnerable. Resilient. Fierce.

I should know better than to touch a caged animal. They're forbidden, therefore beautiful and desirable to all who look upon them. But it's their cage that makes them desperate and unpredictably deadly when necessary.

I left the club with a serious case of blue balls and a new assistant. Whatever this thing is that Conti is doing with her, I don't think she's in on the scheme. At least not yet. She tried to warn me off. It was kinda cute, really. But I wasn't kidding when I told her she was the girl I'd risk everything to save.

At least, she could be.

She could be part of my penance. Another way to try and shift the karmic tide. I'll never be able to undo what I did—some mistakes are too big to fix and some deeds too egregious for forgiveness. But I can still help her. I can play both sides of this game. Even if I don't come out the winner.

"Good morning, *Isabel*," I greet her, catching the tiniest hint of a smirk at the use of her real name.

"Good morning, Mister Sinclair."

"Have you met with HR already?" She nods and holds up an ID badge. "Great. Then drop your shit and come with me." I guide her to her new office. "Don't bother looking around, you'll be back soon enough." She tucks her purse and ratty, black coat into her closet, then turns, waiting on me for further instructions. That makes me blissfully happy in ways I don't want to think about. I place my hand on her upper back—in the office-approved neutral zone—and guide her back toward the elevator.

She glances all around and then up at me, her eyes wide with surprise. "Where are we going?"

"Down to one of the shops in the galleria. It won't open for another hour, which is perfect."

"But . . ." she trails off as we step onto the elevator. "Wait. I thought I was going to be your assistant. That's what you said." Her dark eyes narrow in on me. "You never mentioned working in the stores. Those places would never hire a girl like me."

And that just pisses me off. "What does that mean? A girl like you?"

Her arms fold across her chest. "A stripper, Maddox. A cocktail waitress. I don't know who or what you think I am, but that's the reality of it."

"You know that's not how I see you, right? That was your job, not who you are."

She rolls her eyes at me like I'm some misguided, naïve fool. Maybe I am. The world is full of preconceived notions, the majority of which are wrong—case in point, Miss Isabel Bogart.

"You're not working in the store," I tell her as we step off the elevator and make our way through the resort, heading in the direction of the shops. "But I can't have you dressed like that, either."

Her head drops to the floor, her teeth sinking into her bottom lip. Her footfalls slow as she slips farther away from me. "I didn't have anything else to wear."

"I know," I reply, because I do. She tried. It shows in the flats and hair and lack of makeup. But she can't wear that dress.

Let me rephrase, I can't be around her in that dress.

"I went to the library on Saturday and googled executive assistants. It said professional corporate attire. I own trashy dresses that I used to wear to work and second-hand jeans with holes in them. That's it. This was the best I could do."

I pause outside one of the closed stores. This part of the resort is mostly empty as nothing opens here until ten. Spinning around, I grasp her shoulders, hoping to catch her eye, but she's still not looking at me. I can't have that. My hand slides beneath her chin, raising it up. For the first time since I met this girl, I see just how hard her life really is. This onion just showed me one of her layers and it makes me seriously want to fight the world for being so fucked.

"I didn't mean to make you feel bad about your dress. I understand you've never worked in this sort of environment before and that's why we're going to go into this shop before it opens and get you some new clothes. Professional clothes. Clothes that don't make me want to rip that skimpy piece of fabric from your body every time I look at you."

A small smirk tugs up the corner of her lips. "Then maybe you shouldn't look at me like you've seen me naked."

"You remember when I told you that I can't help but hope?"

She nods, her smirk growing into a smile.

"Well, certain things I can't forget. But I'm trying here, and if we're going to make this work, we have to fix this."

She makes a tsking sound, dramatically shaking her head. "You men are all the same. So damn easy, we hardly have to try. But according to the information HR provided me with this morning, you're not allowed to speak to me like that. I can sue you for sexual harassment."

I let out a harsh laugh. "That dress is sexual harassment. Now come on."

She resists when I try to guide her in. "I can't afford anything in that shop."

"You're not buying them, I am."

She shakes her head adamantly, taking a step back and out of my reach. "I'm not letting you *Pretty Woman* me."

"What?" A bemused laugh slips past my lips. "What the hell is that?"

"*Pretty Woman*. It's a movie with Julia Roberts and Richard Gere."

"Okay. I still have no idea what that has to do with buying you new clothes."

Isabel huffs out a loud, exasperated breath, her hands fisting on her hips. "I'm not your whore. I may have accepted this job, but that doesn't give you dominion over my life. I don't want to be indebted to you."

Wow. This girl really does not have an ounce of trust in her. And why should she? I've done nothing but touch and smile and flirt with her. The same as every other asshole she encounters. And considering how she got here, I know she's under Conti's thumb for some reason. She's already owned. Or was. She told me so herself. He may say he wants her out of his life. But that remains to be seen.

"Isabel, almost every employee who works for Turner Hotels, whether here in Vegas or anywhere else in the country, wears a uniform of sorts. Everyone from the cleaning staff to the dealers to the bartenders to the pool staff. Me?" I point to my dress shirt and slacks. "This is a uniform. I hate dressing like this. And if you worked at the pool, we'd provide you with a uniform. But you don't work at the pool. You work up in the corporate office and that requires a different sort of uniform. Does that make sense?"

She considers me for a moment as she absorbs what I'm trying to tell her. "So, you buying me clothes in this very expensive shop is your way of providing me with a work uniform?"

"Exactly. And I get a discount here, so it won't be as expensive as you think."

"Okay," she finally relents, but I can see how difficult it is for her. I'm dying to ask her about her relationship with Conti. It's something, all right. "I'll let you buy me my uniform."

I nod, relieved that she isn't fighting me further on that. But first . . . I take a firm step toward her and force her gaze up to mine once more. "I don't want to ever hear you refer to yourself as my whore again. You are not a whore and I do not own women. You are not indebted to me in any way and you never will be, regardless of what I buy for you. Am I clear?"

"Yes."

"Good. Now, let's go."

I want to take her hand and lead her in. I want to present her to whomever is inside this shop and tell them to spoil her because I'd be willing to bet no one ever has. But this is not the time for that. She is not my girlfriend. She is not my lover or even my friend. She's my assistant. My chess piece in a way. Except, I'm not the only one using her in this game.

"How old are you, Isabel?"

She growls under her breath. "Nineteen." Fuck. That's so young. *Too* young.

"Nineteen-year-old girls don't use words like dominion and indebted." Nor do they read textbooks on calculus, chemistry, history, and business. They also don't have books on learning Spanish, French, German, and Italian. This girl is an enigma. A fascinating one.

"Maddox, in case you haven't figured it out yet, I'm not most nineteen-year-old girls."

I smile at that. She certainly is not. I lead her into the store and tell Paula what Isabel needs. I ask her to put it on my account and then leave. I don't stay to play dress-up. Attraction is a unique weapon. It can be used against you so easily, has the power to manipulate the senses. I need to be focused. And from this moment on, there will be a division between us.

Boss and employee.

I text Jake and tell him to meet me in the security tower. All weekend I thought about Conti's favor. I recounted every detail about that night Starshine sat beside him at the club after she danced. I mulled over my exchange with him in his office and then that hour at the club in the champagne room. It was a lot to go over. A lot of fine details to sort through.

I reach the tower first, give Cash—our resident security ace—a nod, swipe an unused tablet and then head for the back room. It's the room where Gavin was waiting for Jake and me the day everything went down with Niklas Vaughn. It's the room that's heard more secrets than I care to think about. I take a seat in the large leather chair, swivel around to face the wall of soundproof glass and log in to the tablet. For full security access, you're required to either have thumbprint or facial recognition and a password. If I enter the wrong password twice, it locks me out for twenty-four hours. There is also a panic password that notifies the police instantly. Another one can shut down all access to every Turner Hotels' employee completely. Jake doesn't believe biometrics is enough. Anyone can be held at gunpoint.

I guess he has a point.

In any event, no one else in this business has a security setup quite like ours. It was designed by Ryan Grant and Luke Walker, old friends of Jake. They're former black-hat hackers, the best the world has seen, before they flipped sides and created an information security company. They've been helpful with other projects, too, and part of me wonders if we'll require their less-than-legal services before all this is done.

Scanning through the system, I locate the store where Starshine is currently shopping. I shouldn't be looking. But I am. The camera is in the ceiling so my angle of her isn't the best. But I do catch her smile when she turns around, her hands full of hangers lined with clothes as she heads toward the dressing room.

That smile . . . It's one I've never seen on her. It's not mischievous or flirtatious or even overtly sexual. It's . . . happy. Genuinely happy. I continue to watch as she talks with Paula. They appear to be laughing and having a good time while she tries on outfit after outfit. Shoes, purses, and even things like earrings are thrown in the pile. *Good.* Paula knows her shit, and I want Isabel to have the works. It's a small price to pay for that smile.

She's not my type, this girl. I usually like them taller, blonder, sweeter. More like Fiona, if I'm being honest. It was her dancing that caught my eye, but the defiant flash in hers is what held me. It's what makes her so damn irresistible.

Five minutes later, Jake enters, giving me a "what's up" head nod. I log out of the system and set the tablet down on the table. The door shuts with a heavy click, but he doesn't sit down. Instead, he faces me, crossing his arms over his chest and leaning against the glass as he waits me out. He's in a suit, sort of like mine, only his is darker and accompanied with a white shirt and a pink paisley tie. And a jacket. I hate wearing those fuckers. "Fiona pick out that tie? You look like a banker."

He glances down at it and then back up to me. "Fi thinks my regular ties are too boring. Too street-thug-trying-to-be-a-CEO."

"You are a street thug trying to be a CEO."

He shrugs a shoulder. "That's what I told her, but she bought me the tie anyway. I hear we have a new employee."

"Yep."

"Where is she now?"

"Getting *Pretty Womanned* or whatever."

"Huh?"

I wave him off. "Never mind. I don't know what it means, either."

He blows out a breath. He doesn't like this. But more than that, I know he feels guilty about it. About what's coming. "Maddox—" he starts and then stops. What can he say that he hasn't said already?

"I'm glad it's me and not you," I tell him, and I mean that. Not only because it's Isabel—that's actually a reason I wish it weren't me —but because he has Fiona, and she needs him. He's the CEO, and Turner Hotels needs him. I'm the lonely hunter. The guy who can never find absolution.

"You always say shit like that. And I'm going to tell you again that I wish it were the reverse. But it's done, and I'm with you, man. This isn't just about you. I'm in this, too, even if it's only from the periphery. Whatever you need. You know that. So, talk to me. What are you thinking?"

"That I'm not supposed to talk to you."

He chuckles, running a hand through his brown hair and latching onto the back of his neck as he waits. This is how we work. How our machine runs. Conti can make a million threats, but I'm not worried about Jake talking. And really, Conti would have to be a fucking fool to go after Jake Turner directly. We know this. It's partially how we got here.

"Are you going to tell me, or should I just continue to stand here like an asshole?" His brown eyes stare into mine. Not hard. Not even questioning or searching. Just focused. Determined. It's why we make such a good team and managed to survive this long. First in Afghanistan and then out here. Niklas Vaughn was not our first rodeo, though we don't typically go out and kill men. Not now that we're civilians.

"Why would he call in his favor using her? He could have had me up to his office, given me his expensive bourbon and simply asked me to hire her. Man to man. I probably would have done it. He has to know that."

"She's a puppet."

I nod. "But why call in *this* favor now? And do it in this way? Why tell me that she's different only to back that up by telling me he wants to rid her from his life? That's superfluous info, right? Window dressing."

"You mean why expose her as a potential weakness only to feign like she's not?"

I shoot at him with my finger. "Exactly."

"He's playing you. Playing us."

"That's a given. But why her? Is he looking for an excuse to kill me? Is he thinking I'll be a dick-led idiot and fuck her first chance I get?" *Well . . .*

"Conti isn't the type of man who needs an excuse to kill people. He's obscenely arrogant and has gotten away with it before. That said, he's after something very specific and knows that if he tried, he'd be opening himself up to a war he might not win. And really, what reason would he have to kill you? You're far more valuable to him alive than you are dead. For now, at least. He placed her here for a reason. My guess is to distract you. Should we have her followed?"

I shake my head. "I assume he's already doing that, and I don't want him to know I'm skeptical of her intentions."

"What about her access?"

"Limited and traced, but not restricted enough that she, or he," I add, "are suspicious of it."

"Agreed." He drops his hands, tucking them into his pockets like he's getting comfortable. Except, there is nothing comfortable about this. This is the beginning of something. Something we knew would eventually come, but still. Jake is right about one thing—Conti is obscenely arrogant. And better yet, the man thinks I'm stupid and blind. "But I still want her badge and code access restricted. I'd rather not find out after the fact that she's been places she shouldn't be."

"If she's a mole, I don't think she knows it yet."

"Probably not, but that's only a matter of time. Can you handle that?"

Good question. My elbows fall to my parted thighs, my face into my hands. I blow out a breath through my fingers as I think this through. "A woman. Why did it have to be a woman?"

Jake laughs at my *Indiana Jones* reference. "Better than snakes."

"She's likely one and the same. And we both know she's the next step in his plan."

"Then we have to watch her closely. And Maddox?"

I raise my head when he doesn't continue.

"Pretty girl with a fucked-up life aside, Conti did call in his favor for a reason."

I nod, because he's right and I know it. "Now we just have to figure out what he's going to do with it."

EIGHT

ISABEL

FIVE SHOPPING BAGS. That's what I ended up walking out of that store with. I told Paula, the saleswoman, that I didn't need this much stuff. That I didn't feel comfortable having Mister Sinclair purchase all this for me. She waved me off and told me to have some fun.

"He told me to outfit you with a complete wardrobe. So, that's what I'm going to do. Enjoy it, honey."

Once I got over the initial shock of the price tags, I did enjoy myself. Because never in my life have I worn anything like what I'm wearing now. It's a black—of course—long-sleeved, sweater dress that stops just above my knees and is form fitting without being tight. The neckline has a gathering to it, so it shows just a peek of skin, but no cleavage. It's made of cashmere and wool and is the softest thing I've ever put on my body.

I'm also in silk—like, real silk, I think—stockings and three-and-a-half-inch heels that are pretty and a little sexy, but completely appropriate for a work environment. Well, that's what Paula told me when she picked them out. I feel beautiful. Not trashy or overly sexy or slutty. I feel like a lady. Like I belong. When someone looks at me dressed like this, they won't know I've danced naked on a stage and that my mother was a drug-addicted prostitute who died from an overdose when I was a teenager. They won't know of the depraved, sick man I belong to.

I make it back up to the corporate floor and that Mallory woman directs me over to my small office across from Maddox's office. It's really just three walls and one of glass that opens to the hall without a door on it. But it's mine, and it's bright and it's awesome. On my desk is a new iPhone, a laptop, and a desk phone. She shows me where to store my new clothes and how to log onto my computer, then she leaves me.

I'm not good with computers. The only ones I've ever used are the public ones at the library and they are limited. And old. This is a new laptop from the looks of it. A Mac. I'm completely unfamiliar with those. I do manage to find the calendar, which has Maddox's schedule already on it, and my email account that has a bunch of welcome to Turner Hotels things in there, so I figure that's a good place to start.

A job. I have a real job.

I'd be giddy if I weren't so terrified.

Maddox steps into my office as I'm searching around on my new computer. I'm sitting, so he can't see my full outfit, but he's inspecting me from the waist up with an indiscernible expression. All my artfully crafted snark and bravado are slowly ebbing. Seeing this man naturally raises my hackles, but now I'm tired and emotionally worn out, and well, thankful. There, I admit it. I watch him watch me and I hate that I care, but I'm desperate to know if he likes what he sees.

He gives a tight nod.

That's it?

Fine.

Whatever.

His opinion shouldn't matter to me anyway.

"Now what?"

"I don't know, Starshine."

I scowl. I hate that he's still calling me that. I liked the way he said Isabel much more.

"I've no idea what to do with you. I've never had an assistant. Never really wanted one before, I guess."

I stand up at that. It practically shoots me out of my seat and I'm rounding the corner of my new shiny desk before I can stop myself, getting right up in his face. He doesn't flinch, and he doesn't step back. He doesn't even look all that shocked, which angers me further.

"Then why did you hire me?" He doesn't answer. "What am I doing here, Maddox, other than playing dress-up Barbie? Tell me the truth."

I don't know anything about this man other than his job title, his name, and that he's involved with Anthony Conti enough for Conti to buy his drinks and offer him whatever he wanted at the club on the house. If that doesn't set off big, ugly warning bells, I don't know what would.

More silence.

Christ, I'm so stupid for pretending this was real.

"Screw this. I'm out of here." I push off him and spin around, going straight for my closet that has my dress in it. I pull out the bags, one by one, digging through them like a fool because I can't remember which one I stuck it in. Maddox is still standing there, observing me while I have a breakdown. I can't take this. Feeling ridiculous is not a new phenomenon for me. But this moment might be one of the worst.

Finally, I locate it, yanking the black spandex fabric out of the bag and standing back up. The bastard is still there, only now his arms are folded as he examines me like I'm a curious spectacle he can't quite figure out. "Why are you leaving?"

"Because I don't like it when people play games with me."

He rolls his eyes, and I'm about ready to kill him. "I hired you because I need an assistant. I might not have wanted one *before*," he emphasizes, "but I do now. I have a lot of work to do for the hotels and not enough time or help to get it done. I just don't know how to start. Like I said, I've never. Had. An. Assistant." He punctuates each word in a rough staccato, practically biting them out like I just ate up the last shred of his patience.

I pause, blinking up at him. "Oh." Heat swarms up my face like a gang of angry bees. "You could have gotten to that point a little quicker. You know, *before* I made a big dramatic scene."

"Probably." He eyes the crumpled dress in my hands. "But now that I know you're willing to walk out on your own, I think we can get started."

Huh?

"Are you going to change?"

I peek down at the dress and then back up to him. If I had my choice, I'd never take off the new dress I'm wearing. If it didn't cost more than my monthly rent, I'd probably sleep in it. I quirk an eyebrow. "My attitude or my outfit?"

His lips twitch. "Both."

"I wasn't planning on it. In either case."

"Good. Because I like you in your new dress. And, if I'm being honest, you're fun to rile up."

I flip him off and he laughs.

"Before you went all bratty teenager on me, I was going to suggest you bring your laptop into my office. We should probably sit and try to figure out this assistant job thing."

He turns on his heel, forcing me to scurry after him. I snatch my laptop from my desk and push through his partially opened door. His office is big. Not as big as Conti's, but still big. It's comprised of a large L-shaped desk with three monitors on it, a sparsely filled bookcase, a brown leather couch, a round glass table with four dark chairs tucked snugly around it, and in the far corner, a private bathroom from the looks of it. The opposite wall is all glass, overlooking the Strip and the mountains in the distance. No pictures of any kind.

Nothing personal at all. The only warmth in here is the sun shining through the tinted glass.

"Have a seat." He points to the couch and not the table and chairs, which I find a little odd but sit on all the same. It's soft and sleek, and I sink into the leather a little too much. I set my laptop next to me on the couch, keeping my mouth shut for once as I await further instruction.

Maddox closes the door and then turns to me, crossing the room with his long legs, until he's kneeling down on the ground directly in front of me, so we're eye to eye from only a foot away. I gasp, taken aback by our sudden proximity. The enticing scent of his cologne is everywhere. The light blue of his beautiful eyes is darker, filled with fiery determination. His strong, chiseled jaw—now freshly shaven—is locked tight. His lips. God, they're right there. Full. Commanding. Devouring. He's the full package. The one girls dream about. Forget movie stars and rock stars, Maddox Sinclair is the type of gorgeous that can make a girl's panties melt with a simple look.

My heart starts to pound, even though I'm doing everything in my power to remain impervious. I don't want to want this man. He's the last man on the planet I should want. Well, one of two. It's just attraction, I tell myself. A natural physical reaction to a handsome man and nothing more.

Mercifully, he doesn't touch me. He barely moves. He's just breathing in and out as he studies me. "You're beautiful, Isabel. There is no denying that." His eyes bounce around my face, feature by feature, before settling back on mine. "You're so stunning you have the power to drop a man to his knees."

He moves in closer until he's mere inches away now. I can't stop my eyes from sliding down to his lips. I wonder what kissing a man like Maddox would feel like. Would he make me feel safe, coveted, and adored with the gentle sweep of his lips? Or wild, passionate, and out of control as he dives in and takes what he wants? He made me feel all of that in my apartment and that was only from kissing my neck.

"But what happened the other night in your apartment and then at the club will never happen again. Our relationship, our interactions, are one hundred percent professional from here on out."

I swallow hard. He watches the roll of my throat as I nod my head, drawing myself away from my dirty thoughts. "Agreed." And thank all that is holy, my voice is calm and steady.

He rises swiftly, gracefully given his size, and then sits behind his desk, affording me the distance I need. "Now that we've gotten that out of the way, let's get down to business."

AN HOUR LATER, we walk out of his office together. I think Maddox finally figured out what he needed in an assistant, and I think I finally saw him as my boss. "Well, now that that's done, it's time for lunch."

"Lunch?" I laugh the word. "Didn't we just start the day?"

"No," he says, as he types something into his phone. "*You* just started the day. I've been working while you were shopping."

"All right," I agree with a shrug. "Lunch. I guess I'll see you later."

"Wrong again. Mallory informed me I needed to take you out. Something about that's what executives do for their assistants on their first day. Honestly, I think she's just saying that to keep you happy. She's thrilled you're here. So are the other assistants. It means less work for them."

I look up at him through my lashes. "You're taking me to a restaurant?"

His gaze shifts away from his phone over to me, and judging by his expression, he remembers our conversation about restaurants. "Yes. I'm taking you to a restaurant." And damn him, he smiles like a triumphant king returning from battle. "Shit," he mumbles, rubbing his smooth jaw. "Now I need to take you somewhere really good. This can't just be any old restaurant. A diner won't do."

I try to maintain eye contact, but it's hard. When he looks at me like that, it's practically impossible. Because this guy? This one right in front of me? He's the one I let drive me home from the grocery store. He's the one I let into my apartment. The one I let buy me dinner and kiss my neck as I sat on my kitchen counter, all the while knowing better. "A diner is perfect. I honestly don't care where we eat."

"You may not, but I do. I have an idea, let's go."

He marches toward the exit and I follow. That might be our new thing.

We walk down the Strip in the direction of The Venetian. I'll be honest, I've lived in this town my whole life and I've never walked the entire Strip. It's over four miles, and when you're a poor girl with very few friends, there isn't much for you here. But Maddox looks at me like I've got two heads growing out a lizard's body when I tell him I've never been inside The Venetian.

"Well, if we had more time and it wasn't considered romantic, I'd take you on a gondola ride." The idea of Maddox climbing into one of those long, narrow boats makes me laugh. He's so big, he'd probably sink the thing. "I told you I'm a Southern boy," he says as he leads me into a restaurant that smells out-of-this-world good. Like butter and grease and spices. My mouth is already watering, and we haven't even been seated. "But I didn't tell you I'm a Georgia boy. Now that I know your real name, I guess I can let you in on my secret." He winks at me. "This is probably as close to good Southern food as I can get around here. It's not quite my mama's biscuits, or my eldest sister's chicken and waffles, but it's damn close."

As excited as I am to eat in a restaurant and despite how good the food looks and smells, I wish he had taken me somewhere else. Somewhere less personal. Somewhere that didn't give me the inclination to really like him. I'm dying to ask more about his family. About his mama—as he calls her—and his sisters. I want to know him, and that's not the sort of desire that leads anywhere good.

We're seated in the far corner, away from the other patrons, and when the hostess tries to hand Maddox a menu, he shakes his head and pushes it away. "No. No menus. We're ordering one of every-thing on the lunch menu as well as everything on the dessert menu."

"What?" both the hostess and I squawk in unison. He has to be kidding. Who orders one of everything from the menu?

He peers over at me with an impossible grin. "It's why I wanted such a big table for just the two of us."

"Maddox, we can't possibly eat all that food," I rush out under my breath, trying not to be rude or ungrateful.

He shrugs, unfazed. "Whatever we don't finish, we can stick in the kitchen back at the office or you can take it home for leftovers. Either way, I want one of everything for us to try."

"I'll tell your waitress," the hostess says, recovering faster than I do.

"You're insane," I accuse once she leaves us.

"It's a special occasion, Isabel. Something to celebrate and all that. Now, tell me, how many languages do you speak fluently?" He leans back in his chair like he doesn't have a care in the world. Who is this man?

"What?" A bemused laugh escapes my lips as I finally relax in my seat and take a sip of my water.

"I saw all the books on your shelf that teach you how to speak a foreign language. You told me you've read all those books, so I'm curious."

I look away from him, out into the restaurant as I set my napkin on my lap. It's fun in here. Loud and busy with tourists and people enjoying their lunch hour the way Maddox and I are. "I don't speak any fluently, other than English. In order to master a language, you have to speak it regularly with someone or be immersed in it. I can read and understand Italian, French, and Spanish pretty well and maybe get by with speaking some of the basics." I turn back to him and smile. "I'm pretty good at sign language."

"Why did you want to learn all those languages?"

"I don't know. Languages interest me. I used to imagine what it would be like to travel the world and speak the language of each country I visited. What?" I ask, tilting my head. "Why are you staring at me like that?"

"Can I ask you something personal?"

"More personal than what languages I speak and why I wanted to learn them?" I challenge with a raised eyebrow.

"Well, you might get defensive about this question, and since this is the longest we've gone without arguing, I don't want to break our streak."

"*Moi?*" I point to my chest in mock indignation. "*Défensive? C'est impossible.*" His lips twitch, but I can see this one is serious and he's genuinely afraid of my reaction. "Okay," I say folding my arms across my chest. "Now you have to ask me."

"Why aren't you in college?"

That seemingly innocuous question just sprayed bullets in my chest at point-blank range from a shotgun. The wind is knocked out of me and I have to look away from Maddox's penetrating gaze before I start making a fool of myself and blubber in this beautiful restaurant. I suck in a deep breath, swallow it down past the lump lodged in my throat, and when I think I have control over my vocal chords and can speak in an even tone I say, "College isn't an option for me."

"Is it the money?" he presses quickly, like he's gearing up for a riveting motivational speech. I'm talking *Rudy* caliber—thousands of fans standing up to cheer and I'm carried out of this restaurant on the shoulders of all the excited patrons who cannot wait for me to go to college and take on the world. Only that's not my life.

"No. It's not the money. College is not an option for me," I repeat, a bit firmer this time, hoping he'll get the hint and stop now. He doesn't, of course. That's not Maddox's style.

"Why not?"

I shake my head, willing him with my eyes to stop pressing the issue.

Recognition dawns on his face, before it hardens into stone and he whispers one word. "Conti."

"Yes," is all I can manage because I can't tell him that when everyone in my high school was applying and getting in to colleges, he ripped up my acceptance letters. I got into NYU—only about two hours away from Justin—and he made it clear in no uncertain terms that I was never leaving. I would never go to college. And if I ever went behind his back like that again, he'd make me regret it more than I already did in that moment of punishment. Not only that, but Justin would suffer as well. Anthony Conti doesn't make threats he's not willing to back up. That day he told me I got off easy.

Didn't feel that way to me.

After that I gave up on pretty much everything. The books and learning languages and pictures of far off places on my walls are the compromise between wishes and reality. But maybe, with this new job, things will start changing.

Or maybe they'll get worse.

NINE

ISABEL

MADDOX AND I EAT. And eat. And eat until I'm so full it actually hurts to move. We barely made a dent, though Maddox did give it his best effort. He made me try some of everything. His favorites were the barbeque stuff and the shrimp and grits. I picked out a few things I wanted to take home for myself and the rest we wrapped up to take back for everyone else to pick at. The food is too good to go to waste and not share. I tried things I've never tried before. Brussel sprouts with pancetta. Collard greens. Fried green tomatoes. And the desserts? Holy hell, the peach cobbler gave me an orgasm right there at the table.

As Maddox and I reach the corporate floor, arms lined with to-go bags, I stop him. "Thank you," I tell him. "That was a lot of fun, not to mention delicious. It's been quite the day so far."

He chuckles at that last bit. "You're welcome. We'll do it again."

His pale blue eyes stare into mine as a smile curls his lips. This doesn't last more than a second. I know it's simple and innocent and that crinkle around the corners of his eyes means nothing. He told me so this morning. But still. A strange, unfamiliar sensation blossoms low in my belly and I quickly push it away before it gets a mind of its own. "I'd like that." *A little too much.*

In the kitchen—which is bigger than my entire apartment—three women are chatting at one of the tables as they drink coffee.

"Afternoon, ladies," Maddox drawls, and I swear, each of them peeks up and bats their eyelashes in unison. "Isabel and I come bearing treats." He drops the bags on the counter and steps back like his work here is done. "Have you ladies met Isabel?"

They shake their heads like well-trained puppets, hanging on his every word.

"Isabel, that's Sarah." He points to the one on the right. "She works in finance. That's Olivia, she's Morgan Fair's executive assistant. You'll meet him next week, because he's traveling now. And that's Carmen, head of marketing. Ladies, this is my new assistant, Isabel."

We exchange niceties as I shake their hands in turn and they welcome me to Turner Hotels. They're as sweet as sweet can be, all warm, genuine smiles and curious eyes. I sidestep their questions about where I worked before Turner, but other than that, they artfully ply details from me one after the other. In a matter of minutes, they know I grew up in Las Vegas, where I went to high school, that I graduated among the top of my class, my age, and that this is my first gig as an executive assistant. Olivia goes on to tell me she's very happy to have me here because now she won't have to do both Morgan's work and Maddox's.

"Ha, ha," he replies dryly as his phone rings. Sliding it from his pocket, his face lights up like a boy on Christmas morning. "Excuse me, ladies. I have to take this. Hey doll," he answers. "No. I'm never too busy for you. What's up?" He throws us all a wave and then walks out of the kitchen, the sound of his laughter trailing behind him.

"Must be Fiona," Carmen clicks her tongue with a knowing grin and wink for me.

Fiona? I'm dying to ask who Fiona is, but I don't want to come across as nosy or a gossip or even interested—which I am. Insanely so. Morbidly, pathologically so.

Instead, I go a different route. "What's Maddox like? Is he easy to work for? I don't know him very well."

"Oh my goodness," Sarah whispers. She's younger than the other two—early thirties is my guess—with blonde hair tied on top of her head in a perfect ballerina bun, sporting a very large, beautiful baby bump. She stands—with some effort—and waddles over to the bags, inspecting them with barely contained lust. "Is this all for us?" Her fingers run along the plastic before she loses the battle of trying to play it cool and opens one up, digging right in. "Fried chicken. Oh, and macaroni and cheese."

Carmen stands up, too, rolling her eyes indulgently. "Great. Now there won't be any left for the rest of us."

"Hey," Sarah snaps with feigned irritation. "I'm growing twin boys. Do you have any idea how many calories twin boys burn? I can already tell these boys are gonna eat me out of house and home just like their daddy."

"Whatever. Just save me a biscuit," Olivia says, rummaging through the bags, her back to me. "Maddox is a good guy. A very good boss. Always considerate and goes out of his way for the employees here." She waves a hand across the buffet of food we brought back. "Case in point. But really, I don't know him very well on a personal level."

"I doubt anyone other than Jake and Fiona does," Sarah chimes in as she shoves forkfuls of macaroni and cheese into her mouth. "God, this is so good." She chews and swallows, sucking the remaining cheese from her fork before adding. "He's very private. Doesn't like to talk about himself much. Especially after what happened a couple years ago."

"What happened a couple years ago?" I ask before I can stop myself.

The three of them exchange glances and then Carmen says, "It doesn't really matter. We're just happy to have you here."

A strange silence falls over us and I turn to Sarah, who is now stuffing her face with fried pickles and moaning in delight. "I know. Those are so good." I nod towards her belly. "Twin boys. That's exciting. When are you due?"

Her face lights up at my question. "Technically in early May, but I have a planned C-section for the end of April. These boys are my third and fourth."

My eyes bulge out of my head. "Seriously? Wow. You look incredible for a mother of four. What are your other two?"

Sarah is blushing now, and I can't help myself. I like talking with these women. The girls at the club were different. Catty. Always talking shit and getting into fights. I mean, not all of them, but there was a lot of competition between the dancers. I usually tried to stay as far away from it as I could. But these women are warm and inviting, and I have no women in my life I can talk to, even casually.

"A permanent headache."

I laugh and so do the other women.

"I have two girls, so these boys are going to be an adventure."

"I'm sure you're a great mom," I say as she lovingly rubs her belly. Sometimes you can just tell with certain people, and Sarah has that doting maternal thing to her. Not that I've ever seen it or experienced it for myself, but still.

"Well, you're like the prettiest thing I've ever seen," Sarah tells me. "I'm seriously jealous. I bet you can even see your feet with that tiny waist."

I laugh, trying to brush it off, but I don't get very far.

"She's right," Carmen agrees. "I'd kill for your hair. It's so lovely, and your skin . . ." She shakes her head, a half-smile etched on her face. "Ah, to be young and beautiful."

"Agreed," Oliva chimes in and my face is a perfect—and not

embarrassing at all—shade of fireball. "If it were anyone other than Maddox who hired you, I'd be worried for you."

My eyes widen of their own volition. "How do you mean?"

"Oh, you know." Carmen shrugs. "Men can never resist a pretty face. But don't worry. Maddox is a bit of a different type than most. Now. Let's get down to business. Are you seeing anyone?"

"Pardon?" My eyebrows hit my hairline and I most definitely have whiplash at the abrupt shift in conversation. Clearly Carmen is a master, because the case is officially closed on whatever the hell happened with Maddox a couple years back, and it's most definitely over about why Maddox is a different type than most.

"Oh no, you don't." That's Olivia and she marches back over to us, breathing red-hot determination, wagging her finger at Carmen. "She'd be perfect with my Chris." She pivots to me. "Because I'm sure a smart, young lady like yourself dates men who are tall, handsome and charming. Am I right?"

Oh lord. These women have known me for all of five minutes and are already trying to set me up with their sons.

"And that's why she'd love my Mateo." Carmen looks at me, tilting her head, her features softening. "He graduated with honors from Brown and is now working in marketing for Caesars. A total catch. Here. Give me your number and I'll have him call you."

Sarah is standing there with a mouth full of food, watching our exchange like we're a daytime soap opera.

Wow. How do I get out of this gracefully? The last thing in the world I want to do is upset these women. "I'm so sorry. They both sound like terrific men, but I'm not available to date at the moment." And that's not a lie, either, which is why it rolls off my tongue with sincerity. Though I can see that they're dying to push the issue, they don't. "It was wonderful to meet you all, but I really should be getting back to work." I force a laugh, hoping it sounds better than it feels. "It's my first day and I feel like I haven't done anything at all."

Mercifully, they all laugh with me, shooing me away.

. . .

THE REST of the day goes by in the blink of an eye. Mallory coaches me through and Maddox gives me the simple assignment of typing up a few documents, because evidently, and I'm quoting here, "I think better when I use an actual pencil and paper." At least his hand-writing is legible.

Even though I'm horribly new and terribly inexperienced and not the best typist in the world, I take on my job with gusto. Even if Maddox has been distant, maybe even a bit cold and dismissive since our lunch. But I'm not focusing too closely on that. He's a busy man with an important job and he doesn't have time to hold my hand or even talk to me other than to give orders. I get it. Because right now, I'm believing in the higher power of delusional thinking. Sense and reason can go find themselves a new play thing. I'm hoping that if I do this job really well and somehow manage to keep my mouth shut, Maddox will keep me here. And my previous employer will, for once in his life, be happy that I'm not stripping naked and will leave me alone.

Maybe, dare I say, forget about me?

Pushing it too far? Probably.

But by Thursday morning with no word from the soulless monster who controls my life, I'm feeling pretty damn good. I arrive at work first thing and make Maddox a cup of coffee even if I don't have to. I'm hoping it will lighten up his grizzly bear mood he's been sporting as of late. I hand deliver it, smiling at the way I managed to safely navigate through their crazy machine—it only took me three tries to get it right. I set it down on his desk with pride oozing from my pores and smile. Maddox peeks up at me, then down at his coffee and then back to me with furrowed brows. "Rat poison or strychnine?"

I roll my eyes. "Har, har. Maybe if you took a sip, you'd perk up. Not be so rough around the edges." But not even his bad attitude can sour my smile.

Maddox eyes me with equal measures of skepticism and concern.

"You're . . ." He tilts his head like he's searching for the right word. "Different this morning."

"Is that a compliment? How very kind of you to notice that I'm . . . different this morning. It's what I've always dreamed of being called."

Leaning back in his seat, he rolls up the cuffs of his light gray button-down shirt and my gaze inadvertently casts down to his muscular forearms. Once he's done with his task, he takes the mug of steaming hot coffee I brought him and brings it to his lips. I'm mesmerized, standing here dumbly as he takes a sip and sets it back down.

"It's good."

I shrug like I don't care all that much, as I mentally fist pump the air.

His hand glides along his smooth jaw as he takes me in from head to toe in a slow sweep. "Tell me, Isabel Starshine Bogart, why are you dressed for an ice cream social at the local teen club in hell, and why are you so chipper at not even eight in the morning? Where is the evil, defiant kitten I'm so used to?"

My cheeks grow warm as I peek down at my outfit. Black leather booties with silver studs on the heels, black leather pants and a black fitted blouse with silver stud buttons that match my boots. My hair is up on top of my head in a sleek, high ponytail and my eyes are lightly lined in black. I felt sorta badass when I put this ensemble on this morning, and now I just feel foolish. Foolish for being in a good mood and being hopeful and getting here early and making him a stupid cup of coffee. I narrow my eyes, jutting out my chin at him as I cross my arms over my chest.

"What's wrong, Maddox? No other giants to berate this morning to boost your over-inflated ego? Or is it that you couldn't find a woman who doesn't know any better to take home last night that's making you so pissy?"

He chuckles, standing up just so he can be imposing with our incredible height difference. The bastard takes another slow sip of his coffee, his eyes trained on mine as he does. He likes this game. This building suspense and giving-Isabel-a-heart-attack game. He's good at it. I'll give him his dues. He called me an angry kitten. I think I like that description because cats are feral, pretty, graceful, unpredictable and have claws that will scratch your eyes out if you're not careful.

"Do you speak to your lord and master this way, or do you save it all for me? Something tells me your pillow talk with him is a bit different."

My warm cheeks turn into matching infernos. Wow, he's really not holding back this morning. Maybe I went too far with my comment. I was angry and defensive, and I snapped back, knowing I probably shouldn't have. Especially to my boss. But . . . "I'm not . . . I mean, he's not my—" I'm at a loss for words. His brutal accusation wraps around my heart, digging its talons in so deep I feel myself bleeding internally.

He thinks I'm sleeping with Anthony Conti? That I'm his mistress?

A wave of revulsion consumes me. I should tell him the truth. Tell him that even broken strippers have limits. That when his lips pressed against my neck last week, it was the first time someone had ever touched me there in a non-threatening way. That despite the whore badge he clearly thinks I wear, I'm as untouched as a woman could possibly be. Conti may own my life, but he hasn't owned my body. Not yet. When he does finally decide he wants to ruin me once and for all and make me his submissive fuck thing, that will be the day I end my life or run so far he'll never find me.

If Maddox were closer, I'd likely take a swing and let the cards fall where they may. That's how fired up I am. Because this bastard didn't just pop my happy bubble, he exploded it into tiny unrecognizable pieces. And for what purpose? To intentionally hurt me? To raise those hackles he knows how to manipulate with skilled fingers? Well, I've had enough of that in my life to just sit idly by and take it from him.

I open my mouth to tell him everything. To let it all pour from my lips like the blood hemorrhaging in my chest, but a swell of emotion chokes me, and I know that as soon as I speak, I'll sob. All I can do is shake my head at him, balling up my fists so tight my bones creak, and turn on my heels to leave. *Don't cry. Don't cry.* I don't. I refuse to give him the satisfaction.

"Fuck," I hear him growl behind me. "Isabel, wait up."

I shake my head and walk faster, heading I have no idea where and not caring as long as it's away from him.

"I'm sorry. Fuck, I'm so goddamn sorry. Shit. Wait!" he yells, as I quicken my steps into a jog. He catches me in no time, his one stride equaling two of mine and then I'm practically swept off my feet, his arm encircling my waist as he swings me around to face him.

He glances around, checking to see if anyone is watching our little encounter, but they're not. It's early and only Mallory is here, but she's down by her office on the far side of the floor. Maddox carries me into an empty office, shutting the door behind him and setting me down on my feet once more. Storming over to the window like a pissed-off child, I stomp my foot as I stare out the window, my back to him.

"I'm sorry."

"Screw you." I know I shouldn't speak to my new boss like this. I know I'm dancing on the line of getting fired, but my pride is eating at me. I want to nail him in the balls, and I can't, and it's frustrating me to no end.

He heaves a harsh breath and I can't help but listen as he abandons the door and moves closer to me. If he touches me, I'll fall apart, so I stiffen my posture, ready to fight off whatever he's about to throw at me. I don't know why his words affected me this much. It's certainly not the first time someone has assumed the worst of me. Maybe it's because for the first time, it felt like someone actually saw me. Cared enough about me to ask personal questions and dig a little deeper beneath the surface.

"Isabel," he starts, his voice soft and lined with regret. His hands drop to my shoulders as he reaches me, and I shudder, stuck somewhere between wanting to shove him off and maintain his touch. "I didn't mean it. I had a shitty night's sleep and then you came in with that coffee for me and that smile and . . ." He trails off like he doesn't know how to finish.

"And what?" I press. "You thought you'd wipe it from my lips? Mission accomplished."

"No." He sighs, squeezing my shoulders. "And yes. But it's not in the way you think. I've been watching you. I've watched you with the other assistants and women in the break room when you go to get a drink. I've watched you when they help you with things. You smile with them and chat. You ask them about their lives. You listen, and they tell you things. I mean hell, Carmen, Sarah, and Olivia cannot shut up about you. About how smart, sweet, and beautiful you are. Sarah even said she has a girl crush on you. They knew you for two minutes, and Olivia and Carmen were trying to set you up with their sons. It's all so very different than the girl I've gotten to know. I just . . ."

He trails off once more, his warm breath brushing over the top of my head. His hands slide past my shoulders and over the top of my chest, crossing just under my neck as he pulls me back into his chest in a backwards hug. I close my eyes. Jesus. Nothing has ever felt as good as being held like this.

"I find you difficult to get a read on, and reading people well is what I do. One minute you're angry and feisty. The next you're broken and despondent. And then you're practically skipping with a smile so wide your entire face lights up. I don't know what to believe is real with you. Tell me what's real."

TEN

MADDOX

ISABEL SINKS back into my chest, her body less rigid. She fits into me so well, her head tucks under my chin perfectly. Her body so easily wrapped up in my arms. It's wrong, what I'm doing right now. All of it. Me trying to draw her off-sides. Rile her up. Her snapping back at me. Me chasing after her. Me holding her like she's something important.

I tell myself that I'm just offering her comfort. That this is my way of apologizing.

But I know better, and I bet she does, too.

Hell, Sarah's cried three times in the office and each time I've just given her a small pat on the back and walked away. I'm not good at that stuff. But with Isabel, it's so easy I don't even think about it. It's not awkward or an uncomfortable challenge I have to rise to emotionally. It's just there. Sort of how it was with Fiona, only different.

I turn her slightly to look in her eyes. Eyes that are alive with disdain and it pulls me to another level. It's enough just to hear the way her voice bites into me. This feisty raven-haired beauty who hates my guts has somehow managed to tug at every string I've got. I wonder how far off I am about her. I feel like I'm the only person on this floor—other than Jake, who hasn't even met her yet—to know the real Isabel.

But that's the question.

Do I know the real Isabel?

I'm starting to think I don't. That my preconceived notions are just that. Conceived.

I've never witnessed hurt the way I did when I accused her of being Conti's mistress. My words didn't stir embarrassment or even contempt. It was as if they broke off that last shred of her pride and flicked it away. I realized then that my assumptions about her might have been wrong. But it was Conti who planted that seed. He referred to her as different. Implied she was someone who was in his life, but now he was done with her. Right? Did I misinterpret that? What really messes with my head—worse than that rat bastard touching her—is that she's only nineteen. He's at least twice her age.

And if she were his mistress, then where are all the accessories that accompany belonging to a rich and powerful man like him? Clothes? Nope, those I bought for her. A nice apartment? Wrong again. She has stacked books as furniture and a couch that's older than she is. She also lives in a shit neighborhood. Expensive jewelry? She wears tiny silver hoops in her ears—one of them is bent—and nothing else.

So, what is his hold on her?

Why is he her great and powerful Oz, puppeteering her life and choices?

Her head falls back, practically tucking itself into the nook where my neck meets my shoulder. Her hair smells like a tropical oasis in the middle of the Caribbean. "Everything I've shown you, told you, is real. And I don't do that, Maddox. I don't open up to anyone. I am a closed, locked box." She releases a breath and it sounds so tired. So defeated. "I'm happy working here. I like the other women in the office, so I ask them about their lives, because I like to know that what they have is possible. I like listening to Sarah tell me about her kids and how nervous she is for twins. I like listening to Carmen and Olivia try to set me up with their sons, even though I know I'll never date them. If they want me to date their sons, it means I'm worthy of that in their eyes. Don't you get that? Can't you see how something like that could mean everything?"

Fucking Christ.

"You think you know me, but you don't. I told you that night at the club. I don't fuck men for money and I never have. There are no exceptions to that. If you want to know something, then just ask me flat out. I'll either tell you or I won't."

"I'm sorry," I tell her, wanting to plant my lips into the top of her head, but resisting. "You told me that night at the club that you can't buy what's already owned."

"So you assumed I'm his whore?"

"Did I assume you were sleeping with him? Yes. That's typically what it means when a man owns a woman. You told me you couldn't go to college because of him. You told me you couldn't date and that you've never been to a restaurant before. You danced in the club and it obviously enraged him enough to punish you for it. I couldn't figure out why a girl like you would let a man like him take over your life like that if you weren't in love with him. If you weren't his mistress."

She laughs bitterly, the sound reverberating through my chest. I really should release her, but I can't seem to get the mechanics of it in motion. She doesn't reply. Not even a deep sigh or a scattered, short, choppy breath or a sniffle of a tear. She stays silent after that laugh is finished, and once again, I hate that I can't get a read on her. It's infuriating.

"Isabel?"

"That's not always what it means when a man owns a woman."

I shouldn't care. That's what I told myself all day yesterday as I watched her. Or even the afternoon before. Or the one after our lunch together. And all fucking night, every night since I met her, I told myself I shouldn't care. There are lots of smart girls who want to go to college and can't. Lots of girls who don't date or have the money for nice clothes or furniture or restaurants. In fact, there are lots of people out there who have it a hell of a lot harder than she does.

So yeah, I shouldn't care.

But I do.

I want to help her, and I can convince myself that's what I'm doing by giving her the job that I was forced into giving her. She'll earn a good paycheck. She'll have benefits. I bought her thousands of dollars' worth of new clothes. She's making friends in the office and learning a profession she could conceivably continue for the rest of her life. But something is seriously fucked with her life and that miserable curiosity is quickly turning into a fascination.

Same as her.

And who has time or space for that in their lives?

"I'll never make assumptions about you or your situation again. Am I forgiven?"

"I suppose I don't have a choice. I work for you." There is a smile somewhere in her voice, I know it.

"I'll take it." When I think my shit is back under control, I release her and step away. She spins around to face me, her dark eyes clear and her smile genuine. Even with this rock-star Brunette Barbie thing going on, she undoubtedly has one of the sweetest faces I've ever seen. "I even have an olive branch to extend. I have to go downstairs to the spa and pool area this morning. I've been asked to take a tour of the new pool retreats they redesigned over the winter and see the new spa. You interested in tagging along?"

"Sure. Sounds fun. But what's a pool retreat?"

I laugh, taking her upper arm and guiding her back toward the door I had slammed shut. "Most of our pools in Vegas are open year-round and heated in the winter with minimal services for guests. But the pools here have gotten a whole overhaul. There are three large pools as part of the property, all with different themes. But we've added on a ten-thousand-square-foot European-style adult-only pool area that's a strange combination of a spa retreat and a nightclub. Plus, we redid the spa because it needed it."

Isabel scrunches up her nose. "I've lived in this town my whole life and I still don't understand it. I'm assuming European-style means topless."

I nod in confirmation. "It's a new trend. There are two sides to it and guests can pick which vibe they're into. There are cabanas in both areas, and we offer a special menu exclusive for this area."

"And why do you have to view this?"

"Because the facilities director asked me to as facilities in all our hotels report to me."

Isabel follows me out the door and down the hall. People are just starting to arrive. In fact, we have to wait for everyone to shuffle off the elevator before we can step on. "I suppose I shouldn't be surprised that this is a growing trend. I just wonder if this town will ever hit a limit."

I chuckle at that. "I highly doubt it."

"And you like this? This life?"

"Yes. I love all the naked women around me. You know, the girls in tiny bikinis who get way too drunk and occasionally pass out in the sun? They're my favorites. Sunburns and vomit breath really turn me on."

She rolls her eyes at me. "Just so you know, your sarcasm is not attractive."

I shrug, poking her in the side with my elbow. "Good thing my face is."

Her face drops to the ground to hide her smile, but I catch it all the same. "Your arrogance isn't attractive, either."

"I believe you've already mentioned my over-inflated ego once this morning."

"Once isn't enough to crush it down to normal human size."

"Baby, nothing on me is normal human size."

She laughs at that. The sound so warm and full of rich color that it stops me dead in my tracks. Literally. A group of tourists in matching hats nearly plow into me as we step off the elevator. She catches me looking at her and twists away, waiting for me to lead her. "Mind the brick wall," she mutters under her breath, and now it's my turn to chuckle.

"How do you feel about getting a massage?"

"What?" Her eyebrows draw together as she stares up at me like I'm speaking to her in French. Which I already know she speaks so she'd likely understand me better than she does this very minute. "A massage?" She's testing the words now. Likely waiting for the punch-line to my joke. Maybe still not catching my meaning. Either way, her confusion is adorable.

"Yeah. A massage. You want one?"

So, true story number one: We have just finished renovating our spa. True story number two: I got a call from the facilities director for our Las Vegas hotels asking me to come down and check it out. True story number three: He offered me free spa services for the rest of the day. But really, I have no time or desire for that crap. And I don't exactly trust Isabel enough to give her a real task to do. So, it's not wrong or even an abuse of company whatever by offering her a massage or a facial or whatever it is girls like. It's simply testing it out on our prime demographic. Right?

Absolutely.

"Sure." She laughs, still thinking that I'm joking. "Right after I take my clothes off and parade around the pool area in just my thong. I mean, I'm here to get the full Las Vegas resort experience."

I narrow my eyes at her, and she tosses her hands up in the air, shaking her head at me with wide eyes like I'm the one not getting it.

"When in Rome, Maddox."

Is it considered wrong or illegal to spank your new assistant's ass red? I swear, a woman has never infuriated me more, and I have four older sisters.

"I'm getting you a manicure and pedicure, too." I grab her by the upper arm and practically drag her toward the spa. Well, drag might be a bit of a stretch. It's just that I have long legs, and while hers are long and toned and sexy as fuck, they're not as long as mine. So, she has to practically jog next to me to keep pace. We enter the spa and I shove her forward, straight into the arms of a surprised girl in a black uniform with a name tag that reads Victoria.

"She's to have a full massage. I don't know what kind you guys have here but give her something that will turn this feral cat into a purring kitten. Then I want her nails and toes manicured. I'm sure she'll pick black as the color, but I can live with that. After that's all over, I want her to eat whatever she wants from the spa menu for lunch. No alcohol since she's underage. When that's all done, make sure she returns to me, so I can hear all about her experience in our newly redesigned spa."

"Um." Victoria appears lost for a beat but quickly recovers. "Of course, Mister Sinclair. It will be our pleasure to ensure Miss . . ."

"Bogart," I supply.

"Miss Bogart has the full spa experience."

Isabel spins toward me. I expect her to be pissed. I expect a rocket launcher to be aimed at my head, ready to fire. I expect her to unleash holy hell, but she doesn't. She smiles sweetly up at me. It throws me for a second before she steps into me, getting up onto her tiptoes as she whispers into my ear. "You're an adorably sexy bastard when you spoil me. You pretend to want me docile, but the joke's on you, *boss*," she emphasizes. "I'm going to enjoy the hell out of this, and you might just get exactly what you claim you want from me. Don't say I didn't warn you."

She plants a soft kiss on my cheek, throws me a wink, then saunters off with Victoria like I don't exist.

Shit, I think, rubbing my jaw as I listen to Victoria go over the spa's new amenities. She might just be right. Then what the hell will I do?

ELEVEN

ISABEL

I GET lucky and catch the express bus that drops me a half a mile from my apartment. This week ended about the same as it began. At least from a job standpoint. Honestly, it's been the best week of my life and sparring with Maddox is only part of that. A rather large part of that. But the lunches out in swanky restaurants and chatting with the other office women and the fucking spa treatments that made me feel like Cinderella? Yeah, best week ever.

But after I returned from my morning at the spa and my lunch in their restaurant, he sat me down in his office to reiterate his set of rules. It's adorable, really, since he's the one who continues to break them. We decided I didn't have to fetch him coffee unless I was getting some for myself. I would start making all travel arrangements, take notes in meetings he attended, field calls and emails. That kind of stuff. Stuff he hadn't really let me do all week. He explained that this would be like a trial period for us. If things went well, and we had a good working chemistry, then we'd expand my responsibilities, and eventually my salary.

I nearly drooled a puddle on his floor at that.

The next day went by in a blur. Maddox took me on a tour of each of the three resorts on the Strip. It's been all work since. Like real professional work without the naughty office banter that fuels my nightly fantasies. I think I've officially read too many romance novels because I swear, I have this whole role-play thing going on in my head and I might have crossed some of that over into my regular day with him.

Oops.

But today there was none of that.

For all the good that chat yesterday did, he hasn't let me do much around the office today. I'm mostly the office bitch, to put it politely. The one helping the other assistants with their menial tasks like picking up dry-cleaning, making coffee, picking out ties to match hankies, waiting on hold, making copies, and perfecting the art of saying, "I'm sorry, Mister Sinclair is not available right now, but I'm happy to take a message for you."

I didn't go to his meetings with him. I didn't weed through his emails. I didn't even make his travel arrangements. I haven't pushed it. I'm still too new at this game. Still learning as I go, and I figure he'll give me more responsibility once I prove myself capable to him.

I text back and forth with Justin on my ride home. We don't talk all that much on the phone—he's a teenager and texting is easier—but deep down, I know it's because we both understand the power of the spoken word when there are potential ears. He's doing well, studying for midterms, and claims that everything is straight on his end. It's a relief. It gives me the sense that maybe things are turning a corner for the better with my life. And it's with this calm, satisfied heart that I enter my apartment, and scream out in terror when the lamp beside my sofa clicks on.

"Christ," I yell, grabbing my chest and leaning back on shaky legs against my now-closed door.

"Nope. But close."

I roll my eyes at him and he actually chuckles for once. "What are you doing here?" I snap, not caring if he doesn't like my tone. Taking a breath, I try to steady my beleaguered heart.

"Did you really think I wouldn't come to see you?"

No. I assumed he'd come to me at some point. I just didn't think he'd be in my locked apartment waiting for me.

"How was your first week at Turner Hotels?"

"Fantastic," I deadpan. A smile spreads across Anthony Conti's face. He pats the seat next to him on the sofa, but I shake my head at him. "No. You don't get to play nice with me. You fired me."

"I saved you. I always save you."

I fold my arms across my chest and take a small step away from the door. He can't actually think I'm buying that. He pats that space again and I reluctantly cross the room, sitting beside him but leaving a large dividing space between us on the small, worn sofa. I want to draw my knees up to my chest and wrap my arms around them. I want to curl up into the smallest possible ball. I don't like being so visible to him. So exposed. He reads me like an open picture book, and no amount of backtalk or sneering hides my thoughts.

"Come here."

I don't move, and I know this will anger him, but tough shit. It's good for him when I don't instantly comply. Keeps him human. Keeps him from believing he truly is the master of the universe and that my position in life is to comply to his every will and demand. His head whips in my direction and he points to the spot directly beside his legs. He's not the sort of man that reaches over and picks you up to move you. He does it with silent force and terrifying threats. Though I'm tempted to see just how far I can push him and what he'll do if I really rile him up, I move to that spot.

"I don't like to be made to wait, Isabel. Don't do it again."

"Yes, sir."

"I see Maddox Sinclair took you shopping. How gallant of him."

"Why did you do it? Why did you fire me?" I tilt my head to

catch his eye, and he smiles down on me with so much love that it jilts me the way it always does. His devotion disgusts me and thrills me and makes me hate myself just a bit more because I know what that love is.

"Because when you were sixteen and I first took you as my own, the club was an easy place to hide you. An easy place I could keep an eye on you. Then you started *dancing*." The word hisses from his lips with disgust, his expression following suit, but I still haven't found regret for dancing. Minus the naked part and lusting men, I actually like the act. "You took off your clothes for strangers, and I cannot have strangers looking at what's meant to be only for me. This last time was the final straw."

"So now what?" I'm waiting for the punchline. For the sick end of the joke that tells me why he's here. Why I've suddenly found myself with a job at Turner Hotels. How Maddox Sinclair came to be in my life and came to offer me a job the same night I was fired.

Life is never that coincidental.

"You set this job up with Maddox." It's not a question. I know it's the truth, but part of me is hoping he'll tell me I'm wrong. That Maddox really could be a good guy and isn't in bed with Conti and that somehow the stars aligned, and he found me at my moment of need and came to my rescue.

"Maddox Sinclair owed me a debt. A large debt. I cashed in on it."

My eyes close before I can stop the action. It hurts even when I know it shouldn't. I figured it was something like that, though the notion of Maddox being indebted to Conti feels infinitely worse than him simply asking him to hire me and Maddox saying yes. Maddox doesn't want me there. Maddox doesn't need me there. He was just trying to pay off a debt and got stuck with the dumb, desperate stripper who didn't know better. All that talk about how I'm the girl he'll give up everything to save was a lie. All those lunches and spa treatments and easy, sexy banter that never failed at making my panties wet and my heart race were an act. I'd even go so far as to bet that this was in the works that day at the grocery store.

He's played me from the get-go.

There are no heroes in my world.

No white knights slaying my dragons.

The only person I can count on is me. I've known that all along, but every now and then I forget. Or maybe just get waylaid with hope and loneliness.

"I thought you'd be pleased."

"I am pleased," I lie. I'd rather be stripping and waitressing, because at least that was honest.

"Is Maddox not good to you?"

I shift my weight, trying to distance myself from him, but his arm wraps around my shoulder, grasping it and holding me firmly in place with a hard squeeze. A warning. "Answer me, Isabel."

"He's fine. I hardly know the guy. I could have gotten a regular job doing anything else. Why did you call in this debt he owed you over a stupid job?"

"Because there is nothing stupid about it. You're the executive assistant to the Chief Operating Officer of Turner Hotels. You see, I cannot get to Jake Turner. Not really, anyway. But Maddox Sinclair . . . I can get to him. He owed me, and I intend to cash in fully. You"— he taps the tip of my nose—"my beautiful Isabel, are going to help me do that."

Ah. And here it comes.

"How am I going to do that?" I bite out after he fails to follow that up.

"I want non-public information on Turner Hotels. Anything and everything. That's why I put you there. My little temptress, I have no doubt he's already eating out of your palm."

I turn to ice as a foreboding chill runs up my spine. Anthony Conti is a deliberate man and nothing he does is ever free. There's always a price. And I've just become the sacrificial lamb.

"How on earth do you expect me to get you that sort of information on Turner Hotels?" I'm trying for incredulous. I'm trying to come across as an annoyed and sarcastic and belligerent teenager. I come nowhere close to meeting my mark.

"You'll do it because you have to, Isabel. I expect you to get me everything you possibly can on Jake Turner and Maddox Sinclair. On the way their operation works. On the way it all works. The rest is for me to handle."

Translation, for me not to know about. That's a blessing, at least.

I shake my head, my eyes burning with tears I don't dare shed. Goddamn him! Goddamn him for doing this to me. For being such a sick, greedy bastard that his billions aren't enough. For trying to blackmail me.

"I won't do it. I *can't* do it. Find someone else to do your evil bidding."

He smirks and my heart sinks. "You can, and you will. You have no choice in the matter. You might as well accept that now."

I shake my head back and forth. "Why Turner?"

"That's not your concern."

"I'm still saying no."

"Then Justin loses everything. His overpriced education. Connecticut. His fake guardian. He's what, fifteen now?" He tilts his head and I want to punch his face. "Three years from being a legal adult. He'll become a ward of the State of Nevada. Bounce from foster home to foster home. Is that what you want for him?"

I knew he was going to say that before I even asked. "I'm nineteen, and thanks to you, I now have a real job. I can petition the State for guardianship of him. He's my brother. They'll say yes, and I can move to a good school district with my new salary."

Conti laughs. He actually fucking laughs. I never realized the man was capable of that. I hate the world. I hate this evil, ugly, corrupt world. And I want to kill the man sitting beside me for embodying all it represents.

I fly off the couch, distancing myself from him before I do something stupid like strangle him with my bare hands. I back up toward the kitchen. My apartment isn't big. There isn't much room to move, but the kitchen gives me the best advantage. He also stands up, so tall and portentously handsome. Dark hair, dark eyes, olive skin. If he weren't the personification of the devil, a girl could almost be attracted to him.

He tracks my movements, knowing I want to kill him and confident that I won't try. "You believe any judge in *my* town will grant you guardianship of your brother? How will you explain what happened to you after you turned sixteen? What you've been doing for employment all these years? How your brother has been getting by with a fictitious guardian? It certainly won't link back to me. I know you're smarter than to try and make it." He takes a step in my direction. "I'm sure the public schools around here are just as good as the private boarding school he's in. The foster home he'll be forced to live in with strangers just as nice as his dorm with his friends."

More of those stupid, insipid tears I refuse to let fall well up in my eyes, obscuring my vision. He has me right where he needs me. Stuck between blind hatred and a hard spot. Blackmail. The man is an artist with it. It's not the first time he's had me in this position. It's just never been so deplorable in the past.

"I hate you," I seethe, slashing my arm out in front of me. "I don't want to be part of your messed up world. I never did. I won't be a player in your sick game."

"You don't hate me, Isabel. Your love for me is as unconditional as my love for you. You're just angry because I'm forcing you to do something you feel is morally objectionable. But you'll get over it. Everyone does." His eyes soften, so sure of everything he's saying. His smile curls his lips up and he stares at me like that love he just spoke of is actually something real. Something tangible. The very thing he knows I've been searching for my entire life. "You're the only one who can do this. Help me, my sweet, darling girl. It will all be worth it in the end. Soon enough, it will be you and me, and all this troubling business will be behind you."

I shake my head, my hands shooting out protectively in front of me. I don't want him to come any closer. Love him? He must be high. I want to kill him and leave his body out on the Strip for all to see. I want to run away and never look back. And I would. If it were just about me, I would do both of those things.

"Maddox doesn't trust me. He certainly doesn't want me. My access to everything is limited, he told me so himself. I'm on a trial period. He doesn't even let me book his travel arrangements."

Conti's smile grows as he advances on me. Why don't I have sharp knives? I don't. I have fucking butter knives and only two of those. I have nothing.

He's right about Justin. I can't take guardianship of him. The courts will never grant it. He has them all in his twisted pocket. And then Justin will end up in foster care. I won't do that to him. He's the only light there is in this darkness. He's in one of the best schools in the country. Far away from here.

Away from Conti.

"I saw the way Maddox looked at you that night in the club after you danced. I watched the way he looked at you, spoke to you, in the champagne room last Friday night."

"He won't touch me. He told me so. His interest was forced and is now completely gone. We're one hundred percent professional and he hasn't so much as strayed an inch from that."

He tilts his head to the side, offering me a sardonic grin. His large, looming body now stands before me, pressing my back into the sharp edge of the laminate counter. There is no warmth emanating from him. No life in his black eyes. "Come now, Isabel. Don't play coy. You're more than aware of the power your beauty wields over weak-minded men like Maddox Sinclair. He won't touch you, because I forbade him, but he doesn't have to for you to get what I need. Your power lies in the temptation, not the capture."

"Don't make me do this," I whisper, so dejected I hardly have the will to breathe.

"Do this for me, my darling girl, and I will pay for Justin's entire education. All four years of high school. Anywhere in the world he wants to go for college and medical school, I will make sure he does."

I narrow my eyes, my heart thundering. "Until you hold that over my head."

He stares intently into me, reaching up to cup my face. I'm trembling, I realize. I'm so tired of feeling weak. Of being scared and alone. I want to be strong, to take charge, but the moment I feel like I'm starting to, the rug gets swept out from beneath my feet.

"I love you, Isabel."

I want to die.

"And I need your trust."

I hate you.

"Your respect."

You'll never have it.

"You're nineteen now. No longer a girl, but not quite a woman yet."

Understatement of the century.

"Do you know how old I am?"

"No." I swallow so hard it's audible. He loves this. This power. This control.

"I'm thirty-nine. Twenty years your senior. You are still too young. There is still too much I need to do before you can truly be mine. But soon, our wait to be together will be over. That's what I'm trying to do. For *us*," he emphasizes that like it's a selling feature. "So you'll never have to worry. So Justin will never have to worry."

Fuck you, you bastard.

"Do this for me," he urges. "For Justin."

I swallow and shake my head, feeling the blackness creep into my soul. I have to do this for Justin. He deserves a world that's clean and filled with potential and hope. I have no choice.

"Keep your eyes and ears open. Get Maddox to increase your security clearance. Make him trust you. Wrap him around your finger. I want pictures, confidential documents, tablets, flash drives, audio, everything you can get from the security towers and anything else you can think of." He brushes his thumbs up and down my cheeks.

My heart sinks and my stomach roils. I wish I had a comeback. A brushoff. A real, solid way to say no and make it stick.

"If you do this for me, if you help me get what I need, I will give you the money to pay for Justin's education yourself. I'll make sure you become his legal guardian within the year. Do this, and I'll never hold anything over your head again."

Oh god. Please, don't do this to me.

"I need more time. To think. To figure everything out for myself."

"I'll give you more time because that will serve as an advantage to me now. But I won't give you forever to decide, Isabel." He leans in and kisses my face. My cheeks. My temple. Never my lips. Not yet, anyway. He has plans for that. "Have a good night, *Starshine*." He smiles as he uses the nickname Maddox gave me. A reminder that he's everywhere, watching everything. "Keep your mouth shut and your eyes in the game. I'd hate for you to lose more than you already have." The ultimate threat. "I know you'll make the right choice. You always do."

Then he leaves me, shutting the door and allowing me to fall apart in peace. What the hell am I going to do now?

TWELVE

ISABEL

I DIDN'T SLEEP for most of the weekend. For a while after Conti left, I sat on the kitchen floor. Eventually, I found my way to my bed, but I couldn't close my eyes. I stared up at the water-stained ceiling and thought, mentally researching every angle. That's pretty much how I spent Friday night through Sunday night. I didn't go out. I didn't speak to anyone. I ate Ramen noodles and buttered pasta and felt like the poor-girl cliché as I did, but I couldn't force myself to go out and buy groceries.

What if I don't have a job, any job, when this all comes crashing down on me?

Option one: I go directly to Maddox and tell him the score. He'll fire me, or use me to get back at Conti, and Conti will pull Justin's school money, then Justin will end up in foster care who the hell knows where.

Option two: I go directly to Jake Turner—a man I've never met—

and tell him what Conti is planning. I'm betting the outcome is the same as option one.

Option three: I play along with Conti. I take pictures, maybe record an inconsequential meeting or two, and find out what I can without extending myself in any way; without stealing confidential documents or giving him intel. I make Maddox hate me, because I don't think I can make him like me—not after discovering the real reason I'm working there.

For that reason alone, I shouldn't care about being on Team Conti. After all, helping him is a means to an end. It's security for Justin's future. Probably for mine, too, if I allow it. So why not help him? What loyalty and honesty do I owe Maddox? None. He's certainly not been particularly forthcoming with me. He's a black hole fashioned to be the sun.

Option four: I go all in. I use everything I have to bend Maddox to my will and help Conti get everything he wants on Turner Hotels.

Except every time I consider that option, I want to throw up. Doing so makes me no better than Anthony Conti. It makes me a thief. A pirate. A despicable human being. I promised myself long ago that no matter the concessions I make in my life—stripping, chronically allowing Conti to have the upper hand—I would not do something that took away my ability to face myself in the mirror. I can justify almost anything. Justin is worth it. But Conti does not deserve whatever it is he's after.

I think I officially just found my limit.

So, I'm back to square one. Or maybe option one. I don't know anymore. I want to feel Maddox out some more. I don't like him any more than I like Conti at this point. I have no idea what that debt he bought into was, but I'm assuming it was something pretty awful. You don't go to Conti unless it is.

I arrive at the office at exactly eight thirty-five. Maddox isn't here yet and the office floor is still fairly quiet, except for Mallory. That woman strikes me as the type who stays late, comes in early, and knows everything. Finding my way to the kitchen in the back of the office, I make myself a cup of coffee, then I play around with the espresso machine, deciding I could use a few shots of that in my coffee.

The day I found my mother dead in our apartment, a needle sticking out of the crook of her elbow and a rubber band constricting the skin above it, was the day Conti entered our lives. He may have been there before, but I have no memory of that. I was sitting on the bathroom floor, staring at my mother in horror, hating her for ruining our lives again. I was terrified. I knew what her death meant for me, for Justin. I was sixteen, he was twelve, and part of me wondered if the moment I called the police would be the last time I ever saw my brother.

I was exhausted. Malnourished. Neglected. Years of scraping by so we could have a roof over our heads and a small amount of food in our bellies had taxed me to my limit. Anything my mother ever had went into her arm. Or her nose. Or her mouth. Her pimps were abusive, her dealers a little too interested in me. And it occurred to me that things were about to get worse for us.

I was crying, wallowing in a pit of self-pity when Anthony Conti walked in like he owned the place. I didn't know who he was, but he introduced himself to me with a smile and promises of a better situation for me and my brother. I took his hand when he offered it and he pulled me up off that bathroom floor. We left that apartment together.

I never went back, and I never called the police to report my mother's death.

Conti told me he had taken care of everything and I believed him.

Justin and I were taken to a new apartment, given food and clothes. A driver took us to school for exactly three weeks. The happiest three weeks of my life. Then came the day that Anthony Conti explained to us that Justin would be going to a private boarding school across the country.

"I don't want to go," Justin had said, his arms wrapped around his chest. My insides had split open as I'd stared helplessly up at

Anthony Conti's stern face. There was no argument to be had. It was done.

But still, I had to try. "Does he have to go? We'll be so good. I promise. We won't bother anyone. I'll get a job. I'll help pay for anything he needs. Please just let him stay."

Anthony's eyes wandered to mine and he smiled at me, cupping my jaw in his large hand. "This is the best opportunity for your brother. Don't you want that for him?"

"Of course I do," I replied automatically. It's all I've ever wanted. All I've ever done was take care of Justin and make sure he had everything he's ever needed. But what about me? Justin goes, and I stay, and what happens to me then? My throat closed in on me, my skin crackled as I fought back my tears. We were to be separated. I couldn't lose Justin. He's all I have.

"Please," Justin cried. "Isabel has to come with me." He covered his face with his hands as he began to shake from his sobs. I wrapped my arms around his narrow shoulders. He was still a few inches shorter than me, enough for my chin to rest on his head when his hands met my back. A perfect fit.

"It'll be okay," I promised, hoping I wasn't lying to him. Hoping he didn't grow to hate me or believe I was pushing him away. "You get to get away from here. You're going to go to this amazing school. Meet new kids. It'll be awesome."

"But you won't be there," he sniffled into my shirt, clinging to me like I was his talisman.

"We'll talk all the time. I promise you. We'll get cell phones and call and text whenever we can. You're my brother and I love you. That will never change." Even though I'm terrified I'll lose him. He's all I have.

"I love you, too. I'm scared, Is."

His words had broken me. I had been scared, too. Of so many things. Turned out, I was to stay behind and work evenings in the club, helping the girls get ready for their performances. I was to stay close to the man who called himself my savior.

Justin cried and clung to me, begging Conti to let us stay together. I sat there, holding in my sobs as I built it up for him and told him how wonderful his life would be at the boarding school. I was devastated at the prospect of losing the only person in the world I had. The only person I cared about. But I was old enough to recognize the possibilities the move would offer Justin, the sweet boy who would always make sure I ate before him, so I wouldn't go without. The boy who'd stepped in front of my mother's pimp when he tried to hit me, and took the blow for himself.

I wasn't Conti's daughter and I wasn't his girlfriend. I was some odd doll he claimed to love in private but barely existed to him in public. His punishments were brutal. His possession absolute. My freedom non-existent. One thing was made abundantly clear to me. I was always under his watchful eye. *Starshine.*

If I followed along with his every request without argument or hesitation, then Justin would have a shot at a real life. We weren't given the option; it's just how things went.

And as the years progressed and I grew older and a little more streetwise, I came to understand just what sort of monster he really is. Beyond what he did to me. I saw more than I bargained for, heard more than he ever suspected. And learned that he was the man who had killed my mother. Conti had ensured my mother received the lethal dose of whatever shit she was pumping into her veins. I wasn't sure if she had wronged him, owed him money, or if there was another reason he felt the need to take her life and disrupt ours in the process.

Whatever it was, I didn't hate him for killing my mother—as far as I'm concerned, she was just as evil as Conti. I hated him for taking away my choices. For eliminating my opportunities. I was not allowed to attend college. I was not allowed to date. I was not allowed to have friends.

He was my curse. My savior. My darkest nightmare.

I only learned how to dance because it was a choice I could make. I went up on that stage as an act of rebellion—seeking a freedom I knew I'd never truly obtain. It was a jab at his controlling ways. A secret I loved owning.

My days were empty and lonely, spent killing time because I couldn't kill myself. By day, I was at the library, surfing the internet or lost in books that allowed me to live vicariously through their pages. My nights were spent in a strip club surrounded by men who viewed and treated me like a whore. But where I deteriorated, Justin thrived. He was at the top of his class, had friends, and excelled at sports.

That knowledge made my life tolerable. Justifiable.

Even though I knew there was a catch hidden in the promise, in taking the job at Turner Hotels, I overlooked it. I believed Maddox's promise to me in the club that night. I let him buy me clothes. I let him explain the responsibilities of my position. I let myself grow more than a little infatuated with him.

It's been a long time since that day in the bathroom when Anthony Conti held my face in his hands and captured my tears, but now I know that I will never be free of him. It will never really be over with him. I'm his prisoner. His slave. He can bend me to his will, not the other way around. But if I can get through this somehow, figure out the perfect plan . . .

"I was starting to wonder about you."

I don't flinch. My heart doesn't even skip a beat. *Don't give up, Isabel. Fight through this and beat them all.* I will. Or I'll die trying.

I have no idea how long I've been standing here, staring sightlessly at the espresso machine, but Maddox looks horribly uncomfortable as he tries for casual. Feigning like he's just stumbled upon me and wasn't watching me. He was. He's like Conti in that manner.

He's leaning against the wall as he works his phone with both thumbs, his posture rigid. I smile at that. I like him uncomfortable. If he were at ease, then he'd be taking this situation lightly.

"What were you wondering about?"

A stupid school-girl laugh is dying to escape from the new position I find myself in and I'm most assuredly not referring to my job here. I liked our power dynamic so much better when I was straddling his thighs and dry fucking his hard cock through his jeans. I wonder how many times Conti watched that video.

I smile like a demon at that thought.

"How long you were going to stand and stare at the coffee maker like it was offering you anthrax."

Jokes. This man is all about them here. But right now with me, he's oh-so-serious as he moves like a predator in my direction. I swallow hard, a nervous bubble of energy rising from within me. *Which way should I go, Maddox? You guide me.* Last week we were cat and mouse, toeing that delicious line between flirty and professional. I loved it. I ate it up and couldn't wait for seconds.

But now?

Now, I don't dare glance in his direction, but that doesn't mean I'm not watching him. I'm full of questions for this man. Why of all the men in the world did it have to be him? Is this town really that small? Maddox folds his huge arms over his even larger chest. I feel the weight of his heated stare on me, on my dress Paula picked out. I didn't argue with her about it even though it edges between work and stripper.

Black. Mid-thigh. Tight. High neck—which is what makes me think I can get away with it at work—and long-sleeved. It has this crazy, gold zipper in the back that extends the length of the dress. Right now, I'd give anything to feel his immense fingers grasping the small clasp. To feel the cool rush of air hit my skin as he slowly unzips it, staring into my eyes as he watches me react to his touch. Will I blush the first time I let a man undress me? The first time I feel hands touch my skin in an intimate manner?

I want to be defiant. I want to raise my chin and stare back, but this man and his perfect face make that nearly impossible. He makes my insides quake and my thighs clench, my heart race and my panties damp . . . and he's not even touching me. I hate that I still react to him this way even after everything Conti told me. *He won't touch you because I forbade him.*

"Why do you only wear black?"

Interesting start to this game. I could tell him the truth—that it started out as a way to blend in when I was young, but then it grew into a cost-saving mechanism because if everything was black, it all matched. Eventually, black became a badge of honor and a fuck you. "I like the way it looks on me." That's not entirely untrue.

His gaze roves over me in a way that lets me know he likes the way it looks on me, too. Maddox steps in closer, a small smirk tugging at his lips. He bends, caging me in like a trapped animal. His eyes lock on mine just as someone clears their throat.

"Hey," an unfamiliar male voice says and Maddox slowly—like he has zero fucks to give and does not care that he was just caught cornering his new assistant—steps back from me. "Good morning, Maddox. I really appreciated your help with setting up the new banner on the website."

Maddox waves the guy off, his eyes still on mine like our inter-loper isn't even in the room. His eyes say we're not finished. I try to convey with mine that we can never start.

"I know you." Pause. "Do you remember me?" the voice contin-ues, undeterred. For the first time, it occurs to me that he's speaking to me. I turn in his direction and find a young guy with blond hair, bright blue eyes, and a charming smile that is most definitely trained on me. He steps forward, blatantly ignoring Maddox. "We met at Infinity a couple of weeks ago. I was there with a bunch of guys for my friend's birthday. You were our waitress."

"How original," Maddox declares with a bored tone. "Asking a waitress if she remembers you."

Only, I do remember him. He came in the night before I was fired. Him and his friends paid for the large champagne room, and he threw around money like the world was ending tomorrow. He was the most polite and sober of the crew. He also left me a phenomenal tip. Waitresses don't forget those.

"You're Morgan, right?" See, I even remember his name. Go me.

His face lights up like a rich kid on Christmas morning. "Yes," he exclaims, maybe a touch surprised. "You do remember. I know your name in the club, but I doubt that's your real name." He smiles wider, chuckling in a good-natured way.

I think I like this guy. I mean, how adorable is he?

I shake my head, trying to hide my amusement. Maddox is giving Morgan a dangerous glare. The type of glare that promises death and dismemberment should he continue to speak to me. Maybe Conti was right. Maybe Maddox doesn't have to touch me to be affected.

"I'm Isabel."

Morgan reaches out and shakes my hand. His eyes have not strayed from my face once. I don't know if he's gay or a gentleman or just not interested, but typically after a man meets you in a strip club, they think you're fair game on the easy scale. Not this one. At least, not yet.

"Isabel. Beautiful name for a beautiful girl."

Maddox makes some kind of sarcastic scoffing sound, moving just a touch closer in my direction. "Sure, you give him your name just like that," he murmurs under his breath so only I can hear. I'd be lying if I said I didn't love that Maddox is jealous. It's making my miserable day just a touch bright and shiny. I still might not have a clue what I'm going to do about Conti and the whole spying thing, but Maddox is the definition of dirty fun, and I want to roll around in him until I'm covered in his filth.

"Do you work here now or are you just . . . visiting?" Morgan glances over at Maddox, who is still giving him the death stare. "I haven't seen you around here before, but I was traveling all last week."

"I work here now. I just started last week."

"Yep. She's my assistant. And we have to be going." Maddox slips his hand to my lower back, a total possessive move if you ask me, and guides me away with a strong push.

"Nice seeing you again, Morgan," I call over my shoulder, giving him a flirty wave and a smile because I can, and I know it will drive Maddox wild.

"You, too," Morgan replies. "And I'm sure I'll be seeing a lot more of you now that you're working here."

"Over my fucking dead body," Maddox grumbles, still leading me away from Morgan, but instead of directing me to my office, we're moving toward the elevator. "Stay away from that guy. He's bad news."

"Says the pot about the kettle."

"Without a doubt. Now, move your ass. I'm late and you're coming with me."

I'm smiling. Oh, Maddox, what naughty thing did you do to put me in your path?

And why do I like being there so much?

THIRTEEN

MADDOX

"WHERE ARE WE GOING?" Isabel asks for the umpteenth time. We're in the back seat of a town car. I have the partition down when what I really want to do is raise it up and plaster her body to the leather. I swear, this one will be the death of me.

I've gotten close. Right up in her face, and I didn't kiss her full, red lips. I didn't tear that miniscule, bullshit excuse for a dress from her gorgeous body. I haven't devoured every inch of her perfect curves. Even when she looks at me as if she wants to know what it feels like to have my dick inside her body. I've passed the I-want-to-fuck-this-woman-and-didn't test. And I've been feeling pretty damn proud of myself for it.

We've maintained our professional boundaries since that episode in the spa.

No touching. No flirting. No taking her clothes off and dancing for me—though that's still at the top of my fantasy chart.

I wish I could say that now that she's wearing professional

clothing and is out of club makeup, she's become ugly or unappealing. That now that we're less adversarial and more professionally friendly, she's become boring. She's none of those things. It's all just added layers I'm dying to peel back and explore.

Then she decided to wear this fucking dress. I swear, she did it on purpose just to mess with me. This girl is a punch to the gut. A visceral reaction. Someone you feel *and* see. It's what made me watch her that first night at the club. It's what had me staring at her as I left and made me approach her in the supermarket. It's what had me mindlessly letting her dance and grind against me when I knew better. Even now, with her as my employee and Conti silently lurking, hidden in the shadows, I can't find it in me to regret it.

Who are you, Isabel? Are you lost and in need of finding? Or are you the wolf, masquerading as a sheep?

"We're going to a meeting," is my only reply as I type on my phone.

Her eyes are trained straight ahead, as if she's afraid to so much as glance out the window. She lets out a nervous giggle. She doesn't laugh very often, at least not genuinely. This odd sound coming from her lips is no exception. "Oh. So you're finally trusting me with those?"

Not even a little, but I didn't want her hanging around the office so douchey McMorgan could get his slimy, nepotistic, intern rich-boy hands on her. Morgan Fair Senior has been with Turner Hotels forever, long before Jake's dad died and left him the company. He's not a bad guy, all things considered. He really runs the operations for the company, even though my title is now COO. I hate that side of things, which is why I think Jake promoted me. Just to piss me off.

I like technology. I like security. I like surveillance. And I most definitely like the dirtiness that comes with running all that for hotels and casinos. I think that's why Morgan Fair Senior and I still get along as well as we do. But his kid can suck it. Especially if he's trying to make babies with my assistant.

"We'll see how it goes," I tell her, my eyes still locked on my phone. "Since we're talking about it, did you dance for Morgan Fair Junior Dick when he came into the club?"

Isabel shifts away from me, looking out the window, but I swear I catch a hint of a smirk before she does. "Would it bother you if I said yes?"

Like a motherfucker.

"Why would it bother me?"

"Why did you ask?"

Because I'm insanely jealous. Duh.

I shrug indifferently as I finish up the email I'm not really paying attention to, then tuck my phone back in my pocket. "Just wondering if I'm going to have to kill him and ruin my relationship with his father, is all. It's not good for business to have your interns see your employees naked."

"*You* saw me naked."

"*Mostly* naked," I correct with a raised eyebrow. "And I'm not an intern. I'm the boss."

She makes some kind of snorting sound, crossing her legs at the knee and shifting once more in her seat. Every freaking time she does that, I'm assaulted with a blast of her scent. It's sweet and floral and spicy and so goddamn good, my stupid dick perks up with every inhale. Not only that, the insanely short hem of her dress hikes up as if to say, *yes, my legs are delicious. Would you like a bite of my inner thigh?*

"That's worse, you realize."

"Probably."

"Where are we going?" she asks, *again,* but now that she's staring out the window, she's realizing we're off the Strip and moving away from Las Vegas center.

"I told you. To a meeting." She throws a glare over her shoulder and I can't help but chuckle. "There's a five-star resort northwest of the city, closer to Red Rock Canyon national park. It's got this whole spa-oasis-retreat gig going for it and is close enough to the Strip that people can do the nature thing and enjoy Vegas for Vegas without being in the heat of it. Jake wants me to check it out to see if it's worth buying. The owners are interested in selling."

"Sounds nice. Do I get another spa treatment out of this? You know, to test things out?"

"Not today, Starshine. Maybe if this deal progresses."

"Do me a favor, Maddox," her voice coasts across me like a pained whisper. "Don't call me Starshine. I'm not Star anymore, and I most certainly don't shine like one."

That's where she's wrong, but I won't argue with her. I get her not wanting to be called by a stage name.

"Can I call you Izzy? Isabel sounds so formal to me."

Isabel glances at the driver in the front, then down to the panel of buttons by her door handle. Her finger presses down on the one that controls the privacy divider and then it starts to slowly climb up until it's just us in the back of this car. Suddenly, things got a whole lot smaller in here.

"It was just a suggestion. You're not about to whip out a knife from a hidden garter, are you?" Isabel cocks an eyebrow and I shrug. "A boy can dream."

She rolls those pretty eyes at me, a small smile playing on her perfect lips. I'm dying right now. This is not a particularly long drive and she just rolled up the barrier. I promised her like, what, a week ago, I wouldn't touch her and now all I want to do is touch her. A lot.

Climbing up onto her knees, she crawls toward me. *Sweet baby Jesus.* My heart starts to jump in my chest, a thin sheen of sweat clamming up the back of my neck. God, she's so damn sexy. My cock could cut a diamond right now, it's so hard. It's been like that since I walked into the kitchen this morning and found her staring at the coffee machine in that dress. Hell, it's been like that since I first saw her. No amount of jerking off has been able to alleviate it. She's a siren.

"Isabel," I warn. She ignores me. The seductress has an agenda and suddenly I'm very interested in finding out what it is. Her knees press into the side of my thigh, her tits hovering right where my mouth is. Swinging one leg over my thighs, she straddles me, hiking up her already insanely short dress in the process and revealing a hint of black satin panties beneath. *Amazing Grace. How sweet the sound. That saved a wretch like me.* Dammit, that's not helping the way it typically does. "What are you doing?" I rasp, my voice thick.

"Looking into your eyes, Mister Sinclair. Checking to see just what sort of man you are."

I don't touch her. I don't grasp her waist and adjust her pussy until it's flush against my dick. I want to. I'm fucking dying to. But I don't. "What's your verdict?"

She stares into my eyes and smiles softly, inching up until we're face to face and the apex of her thighs brushes the very tip of my cock. It's a tease. It's a taste. And it feels so good I have to swallow to stop myself from groaning.

"That you're a dark man. A man of profound secrets." Her fingers come up, raking through my short hair, dragging along my scalp and now I do moan because there is absolutely no way to stop it. "But are you a good man? A man of integrity and honesty?"

"I try to be," I tell her with all sincerity. "But that doesn't mean I'm not the former as well, because I am. Everyone has secrets, Isabel. I'm betting you can appreciate that more than most."

"I want to kiss you."

Christ. "I want to kiss you, too."

"I'm thinking it's a bad idea."

"It most definitely is."

"This could break my world apart or save it." I have no idea what she means, but the way she says it, it's a warning. A plea for understanding.

Reaching up, I brush her long, inky hair back and over her shoulders. Then I cup her face in my hands. She stills, her eyes glassing over, and I wonder how impossible it is to be her. If everything in her life is the equivalent of walking the tightrope from fifty feet in the air without a net. "You can trust me."

She shakes her head in my hands. "I don't trust you."

"Ditto, babe. But that's earned, right?"

"You don't understand. I don't trust anyone, Maddox. It's not even one of those things that's earned or built up over time with me. Everyone has their own agenda. Everyone will stab you in the back if and when it's needed."

That's quite possibly the saddest thing ever. It's so much like how Fiona was when I first met her. Talking about shattered promises and worlds falling apart. Similar to Isabel, but different. It occurs to me that this might be how Jake felt with Fiona. How he wanted to be the man she placed her trust in. How he would have done anything to earn it. How he wanted to slay every damn dragon that came her way. But I'm not that man. I'm not a Jake. I need to save the girl, but I'm not the one they should end up with. It's why I set Jake and Fiona up instead of keeping her for myself.

It's the way it's supposed to be. But suddenly, staring into Isabel's dark eyes, I'm not so sure anymore.

"You might be right, but I'm gonna try like hell to prove you wrong."

"Don't make promises you can't keep, Maddox. It'll only make me hate you when this is all over."

When this is all over. What a very deliberate and telling choice of words.

The car stops, and our driver gets out. He doesn't knock on the window and he doesn't rush us. He just stands there beside the door, patiently waiting. I slide my hands through her hair and down her back, all the way down to her waist, then lift her off me, setting her back down beside me on the bench seat, before I lean across her to open her door. We're hit with a blast of mild air, not exactly warm and not quite cold. Sometimes, winter in the desert has its advantages.

She steps out of the car and I follow, the driver shutting the door behind us. I tell him we'll be about two hours, and then when Isabel and I are out of hearing range, standing directly under the overhang that leads into the luxurious and spacious marble lobby, I lean into her and whisper, "It'll only end if we let it. And I'll never make you promises I can't keep."

I pull back and catch her eye, just as a group of hotel employees and the owners come out to greet us. Isabel is completely professional during our time here, and I'm grateful for that. This thing with us . . . it could go either way. It's already teetering precariously close to the edge. And falling over into the darkness doesn't have the same feel this time. It's a rowboat in a hurricane. She knows it. I know it.

FOURTEEN

ISABEL

I'VE NEVER LIKED PLAYING games. They always felt like a waste of something better to do. But now, it feels like that's all I do. Games. My problem? I like Maddox—more than I should. His problem? Certain things in life are bigger than like. I like Maddox. But I love my little brother. I love that he has a shot at something real in this world. Something for himself. I love that he could go to college and medical school—his ultimate goal.

I get that my situation will likely never be that easy.

I'm a kept woman without the physical obligation. At least, not yet. That's still to come. It's why rationalizations are the bread to my jam. They are my tonic. The elixir I drink down like water after running a marathon.

I'm not selfless. I'm not altruistic. I'm not a good person.

I'm a realist, living in a fucked-up world of demands and crappy non-choices.

And with that comes the inability to lie to oneself. Hence the rationalizations, because they're not lies. They're force-fed bits of grain in the form of life-sustaining sustenance.

I raised Justin. I made sure he got his vaccines. I took him to the doctor when he was sick. I signed his school forms and purchased the groceries and clothes that kept us going. And I don't regret that. I'm glad it was me and not our mother. She would have just fucked it all up.

Justin was just a kid when our mother died.

Conti bought him braces. Conti sent him away to school. Conti gave him the chance to touch the world and one day hold it in his hands. I'm grateful to him for that. I really am. And if he dropped dead tomorrow, a part of me would mourn his loss.

But I also hate him.

Aside from being an evil man—which he is—I'm the reason for his 'kindness.' Me. My body. My lips. My hair. My eyes. My face. My personality? Superfluous.

I'm a doll. And when he figures I'm old enough and he's ready enough, I'll become his slave once and for all. He told me as much last week in my apartment. He doesn't care that I might have once had dreams of my own. Aspirations beyond living in my mother's version of a crack house. Beyond this town. He sent Justin off, leaving me here, alone and underage and in need. He made me dependent on him, and now that dependence is a weapon.

So yeah. Liking Maddox is pretty damn insignificant.

But at the same time . . . I want to believe that Maddox will never make me promises he cannot keep. That he'll try to put it all on the line—even though he's likely as beholden to Conti as I am.

It's the way he touches me—like I matter.

It's the way he looks at me—like he doesn't see anyone else.

It's the way he makes me feel—like I'm worth it.

I settle into my desk this morning earlier than I typically do. It's still quiet and I find that's when I like being at work the best. No one bothers me here. I think they're still not used to Maddox having an assistant, and unless I'm walking around the floor or running an errand, I'm forgotten. I chat with the ladies in the kitchen or at their desks, but mine seems to be a no-go zone.

"Hiding out?" Maybe I was wrong about that no-go zone.

I peek up to find Sarah smiling down at me, her belly even larger than it was the other day. "Absolutely," I tease, and her smile widens. "Just about to dig into Maddox's emails."

"Oh, then I won't keep you. I just wanted to make sure you're coming to my baby shower."

I sit back in my seat, my eyes widening a bit. I heard people mentioning it, but I never assumed I'd be invited. "You want me to come?"

"Of course!" she exclaims, and I can't help but return her emotion. "It's tomorrow morning in event room C. Don't you dare bring me a gift." *Shit. A gift.* "I mean it. I just want you there. It'll be fun."

"Okay. Thank you so much for thinking of me."

She waves me off and then leaves me to my work. A baby shower sounds fun. I'm actually looking forward to it. I'm sure I can figure out something to get her.

Logging onto my computer, I hum a little song, suddenly in a great mood. I weed through Maddox's emails, well, his crap emails. Most of them are just solicitations in one form or another. I doubt I get the real ones. Those go to some other inbox I don't have access to. It takes me forever, but eventually I finish flagging the ones he should perhaps take a look at—probably more than he should, but that's going to be a learning curve for me—when my phone vibrates on the side of my desk. Glancing at the screen, my breath catches in my throat and my heart follows it. ***Tuition due in 24 hours. Tick. Tock.***

Way to kill a good mood. I stare at the text, debating if I should reply. But there is no reply to that. It's not a hint. It's coercion. It's forcing my hand in a position it doesn't naturally want to bend in. This is why I hate the bastard. I was hoping for longer than a week to make my decision.

He's never texted me before, and he rarely calls me directly. I have to do something, or Justin is going to lose everything. Anxiety creeps up my spine like a spider about to bite. I slam my phone down on my desk, shoving it off to the side, as if the further away from me it is, the less I have to think about that text. Only there is no erasing it. It's do or die time and I'm officially on the clock.

Maddox is still not here and that makes my stomach stir uncomfortably. He told me last night when I left that he'd see me in the morning, and we'd be attending a meeting together—my first official meeting. Monday at the hotel near the desert didn't count.

I check his schedule and find the meeting. But I'm not there with him. And there is no text from him on my phone or email from him in my system. It's just about ten and the meeting is slated to begin now. Do I go there alone without him? I have no idea how any of this works.

"Hi," a chipper voice startles me out of my small breakdown. Glancing up, I find a tall, slender, absolutely stunning woman with long blonde hair piled on top of her head and pale green eyes. She's wearing cropped hot pink yoga pants, a powder blue sports tank with stripes of the same matching pink on it and a brilliant smile.

"Hi," I reply trying to match her smile and falling way short. "May I help you?"

"Sorry if I startled you. I'm Fiona."

Oh! I stand up. "Isabel."

She shakes my hand with the type of warmth and affection I didn't realize was possible in a handshake. Fiona. I had forgotten all about her since she was first mentioned.

"Maddox sent me to fetch you for whatever meeting you have this morning. He's running late because I worked him hard in the gym and then made him buy me breakfast after." There's a prideful, wicked gleam in her eyes, but other than that, there is nothing but sugar and sunshine and rainbows coming from this woman.

"Oh," I say, because that seems to be all I'm capable of. My eyes pop open wide. For the first time since I met him, I consider that she's Maddox's girlfriend. A very beautiful, bright, perky girlfriend. A girlfriend who is the complete opposite of me in every way possible. I was jealous of her when he picked up the phone last week, but it never occurred to me that they could be something real. Something serious. She shifts her position and a flash of something blinding hits my eye. My gaze drops to her hand and I catch the sparkle of a huge engagement ring positioned atop a row of pretty diamonds in the form of a wedding band.

Wow. This is . . . unexpected. And so totally fucked up that I think I've officially lost the ability to swallow or breathe or speak. He doesn't wear a wedding band, but then again, lots of men don't. Especially when they have something to hide. Like a wife. Or a dirty little secret like me.

He never did anything wrong with me per se. I mean, he asked me for a date and kissed my neck in my apartment. So there's that. I stripped and danced a bit and he sat there watching—and asked me to stop. We've been flirting. Or maybe we've just been at each other's necks and not actually flirting? And then there were those times he cornered me and invaded my space with desire flashing in his eyes. At least, I think that's what that was. Honestly, I'm not so sure now. I'm the one who danced for him when he told me he didn't want me to. I'm the one who straddled his lap in the car the other day. But nothing ever happened between us and he certainly made his stance on our relationship clear from day one when he told me that we're strictly professional.

My crush is married. How unfortunately appropriate.

A stab of ugly and unwelcome jealousy slices my skin.

A wife. Christ. That . . . sucks.

"You weren't expecting me," she surmises with a laugh since I'm frozen here like a deer in headlights staring at her as I imagine just how perfect and blissfully happy her life is. "Sorry. I asked him to text you, but clearly he didn't."

She rolls her eyes in a good-natured way. Like "oh, isn't my husband so adorable when he forgets to text his new assistant who doesn't mean anything more to him than paying off a debt?" Clearly, I've hit the bitter stage of jealousy.

"Come on. I'll walk with you, if that's all right?" She waves her hand for me to join her. I wish she weren't so likable. I pick up my laptop and work phone sans text from Maddox, my personal phone with a threatening text from Conti, and follow her. "Maddox mentioned he just hired you. I think it's fantastic that he finally has an assistant. He's been pulling too many long hours."

I hum something out that sounds like an agreement as I walk miserably beside her. I'm desperate to ask how long they've been married. If they have children. *Oh god, children!* What their life together is like. But I keep my mouth shut. It's none of my business. I'm here to do a job. Well, now two jobs, right? I glance down at the plethora of electronics in my hand, at my personal phone. Conti tracks this phone. I know it, because there have been too many coincidences for him not to—knowing about a particular text I'd sent Just, or what I'd googled, or people I'd called and locations I'd been to.

It's why I go to the library and use their internet to look things up.

It's why I only text the very basics with Justin.

It's why I never go anywhere or do anything with my phone that I don't expect him to know about. And I brought it with me. All I have to do is hit record during this meeting. It's that seamless and that simple. Any pictures I take, phone calls or recordings I make, are all there for Conti to see.

"What were you doing before this?" she asks, all naïve and innocent because her husband never told her about the stripper he was forced to hire.

"I was a cocktail waitress at a club." It's not a lie, but for some reason, I don't want her to know my ugly. My irrational and misguided hurt, coupled with that ugly, ugly jealousy, are keeping the finer details a secret. My pride is suddenly getting the better of me.

"I was a bartender for a while when I first moved out here. I still pick up a few shifts every now and then for fun."

"That sounds nice." And it does. Working for the fun of it.

"This is us," she says as we reach a set of closed tall oak doors. "It was very nice to meet you, Isabel. I hope to see more of you now that you're working so closely with Maddox." I stare into her eyes, searching for a hint of resentment. A spark of jealousy. A flash of sarcasm. Something that would make me hate her just a little. Nothing. She's genuine and perfect and I'm about to do something that will make living with myself nearly impossible.

"You, too, Fiona. Thank you for walking me down here."

"Any time. Have a good rest of your day." She throws me a friendly wave and heads for the elevator at the opposite end of the hall, smiling and politely greeting people as she passes. I stare after her longer than I should. Long enough that I'm hoping by the time I enter the conference room, I'm mentally detached enough to hit that record button.

You have no choice. You're doing this for Justin.

I release a long-suffering sigh and turn the knob for the conference room. The meeting hasn't begun yet. At least, I think it hasn't since everyone seems to be having small, private conversations as they make cups of coffee and pick at a tray of fruit and pastries in the center of the large oval table. Maddox glances up when I enter the room and points to the seat beside him. He's wearing a dark gray suit, a light blue shirt that matches his eyes, and no tie. He's so gorgeous it hurts, and I think I hate everything about him. My heart begins to thunder in my chest and it's not because of the swarm of eyes that suddenly feel like they're burning into my back.

I swallow hard and sit down, placing everything on the table in front of me with precision as if I'm setting out surgical instruments. Breathe in. Breathe out. My eyes glue themselves to my personal cell phone when I feel Maddox shift beside me. Feel his warmth brush across my exposed arm. "Everything good?"

I nod.

"Did Fi bring you here?" *Fi*. That must be what he calls Fiona. His wife.

"Yes."

"Good. She was very excited to meet you."

"Because you told her nothing about me," I bite out in harsh whisper. I don't know why I'm upset about any of this. I know the situation. I know the score. I know all of it. Because you started to like him, my inner bitch reminds me.

He grabs my arm, squeezing hard enough for me to take notice but not hard enough for it to hurt. "What did you want me to tell her?" he barks in my ear.

"Not the truth, certainly. We should all be so very ashamed of the truth." My voice is strangled. Hoarse.

I've given up so much of myself over the years. I let Conti convince me that not having a guardian or being in the system at the age of sixteen after my mother died was the way to go. That allowing him to send Justin—my only remaining family—off to a private school across the country was for the best. That my working in a strip club was the only way I could earn real money without being questioned. That allowing him to own me, control me, ruin me day after day, was the only way to survive and keep Justin safe.

And now this.

I continue to stare at my phone. I have to do this. I have to hit record. I shake my head, not even caring if everyone around me thinks I'm nuts. If I do this, it's a slippery slope. Giving Conti what he wants is like playing with a live grenade.

Maddox is still holding onto my arm. He's still bent over in my direction. "I'm not ashamed of the truth. Of who you are."

I shake my head again. Because that's not the truth I meant. I wonder if he knows that and is playing games, or if he's genuinely clueless.

"Doesn't matter. She was nice. I don't like you. Everything is as it should be."

Morgan Fair Senior clears his throat. He's an older man with more salt than pepper hair, bright blue eyes like his son's, and dressed in a power suit to end all power suits. I open my laptop and pull up the slides I was emailed. I read through the first few and then I hit record on my phone.

FIFTEEN

ISABEL

MY BREATH, I can't catch it. *I'm not cut out for this, Anthony Conti!* This dealing with the devil crap. It's throwing everything about me off balance. It's giving me a goddamn panic attack, is what it's doing. Can a person develop an ulcer before they're twenty?

I'm half a beat from bat-shit crazy. It feels like the walls of the mammoth place are closing in on me. That everyone is staring at me, watching me. The piece of shit has turned me into a raving lunatic, and it makes me so enraged that the fires of hell have nothing on me. I don't do weakness. I'm the ultimate fighter. I'm mean and scrappy and don't play by the rules.

I just recorded an entire conference and sent it to Conti. What have I become?

Launching myself out of my chair, I rush out of the conference room, not even sparing Maddox a second glance. Air. I need air. Once I clear the conference doors, I turn right, only to slam directly into someone. The force of the blow knocks me back a step as strong hands grasp my arms, trying to steady me.

"Whoa there," Morgan Fair Junior says. "You okay?"

I nod numbly, my eyes still locked on the floor.

With his hand on my biceps, he spins me around, marching me toward my office. I don't want to go there. I want to get out of here. I want to run away and never look back at any of these people. Maybe if I move to Connecticut, petition for guardianship there, get a job and apply for financial aid, Justin can stay in school?

You'll never be able to do any of that in the next twenty-four hours.

Christ. If dejected had a picture in the dictionary, it'd be my miserable face.

"I need to get out of here," I tell Morgan, not caring how my voice sounds.

"We will. I just wanted to drop these papers in Maddox's office."

"What?" I blink up at him before dropping my gaze back down to the papers in his hand. Confidential is written across them in a watermark. Confidential. "I can take them." I set down my laptop and phones. Morgan gives me a sideways glance and a small smirk. Then he hands me the confidential papers. "Just make sure he gets them."

"I will."

After I read through them and take a picture. God, I suck at life.

"Do you want to go for a walk? Get some air? You look like you could use a break after that riveting meeting."

I laugh at his sarcasm, though I'm sure he can tell just how fake it is. "Yeah. I . . . uh." I look up at Morgan, right into his bright blue eyes. He's always looking me in the eyes. He doesn't eat my body up for sport the way Maddox does. Maddox. Married Maddox. Sucking in a silent breath, I smile despite the pounding of my black heart. "Sure. That sounds good. Just let me put this in my desk for safe keeping until I can give it to Maddox." *And join Anthony Conti in hell.*

. . .

THE ELEVATOR DOORS part and we step on. Morgan presses the button for the lobby and down we go. Closing my eyes, I take a deep, steadying breath. *Get your shit together, Isabel.* I do. I'm a big girl, after all.

"How do you like working with your father?" I ask Morgan, needing to fill the space between us with idle, inconsequential banter. If he's going to be my newest version of a work buddy, I might as well get to know him. Sarah doesn't usually stop talking. Neither do Oliva and Carmen. Mallory is always too busy to chat, so I don't try all that much with her. But Morgan doesn't usually offer up a whole lot. I get smiles and waves, but we haven't talked much since Monday in the kitchen before Maddox shooed me out.

"You mean *for* him. I don't work *with* him." I can't help but note the bitter tone in his voice. "My father doesn't believe in nepotism or even giving his only son a helping hand. He feels I have to earn everything in this world on my own. Graduating from college with a degree in business and finance evidently didn't earn me this bullshit paying internship because it wasn't an Ivy League school and I wasn't top of my class the way he was."

Yikes! What do you say to that? I peek over at him as we step off the elevator onto the ground floor of the hotel. "He obviously gave in, though. And I'm sure he sees how hard you're working."

Morgan turns away from me, staring out in the direction of the casino. "I guess. I don't mean to sound ungrateful or resentful. Just a crappy morning." *Tell me about it.* "He was pushing my buttons hard before that meeting. But it's fine. How do you like working here instead of at the club?" he asks, changing the subject quickly. I don't push it. I don't know him well enough to delve into anything personal, and family dynamics are notoriously tricky. "You seem to be having a rough morning, too."

A burst of nervous laughter flies out of my mouth. "I guess you could say that."

"Anything you want to talk about?"

I shake my head as we walk in the direction of the atrium where I went shopping that first day for clothes. "No. I just needed some air. Who knew meetings lasted that long and were so boring?"

"You have to learn how to play games on your phone and not make it obvious. I was switching off between Roblox and Scrabble."

I smile up at him, at his adorably boyish face. All-American good-looks and sweet charm. Yeah. I definitely like Morgan.

The lobby of the hotel isn't all that crowded. No more than usual. I have no idea where Morgan is leading me, and I don't care in the least. We're just walking. Past the coffee shop and a couple of restaurants and some weird, glass sculpture thing that looks like it's illuminated from within. It's the sort of thing you'd only find in this town. Maddox hasn't called me to find out where I am—well, it's lunchtime, so whatever. As we pass an open bar area that leads into the atrium, I know why. He's leaning an elbow against the bar, a glass of something that's likely water in his hand as he converses intently with another man. His back is to me, but I'd know him anywhere. He's impossible to mistake.

His companion is standing straight and the dark amber in his glass—it's not yet noon—all black casual attire, and bored stance manages to pull a small smile to my lips. Maddox is all words and this man is very few. He shifts, pivoting his head at the right moment and catching my eye. His eyes are green and piercing and strangely familiar, though I'm positive I've never seen this man before. He's the sort you'd remember. The man runs a hand through his dark hair, mussing it up further. He's beautiful, in a dangerous sort of way—maybe that's why he looks so familiar to me.

His lips move, obviously alerting Maddox to my presence because Maddox raises from the bar and stares me down, his gaze so brutally cold, I shiver.

"Earth to Isabel," Morgan says, snapping me back into the moment, though not enough to drag my attention away from the two men who are still speaking as they watch me. Green eyes is curious. Maddox is angry. And I wonder how much longer I'll be working here. He must know. That look . . . he must know. "Did you hear what I said?"

"No," I admit. I asked Maddox if he was a man of integrity and he said he liked to think he was. I'm narrowing my gaze and spitting venom at him before I can even take my next step.

"Ah," Morgan drawls in a knowing tone that makes me want to simultaneously roll my eyes and cringe for being so obvious. "Bossman being hard on you, too? That explains the way he was speaking to you before the meeting started." I didn't even realize Morgan was in that meeting. I just kept reading slide after slide, listening to his father and Maddox speak, and recording everything they were saying.

"Something like that," I deadpan. "I don't think he likes me much. I doubt I'll last long with him for a boss." Before I can make sense of anything else, Fiona comes up to them, wrapping her arms around the dark stranger. He cups her face in his hands and smiles the type of smile that would make any girl's heart skip a beat.

"How long have Maddox and Fiona been married?" I ask before I can stop myself. I hate that I care. I hate that just the sight of her near him makes me crazy with jealousy.

"You mean Fiona and Jake, right?"

I rip my gaze away from Maddox over to Morgan, my eyebrows pinched together so tight I probably have a unibrow. I shake my head but can't seem to formulate words as I think it all through. Fiona and Jake Turner. Fiona *Turner*. That's ringing a small jingly bell in the back of my head.

"Fiona and Jake?" I parrot, and Morgan nods at me like I'm an idiot. Laughing a little at my stupefied expression, he nudges his elbow into my side, rubbing it up and down my arm a few times for good measure. It's flirtatious. So is his arm dropping around my shoulder, pulling me closer into his side, but I don't care right now. I'm too preoccupied with this revelation.

"Jake and Fiona have been married about a year or so, I think. Honestly, I'm surprised a Vegas girl like yourself doesn't already know this. It was this whole big thing a couple years back. Fiona's ex-husband was abusive, or so she claimed. He came to Las Vegas to find her after she ran off on him. Tried to get her back, I bet. Anyway, however it all went down, Maddox killed him."

I stop. Dead in my fucking tracks. Like to the point where the woman behind me bumps into my back and snaps something at me that I don't care about enough to pay attention to. *Maddox killed Fiona's husband?* Then it comes back to me in flashes.

"Niklas Vaughn," I whisper. It was all over the news a year and a half ago. I remember the girls at the club talking about it. I don't have a computer or cable—my television only plays DVDs; archaic I know —and I believe I already mentioned my inability to do internet searches on my phone, so getting the news isn't all that easy for me. But the girls at the club like to gossip and the shooting of Niklas Vaughn—a billionaire who was married to Fiona Ramsey-Foss, an heiress in her own right—made the top of the gossip mill.

I just didn't realize it was Maddox who did the deed. His name was never mentioned. Not once. Why him and not Jake? Or Fiona, for that matter? My heart softens to her further. God, she ran from an abusive man and he came after her. And Maddox killed him. A man who is not her husband or even lover. What's their relationship like? He risked it all for her. Like he said he'd do for me.

Morgan shoots me with his finger, chuckling under his breath like the gesture, given the topic, is hysterical. But I can't get past Maddox Sinclair shooting, *killing*, a man. It had to have been in self-defense. How else could he be walking the streets? Unless . . .

"Crap," I mutter, snapping my fingers like I just remembered something. "I completely forgot I have to do something for Maddox. If I don't get it done now, I'll be fired for sure."

"Oh. Then you better go. I'll catch up with you later."

"Definitely." I leave him in the atrium. He's obviously in no rush to return to the corporate floor, but I need a moment alone to think, and I can't do that with all these people around me and Maddox himself lurking somewhere close.

I head directly for Maddox's office. To my surprise, it's unlocked. I glance around the floor, but I can't find him, and the ladies' room is all the way down the hall and around the corner. It's just too far and too public. But Maddox has a private bathroom and he's not here, so I go for his. His office is the same sterile environment it always is, and his bathroom is no better. It has a shower. Why on earth would someone need a shower in their office bathroom?

I don't get this place. These are not my people.

Turning on the faucet, I cup my hands and allow the cool water to pool up before I splash it across my face. It's not the cure, but it is a start. I do it twice more, washing off all remnants of mascara in the process. My breathing calms and my heart slows, and I drop my head, staring down at the water as it slides down the white porcelain and into the drain.

"I don't think I can do this."

Blowing out a long, slow, exhausted breath, I raise my head and jump two feet in the air, screaming out as I do. Jesus. Can't these men announce themselves for once?

"What can't you do?"

"Work for egomaniacs like yourself. It's giving me high blood pressure already." The lie slips past my lips smoothly. Effortlessly. I want to taunt Maddox Sinclair. Possibly for being indebted to Anthony Conti in the first place. Possibly for dragging me along for the ride. Or possibly to get him to fire me. Right now, I can't decide. Because I think I've finally got it all figured out and it's driving me wild. He sacrificed everything for Fiona, and even though I know he's not her lover, I'm still psychotically jealous of her. Of all that she has.

"You work for him." It comes out as an accusation.

"No," he replies quickly and with more force than I would have expected given the situation we find ourselves in. "I'm the Chief Operating Officer for Turner Hotels." He pauses here, reading me intently through the reflection in the mirror. He reaches around me, shutting off the faucet and removing the only sound between us other than the blood thundering in my ears. "I owed him a debt."

I nod my head because I know all of that now. I can add one and one with the best of them.

"And you working here is his way of cashing in."

I turn away from him at that. I don't know why, but for some reason, his easy truth bothers me more than when Conti told me. It's as if he just admitted he's not invested in me being here other than for the obvious reasons. Like everything else between us, all those stolen moments, all those heated gazes and lingering touches, were a lie. If it were strictly up to my pride, I'd walk right out of this job. He never wanted me for it anyway.

Can you blame him?

"Is that going to be a problem for you?" His fingers clasp my chin, dragging my face back toward the mirror and up until my eyes lock on his once more. "It doesn't have to be. I really do need an assistant and you really do need a job. Nothing has to change."

Except everything has changed.

Guilt captures me, seizing the air from my lungs. *I'm a horrible person, Maddox. Lock me out and throw away the key.*

"Is that why you don't like me anymore? You found out the real reason I hired you?" Much to my chagrin, he chuckles. The man finds me amusing when I feel anything but. Maddox is my undoing. The one who picks at the loose strand of yarn and pulls. Suddenly, I wish he were actually married.

"You're not a very likable guy, Maddox."

His smile is broad and charming and showcases all his perfect white teeth that I want to punch in. "You're disturbingly young looking without makeup on. Why are you washing it off in my bathroom?"

"And you're frighteningly old looking with those gray hairs and crow's feet, but I'm not judging, and you shouldn't, either. Why didn't you tell me about the debt?"

"Why are you answering my questions with a question? Last I checked, I'm the boss and you're the employee. I don't answer to you, and I sure as shit don't owe you any explanations. Remind me next time I'm out to lock my office door. You're ruining my white towels with all that black shit."

A groan sears past my lips as I roll my eyes. But the truth is, with his intense scrutiny in the reflection of the mirror, I feel fearless for the first time in my life. Or maybe reckless is the better term for this bubble in my chest. I want him to see me. To look at me with those crystalline baby blues and boyish smile and cut past all my bullshit.

Call me out, Maddox. I dare you. Or better yet, let me be your Fiona. Yep. I went there. I don't even feel bad about it. I can't stand the man, we fight more than I've ever fought with anyone, yet he's all I think about. Dream about. This crush is a killer.

He doesn't, of course. How disappointing. He just continues his game of who will blink first.

"Your bathroom is nicer. And closer."

"I don't remember giving you permission to enter my space without me."

"Ouch." No, really, that hurts. He might be right, but still. "If I wanted to be treated like nothing, I would have continued taking my clothes off for money."

Maddox has the audacity to laugh. "As I recall, you were fired from that."

I jut my ass back, trying to bump him back a few pegs. The wall that is Maddox doesn't budge. Does he have to smell so good? Stand so close? Push every one of my buttons?

"True. It's such a shame that Infinity is the only strip club in Las Vegas. What's a sexually starved man like yourself to do when he's hard up for the champagne room?"

"Are we done with this? It's like we're going around in juvenile circles, playing duck, duck, goose. Can we get back to work?"

"You're funny, Maddox. All these kid jokes are a laugh riot. And what do you think I've been doing all morning?"

"Walking around the atrium with that fuckstick Morgan. I believe I told you to stay away from him."

So, that explains the angry look he was giving me downstairs. "You're my boss, not my keeper."

I toss his reflection a saccharine sweet grin and turn to leave, needing some air that doesn't taste like desire and sin. Suddenly, everything spins in place and before I can make sense of anything, I'm hoisted into the air, my feet dangling, a squeal of surprise flying past my lips just as my butt lands hard on the stone counter of the sink.

Maddox stares down at me, his hands sliding to the smooth marble on either side of my thighs. He leans in and whispers, "That's where you're wrong, Isabel. And as long as you work for me, you're going to stay away from Morgan Fair Junior. In fact, you're going to stay away from every stupid, punk-ass, adolescent boy, man or whatever the fuck. I don't discriminate, and I don't care. No exceptions."

His hands meet my hips, sliding my ass forward on the counter until I nearly fall off. He steps into me, spreading my legs with his hips and inching so close I can taste the mint on his breath. Feel the heat of his skin. Note the hardening length in his pants. God, that's a turn-on like nothing I've ever experienced. Nothing has ever made me higher than doing battle with Maddox. Than straddling this thin line between love and hate.

Only there is no love in this war. And nothing about my situation is fair.

I press my hands to his muscular chest, taking a second to appreciate the way his heart pounds beneath my palm, betraying his cool façade. Leaning up, I drag my lips across his cheek toward his ear. His self-control is hanging on by a thread. I feel his restraint in every tight muscle. In the way his hands white-knuckle the counter. It's empowering and sexy as sin and I need so much more. Waves of anticipation course through my body. What would we be like together if we finally gave in to this?

Explosive.

Consuming.

Deadly?

"Is that one of the promises you intend to keep? I wonder, Maddox, what will you do to me when I break your rules?"

Drawing back, I push against his chest and slip off the counter, leaving the bathroom and him behind. I just struck the match to ignite our fuse.

SIXTEEN

ISABEL

"OH MY GOD, these are the most adorable onesies." Adorable is a bit of a stretch. The onesies read, 'We're what happened in Vegas.' They came with bibs that say, 'Vegas Babies.' They're both a bit cliché, if you ask me, but since no one did, I don't comment other than to smile and clap along with everyone else. Baby showers are a spectacle. There is a whole onesie decorating station, a scrapbook page-making station, and we've already played the weirdest game where people are handed a sheet, and everyone had to 'find the guest' that matched the item on the sheet. The questions people kept asking me made me laugh.

I didn't play. I was a happy spectator.

I didn't have time to buy Sarah a baby present, and honestly, I don't think I could have afforded the type of swag this girl is walking away with. Who needs silver baby rattles? Like the babies care if they're Tiffany's? But last night when I went home, Evelyn cornered me to chat outside our apartments and I told her about the shower.

We spent the following two hours baking cookies by the dozen. Apparently, Evelyn's grandmother owned a bakery in Brooklyn a million years ago, so she knows what she's doing. Good thing, too, because I had no idea.

Sarah gushed over them, which is why I like her.

They're regular old chocolate chip, but she oohed and ahhed as if they were gourmet.

I always assumed baby showers were a female-only thing, but not this one. Our entire floor, men and women, are here, including Jake Turner. His wife, Fiona—talk about a girl crush—is the one responsible for the fete. But those two are inseparable. I've been watching them out of the corner of my eye. He's always touching her and she's always smiling up at him, and they're always stealing kisses whenever the moment strikes them. Jake Turner is a looker. And now I sound like Evelyn. Awesome.

I learned Fiona is in college, getting her Bachelor's in psychology because she eventually wants to be a social worker. She's best friends with Maddox and she, Jake, and Maddox are some kind of close-knit secret unit. That's what Olivia called them. "Even Morgan Fair Senior, who has been part of this company forever, knows nothing about them."

I shouldn't care. I shouldn't be jealous—I'm starting to realize I'm a very jealous person—but I am. I've told myself over and over again that I cannot like Maddox. That he's potentially just as bad as Conti.

Only, I don't think he is.

I think he risked everything for his best friend. For his best friend's girl. And Conti is how he managed to walk away. He risked it all for her, for them, and he promised to do the same for me. So yeah, that whole not liking him stuff? Well, I'm working on it. Because he is clearly the better person in this scenario. I'm the black-hearted thief. When he eventually learns what I'm up to, he'll hate me. So will Fiona and Sarah and Olivia and Carmen. I've seriously wondered if Maddox, or Jake, will have me arrested. Will I have to call in a favor to Conti?

Is this where my life is headed?

Just as I'm feeling about as low as a person can possibly feel, I get a text from Justin. It's a picture of him holding up his mid-term test with a big A+ circled in red ink on the top, my brother's smile is unstoppable. *Thanks, Justin.* I totally needed that. I shoot him back a text that tells him how proud I am of him. How much I love him. Lots of super cheesy emojis, too.

Love you, too, Is. Miss you!

Damn him. Now I'm getting choked up in the middle of this stupid baby shower.

"Don't tell me it's that Diaper Genie thing that's making you all misty-eyed." Maddox's soft breath washes over my exposed neck. It gives me such a thrill, and thank Jesus I decided to wear my hair up today.

"Why does someone need a special trashcan for diapers?"

"You're asking the wrong person here, Izzy. I don't understand any of this stuff, but then again, I'm the baby of five."

I smile at that. Personal information on Maddox Sinclair? Check. Only something tells me that Anthony Conti could give a rat's ass that Maddox has four older siblings.

"How long do we have to stay?" I ask, still feeling a bit down after my twentieth pity-party in the last week. I don't know what I can't stand more, the fact that I'm feeling so sorry for myself or the fact that I'm legitimately scared of what will happen when it all comes down.

"Anxious to get back to work?"

I shrug. "Sure. If that's what you need."

"Let's go take a walk."

I stare at Sarah who is in baby gift heaven and ask, "Won't we be missed?"

"Nope. And if anyone asks, I'll say we needed to do something. It is a work day, after all."

"Right. Work." I spin around on my heels and peer up into his blue eyes. "So, where are we going on this walk?"

"Wanna go swimming?"

I laugh, smiling stupidly up at him. "This isn't more of that European-style thing, is it?"

"Absolutely not. Your days of showing off your tits are over."

I shake my head at him. "I don't have a bathing suit. And for the record, this is the weirdest place I've ever worked, and that includes Infinity. What kind of job is this where we can go swimming in the middle of the day or get massages and pedicures?"

"No swimming, then? We can dip our feet in the water. Come on." He takes my upper arm like he's dragging a wayward child out to punish them. "It's warm and sunny out today. I don't want to be here, and neither do you. Let's sneak out and play hooky."

"Yes, Boss. I'll sneak out and play hooky with you." I roll my eyes at him, huffing out an exaggerated breath. "You're such a tyrant. Always giving me the worst jobs to do."

My steps falter as we walk along the hall that leads away from the event area and back toward the main resort. I want to tell him, but there is no way I can. I glance around us, and though we're completely alone, I don't trust it. We reach the sunshine, and suddenly I find myself standing on the edge of a deserted pool area. I have no idea how we got here so quickly without my noticing, but that's where we are. The pool is beautiful and huge. Glistening blue ripples against the gentle breeze. The sound of water lapping gracefully against the rocks as it glides down the manmade waterfall reaches my ears. White loungers arranged in rows and columns extend as far as the eye can see. It's almost eerie out here, seeing as how we're the only two people. Maddox told me that all the redesigned pools are set for their soft opening next week and their grand opening the beginning of April.

And maybe I've watched too many movies or been hanging out with the wrong people, but I have to ask, "Did you bring me out here to kill me?"

"If I were going to kill you, I certainly wouldn't do it out here in broad daylight at our newly renovated pool. Blood would stain the stone and be a bitch to get out of the water."

"You're supposed to laugh when you say that, Maddox. Not sound so serious."

"How about we sit down, and I promise I won't kill you? Is that good enough?"

"Not really," I grumble, wondering where fun Maddox from the party went.

Slipping off my heels, I sink down to the warm stone, my bare feet sliding into the water. It's cool but not cold, and I scissor my feet back and forth, reveling in the way the water feels like flowing silk against my skin as I move. It's casual Friday, so Maddox is wearing jeans, which he rolls up to his knees, then takes a seat directly beside me. For a long time, we're silent, enjoying the warming rays of the sun on our backs and the cool water on our feet.

"You've been here almost two weeks," he starts, and there is something in his voice I can't quite place. "How do you like it so far?" Yep. That's a loaded question.

"I like it a lot," I tell him honestly, staring up at his perfect profile. "I like the people. Lunches and pedicures aside, the stuff you do is interesting. At least, the things I've seen and been a part of." Leaning forward, I try to meet his eyes, but he's staring out at the stone water-fall in the center of the vacant pool and not at me. "I'm not asking for more, though. I understand that will take time." *Please hear the plea in my voice. Don't give me anything of use.*

"How did you meet him?" he asks, after an eternity of silence. His mercurial mood shift makes me uneasy. He wants to talk about Conti again, and Anthony Conti is the last man on the planet I want to talk about. Most of the time, I like to pretend he doesn't exist. But after the way I accused Maddox of working for him yesterday, I suppose he's entitled to his questions.

And then it hits me. He knows I've spoken with Conti.

I accused him of working for him. I made it clear I was aware of the debt. I tipped my hand, and now Maddox is suspicious. He should be. He should be very, very suspicious.

"My mother died of an overdose when I was sixteen. He was there the day she died."

"What does that mean? There?"

Dammit, Maddox. Don't do this. My face drops as I stare at the clear blue water circulating around my lower legs. "He walked into the bathroom of our apartment where I was sitting with my mother's body. That's how I met him."

"That was the first time you met him? He just walked in?" He's incredulous, though his voice barely rises above a gentle purr. Hardly audible above the sound of the waterfall. I assume that's intentional. I nod, and even though he's not looking at me, I know he saw it. "So . . ." he trails off like he's trying to work this all out. "He knew she was dead even though she had just died."

"Yes." Because that's how I figured it out, too. That he killed my mother. The timing was too perfect and there are no coincidences. Not from my experience.

"Who was your mother to him?"

"No idea. I've asked, and he's never said anything more than that she was a junkie whore."

Maddox's jaw clenches, his fists balling up in his lap. I realize now that this is why he brought me out here. Why he asked me to play hooky and go swimming. It was to get me completely alone and ambush me. I should mind. Part of me does a little, but not enough to get up and leave or stop answering his questions. I want Maddox to know everything without me having to offer it up.

"So, you've . . . *belonged* to him since you were sixteen? Since he walked into that bathroom and claimed you as his own."

I swallow hard, the thought as revolting and sick as his tone suggests. I hate how quick he was to figure it all out. "Yes." I close my eyes, too terrified to watch his reaction. I don't want Maddox to think less of me. To think I'm stupid and weak for allowing myself and Justin to fall under Anthony Conti's control. In my defense, I was young and alone and scared Justin and I were going to end up in foster care. I didn't see evil when I looked into his dark eyes that day.

I saw a way out of our horrible situation, and I took it. Still, it's hard to regret it now. Justin's elated smile as he held up his A+ springs into my mind.

We fall silent once more. I don't mention Justin; he's never asked me about siblings.

"What do you think?" he finally goes for. "Should we hop in the pool?"

I smile so big all my teeth show. "In our clothes?"

His gaze finally, freaking *finally*, meets mine. "You afraid?" His eyes drop to my thin black blouse and I feel my nipples salute him. I shouldn't like the idea of being wet in an empty pool with Maddox, *my boss*, as much as I do. I didn't tell him I was stealing intel for the enemy. I'm duplicitous to the worst degree and I should not interact more with him than necessary for work. It's wrong. But it feels so good I don't know how to stop.

"I don't know how to swim."

"I won't let you drown."

"Prove it." I jump in without a second thought, coasting back until I'm nearly in the center of the pool.

"Fuck," I hear him hiss before he dives in from a sitting position, swimming over to me as my movements start to falter.

I really can't swim. That wasn't a lie. Swimming lessons are for rich kids who have access to pools or live by the ocean. I was neither. He swims over to me quickly, grabbing me around the waist and hoisting me up over the break of the water. "Are you trying to die?"

"Maybe I just wanted you to save me."

He grins up at me and the way my heart flutters in my chest tells me I'm more than in trouble. This crush, this thing I have for him . . . it's turning into something real. My wet hair brushes across his face as he holds me up. Rivulets of water run down his cheeks and my breath stalls at just how handsome he is. I grip his shoulders, holding on tight.

"My hero."

"No, baby," he says, his blues locking on mine, so eerily calm, his full lips holding not a hint of a smile. "You don't need me to save you. You've been fighting your own battles over and over again. It's about time you start owning that."

My throat thickens and I'm desperate to move, to squirm out of his arms and get away. Instead, I stare at him, paralyzed. Was I saving myself all this time? Have I been saving Justin? Is that what this burn in my stomach is? Fire? Grit? Determination?

Maybe, he's right. Maybe I don't need a savior. Maybe I just need myself. But that doesn't stop me from wanting him. Does it?

SEVENTEEN

MADDOX

THE WORST PART about living in Nevada? It's a landlocked state. No ocean. Hell, it's a fucking desert climate, so there's not much water other than the fake-ass features in front of the casinos. I didn't grow up in Australia or California. I grew up in Georgia, and beaches on the east coast aren't particularly known for their surfing. Plus, I'm six-six if I'm an inch, and broad, which means my center of gravity is decently fucked. Not all that conducive for surfing.

But that didn't stop me from trying.

Didn't stop me from loving the hell out of waking up at five a.m. on weekends and making the thirty-minute drive from Savannah to Little Tybee Island to hit the waves with my wetsuit and board. It was the only place I couldn't think. The only place that eliminated everything beyond basic survival instincts. You couldn't hear past the roar of the water and you couldn't see past the wave while trying not to drown.

I lost my virginity on that beach.

I got drunk and stoned for the first time there, too.

It's where I first told a girl I loved her. And meant it.

And even though I wasn't going to be doing any surfing, that beach is where I was headed the night my entire life changed in the worst possible way.

Exactly eleven years ago today.

It's why I'm still sitting in my office under the bullshit pretense of doing work, even though it's close to six-thirty now. I can't go home. I can't be alone with myself or my thoughts. Visions of that night flash through my head, one after the other like a taunting masochistic collage. They're always there. Always lurking in the background. And no matter how many things I've done, how many people, women, I've saved, there is no righting my wrong.

And I no longer have a place to go to remove my ability to think. Hence why I'm still here.

Spinning around in my chair, I face the window. I'm restless, overly edgy, and incapable of sitting still for too long. The sky is echoing my mood—stormy, dark, hateful. I want to stand up and smash my head against the glass. I want to feel it shatter and cut me open. I want to punch it. Punch something so hard until the earthquake of emotion inside me settles back down into a manageable rumble.

My phone chirps from my pocket and I take a few extra moments to reach for it, too busy watching the lines of tears streak down my windows and the flashes of lightning erupt across the sky.

Jake.

The considerate bastard gave me a wide berth all day.

Go home or come over or go to the gym. But leave the fucking office.

Or, if you'd rather go hunting to burn the energy, I'm with you. Whatever you want.

A half-hearted grin crawls up the corner of my lips. I know he's with me. To say we have each other's back is an understatement. Ours is the level of trust that's earned in battle and happens when you believe the man next to you would risk his life for yours and knows you'd do the same for him without hesitation. Our friendship is a brotherhood. And though we only served for two years together before Jake was shot in the shoulder, it was enough for us. Not that I go around sharing my shit freely. Jake's the only one who knows my dark truth, and that's simply because I got shitfaced one night in Afghanistan and told him.

Hunting. He's not talking about deer, either. He's talking about running recon. Gaining intel. He's talking about Conti. As much as that's a necessity, now more than ever, I'm too distracted tonight to focus on that. I don't reply. I don't have to.

Last year he wrongly assumed smothering me in human interactions was the way to keep me from ending up face down in a bottle. I think he learned his lesson this year.

Before I became the COO, I was a dealer, a bouncer, the head of casino floor security—Brian's current job. And as I sit here in my executive office, staring out my corporate window and wearing a three-thousand-dollar suit that makes me feel more like a monkey than a man, I wish I could return to that. I don't feel powerful in suits like these. I don't need them to earn respect or intimidate. I don't need them to negotiate a deal or prove I can roll with the big boys. And they sure as shit don't hide my particular brand of crazy. At least not today.

"I'm going home now," Isabel murmurs from where she's hovering at my door. She should have left over an hour ago. Honestly, I didn't realize she was still here, or I would have told her to go.

"Have a good night."

"Do you need me to do anything before I go?"

"Nope."

"Do you want me to stay?"

Isabel. I want so many things from you.

"Nope."

"Okay then."

"Okay then."

I don't bother turning around to face her, but I note her heavy sigh and sweet scent that is uniquely hers. It's not perfume. It's just Isabel. Her warmth hits my back even from across the room. The moment she leaves, everything wonderfully distracting that came with her does as well.

I think I frightened Isabel.

She's been silently lurking all day, sitting at her desk and quietly doing her work, only communicating with me via text or email, even though I was directly across the hall from her.

Isabel. My Starshine. She called me her hero. She might hate me when this is all over and done, but the way she looked at me when she said that . . .

She's the one girl I can't fall for and the one girl I can't stay away from.

"Fuck this."

I already spent two hours in the gym this morning, and honestly, all I want to do is eat a shit-ton of greasy food, drink some really expensive tequila, and watch mindless sports. Alone. That actually sounds like a pretty damn good pity party to me.

Dialing up takeout from my favorite barbeque place, I order one of almost everything from the menu. That's going to take a while given the size of the order, so I head downstairs to my favorite bar, Valaria's. It's where Jake and Fiona used to work together, and if I wasn't so into being alone, I'd probably sit at the bar and do my thing here. It's Wednesday or some shit, but I swear, this place is always crowded, even in February during a crazy ass storm in the middle of the week.

Walking behind the bar, I snag a full bottle of Gran Patron from the top shelf. "I'm taking this," I tell Diamond, one of the bartenders. I drop three hundred dollars on the counter and walk out. She can keep the change for herself. I don't even care.

I set the bottle on my passenger seat, start up my Jeep, make sure the top is up, and then pull out of the garage. Heading south on Las Vegas Boulevard during rush hour is a nightmare on a good day. In the middle of a rain storm is ten times worse. My wipers are barely keeping up.

As I creep along, suddenly, everything stops.

My car. My patience. The world.

Because there, sitting at the bus stop in the thunder, lightning, and rain, blatantly being harassed by a gang of assholes coated in tattoos and a death wish, is Isabel. There are three of them and she's sitting with her legs crossed, arms folded, no longer wearing the pretty black sheath dress she had on today. Nope. She's wearing a black blouse of some kind, with her black leather pants and black boots. Her hair is down and wet and sticking to her body—as are her clothes—and she's yelling something at them that I can't hear. I'm going to kill them all because one of them just touched her arm.

These assholes picked the wrong girl on the wrong fucking day.

I'm out of the car before I even get my next heartbeat. Horns honk, blaring their aggravation behind me since I'm now parked in the middle of the right lane. I don't care. I hardly notice, except the punks at the bus stop do. Their pinheads all swivel at once in the direction of the orchestra of sound. That's when they spot me. One of them smiles tauntingly, as if to say, "game on." One takes a step back, his expression filled with uneasiness as he glances to his friends for their next move. The last one shifts to stand in front of Isabel, as if marking his territory and protecting his property from the psycho headed their way.

"Get in the car, Starshine," I bark, not wanting to use her real name and give these goons anymore bait. She moves to stand, but the guy in front of her pushes her back down.

Fucking idiot.

"Sorry there, *friend*," the guy says smugly. "But we saw her first."

I don't stop until I've reached him. I wrap my hands around his neck, lifting him off the ground and slamming him back into the plastic barrier, his head bouncing off an advertisement for Cirque du Soleil at The Mirage. I give his neck a good squeeze and he makes an extremely satisfying gurgling sound as his feet dangle from the ground, thrashing back and forth, attempting to kick me. He grips my wrists, his minimal fingernails digging into my flesh. The small zing of pain drives me on. He's smaller than me. They all are. Then again, so are most people.

The stupid ass is still smiling like he has the upper hand. Some people really don't know when to cut their losses and run. He puffs out a breath and I catch the rancid stench of beer. They're drunk. Fantastic. I squeeze again to let him know I mean business and his smile begins to falter. His bug eyes widen into genuine fear like I might actually strangle him to death in the middle of Las Vegas Boulevard. Again, fucking idiot.

One of his friends comes up to my side, grabbing hold of my wrist, trying to pry his friend's neck free. My eyes cleave a path of murder in his direction and the coward steps back, throwing his hands up in surrender. They could have weapons. Knives or guns. But somehow, I doubt it. Their tattoos are custom, not prison. Their clothes are designer, not second-hand. The diamonds in the ears of the asshole I have strung up are real. And they're too scared and stupid to be made men. They're rich boys with too much time and money, with too much arrogance and zero repercussions for their evil deeds. My bet is that they're tourists, here for a good time and thinking all girls in this town are easy prey.

"Come on, man!" one of the dude-bros yells, pulling back on my shoulders and getting nowhere with his attempts to disengage me from his friend. "Let him go. No harm, no foul, right? We were just having some fun." He's yelling because his friend is turning redder and can't speak or breathe much past his constricted trachea.

"I'm going to tell you this once," I spit in his face. "You don't touch women who say no. You don't harass women who say no. You don't look at women who fucking. Say. *No*. It's not a joke. It's not having some fun. And it most definitely doesn't make you more of a man." I release him before he passes out and step back. The guy falls to the ground in a heap, clutching his neck and coughing as he sucks in air. His friends aren't smiling anymore. They're standing back, giving me a wide berth, jumpy that I'll unleash my crazy on them next.

Isabel is staring at me with an indiscernible expression, half in the rain, half under the protective barrier of the bus stop, her arms wrapped around her chest as if staving off the cold and wet. She's soaked and quiet and so pretty my chest hurts.

"If I ever see any of you near her again, I won't be so forgiving. I live on this Strip. I own this motherfucking Strip. Don't come back."

I turn around, take Isabel's hand and walk her to the passenger side of my Jeep. Opening the door for her, I grab my expensive bottle of tequila and help her in. Her eyes find mine as I shut the door. I feel her following me as I round the car, set the bottle in the backseat and get in. I feel her eyes on me as I buckle my seatbelt and throw the Jeep back into drive. And when I glance in her direction and find her practically leaning against the door, it occurs to me that I might have scared her.

"Are you okay? Did they hurt you?" I ask, trying for soft and unintimidating. "I'm sorry I don't have a towel," I continue when she doesn't answer. I turn up the heat, pointing the vents in her direction because she has to be cold. She's soaked through. Her backpack on her lap is in no better shape. I let out a harsh growl. "Why were you taking the bus? Don't you have a car?" I already know she doesn't and it's driving me up a wall that I didn't consider that before.

Lightning flashes across the sky, followed by a loud crack of thunder. It's only pissing me off further. Why the fuck was she out in this? We're slowly crawling along the Strip. All I wanted tonight was to get my food and take a few shots and watch some basketball. Now she's here. And now I can barely breathe I'm so fired up.

She doesn't answer me. *Fucking answer me!* "Why don't you have a car, Isabel?"

"They're expensive, Maddox."

She's taunting me. Her mocking tone is taunting me, and once again, I want to spank her ass red. No one makes me as crazy as this woman does, and I love it as much as it drives me wild. I shake my head. Conti, whatever the hell he is to her, is a billionaire and he lets her take the bus? "I'm going to give you access to a company car."

"No, you're not. I don't want your charity."

Christ. This girl. This beautiful, stubborn girl. I wonder if that's why Conti never gave her a car. I wonder if she makes him as nuts as she makes me. I run a hand through my hair, shaking off the remaining drops of water that linger on my short ends.

"Next time it's raining or it's late or dark, you're going to drive a company car home or I'm giving you a ride myself." She opens her mouth, no doubt to protest, but I cut her off. "Don't argue with me on this. It's non-negotiable."

"Last I checked I'm a grown woman fully capable of making her own decisions. You're my boss. That doesn't give you the right to dictate how I do things."

We're back to this shit now? "Isabel, I swear to God." I turn to look at her. "In case you haven't noticed, I'm not someone to fight with today. It's for your safety and my sanity and that's the fucking end of it." She huffs out a breath, but she's smiling. "Why are you smiling?"

"Because you're cute when you're angry."

"Cute?" I puff out incredulously. "I don't think anyone has ever called me cute before."

"That's because they're afraid of you."

"And you're not?"

"Nope." She shakes her head at me, that smile spreading into something whole and uninhibited and unbelievably sexy. "Not even a little."

"Good." That's the extent of my super brain power right now. That smile, man. *Jesus.*

"This is not the way to my apartment."

Here's the thing: I don't want to take her home. I know I should. I know I should give her as much distance as I can, especially outside the office. I'm infatuated with her ass—and all her other parts—and man enough to admit it to myself. That raw truth doesn't make it easier to manage. If anything, it makes it harder. But it's been a really shitty day and I'm suddenly not so anxious to go home and eat all that food and drink all that alcohol and watch all that basketball alone. "I ordered a lot of really good barbeque and I bought that bottle of expensive tequila in the back. Any interest in sharing them with me?"

I feel her shift in her seat, crawling closer to me on the seat. Her fingers reach out, swiping a drop of water from my ear. Everything inside me stirs to life. Her touch is warm and wet and unexpectedly wonderful.

"I don't drink."

"Like ever?"

She shakes her head.

"How come?"

"Junkie mother whom I don't want to end up like. Addictions run in families. Why are you hell-bent on destroying yourself today?"

I glance over at her and immediately back to the road because now we're finally off the Strip and starting to move, and I'd rather not end this miserable day with another accident. "You don't drink, but you do eat barbeque, right?"

"I can't tonight. I need to go to the grocery store for Evelyn."

"You don't have a car."

"I either Uber or take the bus."

"Is that the only reason you can't?"

"It's the only reason I can't." Pausing, she lets out a breathy sigh, shifting away from me until she's facing forward again and staring out the windshield. "But it's not the reason why I shouldn't."

I grin. It's definitely the first time that's happened today. I pull into the parking lot of the barbeque place and slide the Jeep into park. I look into her dark eyes and my smile grows a bit wider. "You're right. I *was* hell-bent on destroying myself today. But right now, I only want to eat barbeque with you." Because there are reasons why she shouldn't have dinner with me. Because I am absolutely crazy about Isabel Bogart and I don't care about that other shit right now, nor do I care about the reasons why I shouldn't be crazy about her or she shouldn't have dinner with me. I want another date with my girl. "What do you say? You in?"

EIGHTEEN

ISABEL

I SHOULD BE afraid of Maddox. The way I am of Anthony Conti. Maddox is big. He's a little unstable. Possibly a bit of a psychopath. But right now, I'm insanely turned on by him. By his brand of protective force. I've never been the type of girl who's all that into macho alpha dogs—the men who view themselves as the masters of the universe. Honestly, I always found that to be a bit anti-feminist. But I think that's because I was going about it the wrong way.

All of the men I've ever encountered have been the likes of Anthony Conti or drunk men at the strip club. Not exactly the best representation of the male population. But Maddox charged into that situation in the name of protecting me. Of protecting all women. It was undoubtedly masculine and insanely hot. It was sexy in the form of total dominance and I find myself not caring, not even a little. I want his dominance if this is the type of package it comes in. He made me feel safer in those thirty seconds at that bus stop than anyone ever has.

He's still staring at me, waiting for my reply to his offer for dinner, but suddenly, I'm not all that hungry. Well, not for food.

Unbuckling my seatbelt, I climb across the center console and into his lap, straddling him again, which seems to be my signature move where he's concerned. Our clothes are soaked, my pants and shirt practically fusing to his.

"What are you doing?" he grinds out, his hands sliding to my hips, his head dropping back against his seat so he can take me in.

I look into his eyes, which isn't all that easy in the darkness of the car. My back is shielding him from the glow of the dash and navigation and outside it's a wild monsoon. But I can just see him enough and what I see . . . "I'm looking into your eyes, Mister Sinclair. Checking to see just what sort of man you are."

The flash in his eyes tells me he remembers the first time I spoke those words to him in the back of the town car. "And what's your verdict?"

"That you're strong enough to fight your own battles and smart enough to win them."

"What does that mean?"

"That I'm done fighting this." My fingers rake through his short hair and I lean in, pressing my lips softly to his. I've never done this before. Never initiated a kiss. Hell, I've only ever kissed two boys in my life and that last one was when I was sixteen. That time didn't end well for me. I'm hoping this is different. Maddox freezes, his body tensing and his hands clutching my hips just a bit harder. "Kiss me back, Maddox. Don't make me beg you for it." I will. I want this that badly.

"Fuck," he growls, his face tilting to deepen the kiss as he tugs on my hips, pulling me closer into him. His lips part mine, his tongue sweeping in, devouring every inch of my mouth.

I surrender. I give in to him completely. Allow him to lead and consume me with his hands in my hair and up the back of my shirt. With his hard cock pressing against my most sensitive area, shooting sprays of electricity throughout my body.

I cup his face, loving the hint of roughness from his stubble against my palms, as I grind forward against him. I may be brand new at this. I may have never done anything more than kiss a guy, but I know how to move my body. I was taught by the best. And judging by the sounds slipping past his lips into mine, I'm doing it right.

We fit together so well. So perfectly aligned. This is it. This is what I've been waiting for. All that angry passion between us bubbling beneath the surface explodes. We're a mess. Wild and frantic. Teeth and hands and moans and tongues. It's kissing the way I always imagined it would be. Full of unrestricted passion. I lose track of how long we kiss like this. It's hours and days and I never want it to stop. He's learning every inch of my mouth. Memorizing the way the brush of his tongue against mine makes me whimper. How the press of his lips against mine makes me dive in for more. Maddox is my drug. He's my high. And I never want to come down.

"Isabel," he groans against me, his arm snaking up the back of my shirt, his hand reaching out of my collar to grip my hair. He tugs down, forcing my head back, my neck to arch. His tongue glides up the column of my neck, nipping at my flesh as he goes. I shudder and shake, pressing his face deeper into me. "We're playing with fire," he breathes against me, causing gooseflesh to erupt in his wake.

"What's the matter, Maddox? Afraid of getting burned?" I moan, my neck stretching back further at the demand of his hand in my hair. It's not painful, but it's not comfortable, either. I love that he's not being gentle with me. That he's turning me into this wanton creature who can't seem to get enough.

He releases my hair, my chin dropping down as he pulls his mouth away. I'm about ready to cry in protest when his knuckles skim my painfully hard nipples poking through the thin, wet material of my shirt. Another moan bursts past my lips, my head falling back once more. *Oh god!*

"Has anyone ever touched you here?"

I don't respond. I just thrust my nipple further toward his capable hand.

"What about here?" His hand skates down my abdomen, the pad of his thumb rubbing the sticky wet leather of my pants, directly over my clit.

"Mmm," I hum.

"Open your eyes and look at me, Izzy."

I do, but it's a struggle. I've never been so wound up.

"Has a man ever touched you like this before?"

I shake my head, biting into my lip. I'm not embarrassed. There is nothing wrong with being a virgin at nineteen. Besides, my life hasn't exactly taken a typical course. But at the same time, I don't want that to be the thing that holds Maddox back.

"I'm not going to ruin you in the parking lot of The Pit."

I puff out an exasperated breath. "Did you ever think maybe you'd be saving me if you did?"

He chuckles, and I puff out another breath. This one beyond frustrated. I think it's safe to say our moment is over. I climb off his lap and back into my seat, buckling my seatbelt before I do something crazy like rip my pants off and ride his face to prove my point.

"Now I remember why I don't like you."

"That didn't feel like dislike, baby. That felt like something that was going to get out of hand quickly." Reaching over, he grasps my chin in his fingers, tugging it over until I'm forced to look at him. "Wanting you isn't the problem. It's everything else that is."

"I get it, okay. I'm an untouchable. You want to fuck me, but don't want to deal with the messy aftermath. You're probably right. This was a mistake. I'd appreciate if you'd take me home now."

"I don't want to take you home, and I never said it was a mistake. It's just . . . I'm . . . Fuck," he growls, slamming the butt of his hand into the steering wheel. "Here." Maddox tears his phone out, pulling up the grocery delivery app he has on it. He hands me the phone and I stare at it like it's a foreign object I've never encountered before. Maddox just handed me his phone. Me, of all people. Is he insane or just totally clueless? "Put everything Evelyn needs into it. I'll pay for whatever extra that costs. Hell, I'll pay for the whole damn order, but you're having dinner with me tonight. Wait here. No running out on me." He throws me a wink and that stupid smile I like so much, then hops out of the car into the pouring rain.

I stare at Maddox's phone in my hand and wonder if I'm making a mistake. It's tempting. Oh, so tempting. *He's* tempting, which is why I'm hesitating. I just kissed him in his car, and he rejected me. Again. How many times do I need to straddle the guy before I get the hint? He. Doesn't. Want. Me. He's paying off a debt and is a guy and easily turned on like all the rest of them. He clearly doesn't want anything to do with the likes of me. I'm not sure I blame him for that. He's right to stay away. A sardonic laugh flies out of my mouth. God, I don't even know what I'm doing anymore.

Trying to fool around with the man you're stealing from is about as low as you can get. Showing him my vulnerable side might be just as bad. I begged him. Christ. We shouldn't be having dinner. I should go home and eat something inedible from my fridge and fall asleep.

So yeah. Dinner. I should make him drop me off at home and leave things at that. But I'm still punching in everything on Evelyn's shopping list. I'm so tired of being alone while I eat. I'm tired of having no one to talk to at night. I'm tired of always getting lost in books and movies because nothing else in my life makes me feel like I'm actually living. Maddox rejecting me was just about the best five minutes of my life, and that thought legitimately makes me want to cry. When this is done, and Justin is finished with high school, I'm going to leave and never return. I'm going to move somewhere far, far away. I'm going to get a job and go to college and start *living*.

Maddox hops back into the car, soaking wet and carrying more delivery bags than I've ever seen. "Were you planning on feeding an army I don't know about?"

"I'm a growing boy." He pats his flat, washboard abs.

"Lord help us if that's true. You already practically have to sit in the backseat to drive." He smirks, that damn delicious mouth of his going crooked as he shakes his hair out, splashing me with water.

"Hey!" I protest, swatting at him. The man is a house made of bricks. He laughs, doing it harder. "You're getting me wet again."

He stops mid-headshake, turning fully to me, and for what is probably the first time in the history of the world, I blush. I'm not easily embarrassed. I danced naked on a stage and was just dry humping his lap mere moments ago after all. You sort of lose your inhibitions when you do that. But after what just happened? Yeah. No. Not smart. "Is that what I'm doing? Getting you wet again?"

The bastard is teasing me now. "Shut up, Maddox, and take me home so I can eat your free food. And no more flirting. There is an imaginary line and you are not to cross it." I draw a circle around my body and point at him, making him laugh.

"No more flirting or talking about making you wet. Got it. But for the record, your rules suck."

I shrug indifferently. "You started it."

"I know. I'm just sorry I can't finish it."

Lust is a stupid, stupid thing.

Maddox throws his car into reverse and we pull out of the parking lot. The rain is slowing down a bit, his wipers not having to work so hard. Fifteen minutes later, he pulls up right in front of my apartment building. We step out into the light drizzle and when I turn around to ask him something, I catch sight of a jet-black Mercedes-Benz S550. It's parked down the road and across the street, and though it's dark out, I see it all the same. The rims shine like diamonds against the street lights.

I only know one person who has that car.

"Maddox," I whisper, fear gripping my throat and filling me with a rush of adrenaline. I clear my throat and speak louder. "Thank you very much for the ride home. I appreciate it given the bad weather and long day." Maddox pauses by the back door of his car, about to retrieve the buffet of food he has in there. His eyebrows furrow, his head pivoting in my direction. "You don't have to walk me to my door. I can manage on my own. I'll see you tomorrow," I add firmly, hoping he gets what I'm trying to convey. *Get out of here, Maddox. Now!*

He stares me down, clearly trying to read me, but I don't dare widen my eyes or gesture in any way. We're likely being watched this very second. "Sure," he says with that hint of a Southern twang. "No problem. Have a good night, Isabel. I'll see you tomorrow."

Maddox shuts the back door to his car, opens the driver's side door and slides back inside. I watch him pull away and blow out a silent breath of relief. That relief lasts for all of two seconds as I climb the steps to my second-floor apartment. I pull out my keys with shaky fingers, sliding them into the locks and twisting until I hear the stupid things disengage. Why he bothers with the pretenses, I have no idea.

I step inside and a hand grips my throat immediately. I can't even scream or make a sound because he is crushing my windpipe. He drags me across my apartment before slamming my back into the wall. I bump the back of my head, making bright flashes of light dance behind my eyes. "Why did it take you over an hour to get home tonight? And why was Maddox driving you home?"

I swallow, feeling my throat roll against his hand. I push against him, but he's not in the mood to be played with. Conti presses his body against mine, his face inches away as he stares into me, darkening my soul with each passing second. "I went to the bus stop. It was raining, and the bus was late." I don't bother telling him about the assholes who hassled me. "Maddox was driving by and saw me sitting there. He offered me a ride home. Traffic was a nightmare because of the storm, and he had already ordered food from a restaurant. We stopped there to pick it up, but it was a large order and wasn't quite ready, so we had to wait a bit. After that, he brought me home."

"Has he touched you, Isabel?"

I frantically shake my head, wondering if he notices my bruised lips. "He barely speaks to me."

"That's not what I heard."

"I swear. Nothing has happened. I've been recording meetings I think you'll be interested in and I sent you copies of those confidential documents. I'm doing everything I can to make you happy."

His hand slowly ebbs from my neck, air forcing its way back into my chest just as my face whips to the left with a sickening *smack*. I stumble back into the wall, sliding down to the floor from the impact of his hand. White-hot heat sears my face. I cover my cheek with my hands, only to feel something wet and sticky against my palm. Blood. The bastard made me bleed this time.

"If you ever lie to me again, Isabel, the consequences will be dire." He's not even breathing heavy. His eyes are hardly narrowed. There isn't even so much as a wrinkle in his suit from pressing me into the wall. That's how in control he is. And that's what terrifies me about him. He stops at nothing to get what he's after. He's unflappable in his unpredictability. Sadistic and ruthless. The man has no breaking point.

"I'm not lying to you," I snap at him. I don't care if he hits me again. I need to yell back, or I'll go insane with this hate bubbling up inside of me. "I'm giving you everything I have access to, which isn't much. Maddox doesn't trust me, and I doubt he ever will."

"I've paid Justin's tuition through this month. That's it. I want more information. Get me what I need. I don't care how you do it, but you better do it, or I promise you, you'll regret it. And if Maddox Sinclair even so much as touches your arm again, he's a dead man."

Anthony Conti doesn't spare me another glance. He turns on his Italian leather shoes and leaves my apartment. The door doesn't slam behind him. He doesn't need theatrics to prove his point.

It takes me a moment to get up. I'm hurt and angry and afraid he'll come back. He doesn't. When I'm sure he's gone, I go to my freezer for an ice pack. My face feels hotter and redder with each passing second. Just as I'm pressing the cold ice against my cheek, my phone buzzes on the floor where I dropped it when I first came in. I flip it off. *Fuck you!*

Except it's not my personal phone. It's my work phone.

Dragging my ass over to it, I bend and pick it up.

Maddox.

***Leave your personal phone in your apartment and
come outside. Walk down the stairs and around the
building to the right.***

Wow. That's incredibly specific. Maddox must know my phone is
being tracked.

I do as he instructs, leaving my personal phone by the door in
silent protest. Opening and shutting my door as silently as possible, I
peek down the street and see Conti's Mercedes is gone. I take the
stairs two at a time, weaving around the building and almost bumping
into Maddox right on the corner.

I keep my head down as he asks, "Are you okay?"

"I'm fine. You should go."

"The fuck I should, Isabel! What the hell happened in there?"
He does that move where he grasps my chin and raises my face up to
his, and when he catches sight of the cheek that Conti hit, his expression morphs from agitated concern to pure, unadulterated blood-lust.
"I'm going to kill him."

"No, you're not," I state calmly, resolutely. "You're going to go
home. You're going to keep your distance from me and I'm going to
keep my distance from you. We're going to go to work tomorrow, the
same way we did today. I'm going to be your assistant and you're
going to be my boss. Do you hear me, Maddox?" I stare at him
beseechingly. "No more touching. No more talking unless it's business related. You have a debt to pay off and I need the job. That's all
there is, all there can be, to this arrangement. Now go. Get the hell
out of here before you get yourself killed."

He stares back at me, his gaze vacillating between my cheek and
my eyes as if he can't decide which one will fire him up more.
"Weren't you the one who told me I'm big enough to fight my own
battles and smart enough to win them?"

I shake my head, swallowing past the thick lump in my throat
that threatens to suffocate me. "I was wrong. So very wrong. He's not
a battle, he's a nuclear bomb. He fights dirty and without remorse or

hesitation. Please. I'm begging you." I step forward and plant my hands on his chest, pushing him away. "*Go.*"

He takes a small step back, his penetrating gaze never wavering from mine. "I don't want to leave you, Isabel."

I don't want you to leave me, either.

"You have to, Maddox."

I watch the bob of his Adam's apple as he swallows. "I'll go. But only because you need to get back upstairs, and I can't go with you. Not tonight anyway. But know this, I'm not very good at following directions. Anthony Conti might fight dirty and without remorse or hesitation, but he's a fool to underestimate what I'm capable of." Maddox leans down and places the softest, gentlest kiss directly above the cut on my face, skimming down over my lips, and then he's gone, running off into the night.

A fool to underestimate what he's capable of?

God, I hope he's right.

NINETEEN

MADDOX

YEARS AGO, I had been in love with the most wonderful girl. She was smart and witty and beautiful and didn't take any of my shit. Not unlike Isabel to some degree. But this girl. . . I met her when she moved to my small town outside of Savannah with her father. It was just the two of them, and since it was a small town, the single father and lovely daughter were instantly taken into the fold of Southern hospitality.

That's how I met her.

My mother dragged my reluctant, surly ass along to deliver a pie and welcome them to the neighborhood. Kim opened the door with a sweet, Southern voice, bright blue eyes, those blonde, springy curls, and I was done. She was fifteen with the body and looks of an eighteen-year-old, and a smile that stopped my heart dead in its tracks. I was a big guy even then, so it wasn't beyond thought for my mother to offer my services to help them complete their move.

And for once, I didn't hesitate. I didn't so much as complain.

Kim and I began dating almost immediately. I wasted no time in staking my claim—I wasn't about to let any of my friends have a crack at her. I fell in love with her from the very start. I think my adolescent heart hit the pavement that first week. While Kim was sweet and wonderful and giving, she wasn't especially forthright. She never spoke about what brought her to our town—her father didn't work— or where she came from before. She never answered my questions about her mother or if she had any other siblings.

Or why she missed so much school.

Or why she occasionally wore long sleeves or pants during the summer.

Why she would never wear bikinis like the other girls.

Why she would only let me undress her, touch her, in complete and total pitch blackness.

Why she would never let me drink or smoke when she was around.

Now, I was a teenage boy—an in-love teenage boy, yes, but a teenage boy all the same. I was playing baseball and football and surfing and hanging out with my boys, smoking pot and getting drunk whenever life allowed it. I did well in school because it wasn't all that challenging, and I didn't give two shits about much else other than getting fucked up and Kim. My mother was a single mom after my father died when I was young and she worked long hours as a nurse. I had four older sisters who were more involved in their own lives than trying to play disciplinarian to me, so I pretty much got away with whatever I wanted.

For two years, that was my life. Kim, sports, and getting high.

During our senior year, things began to change. Slowly. So slowly at first that I hardly noticed the shift. Kim was more withdrawn than usual. While we were all applying to colleges, she shrugged it off. Then right before Christmas break, she came to my house in tears, sporting a black eye and a busted-up lip. That was the night I found out why Kim was the way she was. Her father was the prototypical abusive alcoholic.

But it was more than that.

She was alone and stuck in a bad situation with a bad father. If she had a mother or other siblings, she didn't know of them. She was also terrified of going to the police, not only because of her father's reactions and the repercussions, but because she was only seventeen and would only turn eighteen after we graduated. The thought of having to leave me, leave our school and town, and go into the system at seventeen, made her cry in a way I'd never seen a person cry.

I spent hours holding her in my bed, murmuring and comforting her with my love. I told her I was going to kill him, that I would go over there and beat her father's ass so hard he'd never touch her again. He was smaller than me. Much smaller. But she made me promise that I wouldn't touch him, and though it went against everything in me, I made her that promise. One I still regret to this day.

That night we formulated a plan.

She'd apply to the same school I was headed for, use my mailing address for it, and then after graduation, we'd run off together. For two months, we planned. We saved up money. We got through it. She was accepted to my school and all seemed to be heading in the right direction.

But on the last day of midterms, everything changed. I was at a friend's house, drinking and smoking weed and generally having a good time. I mean, life was motherfucking great, right? I was in love with a girl and we were set to run off in a couple of months. I was set to graduate second in my class and go on to Georgetown to play some ball. So, when she called me crying, begging me to pick her up, I didn't hesitate.

I should have.

At the very least, I should have called my mom. Or one of my sisters. Someone sober. Someone grown-up.

But I didn't.

I left my friend's house and drove to the spot where she told me she was waiting for me. I picked her up and headed out toward the beach, thinking that no one and nothing would find us there. She was a mess. Her clothes were torn, her face bloody, her arms and body littered with fresh bruises. I was drunk. I was high. I was fucking insane with my rage. As far as I was concerned, we were done with school. Screw graduation, we were leaving town that night. It was either that or I was going to kill that sorry son of a bitch with my bare hands.

That's when her father tried to run us off the road.

He came out of nowhere, flying past us on the two-lane highway. I sped up, not allowing him the advantage. Kim was crying. Screaming. But I was out for blood. His car bumped mine and my truck bumped his right back. It continued like that for more than a mile. Back and forth. I saw red. That was all there was to it. I was careless. I was reckless.

I was devastatingly stupid.

I should have turned around and driven to the police station. To the hospital where my mother was. Anything would have been better than playing chicken on that road.

We were quickly approaching the causeway over Bull River when he managed to find a clear path and cut off my ancient truck with his much faster Mustang. He swerved in front of me and slammed on the brakes. I panicked. I overcompensated. We spun in a three-sixty, tires skidding, before my truck flipped over and over and over again, into the row of trees that lined the side of the road.

The last thing I remember before we smashed into a tree was Kim screaming my name.

That was also the last sound I ever heard her make.

I woke up a week later in the hospital, and immediately upon release, I was charged with a slew of felonies and misdemeanors that threatened to put me behind bars for years. I pled my case to the judge directly—I refused to let my mother pay for an attorney. I made the mess. It was not her job to clean it up. Kim's dad was in jail, but he wasn't going to be there for long. As luck or fate would have it, the judge believed me.

He gave me a few options.

One: Sixty days in rehab.

Two: Sixty days in jail.

Three: Join the Army after graduation.

I chose option three. I couldn't go to college without Kim. I couldn't function without Kim. I hated myself. I hated life. I hated the motherfucking world. I went into the Army to blow shit up and try and save some lives. Years later, I found Fiona, homeless, crouched on a recliner by the pool, asking me if I was going to hurt her. And today, on the anniversary of Kim's death, Isabel walks out of her apartment with a red cheek and a cut.

Today. On the anniversary of Kim's death . . .

By the time I reach Jake's apartment, the rage inside me at Isabel being tied to a man like that is almost too much. "I'm planning a murder."

"Awesome," Jake deadpans, greeting me at the elevator doors that lead into his penthouse atop The Turner Grand Hotel. "Is that from The Pit?" he asks, eyeing the bags of food I wish I were sharing with Isabel and not with him. Fiona's okay. I can share with her, but Jake relentlessly hogs all the pulled pork—pun intended.

"It is. But I only have so much, so remember that when you dig in."

"Fiona won't eat much at this hour. You know, since it's like nine o'clock and we had dinner over an hour ago, like most people on a work night."

I set the bags down on the marble island in his kitchen and throw him a glare. "Is today the day you want to fuck with me? I'm thinking no, but we can roll the dice and see how they land."

He takes the bottle of expensive tequila from my hand and walks over to his built-in bar. "Do you want to talk about it somewhere or is here good?"

"Fiona will be even more on board about this particular murder than you are."

Jake bobs his head as he pours the shots, but he doesn't like that response. He tries to shield Fiona as much as he can, and I don't blame him. But he has to know that the reason I helped Fiona that night when I found her out by the pool, scared and alone, was because of Kim. He has to know that I can't do this shit again.

That Isabel, fucking pain-in-my-ass, stealing-our-shit Isabel, might just be the woman I'm falling for.

"We should call Gavin."

"I already did, and he'll be here in like twenty, so we should probably eat before he gets here." You can only share the food from The Pit with so many.

"Ah," a voice calls out from behind us, "I see Captain America is here to play with Tony Stark. It's cute that you boys still have play dates." Fiona walks into the kitchen wearing black shorts, an oversized pink—this chick is always in pink—tee, that says, 'Sorry I can't, I have plans with my books,' and pink, knee-high fuzzy sock-like slippers.

"Lookin' good, doll. Super classy."

"That's me." She gives me a wink, and that's why I love this girl so hard. I mean, she's been through hell, right? Abused her entire life until she met Jake. *And me.* But she dishes it out now like it's ice cream with pie. "I see we're doing barbeque with shots of tequila. And here I thought this was a Wednesday. Are we allowed limes and salt or are we too cool for that?"

"Damn," I say, rubbing my jaw. I want to hug her after the night I've had, and I'm not a hugger. But she really is sunshine. Jake might have created the most perfect nickname in the history of nicknames for her. "Too cool for that. If you're gonna play with the big kids, you have to drink like one. Maybe even swear like one." I cock an eyebrow.

She flips me off, but she does not swear. It's the debutante lady in her.

I grin, but it feels so off I'm having trouble force-feeding it. Fiona, the ever-perceptive woman that she is, walks over to me and places her hands on my chest. Staring up into my eyes, her green ones are just a bit darker as she says, "You don't drink often."

"Not often."

"And tonight is one of those nights that you do." It's not a question. And really, it's irony at its best. I was drunk the night Kim died. If I wasn't, she might still be alive. Kim hated alcohol. And yet, today is the one day a year I really lose myself and drink, because I can't handle the pressure in my chest. Because I hate myself all over again and drinking is a form of masochistic punishment.

"It is."

"Then let's have a drink and eat some barbeque while we wait for Gavin to get here."

"You hear too much, Sunshine."

Fiona glances over at her husband and shakes her head. "I'm not a fragile doll. You boys might fight dirty, but we girls do what we have to do to win. Remember that." She directs that last part at me. "And don't hate her for it."

"Couldn't if I tried." But she might hate me when she finds out just what I'm up to.

Jake hands us each a shot and we shoot them down. Fiona grimaces, even though this tequila is smoother than a baby's ass. Jake looks contemplative. And me? Well, I'm the man with the plan. The tactical guy. The one who always likes to be three steps ahead. We knew this was coming. It was just a matter of when. And like I said, I'm always three steps ahead.

We finish our barbeque just as Gavin comes strolling in like he owns the place, though I know Jake has never given him a keycard or passcode. I don't ask how he got in and neither does anyone else. Gavin came into our lives by way of Niklas Vaughn, Fiona's ex—now dead—husband. Niklas hired Gavin—a guy he knew from long before he met and married Fiona—to find Fiona. He found her all right, but what Niklas didn't know was that Gavin wasn't on his side of the game.

"I see the alliance of intergalactic heroes are all here," Fiona says as she greets Gavin with a hug. Gavin isn't a hugger, either, but you don't say no to Fiona. It's impossible, I've tried.

"You're a nerd," I tease her, and she shrugs a shoulder, not both-ered by it in the least.

"That I am. Speaking of which, I'm leaving you all so I can read and pretend like you're not about to talk ugly business."

Jake's expression grows sour, and he walks over to her, cupping her face with so much love and devotion it's almost hard to watch. "Do you want us to go?" Jake asks. "We can talk elsewhere."

Fiona shakes her head, her green eyes staring into her husband's. She smiles up at him, firm resolve written all over her face. She peers at him for a beat longer, then at Gavin before resting those green eyes on me. "No. It needs to be done and this is the safest place to talk."

I give her a firm nod. She wasn't lying when she said girls do what they have to do to win. "Love you, Fi."

"Love you, Maddox."

Jake kisses his woman and walks her back into their bedroom, leaving me with Gavin.

"It's totally fucked, bro. We'll have to change everything up if we're going by that crazy stare you've got going on."

"I know." I stare into his green eyes. "But he hit her tonight. And she's stuck."

Gavin gives an indifferent shrug. "You know me. I like playing dirty. Not like the guy doesn't have it coming."

And how easy would it be to kill Anthony Conti. Like really. I could ask Gavin to do it and he would because he's that type of guy. Then it would be done. But then what? And would justice really be served? I don't just want this man dead; I want him buried. If he dies after that, then so be it.

Jake rejoins us, and after taking one look at my face, he motions for us to walk out onto his balcony that overlooks the Strip and the mountains. You don't see many balconies in this town—at least not as part of hotels.

We don't say a word as we walk until we're at the end with nothing but glass on one side and open air on the other. It's like déjà vu as the three of us meet in a place with no outside ears.

I look at Jake and Gavin, then state matter-of-factly, without any inflection to my voice, "I'm going to take the motherfucker to the ground."

"Agreed," Jake says.

"Agreed," Gavin says.

I've thought about this since I left Isabel's apartment tonight. Since I entered Anthony Conti's office. Since I made that phone call after we killed Niklas Vaughn a year and a half ago. Since the moment Jake became the silent CEO of Turner Hotels and I became his silent second.

"We knew it was going to happen. Now is the when."

"The key to this job is to keep it simple," Gavin tells us, leaning against the wall of glass, his dark hair blowing around the strong breeze. "Use him against himself. Anthony Conti is too connected. Too interconnected. Complicated will not be to our advantage."

"The man has his weaknesses," I state simply.

"They all do," Jake agrees. "Money. Power. Sex. He's no different than any other asshole we've dealt with."

"Then we'll take his particular weaknesses and use them. We'll spin them around until he's choking on his own design." That's Gavin. I can already see the wheels of sadistic pleasure coursing through him. I don't make it a habit to deal with and befriend professional killers. They're not always known as the most trustworthy of people, not to mention they have a questionable moral profile. But Gavin is a different sort. And simply put, we need him.

He's the unknown to our party.

Because from the outside, Jake comes off like a perfect, charming, good-looking guy. The rich, Ivy League kid who inherited the empire and became CEO of Turner Hotels by family and default. Married to the beautiful Fiona Ramsey-Foss, they are the highest crust of Las Vegas society, in on every 'in' circle and admired by everyone.

From the outside, I'm the big, easy-going, mindlessly loyal best friend of the CEO. I'm the one no one takes seriously. More than likely not the smartest guy in the room. A dumb jock, former-Army misfit who was only given the job of COO because my best friend runs the show.

Make no mistake, these roles are deliberate and have served us well.

But the truth is we are more brilliant, ruthless, cunning, and deadly than Anthony Conti. And between us, with Gavin as our ace up the sleeve, I have a plan. A plan that will, in fact, take that mother-fucker to the ground.

TWENTY

ISABEL

"MORNING BEAUTIFUL," Morgan says as I enter the kitchen in search of some much-needed coffee.

"Morning," I grumble, ignoring him as best I can while keeping my heavily made up cheek out of his sight. I didn't sleep well last night. I just kept replaying everything in my mind. Last night was not the first time Anthony Conti has hit me. I've been on the receiving end of his violence, his aggression, before. He's brutal when he wants to be. That's no secret. But it hasn't been like that in a while, and it caught me off guard.

I don't know what that was about. Why did he show up in the first place?

That's not his typical MO. I mean, sure, he's come over to my apartment before. Many times even, but never like that. I don't know what he's after here, but I can guess. It doesn't take a rocket scientist to know that he wants Turner Hotels. That he wants to drive out Jake

Turner and Maddox Sinclair, stick a proverbial flag in the ground and claim this land as his own.

But why? And why now? And why use me?

"Long night?" Morgan asks, a snicker in his voice. Peeking over at him, the suggestion of naughty doing is written all over his face. He thinks I was up all night fucking someone. Ha! If only.

"Nothing like that. I just didn't sleep well."

Morgan crosses the room, turning my face to his. His eyes turn to slits and I draw back, shifting away, attempting to hide what I know he's already seen. His hand drops from my face and his fists clench. "Did Maddox do that?"

"What?" My eyes pop open wide, a bemused, humorless laugh crossing my lips. "No. Of course not. Why would you think it was him?"

"I don't know. He seems like the possessive, unstable type. And he was a monster all day yesterday."

I roll my eyes, going back to my coffee, hoping we could brush this whole thing off. "He's not my boyfriend, Morgan. He's my boss."

"That's not how it always looks."

Honestly, I don't know what he's talking about. Most of our moments have been in private. When we're in public, we're nothing but professional with each other. I mean, yeah, Morgan saw that morning with Maddox and me in the kitchen, but nothing happened, and Maddox wasn't even touching me. Other than that? I don't know.

"Well, that's how it is. Nothing is going on between me and Maddox." He stares at me dubiously, folding his arms across his chest. "I swear," I say indignantly. "Maddox is nothing but professional with me. It wasn't him."

"Then who was it?"

"Who's to say it was someone at all? Maybe I fell."

Morgan steps into my side, pressing his arm against mine. "That's the line you can tell everyone else. But you and I both know someone hit you." Morgan turns me back to him, his hand on my shoulder, squeezing gently as he tries to catch my eye. "I'm your friend, Isabel. Someone you can talk to."

Only I can't talk to him about this.

"I'm fine, Morgan. That's all you need to know."

Morgan tugs me into his arms and hugs me. It's so unexpected and needed that I start to choke. "It's going to be okay. It's you and me, sweetheart. We're in this together."

I have no idea what that means, but I hug him back with everything I have. "Thanks, Morgan. It means a lot." I step out of his embrace. I don't want anyone to see us hugging and then see my face and think something they shouldn't.

"Good. Because I mean it." His eyes meet mine and in them I see that he does mean it. He wants us to be a team, and maybe that's what we are a bit. "The intern and the new assistant, right? Bottom of the pile." I guess he's right. Both of us are just a bit lost.

"Isabel?" Maddox picks the worst moment in the history of the world to come into the kitchen. I take that back; ten seconds before would have been worse. "If you're done making coffee and chatting, I need you to grab your laptop and come into my office. I have a bunch of crap to go over and not a ton of time to get it done. Today *is* a work day, right?"

Okay, then. I guess we're getting asshole Maddox this morning.

"I'm coming," I tell him. Maddox doesn't wait around. He turns on his heels and marches back down the hall. "I gotta go."

"You call that professional?"

I glance over at Morgan as I grab my cup of coffee. "No. I call that my jerk boss, but it is what it is, and I need this job."

"Fine. I'll see you later." Morgan leaves in a huff, and all I can do is shake my head.

"And they call women emotional," I grumble under my breath, making my way down the hall towards Maddox's office. Part of me was tempted to call out sick. I know what my face looks like and there is only so much makeup can do to cover up what Conti did. Morgan is proof of that. But it's more than that. I don't want to be here. I don't want to look Maddox in the eyes as I do underhanded things. I don't want to deal with his mercurial temperament. I don't want pitying looks from Morgan, and I don't want to have to lie to everyone when they ask what happened to my face.

Such is life. Suck it up and deal.

Right. Thanks. Awesome pep talk.

Maddox's door is open, but I knock anyway because it feels like the sort of morning for knocking. "Come in," he barks.

I roll my eyes before I enter. He's behind his desk, his face partially obstructed by one of his monitors. "Close the door."

I do, but before I even get a chance to sit down or set my laptop down, he's out of his seat. In a flash, Maddox is rounding his desk and cupping my face in his hands. It all happens so quickly, so unexpectedly, that I gasp, taking a small step back and nearly dropping my laptop and coffee. Maddox grabs both from my hands, setting them down on the round table and then returning to me, staring intently into my eyes. Right now, I'm lost. This man. He's my salvation and I'm his ruination. How's that for heartbreaking?

"How are you this morning? He didn't come back, did he?"

I glance over my shoulder at the door and then back to Maddox, nervously chewing on my lip.

"My office is soundproof."

Oh. That's good to know.

"No. He didn't come back. I'm fine."

Maddox shakes his head like I'm trying his patience with that. His thumb brushes gently across my smarting cheek. "Nothing about this is fine."

Then his mouth dips to mine.

At first, I freeze at the unexpected brush of his lips. At the way they don't devour me hungrily—like they did last night—but kiss me sweetly, gently. It's the sort of kiss that makes your knees weak and tears spring to the back of your eyes. It's the sort of kiss that makes you silently sigh to yourself as you think . . . *perfect*. "What are you doing?" I mumble against him. "I thought I told you this can't happen."

"And I told you I'm not very good at following directions."

I shake my head as he presses me further into his door, his hips locking me in. "Do you have a death wish?"

"Maybe." He chuckles, but the sound quickly dies as his lips meld themselves to mine once more. I take his full bottom lip in my teeth, biting down hard enough to let him know that this is epically stupid. "But you might be worth it."

Damn him. I'm falling in love.

"Did you not hit the reject button last night in the car? Something about not wanting to ruin me?"

"Was that me?" He pulls back and stares at me with his head tilted and his brow furrowed. "Are you sure you have the right guy? I don't think I would ever hit your reject button. Other buttons, yes, but not that one."

"That did happen, right? I know I didn't imagine it. Maybe it's the head trauma. Or am I taking crazy pills and thinking they're Ibuprofen?"

"You might be. Are they prescription or over the counter? You should check the label."

I roll my eyes and he smiles.

"I've been wanting to kiss you since I first laid eyes on you."

"That's because I was naked."

"*Mostly* naked. I haven't seen everything. Yet."

I plant my hand so firmly into Maddox's chest, my nails will sprout leaves soon. "This isn't a game. It's not a joke. Office politics and sexy stuff aside, that warning I gave you in the champagne room is real. The evidence is on my cheek. You can't touch me."

"Do you really think I don't know?"

"Then what are you doing?"

"Making you mine and not his."

Something inside of me cracks. Fissures. Splitting me in two. The bastard just broke me. I'm constantly alone and scared. And I'm tired of it. So very tired of waking up like this. Of walking through my days, counting the seconds until they end. But suddenly, it doesn't feel like that's my life anymore. At least, not the alone part.

I press closer against him, until my chest is flush with his. Then I kiss him. I wrap my arms around his neck and lean up on my tippy toes and I kiss him. My lips slide against his, begging, pleading. *I need this*. He forces my lips from his, looking into my eyes, our breathing ragged, our hearts pounding. He feels it, though. He feels that I'm no longer whole. That I'm something ugly and dark and twisted.

"What's wrong?"

I begin to shake. My body trembles and my bottom lip quivers. Before I know what the hell is going on, I start to lose it. Ugly tears threaten to stream from my eyes like rain falling from the sky. I shake my head, trying to stop the onslaught before they hit the ground running, but it's not working. I close my eyes and suck in a deep breath—anything to regain my composure. He releases my hair and cups my face once more.

"Isabel?" he whispers my name this time, like he doesn't know what to do with the sound on his lips. With the girl begging him. He holds me so tenderly, so passionately, so . . . lovingly.

"Please," I beg, only now I don't know what I'm asking for. I'm not this girl. I'm not this weak, sniveling, begging girl, but I don't know how to make it stop. "I don't know how to make it stop!" I scream, shoving him back. What the fuck did I let him do to me? "Is this all a game? Are you using me?" I swear, one second he wants me, the next he's stopping me. I can't keep up anymore.

Maddox takes a step back, his blue gaze thundering through me. "Isabel," he starts slowly, like he needs the extra few seconds and some oxygen to calm himself down. "I've done many things in my life that I regret and am not proud of. But I have *never* used a woman."

"I'm a thief and a liar. I'm doing his bidding. Don't you get that? Don't you see?"

"I already know that."

"How?"

He runs his hands through his cropped hair and down his face, heaving a harsh breath into his palms. "So, I've been playing this game, right?" he starts, pacing in a small circle. This is not my usual zero-fucks-to-give Maddox. This Maddox is slightly unhinged. "The one where I make it seem like I'm not stalking your ass. Like I'm not hacking everything he's hacking. Like I didn't have your apartment bugged."

I blow out a breath.

"And the biggest part of me knows I need to keep my mouth shut. That I should continue to let you come after whatever it is he wants so that I can hold it over his head later. That's the killer part of the game. The one that makes me the winner and him the loser. But I don't know how to do that right now. Because you have a cut on your face and a bruise on your cheek and he's holding shit over your head, and that's not something that sits well with me, win or lose."

I laugh, and the sound is so goddamn bitter I'm surprised I'm not vomiting all over his carpet. Wow. He's been stalking me like a grade-A psycho. I really have a knack for meeting the best sort of men. Not that I'm much better. We make quite the pair, the two of us.

"I don't have a choice." It's the truth, but I'm not sure how much it matters.

"I know." He spins around and crosses the room until I'm in his grasp once more. "I know all about your brother. I know what Conti's blackmailing you with. I know it all."

I shrug him off me, trying to think this through.

I should hate him. He's been tracking me the same way Conti has been. He bugged my goddamn apartment. I should *really* hate him for that one. And maybe this makes me stupid, but I don't. I'm relieved that he knows. I'm relieved that he's been on to me this entire time and hasn't allowed anything into my possession that he didn't want there. I don't want Anthony Conti to win, but I don't want Justin to lose.

"Do you hate me?"

He laughs at my question, and I laugh with him. It's too ridiculous not to. I mean, what the hell? "No, Isabel. I think I'm crazy about you, which probably just makes me crazy at this point. Do *you* hate *me?*"

"I don't hate you." I blink up at him. "Crazy, right?" I groan. "This is so crazy."

"That's one word for what this is. I'm sorry I've been doing all that behind your back."

"Ditto. Like times a million. But I like you too much to hate you and I only gave him stuff I didn't think was important. Maybe we'll share a padded room at the institution. If we don't end up buried in the desert, that is. You have pretty eyes, Maddox. It would be a shame for Michael Corleone to shoot you in them the way he did Moe Greene."

He chuckles, running his thumb over my bottom lip. "We're quite the pair."

Funny, I was just thinking that, wasn't I?

"I won't jeopardize Justin's safety or his future."

"I know. I'm not asking you to. But we're at the point where there is no going back."

I don't know what that means, and I don't want to. No one likes to lie under oath, and Anthony Conti is quite the cross-examiner.

I look up, falling into Maddox's ocean blue eyes, allowing myself to drown in them completely. We've stopped talking, and now we're just staring. His knuckles burn down my skin, skating from my jaw to my neck as his warm palm covers me, feeling my pulse thrum against his skin. He smirks when he feels it racing and then he continues, moving lower. His hands skim past the sides of my breasts. My nipples pebble in response, my breath coming out in short, tight bursts. And still, he watches my face. Watches what his simple touch does to me.

He rocks into me. Not a lot . . . just enough to let me feel how hard he is. As if he's telling me, *feel that? That's how wild you make me. How uncontrollable.* I need his mouth back on mine more than I need my next breath. My palm flattens into his chest, directly over his heart and the wall of muscles that separate me from it. It's pounding, just like mine. I return his smirk, wondering how long this will last. Which of us will crack first?

Fuck it.

I reach up and wrap my arms around his neck, then jump, startling him. He reacts quickly, catching me as I snake my legs around his hips, resting my feet just above his perfect ass. Damn this man. He's a prize waiting to be unwrapped. And I think he might just be mine. I'm most definitely his.

His lips slam into mine and our bodies in turn, slam into the hard wood of his door. He presses into me, our chests perfectly aligned from this position as he ravages my mouth with his full lips and commanding tongue and sweet breath. He's all I see. All I smell. All I ever want to taste. In fact . . .

Untwining my legs, I slide down his body. His eyes pop open wide, shocked to find me suddenly on my knees before him. "What are you—" His words die on his lips as my hand rubs his hard length over his soft gray pants. "Isabel?"

I answer his question by unlooping his belt and setting to work on his button, followed by his zipper, sliding it down with tremulous fingers. I'm so nervous right now. I wonder if he can see that in my eyes.

"You've seriously never done this before?"

I shake my head.

"Fucking hell woman. You have no idea the kind of turn on that is."

"I think I can guess," I tell him coquettishly, reaching into his boxer briefs and squeezing him. It's not just that I've never given a blowjob, I've never actually touched a penis before. Maddox is huge. I mean, I think he is. Long and thick and smooth and hard. Before I can think too much, I slide it forward and into my eager mouth. He lets out a groan mixed with a growl and that sound causes a rush of wetness to pool between my thighs.

I never realized how sexy and powerful doing this could make me feel, but wow.

Continuing my stroking, I do my best to take him into my throat.

"That's right, baby. Just like that. You look so hot on your knees with my cock in your mouth." I can tell he's restraining himself, standing perfectly still and letting me do all the heavy lifting. He wants to fuck my mouth. He wants to grab my hair and let himself loose, but instead, he cups my cheek and tells me how beautiful I am. Tells me how I'm doing it just the way he likes it. Calls me perfect, and that's exactly what I want to be for him. I want to blow his mind —pun intended. I want to rock his world, so he never even thinks about another woman again.

I never realized I had such a possessive, jealous streak until Maddox Sinclair came along, but now, I don't even bother to fight it. His head falls back, but it doesn't stay there long. He likes to watch, but I can tell by the way his thighs tense that he's getting close. I pump him harder, suck him deeper, and when I swallow and moan around him, he loses his last shred of control. His hips jerk forward, thrusting deeper into me, and with a warning of my name on his lips, he explodes in my mouth. I swallow him down, savoring the way he looks as he comes undone.

Wiping my mouth with the back of my hand, I sit back on my haunches, a satisfied smile of my own etched on my face. It doesn't last long. Maddox jerks me up to my feet. He tucks himself back in his pants and then kisses me with such force, my knees threaten to give out.

"Now there really is no going back," he hisses against me and all I can think is, *I hope you know what you're doing.*

TWENTY-ONE

MADDOX

ON A GOOD DAY, I can convince myself I'm not a total moron. That everything I'm doing serves a greater purpose. Helps to meet my, *our*, end-goal. That's on a good day. On a regular day, I am the ultimate fool making the ultimate mistake with the ultimate bad girl.

And then there are the days like today . . .

Standing across the street, I have the perfect view of Isabel at the bus stop. She's sitting there, legs crossed at the knee, head cast down, eyes tracking the lines of her worn paperback. She's absently smiling at something she's reading, and I'm hypnotized, paralyzed and stupid. I should be down the street. I shouldn't be standing here, or I'll fuck this entire plan up, but I still can't move.

The left side of my pants vibrates, and as I reach into my pocket to retrieve my burner phone, my view of her is obstructed by the bus she's waiting for. I force myself to turn and walk in the direction I need to be in. If it weren't for traffic on the Strip, I'd be late. "What's your situation?" I ask Gavin upon answering the phone.

"Secured the Diamond suite, directly below his office, under the name Alexander Chase."

I smile as I cross the street at the light, jogging up a few blocks so I'm ready. "And?"

"And it's bug free with thin ceilings. The arrogant fuck really should have done his due diligence when he constructed a building and his office from the ground up. Seriously. I drilled up and in between the steel beams holding this place together, and it's like builder-grade insulation. The man didn't even soundproof or wire his own office."

"Clearly he didn't attend the Jake Turner school of paranoia."

"No. My guess is he truly believes he's invincible. In any event, everything is in position and set up. At eighteen-thirty I'll be playing blackjack near the west entrance."

"Awesome. See you then."

I should probably still be at work, waiting it out there. But I'm not. Instead, I stand here like a bitch for a solid five minutes. No one is stalking me, which surprises me some. I expected to be tailed like a cheetah after a gazelle, but no. He has his guy on Isabel. I saw him when I was across the street from her. He was standing behind her and off to the left, staring at her more intently than I was. So much so that he didn't even notice me. Conti really needs to up his goon-training program, because thus far, I'm not impressed with their level of service.

The guy didn't get on the bus with her.

That's not exactly needed since Conti tracks her phone and her every damn move, but I'm guessing he likes the occasional visual as well. He likes to make sure she's alone at the bus stop at the end of the day. I've seen his man there all three times I've followed her. But he never rides with her.

Which is why when the bus comes to a screeching halt in front of the stop I'm waiting at, I step on. This falls under the moron category I previously mentioned. Why? Because not only is this very public, but I was summoned to Conti's office later for a meeting. On a Friday evening, no less. The bastard really has a flair for the dramatic. And if Gavin is correct, Conti thinks he walks on water. I'm sorta hoping that's the case.

The bus starts to move right after I get on. I'll be honest, it's been a long time since I've ridden a public bus. It doesn't smell all that great. And it's on the dirty side. At least this one is. Glancing around, everyone's face is buried deep in their phones, but it doesn't take me long to find Isabel. She's near the back, tucked into the window seat with no one behind her or in front. And wow, just how perfect is that? I couldn't have orchestrated it better myself.

I do my best to contain my smug grin as I make my way to the back of the bus. Without asking if the seat is taken, I slide in next to her. She startles, her head snapping up to mine. Her eyes are wide, and her lips are parted, and I don't waste time, the opening is just too perfect. I lean in and press my lips to hers. "Evening, pretty lady," I whisper against her lips. "Mind if I sit here?"

"Maddox," she hisses under her breath, her movements frantic as she glances around like any second someone is going to pop out with a camera to snap our picture. "What are you doing?"

"Kissing you. I thought you would have figured that out."

She shakes her head, pushing me back. "Do you have a death wish? Are you trying to get us both killed?"

"Baby, no one is going to hurt you. That's a fucking promise and not one I make easily."

"Fine, but can you make the same promise for yourself?"

Good question. "Probably not."

Her eyes glass over as she stares up at me. "Then get off at the next stop."

"Isabel," I start, taking her hand that's resting on her lap and giving it a squeeze. "I am very good at what I do, and I'm not just talking about my job at Turner Hotels. No one is watching us on this bus. The man who stalks you at the bus stop never gets on with you. It's just you and me right now."

Her head falls to my arm as she presses herself into me. I don't know exactly when we made this transition from enemies to lovers. I'm thinking it was that night in my car when she crawled on my lap and kissed me. The night that fucker crossed the ultimate line and hit her. Before that, I was willing to play fair, even when he wasn't. But now . . .

"I'm glad you're here, even if you shouldn't be."

I smile at that. I'm not too much of a man to admit that the tightening in my chest might mean I'm in more danger than I previously thought. I know I don't deserve her. I don't deserve any woman. I took Kim's life, and for that, I deserve to be alone and miserable for eternity. I accepted that fate long ago. But with Isabel, I'm finding it very difficult to hold myself back. Who am I kidding? I've never been able to hold myself back with her.

I plant a kiss into the top of her head, and she lets out a weighty sigh.

"There's this place I really want to take you. It's a long ass drive, but well worth it once you get there."

I can hear her smile when she asks, "Where is it?"

"The Grand Canyon."

She snorts out a laugh. That's what I was after. Her laugh. Her smile. "Grand Canyon, eh? Why there?"

"Because those pictures you have on your walls should not be your dreams, they should be your memories."

I feel her shudder against me, and I know I've hit my mark dead-on. This girl is filled with so many hopes and dreams she doesn't think will ever come true. And that kills me.

She clears the emotion from her throat before she says, "And what will we do once we get there?"

"We'll hike around, obviously. It's one thing to see it from the top, it's another to actually venture in. And once I have you all worked up, sweaty and dirty—"

"From our hike?" she interjects in a cheeky tone.

"Of course. What else will it be from?"

"Continue."

"Thanks for the permission." She nudges me in the flank with her elbow and I pull her in tighter against me. "As I was saying before your rude ass interrupted." I get another flank shot and I'm smiling so goddamn big. Like a stupid bastard in love. "Once I have you all dirty and sweaty, I'll take us up to our hotel suite for a shower. Then you'll get another massage, since I know how much you like them, to work out your stiff muscles from our hike."

I fall silent for a beat, thinking about all of that. Wondering if this is just a dream scenario. Things could so very easily go the wrong direction between us.

"Go on. I'm listening."

"After that we'll take a helicopter ride over the canyon at sunset." She blows out a wistful breath. "Then dinner at a nice restaurant, followed by me taking you to bed for the night."

"And what will we do in bed, Mister Sinclair?" she questions suggestively, her voice dropping an octave and making my blood hum with lust. Christ, I'm easy when it comes to her.

"We'll do this." Clasping her chin in my hand, I raise her face to mine and kiss her. Not hard. Not rushed. But enough so she feels my intent and craves it as much as I do. Releasing her chin, my hand skims down her silky black blouse, past her hardening nipples, all the way down to her skirt. God love her for wearing this because it's short and stretchy enough that she can spread her legs perfectly for me.

Tucking my hand beneath the backpack she has folded on her lap, I seek out the creaminess of her inner thighs. They're warm, trembling with desire or nerves or both. She knows exactly what I'm going to do and her pretty dark eyes betray the inner war she's waging. *Do I let him do this to me or do I stop it?* Her gaze holds mine as I slide my palm slowly up her thigh, all the way to her panty line. I toy with the thin satin at the apex of her thighs and her lips part on a silent breath. Time slows as my pulse pounds through my ears.

"You're so fucking gorgeous, Isabel," I whisper. "Your face alone knocks all common sense from my mind. But you're so much more than that to me. I'm a teenager all over again, staring at the girl he'd do anything to get and keep." That's how she makes me feel. Like I need to scale mountains and slay dragons. Like she's my do-over. My chance at righting my wrongs. I will slay those damn dragons and scale those mountains if she's there on the other side for me.

My middle finger slices up the center of her panties, right between her pussy lips, and hell, she's already so wet for me. I watch as a flush ascends her neck and cheeks. Her eyes grow impossibly black and hooded, her head nodding back as if the pleasure from just this simple touch has the power to overwhelm her.

"More?"

She nods, almost hypnotized by the finger I have sliding up and down her, but then she remembers exactly where we are. Her eyes blast open, her head thrashing around.

"No one is watching," I promise her. "I'd never let anyone see you."

"Then I want more."

Her trust floors me. It was placed in my hands so delicately. So simply. For a woman who once swore she didn't and couldn't trust anyone, I can barely breathe. Peeling her panties to the side, my eager fingers dive in, unable to hold back. I find her clit, swollen and sensitive, my touch forcing a reluctant moan past her lips.

"More?"

"Yes," she pants, those gorgeous eyes heavy once more. "Don't stop."

My cock strains against the metal zipper of my pants, biting into me as my middle finger finds her opening and slips inside. "Motherfucker," I bite out before I can stop it. She's so tight, I can hardly think past it and that's just my damn finger in there. She'll never be able to take my dick. But, hell, do I want to watch her try. I pump in and out slowly, gently. The last thing in the world I want to do is hurt her, so I slide smoothly and watch as she comes undone beneath my hand. My thumb caresses her clit and my girl bucks against me, searching, reaching for something she's not even sure of. I know she's touched herself. I know she's gotten herself off.

But never in her life has a man been at the helm.

She's quickly learning the difference between fantasy and reality.

"Maddox?" she presses desperately, so wary of her voice and movements.

"Give in to it, baby. Relax and enjoy my touch. I won't steer you wrong." And I won't. I never would. I want to watch her face as she comes, but I'll make sure I'm the only one who does. "My girl," I hum against her lips, our eyes still open wide, watching. "So pretty and perfect. This is only a snapshot of what we'll do after our date. A sneak peek at the beginning. I'm going to worship you all night, Isabel."

She moans, and I suck it down my throat, my lips fusing to hers as she bucks wildly against me, gasping and quietly crying out. "I'm coming," she pants on a whisper. "Yes. I'm coming. Please more."

I give her exactly that. I pump in and out of her with my finger while rubbing her clit in circles to the rhythm of her body. She explodes on me, her wetness coating my finger and the top of my hand. Her eyes shutter closed, her head tipping back and I angle my body, blocking her from any curious eyes. I watch her. I watch her shatter beneath my touch and suddenly, I'm fucking ready to scale those mountains. I can destroy those dragons with a simple glare. And this man? The one who seems determined to destroy Turner Hotels and my life and Jake's life? Well . . . he's going down. He just doesn't know it yet.

THE BUS STOPS a block from Isabel's apartment complex and I reluctantly let her go without me. I haven't told her about my meeting, but she knows I can't join her. She doesn't even ask me to, and how badly does that suck? This bus runs on a route and it eventually makes its way back to the Strip, where I hop off like the cool kid in front of The Conti. This building is in the shape of a big Y. That's not uncommon among Vegas hotels, but Conti's office is in the top right of that Y and the Diamond suite Alexander Chase is currently occupying is directly beneath. Alexander Chase. It makes me laugh, thinking about how many aliases Gavin has. I wonder if he was bull-shitting a bullshitter when we pulled the name Gavin Moore from his computer way back when. It never occurred to me that might not even be his real name.

I step into the cool, overly air-conditioned building and move toward the main bank of elevators. He's so unlike Jake, I realize. Conti, that is. The man hangs out in the regular dude elevator. No special code or key required. He doesn't soundproof or bug his own office. I used to think Starshine was his weakness, and given his antics, she still might be, but I'm starting to believe that his ultimate weakness is himself.

Glancing to my left, I spot Gavin sitting at the blackjack table as he said he'd be. Only, he looks so damn different than he typically does, it takes me a solid beat before I realize it's him. Blond wig, dark eyes, glasses, and a beard. Boy sure can blend and it's scary to see how natural it is on him. Trained killer genuinely does spring to mind. It's one thing to know and even understand who a person is, it's another to see it in the flesh.

He glances up at the right moment, like he knew I'd be there just then. I get the most infinitesimal of nods, before his gaze shifts right and blows right past me. He's thinking about his hand and not me, which is how all the cameras will see it. Me? I don't waste a second look on him. He's here for backup in case I need it. It's all wired through a button. Super old school, per Gavin. My cufflinks are wired. The right one with a GPS device that alerts my boys to my location. You know, for when they need to find my body after Conti kills me and dumps it somewhere like the Mojave and I don't have my cell phone on me. Because I'm dead. The left cufflink, if pressed, will set off a panic message and shit will get real, fast. The goal is to press that one before we get to the body-dumping stage. And it's not like I'm not armed. Of course, I am. Same as I was when I came here the last time. But sometimes being armed and wired isn't enough. In this case, I'm going to assume it's not.

Conti's office is already bugged. Gavin took care of that earlier and I know he—and probably Jake—are listening to whatever is about to go down.

I hit the button for the elevator and I'm silently flanked by two goons. It's almost comical how it's all choreographed, but here it is. The dance I'll weave with Anthony Conti. The delicious scent of Isabel still heavy on my fingers, her taste on my tongue, after I licked her off my fingers. It almost makes me want to shake Conti's hand, though I know he won't offer to.

"Evening boys." Silence. "Ring up to the grand master and let him know that I'd like a bourbon on the rocks." *Finger fucking his weakness to orgasm has made me thirsty.*

I step off the elevator and waltz down the hall. Maybe I should be nervous about this impromptu meeting, but I'm not. He won't touch me here. He'd be a damn fool to. No, this meeting has a very distinct purpose. Isabel. He doesn't know that I know, or however this goes. But I do know, because Isabel likes me more than she likes him. And well, I'm a much better hacker than he is.

I open the door to his office without waiting for an invitation and find Anthony Conti sitting behind his desk, the same way I found him the last time I was here. "Hey man," I say as a greeting. He waves his hand like he's being magnanimous, gesturing for me to take the same seat I took last time. It's like a bad case of déjà vu. Even though I know the game and the score, and I might even be up a run, I don't feel like I have the lead.

"Maddox. It's nice to see you again."

I sink back down into my requisite seat and that bourbon I requested is practically thrust into my hand before I can make myself comfortable. One thing I will say, his men in his primary area are trained well. The lackeys down the line are another story.

"Thanks." I nod at the dude and then turn back to Conti. "What's up? Why all the man of mystery invitation stuff?"

And it was man of mystery. I received a text from an unknown, unreturnable number that read, **6:30 in my office.** That's it. If I were a real wiseass, I wouldn't have shown and played stupid. But pissing him off is not to my benefit.

I take a sip, dropping my ankle onto my opposite knee. I'm the ultimate picture of relaxed. The last thing on earth I want to come off as is nervous.

He eyes me for a beat, that hard gaze glaring past each of my insulting features until he decides this is just who I am. I see it happen and I smile inwardly. "She's been working there for about a month now." I nod and take another sip, though I really don't want to drink right now. "How is she working out for you?"

Oh boy. That's a loaded one. "I thought you didn't care," I tease, like the dumb fuck I am. "I thought you told me you wanted her out of your life and that she was my problem now."

His eyes narrow into beady slits and I can almost catch him hitting the remote on the TV to flash my life before my eyes on seventy-five inches in high-def. This is the part where him thinking I'm the stupid loyal fool comes into play. I think we already mentioned this ploy.

"Whatever." I shrug and drink some more. "She's fine. Quiet and easygoing now that we've worked out our kinks. She does the busy work that I don't want to be bothered with and is generally well-liked in the office by the other staff. We fought a bit at first," I explain because I know, I fucking *know*, he already knows this and it's not from Isabel. "But now I think we've found a mutual respect and trust." I pause here after the word trust. "It works. Why?" I tilt my head, like I'm suddenly curious. "Are you taking her back? Is my debt cleared?"

"No," he replies quickly. *Too quickly*. The smallest baby's ass of a hint of a smile is quirking up his lips. "I don't think a month is enough to clear away the help I provided you."

"Okay. I can understand that." I nod in agreement, showing him the deference he believes he deserves. In this instance, he deserves some. "She's a good kid, and like I said, she makes my job easier. So, thank you."

"You're welcome. You said you two fought at first? I take it that's behind you and you're on much better terms now."

Ah, the bait and switch. Nicely played Mister Conti.

I shrug and down the rest of my drink, clumsily setting the crystal back down. "I think it was more that she wasn't happy with the tasks I initially assigned her. She was anxious for more responsibility. To have a larger role in my daily work. I've heard she calls me her 'jerk boss.'" I laugh at that and his baby of a smile grows into a toddler's at my setup. He can't be that easy. He just can't be. "In any event, since I've started increasing her position, allowing her to attend important meetings, etcetera, she's been much happier."

"And your relationship with her? Has it been strictly professional?"

Wow, I can't believe he just did that. So openly. So boldly. It's one thing to tell a guy to stay away from someone who you used to screw around with—he didn't, but whatever—but it's another thing entirely to ask that type of question point-blank. Weakness, indeed.

"My relationship with her?" I point to my chest, because I'm curious as a cracked-out kitten. I pause here for dramatic effect. Leaning forward, I prop my elbows on my thighs, my expression severe like I'm about to deliver a cancer diagnosis. The natural darkness of his eyes turns red, alight with fire and death and promises of pain. "Of course it is, man. I wouldn't do that to you. And anyway, she is far from my type. I like them perky and blonde. She is most definitely not that."

He considers this for a very, very long minute. Finally, he gives a slight nod and then says, "I hear you're seeing someone."

He shoots, he scores! I laugh him off, shaking my head like I'm slightly annoyed for him being so up-to-date on my love life. "Yeah. Maybe. But I wouldn't say I'm *seeing* her. She's just a woman I've gone out with a few times and am having some fun with." He's talking about Gavin's super-secret chick, Sabrina. She's a French-Canadian blonde I've been out in public with a couple of times. It's a ruse. A necessary one. In any event, the hot lesbian is super cool and fun to hang out with, so that part isn't a ruse. She likes to bowl and play video games and eat, and I'm down with all of those things. But she *is* hot, and to someone like Conti who is having me watched to make sure I'm not deflowering his flower, Sabrina is perfect.

What would not be so perfect is if Isabel found out about it, so I have to play this one right.

He makes some sort of humming sound out of the back of his throat, tapping his bottom lip thoughtfully. "So, everything is working out then with Isabel?"

I nod. "Everything is working out."

"Excellent. Then we'll meet again in another month." He eyes me hard. "If not sooner."

Oh, I have a feeling it will be sooner.

TWENTY-TWO

ISABEL

STARING up at the cloudless sky, I let the minimal amount of vitamin D seep into my pores. It's not warm out. At least not by Vegas standards, but it beats the hell out of sitting in my office or in the break room to eat lunch. I'm in the back of the building, down by the conference area. Since today is a rare day that there are no conferences, I can sit here, on this bench, in peace.

The girls—Sarah, Carmen, and Olivia—like to go out for lunch. I feel bad declining every time they ask, but I can't afford it and I'm certainly not going to let them pay for me. I'd like to go out with them. I'd like to sit there and listen to them chat about their families. I love doing that actually, but the situation is what it is.

Taking a bite of my peanut butter and jelly, I wash it down with my free Diet Coke. One thing I'll say for the corporate types, they don't mind splurging on soda. The vending machine upstairs is free for corporate-level employees. Today is Friday, and while this has been a relatively quiet week, I still can't help but think about what Maddox did to me last Friday on my bus ride home.

I think about it, about him, more than I should. I replay his words on an endless vicious cycle. I imagine that date at the Grand Canyon with him. I've fallen in love with the man and I don't know what to do about it. Falling in love shouldn't feel like this. Shouldn't feel so hopeless. I should be jubilant with a nonstop smile smeared across my face as I randomly giggle over nothing. All the previous inconsequential things—songs, books, movies—should now appropriately reflect my every dumb, lovestruck thought. I should be consumed with happiness, dammit!

But I haven't seen Maddox outside of work since last Friday.

He hasn't followed me. I know, because I've been looking for him.

He's been one hundred and ten thousand percent professional. No secret touching. No sly glances. No whispered words. To say it's messing with my head is an understatement. I thought he was in this with me, but maybe it's only been about the fooling around and all his promises were just flowery words to peel my panties from my body. He's making my confidence flounder and part of me is beyond furious at him for that.

For all of it.

For sucking me in. For making me fall for him. For kissing me that day in his office. For touching me on the bus. For fucking promising me that there was no going back for him!

So yeah. Friday. Yay, rah, rah. While I should be looking forward to a weekend of physical and mental space and freedom, I'm not. I used to spend my weekends waitressing, but now I have nothing to fill the void.

My phone rings in my bag, yanking me free of my dark thoughts, and when I slide it out, my face lights up. "Hey," I answer, unable to hide my joy. I haven't spoken to Justin on the phone in over a week. We try to limit our interactions, but it hurts. He's only fifteen, he was twelve when he was sent away, and I see him so infrequently I'm afraid that the longer this goes on, the less he'll remember me. The less he'll want me in his life.

"You're not going to believe this," he says by way of greeting, and the enthusiasm in his voice is contagious.

"What? Am I supposed to actually guess or are you going to tell me?" I laugh the words, that's how happy talking to my baby brother makes me. It also fills my chest with that familiar ache brought on by longing and loneliness and even a touch of a jealousy that I wish I didn't feel.

"I made varsity on the lacrosse team for this season."

My eyes widen. He's a sophomore and I know their team is very competitive. "That's fantastic! I'm so happy for you."

"I can't believe it, Is."

"I can. You work your ass off."

"Playing varsity means I get to travel with the team. I'm not sure if they'll start me, but I don't care. I'm so damn excited."

"As you should be. But wait." I sit up a little straighter, staring out at the green of Las Vegas, knowing his landscape is much different than mine. "Are you guys already practicing? Isn't it winter in New England?"

He laughs into the phone, filling me up with a warmth that flows through my veins like the most addictive of drugs. My mother had it all wrong when she shot up. Justin is far better than any of that crap. "Yeah. It's snowing today, actually. We practice indoors, though we do run outside when we can."

"Snow," I muse, trying to picture it. I've never seen snow in real life. I think it's snowed in this town a record total of three or four times ever. "Wow. I'm sitting outside in the sun and sixty-five degrees."

He groans. "That sounds really nice right now. I practically froze my ass off on my way to class this morning."

That makes me frown, shifting my position on the bench so I'm sitting up straight. "Didn't you get the new coat I sent you?" The one he had before was from last year. Old. Ugly. And very secondhand.

This one is new. And it made me so happy to buy it for him, even though it cost a ton. My new paycheck is quite nice, though I'm not sure this job will last that much longer.

He blows out an exasperated breath. "Yeah, I did. I'm sorry, that's not how I meant it. I hope you know how much it means to me that you sent me that. I'm wearing it and it's warm and I love it. But it's still only about twenty degrees here, so even the warmest coat doesn't do much without a lot of layers under it." He clears his throat and I can hear the reluctance in his tone. "How did you afford it, Is?"

"Tell me about the girls," I tease, changing the subject. He hates that I buy him stuff, but someone has to. He grows like a weed and needs shoes and boots and clothes for school—they have a dress code —and clothes for weekends and winter gear and lacrosse gear and that adds up. I don't mind buying him that stuff. I like to. It makes me feel like I'm still taking care of him in my own way. If that means I use books for furniture or eat buttered spaghetti, then so be it.

He chuckles. "No girls here, remember? But there is a dance this weekend with the girls' school down the road, so maybe that will change."

"Has anyone caught your eye?"

"You sound like Evelyn when you say stuff like that."

I roll my eyes because he's actually right. I really do.

"But I'm pleading the fifth on that. I'll tell you more if there is something to tell after the dance. Tell me about the new job? Still going well?"

I practically choke on my tongue and saliva. I haven't told Justin how I got this job or why I have it, nor have I told him what I'm doing to keep it and him going. I haven't told him how I feel so naïve for falling for my boss, who could quite possibly just be using me to get to Anthony Conti. Again, Justin's only fifteen, and as much as I can keep him sheltered from my world, the better.

But he knows Conti is involved—I'm sure he does—since he knows he's involved in every aspect of my life. "It's good," I exclaim, hoping I come off as upbeat and confident. "I'm still learning, but so far, I like it." It's not a total lie. Just a partial. "It's interesting, though my boss can be a bit of a jerk sometimes." I smile inwardly at that. "Anyway, it's way better than waitressing at the club."

"Do you think you'll be able to scrape together enough money to come to family weekend in May?" he asks hesitantly, an undercurrent of hope lacing his tone. "It's right before the end of the semester."

I close my eyes, my chin dropping to my chest. "I'll try my very best," I promise him, clutching the phone to my ear just a bit tighter. "Just keep kicking ass and taking names with school and sports, and kiss the girl you like but won't tell me about at your dance. And be respectful."

He laughs, and it hurts so much, I want to cry.

I don't know how much he remembers of our life before our mother died and Conti came into the picture. Whenever possible, I tried to hide him from her and the things she did and the men she allowed into our world. "And I want a picture of you in your new varsity jacket when you get it."

"Promise," he says, and right now, I'd give anything to hug him. "I gotta get to class, but we'll talk soon. Love you, Is."

"Love you, too."

He hangs up and I let the phone slip from my fingers. It clatters against the bench beside me just as it starts ringing again. I let it ring two more times before I reluctantly pick it up, not even bothering to check to see who it is. No one calls me. I swipe my finger across the screen and bring it up to my ear, not speaking. I don't have to.

"Justin sounds happy," is all Anthony Conti says.

"Yes." I wonder if he can hear my heartbreak.

"Your face looks all better."

I have no idea how he would know that. If he's watching me now, I can't see him. If he followed me to work, then I missed him completely. Or maybe when he's having me followed, his goon is snapping pictures of me. I don't know, and I'm not sure how much I care right now. I'm not sure how much I care about anything anymore

—other than Justin. I toss the last of my sandwich down on my reusable bag. I've completely lost my appetite, and it nauseates me just to hold the rest of my sandwich.

"Do you want to go to family weekend, Isabel?"

"Why are you asking me that, Anthony?" I snap. "Is it just to torture me?" My voice rises an octave as I reach the last word. "You know I can't afford a plane ticket, rental car, or hotel."

"You're angry."

Angry? Is he freaking kidding me right now? Angry is a kitten swatting a string she can't reach. I'm a goddamn lioness stuck in a not-so-gilded cage. "Yes, I'm angry. You stalk my phone and have me followed and break into my apartment and hit me. You hit me! *Again,*" I spit the word out. Because evidently, this is what rock bottom looks like. "Even though you told me you'd never do it again after the last time. So fuck you. Do you hear me? I'm so sick and tired of being treated like I'm nothing. Usable waste to be disposed of when you're done with me." *You hear that, Maddox? Are you listening? Yeah, that's for you, too.* "I'm doing what you asked of me. Now it's time you start keeping your promises."

"Ah, Isabel. My beautiful, darling girl. You are not nothing to me. I'll never be done with you. I lost my temper. That's all there is to it. Your face has healed."

"You think I care about my *face?* I want Justin. I want my brother."

"You're not giving me what I need."

Does he have to be so calm when I'm anything but?

"That's because you don't give me specifics." I feel like a broken record. "I give you what I get. What I have access to."

"Then maybe it's time you get what you don't have access to." He pauses, and I suck in a silent shaky breath. "You do that, and I'll keep my promises. I'll give you guardianship of Justin and the money to pay for his education. I'll take care of you forever. Make you mine permanently. I'll even throw in family weekend with Justin if it makes you happy."

I shake my head, my forehead dropping into my palm propped up by my elbow digging into my thigh. How can this man be so brutal and unfeeling and reckless with my emotions? With my world?

"Do you love me, Isabel?"

Is he fucking insane? Oh right, I forgot, he is.

"Yes. Of course I love you." Bile climbs up the back of my throat as the words slide past my lips.

"Then get me what I need, and we'll both have what we've always wanted."

Yeah, but will I be able to live with myself once I get it? He disconnects the call and I sit here, staring out at nothing, my thoughts scattered, my heart heavy. Maddox stalks my phone. He likely heard that entire exchange. That didn't bother me so much at first, but it's starting to now. Suddenly, I don't want Maddox privy to everything I do or say. Anthony Conti is offering me everything I need. Justin made varsity lacrosse. Justin has a dance this weekend, and maybe he'll kiss the girl he likes. Justin is going to classes and eventually college.

There is no winning for playing.

Because Maddox knows everything I'm doing. And will no doubt keep what I need from me. And Conti won't give me Justin or the money for his education unless I get him the unobtainable. And at the end of this, no matter how it plays out, I lose a part of me.

Now what do I do?

It's one thing to hit record on meetings I'm already sitting in. It's one thing to snap a quick picture of a document I'm freely handed. But now, he wants me to become a real thief. When Maddox catches me, which I know he will, he'll have to fire me. Maybe even have me arrested. He'll hate me. Despite my ire, that leaves a sour taste in my mouth. I can't stand the thought of him hating me.

Me hating him is completely different.

"Hey," a voice says softly, almost as if he's afraid of rattling me. Too late for that. I glance up and find Morgan Fair staring at me with a smile that makes his blue eyes practically glow. "I've been texting you. You're late for a meeting." Oh. Not sure how much I care. "Maddox sent me to get you."

"Maddox sent you to get me?" I'm incredulous. What happened to 'stay away from that fuckstick?'

Morgan shrugs a shoulder. "Intern, remember?" I pull my sorry ass up off the bench, throw out the rest of my lunch and follow him back into the building. "Why were you hiding out here?"

I give him a sideways glance. "Just not feeling all that great. I have a headache." Understatement of the century.

He bobs his head up and down as if he's moving to a beat I can't hear. His arm loops around my shoulder, rubbing me in a way that feels like comfort and I willingly accept it. "For what it's worth, I think you're doing a great job."

"Really?" I ask, my eyebrows furrowing, my lips peeling into a reluctant smile.

"Absolutely. Your boss is worse than mine." He throws me a wink and I laugh, leaning into his side. "But I'm giving you a warning. Maddox was not happy that you're late for the meeting."

"Fantastic," I deadpan. "What's this one about anyway?"

A wicked gleam lights up his face. It's quick. It's dirty. He gives me a wink. "The executives from Grant Technologies are here to talk about the new security enhancements for the security towers."

I pale, my stomach roiling.

"My father couldn't make it, so I get to sit in, which is pretty great. Jake and Maddox are waiting."

"And Maddox wants me there? To talk about the security towers? And Jake Turner is there?"

Morgan stares at me like I'm insane.

Oh god. I thought stars only aligned in fairytales. Not in nightmares.

"Do you have a boyfriend?"

I quirk an eyebrow at the rapid change in topic. And then at the actual topic, I grin despite myself.

"I know you had a run-in with someone, but I'm curious."

Now I raise my eyebrows and he treats me to this adorably boyish dopey smile, his cheeks perking up with a flash of pink.

"Seriously? We're doing this?"

He shrugs. If I wasn't tragically in love with the wrong man or beholden to worse, I could see the appeal. "We could. I'm a nothing of an intern and you're an assistant with an asshole boss. We make sense when you think about it."

We do. He's way more my speed. Where was he a month ago when I needed him?

"You want to date me?"

"I'm so glad you asked me first. I didn't have the guts to ask you straight up like that."

I laugh at his cheeky response and smack his shoulder. "That's not what I meant."

He shrugs, unconcerned, and I swear, I really can't take much more. "It'd be fun."

"And you want that with me?" I point to my chest. I feel like I shouldn't be as surprised as I am. He's been more than just a bit friendly. Touchy-feely. But that's it. Honestly, he never seemed all that interested.

"I absolutely do. You're smart, ironically funny, sweet, and so beautiful it's unearthly."

Unearthly? That's a new one on me. "I really appreciate the offer, Morgan. In fact, I'm seriously flattered. But I'm not dating right now."

"That's what I figured you'd say. I'll keep at it, though."

He throws me a wink and removes his arm from my shoulder as we enter the conference room together but separate. I don't have time to analyze his response. Before I can right myself, I make the mistake of looking up at the absolute wrong time.

Maddox is staring at me so hard my insides quake.

TWENTY-THREE

ISABEL

MADDOX'S EXPRESSION confirms he's supersonically pissed at me. Whether it's for being late or some other transgression, I don't know. I slink over to his side, my head ducked and my stomach in my feet. I slip into the seat beside him, blow out a silent breath, and set my phones on the table. I don't even have my laptop with the slides. Crap. I'm really slacking today.

That's when I feel it.

His foot. Maddox's foot slides beside my heeled one. It doesn't just slide, it *presses*. And when I feel that press, I remove my heel and slide my barefoot back against his shoed one even though I shouldn't. Even though I just told myself that I'm mad at him and that I kinda, sorta hate him. I know he's more than likely making me the fool. I let the man finger me to orgasm on a public bus and then he proceeded to ignore me for a week. A fucking *week*.

I'm playing Russian Roulette with a full chamber. A bright yellow warning sign decreeing DANGER AHEAD is flashing, and yet, I'm plowing right past it. I pull the damn trigger. Again. If I could smack myself in the forehead without people staring at me, I would.

"You must be Isabel," the man across from me says, and when I shift my gaze in his direction, my breath gets stuck in my throat and I can't reply with anything more than a primitive grunt. It's Jake Turner. Even though I've seen him around, like at Sarah's baby shower, I've never formally met him. I stare back, my eyebrows pinched. When he doesn't smile, I frown.

"Glad you could finally make it."

I swallow. *Nicely done, Isabel. Pissing off the CEO is a classy move.* "I apologize for being late," I say. "It wasn't intentional."

He smirks, shakes his head at me, looks to Maddox pointedly, and then shifts his attention back to the front. Something in that look he just gave Maddox feels . . . off. I don't know. That look had a meaning beyond annoyance over Maddox's assistant being late. I blush from head to toe for no other reason than the confusion taking over.

"Are you recording this?" Maddox asks, his voice low, his tone glacial. I swallow and stare down at the smooth wood table, unable to meet his eyes. "Go ahead," he whispers in my ear. "It's why I wanted you here today. Press the button, Isabel, and accept this as my gift to you and your beloved."

My eyes close. I can't do it. If I press that button, it's me saying goodbye to Maddox. If I don't, it's me risking Justin's future, Justin's life. I won't do that. No matter the personal cost.

"If you listened, then you know I have to," I utter, unsure if he hears me. *Just don't hate me, Maddox. I can handle almost anything, but that's become another hard limit for me.*

I press record, my insides bleeding, my heart empty at the loss of blood flow.

Maddox makes an angry sound in the back of his throat, and it's only then that I realize there are two men standing at the front of the room, talking.

But that's how this meeting goes. Maddox doesn't acknowledge me. He doesn't so much as glance in my direction. He leads it with some IT guys I don't know but am quickly introduced to. Ryan Grant is tall and nerdy hot, with black hair and green eyes and black-framed glasses. The second guy, Luke Walker, is a little shorter, but no less impressive, with thick brown hair and matching eyes. Luke is talking directly to Maddox and Jake, explaining how weak our security posture is. They're explaining high-level things, important things, but all I feel is Maddox's foot. And my heartbeat. And those damn, sickly drunk butterflies.

The meeting drags on like church on a Sunday during communion. I let it go. I let my mind clear, knowing that this is the end of things between me and Maddox. I'll likely be fired after this. He's done with me. How could he not be?

"We've switched up all your software in the towers," Luke says. "The previous restrictions have been removed. This enables total application access with minimal authentication requirements for quick, seamless navigating. Simply put, you'll have access to everything within Turner Hotels' systems from there."

"Fantastic," Jake booms, his dark eyes alive with excitement. He leans back in his leather chair, bouncing a few times. "And that access is also available on the new tablets we purchased? If there is an event we need to handle, I'd like to be able to do it on the go and as quickly as possible."

"It is," Luke continues. "Anything you'd like to locate or direct, you can. Those tablets are loaded with all your latest tech. Everything from the casinos to HR to guest registration to events. Everything for each hotel is on there, all organized into their own individual app."

My heart starts to pound as I realize what this meeting is. What information they're knowingly giving to Anthony Conti. I glance over at Morgan, who is watching the two men at the front of the table with rapt attention. It's just us in here. These men, Jake, Maddox, Morgan, and myself. Sickness brews in the pit of my stomach as I rewind Maddox's words. *Press the button, Isabel, and accept this as my gift to you and your beloved.* Why would he do this? Even angry and spiteful, I can't imagine he'd knowingly compromise Turner Hotels.

"And those only require a password or a thumbprint to access, right? Not both. Please, tell me not both," Maddox asks, leaning back in his chair and tapping his pen on the edge of the table. "If I have to try and remember another password, I swear . . ." Maddox chuckles, dropping his pen on the table and running a hand across his smooth jaw. "I can't stand that crap. There's a reason we hire you guys to do all our security. So I don't have to think about it."

Everyone in the room laughs. I don't. Instead, I press my foot further against his. It's a question. It's a what the fuck? He completely ignores me. But this is not my Maddox. My Maddox is a psycho when it comes to security. These guys have crazy locks on their doors that require six-digit codes to enter. They have badges with person-specific access. There are cameras everywhere!

"That's why you're the operations guy and not the technology guy," Jake jokes with a wry grin.

"No shit," Maddox laughs harder.

"You don't have to worry about it," Ryan promises. "We've gone over everything and made it as user-friendly as possible. I will say, this is not how we typically set up our systems, but we still believe there is adequate protection, given the difficulty in getting into the towers in the first place. With everything being run from that one central location, you'll be secure."

"It's true. You don't have to worry about the wrong people gaining access. They'd still require either a biometric or a password."

"Good stuff, gentlemen," Maddox declares with a loud clap of his hands.

"Absolutely," Jake agrees, his eyes skating over to me for the barest of seconds. "I'm thinking we should take a spin around the security tower. Check it all out before you guys have to fly back to Seattle." He shifts to Morgan. "I know you're just an intern and filling in for your father, but you want to join me?"

Morgan's expression flashes darkly for a moment, before he pulls himself together and forces a smile. "Sure," Morgan says slowly, his voice level. "I'd love to see the security tower here."

"Awesome," Ryan declares. "That way Luke and I can walk you through how it all works."

"I'm gonna leave all that up to you guys. Jake can walk me through it another time." That's Maddox, but before I can make a hasty escape, his hand finds my thigh under the table, holding me in my seat with a firm squeeze. The moment everyone exits and it's just the two of us left, he barks, "I need you in my office. Leave your phones on your desk."

Bastard. "You have no right to listen in on my personal calls."

He pivots to me and our eyes lock. "In. My. Office. *Now.*"

I rise quickly and leave the conference room first. I'm tempted to make a run for it like the coward I'm desperate to be. But I don't do that. He's known all along what I've been doing, though something has clearly changed. I can't swallow this. I can't tell him, and yet he knows, and Conti wants me to go beyond what I'm doing, and I don't know how.

I make my way to his office, dejected and miserable. Not a new state, but annoying all the same. I stand in the threshold of his doorway, on ungraceful legs. I'm a lost lamb while he urges me in, shutting the door behind us. The wolf ready to attack. I'm frozen as he retreats to the window, peering out at the view that is Las Vegas. "You were late. I put that meeting on your calendar before lunch. You should have been there long before it began."

"I'm sorry. I didn't mean to be. I didn't check my calendar and I lost track of time."

"I had to send Morgan Fair after you. You know how much I hate that?"

And because I'm angry with him and the world and need to be fucking acknowledged instead of ignored, I say, "Morgan asked me on a date."

A growl. The man growls like a caveman and I'd be lying if I said I didn't feel that growl hum across my skin like the needle of a tattoo gun. "Then that boy really is as fucking stupid as he looks." He blows out a breath, still staring straight out the window.

"What was going on back there? What was that whole meeting about? Was it bullshit? It had to have been, right?" But why would Jake bother attending if it was? And why fly in their security guys all the way from Seattle if it was?

"Take off your panties. Set them on the floor next to your feet. Turn around, press your hands against my wall and spread your legs."

"I'm sorry?"

"You heard me. And by the time I turn around, you better be in that position, Isabel."

Christ. I can't think, let alone move. A flush creeps up my body at the crude—and honestly unexpected—request. He ignores me for a week and now this? I should tell him no. I should turn around and storm out of here.

But he owns me, body and soul, and we both know it.

Sliding off my panties, I turn around, pressing my palms against the wall. I'm so turned on I can't control my breathing. Maddox hears me panting. He has to. I have no idea what he's doing with me right now. He's insane. That's all I can come up with. Conti, my psycho puppeteer is advancing. And yet. *And yet!* Here comes Maddox Sinclair.

What are you going to do, Maddox?

Make me pant? Make me beg? Make me cry out for more?

I want it all. I want to *feel.*

I catch the faint tap of his footsteps. One. By. One. My pulse thrums, my body a live wire of anticipation. I want his hands on my ass. I want his hard length pressed against me. I want him to dominate every inch of me to the point where everything else but him shuts off. This man with his hard muscles and imposing form can do whatever he wants to me right now. That's how badly I want it.

His palms clasp my inner thighs, gliding slowly—*so damn slowly* —up, heading toward my center before he stops. *Tease.* His chest meets my back, his hot breath rasps against my ear. "I heard everything," is all he says. That's it. No following it up. No room for questions. No advancing on his king. He just checkmated me and I have no play.

"Fuck you."

He chuckles, wrapping my long hair that's tucked up in a ponytail around his fist and tugging it back. "Fuck me? Maybe. But this is not the place for that first. Or was that another lie?"

"God, I hate you. You have no idea. No. Idea."

"The fuck I don't," he hisses in my ear. He drops to his knees, sliding my dress above my ass, exposing me fully to him. "I love this dress. Is that why you're wearing it?"

"Yes," I admit, because it is. Anything else would be a lie. It's the black short one with the scoop neck and the awesome gold zipper up the spine of my back.

"Spread your legs."

I do, gasping when his face goes between my thighs from behind. His tongue licks me from my tight bundle of nerves in the back all the way up to my mound. He hums into me and my legs go weak, my body slack to the point that I tighten my palms against the wall just to keep myself upright. Holy shit. *Ho-lee shit!* Is he supposed to lick me like this? Is it supposed to feel *this* good?

"So sweet. You are so damn sweet for such a wicked devil."

"Don't stop."

He laughs into me and that vibration . . . Lord. I'm taking all kinds of names in vain right now.

He smacks my ass. Not too hard. Not necessarily as punishment, but as a directive to stop talking and pay attention to what he's doing to me. He spreads my ass cheeks and dives in, taking over everything, eliminating my ability to think or rationalize. I don't care if I get caught. Death? What's death after living like this? His tongue slides into my opening, thrusting over and over and over again. He fucks me with his mouth until I'm so wound up I start to crumple, my knees giving out on me.

In the next second, I'm off my feet, being carried over to his couch and laid flat. Then, without warning, he spreads my thighs wide open, and his mouth is back on my pussy. He sucks on my clit, flicking it with his tongue. His finger slides into me just a little, toying with me when I need so much more. "Fuck, you're so tight. Have you missed me, Isabel? Is that what this dress is?" His finger slips from my opening, wet with my arousal, before rubbing it along my asshole. I squirm against him, the sensation too foreign, too taboo for me to get my bearings. Still, I moan as he presses in with the tiniest amount of pressure. "You are not his."

I shake my head.

"Tell me."

"I'm not his."

"You are *mine*. All of you." He finds my pussy again, sliding two fingers in this time, as if to prove his point. I've never felt so full. So stretched. I can't get enough. I want more. I want him inside me. "And I take care of what's mine."

God, yes! His tongue goes wild on me, flicking and sucking me with abandon. His fingers pump in and out, and I come. Hard. I cry out and grab at his hair and claw at his upper back, thrashing around without any control over my movements.

"They can't hear you. Scream it out."

I do. I've never understood the true possession of an orgasm until Maddox. It feels almost tragically pathetic to be this consumed. What do I do with myself now? As I start to come down from my glorious high, Maddox climbs up my body. His lips crashing into mine, kissing me with total abandon, forcing his tongue into my mouth. I taste sour and sweet and like a crazy woman who just lost her mind.

He pulls back, nipping at my bottom lip as he does. "You're not going on a date with Morgan Fair."

I quirk a challenging brow and his eyes harden into twin pools of heat and powerful determination.

"Don't try me on this."

"You haven't exactly seemed too interested lately. I didn't think you'd care."

"I am, though. I'm very fucking interested. And I care like crazy."

"I told you this can't happen between us." I smirk, biting my lip.

He grins back at our familiar turn of phrase. His forehead presses to mine. "Way to sell it to me."

"You have a death wish?"

"I must," he muses against my lips with that smile. *That smile.* "Do you really love him?" he asks, and I freeze.

Staring up, I tell Maddox the only truth I have left. "No. He's not the one I love."

He holds me captive for the longest of minutes before his lips meet mine once more. This kiss is different than its predecessor. This kiss is tender. Passionate. He drops down onto me and holds me so close, covering me to the point where I don't even care if he's crushing me a little. It's as if he's telling me he loves me back without saying the words.

He draws back, searching me. "Just so you know, I don't listen to all your calls. I don't read all your texts. I try very hard not to completely invade your privacy. I know it probably doesn't make a difference when you get down to it, but I only look and listen to the stuff from him."

It does make a difference, actually. Maybe it shouldn't, but it does. "I'm sorry I hit record." Maddox gives me a sly grin. My eyebrows furrow into a V. "It was fake?"

He neither confirms nor denies.

A lump the size of Texas clogs my throat.

I shake my head. "It's just business to him. It's not even personal. I don't understand why all this is happening."

"I think we both know that's wishful thinking. Everything is personal to someone, Isabel. And some things aren't brushed off so easily. Conti is enjoying every second of this. And he knows precisely what he's doing."

"Jesus," I breathe out. "I don't know what to do anymore or who to trust."

He cups my face and stares deeply into my eyes. His face is so close to mine, I can feel his breath on my skin. "Me. You can trust me. Because everything I'm doing has a purpose behind it. Everything I say is planned and well thought out. So if I ever tell you to do something, you do it without question. If I ask you to run or hit record on your phone or follow me or even to hide, you do it instantly, because you know everything I tell you to do has a reason behind it. I can't always tell you everything. There are things I'm holding back, but my ultimate goal is to keep you safe and protected and *alive*." His eyes bounce back and forth between mine. "Say it. My ultimate goal is to keep you safe and protected and alive."

"Your ultimate goal is to keep me safe and protected and alive. But what about Justin? Where does he factor into your plans?"

"I already told you, everything I'm doing has a purpose behind it. Trust. That's the name of our game. Now, get yourself dressed and back to work."

"Yes, sir." I smirk, pushing against his chest, to get up and get myself together, the intense interlude between us breaking. But in truth, I'm scared. I'm scared for Maddox and Justin and even myself. Because one thing is becoming abundantly clear. A storm is heading our way. And it's a dangerous one.

TWENTY-FOUR

MADDOX

THE REST of the day went by in a blur. I got a call from Jake thirty minutes after I was done feasting on Isabel. Conti took the bait, hook, line, and sinker. "There were nips at our backdoor. Super obvious ones. It took Ryan and Luke seconds to catch them. At least he bought it, but I don't think this was his go at a real attempt. This was a test."

"Maybe it's enough to get him off Isabel's back for a while."

"Maybe. I'll give your girl credit, she's brave."

I smiled at that. My girl is brave. So goddamn honest. And tastes like my own personal version of heaven. She's far too good for me.

"We should have this locked down in no time. Luke said he'd let us know if he gets some nibbles."

We ended the call and I shot off a text to Gavin to let him know where things stood.

Since my last meeting with Conti, I've kept my distance from Isabel, knowing I've been watched closely. Closer than usual, by two assholes who don't know how to play cat and mouse particularly well. They tagged Sabrina and I out to a few places, and when I knew they were snapping pictures, I pecked her lips. Hardly a kiss for the ages— my mother kisses me with more feeling. But when my lips met hers, I felt nothing.

When my lips meet Isabel's, I feel everything. And that everything is all the difference I will ever need to know she's it for me.

Yet after hearing Isabel tell Anthony Conti that she loved him, my blood ran hot. It was jealousy. It was rage. It was a need to command and claim the woman who will always be *mine*. She told the bastard she loved him out of necessity. At least, that's what I forced myself to swallow as I listened, feeling like the bastard I was for doing that in the first place. But when she told me, face to face and eye to eye, that he's not the one she loves, my chest squeezed so tight, words were no longer possible. I only hoped I conveyed with my kiss what I was incapable of saying.

Those depthless, dark eyes stare up at me like I can save her from the world, and they haunt my dreams. The way she tastes, innocently sweet and erotically sinful, stars in my late-night fantasies. The way she responds to my touch and exploded under my tongue makes me hard every motherfucking time I look at her. Isabel has turned into a habit I'm finding impossible to break. It's not even her mobster or the slapped cheek that's been pulling at all my chords.

If anything, it's her challenging my status quo that drives me to my constant breaking point.

Where would screwing this girl ten years my junior get me other than dead? Or killing a man who admittedly deserved to die?

But now, with so many external forces pulling every which way, with the hard-earned knowledge that life is miserably short, I find myself lurking in the shadows of her building. It's not the first time I've been here in the past week. I've come under the pretense of ensuring that Conti or one of his goons didn't. I even left Sabrina at my place, letting Conti's guys think she was spending the night in my bed with me. And every single time, I've talked myself out of tapping on her door.

Creeper.

Stalker.

Unworthy.

Tonight is different.

Tonight, there is no more holding back.

I need Isabel. I need her body wrapped around mine. I need her breaths ragged with the pleasure I give her. I need my name to spill from her lips. But more than that, I need to know, once and for all, that she's as in this with me as I am with her. No more arguing or stolen fleeting moments where we're forced to flip the switch back to professionally indifferent in the next second.

Not tonight.

When I'm positive there is no one and nothing here, I slink my way along the wall of the first floor, allowing the shadows and gaps caused by the dismal fluorescents that poorly illuminate this place to cloak me. The stairs are another matter since they're open and directly in front of the building, but I take them quickly, as silently as possible, until I'm back in the shadows and directly in front of her door. I don't knock, unwilling to make a sound that could alert her neighbors—particularly nosy Evelyn—to my presence. Instead, I text her work phone.

Open your front door.

Fifteen hellishly long seconds later, the door cracks open and her beautiful dark eyes seek me out. They widen when they find me, as if she didn't truly expect to find me here lurking. "What the hell are you doing?" Her wild gaze flies in every direction, peeking beyond her door toward the street.

"No one is around. May I come in?"

She steps back, allowing the door to part just wide enough for me to slip through before she closes it back up and locks it tight. "Maddox," she starts with that tone of hers, instantly laying into me the way only she does. "You are absolutely insane. I know I've been teasing you about having a death wish, but I think you might have just proved to me that you have one."

I cut the distance between us and scoop her up into my arms. She lets out a startled yelp, clutching onto my shoulders as I spin her around and march us over to her worn couch. What I wouldn't give to get her out of this dump. Into my home. Once I set her down, she shifts to make room for me, but instead I kneel before her, my hands on her thighs. She tracks my movements with suspicious consideration, unsure of my motives for this impromptu visit.

She's changed since coming home from work, now wearing a threadbare black Misfits tee and black and gray flannel pants. All her makeup is washed off and her hair is down, sorta all over the place. Unbelievably sexy. With her dark hair like this and her fresh face, she's the most gorgeous woman I've ever seen. My hands slide up her thighs until I'm gripping her hips, drawing her closer and forcing her thighs to part to allow my body to fit between them.

"I need to ask you something and I need you to tell me the absolute truth. Can you do that?"

Her eyes vacillate back and forth between mine, her expression a perfect cocktail of confusion and apprehension. She swallows hard and nods her head slowly. "Yes. I can do that."

"Is the only reason you're helping him because of Justin?"

"Yes," she replies automatically, without even the smallest flinch or shift of her eyes.

"Is being with me part of a bigger scheme you have going on with him?"

She rears back. "No," she pushes out adamantly. "How could you—"

I lean in and press my lips to hers, cutting her off. "I just had to be sure."

"Is that what you're doing with me? Using me to get to him?"

I quirk an eyebrow, giving her my best stern face. "You know I'm not."

"But you believe me?" She searches my face, her hands on my cheeks as mine are on hers. "I wouldn't do that to you. I couldn't."

"I know, baby. I believe you." Her eyes meet mine as she smiles, and all the air escapes my lungs like someone just kicked me in the chest. The best heartbreaker I've ever met. "Things are always different on the inside than they appear on the outside. That's why it's called perception and not reality. I just had to be sure."

She emits a small, aggravated humph. "You looking for something real, Maddox?" She pushes me until I fall on my haunches, my chin tipping up to follow her as she stands. Her shoulders square as an impish spark flickers in her eyes. She winks at me. Then in one swift motion, she slides her shirt over her head, tossing it back onto the couch. She's not wearing a bra, her full tits with those perfect pink nipples are practically staring me in the face. The temptress continues to hold me captive as her hands come up to cup them, their fullness overflowing her hands. I wonder if they'll have the same issue in my larger ones. I haven't properly worshiped these beauties yet. A fact I intend to remedy shortly.

"I think I'm dying."

She smirks. "Does that make me your salvation?"

Reaching out, I loop my fingers into the ribbed edge of her pajama pants. She makes a tsking sound as she continues to play with her breasts, but I ignore her, sliding her pants down. "You don't get to have all the fun. Undressing you is something I've been looking forward to for what feels like months."

She leans down, her face an inch from mine. "Then follow me." Isabel steps out of her pants and walks toward her bedroom without a backward glance. She's wearing a thong. A black—always fucking black—lace thing that rides right up her ass. An ass I'm most definitely going to have to explore further. I sit here for another minute because *fuck*. That's one hell of a view. This girl is the sexiest thing I've ever seen, and right now, I'm in dangerous territory of exploding in my pants like a fourteen-year-old looking at his first naked woman.

"You're too young for me," I call out.

"You'll get over it."

"You work for me."

"Your complication as my boss, not mine."

"My thoughts about you are too dirty. I'm not sure I can be gentle."

"You will be. Now, either get your ass in here, Maddox, or leave. Either way, I'm getting off."

Damn. I'm so outmatched with this one. "Yes, ma'am." I stand up, adjust my junk so I don't scare the poor virgin waiting to defile me, and then I head into her room like the eager man I am. I haven't had sex with a woman where it counted since Kim. That's no lie. For the last eleven years, I've been the definition of casually indifferent sex. But I am not casual or indifferent with Isabel. With her, I'm owned, and I don't want to hurt her. It's why I've held off from tapping on her door all damn week. I wasn't lying when I said my thoughts about her are dirty. I'm a fucking animal when it comes to her, and I'm dying to take her like one.

But Isabel is a virgin, and as such, she needs me to be gentle. She needs me to be tender. She needs—

"Maddox, your shirt is still on, as are your jeans. You're boring me with all these clothes."

Okay. Maybe I'm wrong about all that. But still. I'm a big boy and she's tighter than a nun's ass. She's lying on her bed, her head resting against the wall because the woman has no headboard for me to slam into the wall. One arm is propped behind her head, the other casually playing with her nipple. Her panties are still on and her legs are bent at the knees, parted just enough that I can see the scrap of fabric between them. "I'm in love."

That should have been much harder to say than it was. I probably also shouldn't have done it while staring at her pussy.

She doesn't laugh. Instead, she tilts her head, her dark hair falling over her shoulder as she eyes me. I meet her eyes head-on and stare at her so she knows this isn't about sex. It's her. All her. "Somewhere along the way I fell in love with you." Everything inside me comes to life. "It's one of the worst mistakes I've ever made."

She scowls at that. "This is most definitely the worst way anyone has ever told me they love me. It actually makes me want to bitch slap you until my hand stings and your gorgeous face is red."

Christ, I really do love her. "It's the sort of mistake that gets guys like me buried beneath the desert," I continue without missing a beat. "But in this moment, looking at you, I realize you're worth the risk. Conti can come at me with whatever he's got. At the end of the day, it's just you and me baby. And you and me"—I shake my head, my patented Maddox smirk curling up my lips—"we're worth fighting a million Contis for."

She smiles. Softly at first, like her lips are testing it out and once they determine it's right and it feels good, that smile spreads like a wildfire. It hits me in all the right places. It's the only smile I ever want her to give me again. This smile is pure, blissful happiness.

"We better be. Now, you've seen me strip for you twice. I want a show of my own."

"Christ, woman. Do I look like a goddamn Chippendale?"

"No," she replies in all seriousness. "You look better." She points to her chest. Her *bare* chest. "Former stripper, remember. Take off your shirt. But I want you to reach behind your head and grab your back collar. I'd like you to slip it over that way. Flexing your abs is optional but appreciated."

"Fucking brat."

"You can spank me for my insolence later. But for now, I want my fantasy, and you, Mister Sinclair, certainly hit that mark. I want you to take off your clothes and I want you to show me how turned on my mostly naked body makes you."

"Isabel Bogart, you have no idea."

"That's why I'd like you to *show* me."

I roll my eyes and she smiles. My damn vixen. She enjoys playing with her toys. But two can play at that game. "Stand up and slide your panties off. Tuck them into the pocket of my jeans before I fully remove my clothes."

Isabel stands on her bed, her eyes cast on mine as she slowly slides that sheer, black lace down her creamy thighs. They catch on the end of her right foot and she hooks them directly at me with the launch of her foot.

"Nice catch," she appraises as I snatch them up, but her voice gets cut off as I make a show of smelling them before tucking them in my pocket. I take off my shirt the way she asked because even though I like being in charge, I also like being her fantasy. My jeans follow.

"Tell me," I start, advancing on her now that my shirt and jeans are off. She said nothing about my boxer briefs, so I keep them on. Her, on the other hand? She's totally bare for me. "How did you picture this moment going?"

"I didn't."

"Turn around, Isabel." She does, and I spank her ass as she stands on her mattress and box spring. Not hard, of course. Just a playful *smack*, which gives me the perfect excuse to rub her gorgeous, round globes with my large palms. "No lies now, baby."

Her breath startles, her gasp making my cock grow even harder. "I'm on top."

"You will be. It's the only way I'll fit the first time without really hurting you. Do you come on my cock?"

"Yes," she purrs as my hands glide along the crests of her perfect ass cheeks. I want to bend my face down and eat her out from behind again. I want to take her ass, but tonight is not the night for that. Tonight is the night I show her that I meant what I said. Reaching around her, I cup her breasts in my hands, pinching her nipples between my fingers. They're fucking perfect. Fit like a goddamn glove and yet, they are more than my large hands can handle. They make me greedy. They make me want to consume every part of her I can't hold in my hands, so no one tries to take what's mine again.

"Say it back."

"No," she replies, and I smile. I'll get it out of her soon enough.

"Are you ready for me, Isabel? I'm about to make you come all over me."

Pushing down on her upper spine, Isabel's hands hit her mattress. Her ass is perfectly positioned in the air. She is absolutely glorious. A vision of warm, pink skin and heady lust. I can smell her. Practically taste her. "I'm going to stretch you. Get you ready for me." A hum passes her lips as my fingers dive in to her wet heat, scissoring back and forth a little, pumping in and out. "Christ. You're soaked." She's also so goddamn tight that no matter what I do, it'll hurt her. My only chance to prevent that is to get her as wet and needy as possible.

"Don't stop," she pants and my cock jerks up, yelling profanities at me for keeping him tucked away in my briefs.

"I'm going to make you come and then I'm going to work you back up to the edge."

She tries to say something, but then my mouth takes over. My tongue juts out, entering her body with a single thrust, loving the way she slides forward and then back. My hand grasps her hip, so she doesn't fall. This is more than eating her out. This is more than giving my girl pleasure. This is my face bonding with her body. It's me acquainting myself with the pussy that I will devour forevermore. The one that will eventually deliver my babies. Yes, that's Isabel. I had a premonition the night I met her, but it's only grown stronger since, and now? Now, I can't envision my world without her in it. Young? Sure. My assistant? Absolutely. Involved with the mob boss to end all mob bosses? Without a doubt.

But right now, it's just me and her, and I need her to feel how much I love her.

My hand clasps harder to her outer hip, my face unable to hold back. She bucks against me. So uninhibited. So wild. The moment I thrust another finger inside her, splaying them out as best I can, she comes, her back arching and her legs shaking as she loses her grip and falls forward. I catch her before she face-plants, savoring the taste as the last of her orgasm releases.

"Please," she gasps, finding the mattress and rolling over to face me.

Breathing hard, her breasts anxiously await my mouth. I drop without thinking about it, pressing her down and covering her nipple with my mouth. Her fingers rake through my hair, scratching my scalp as I gently bite on one, sucking on the tender flesh until it's nearly purple. I switch to the other, marking the hell out of them, loving the way she squirms and moans beneath me. But I need her ready. I need her ready to explode again before I can enter her.

"Maddox, I need you now. I'm ready."

"Rub your clit." She does so instantly, and I pull away from her chest to watch the show. Her hooded eyes lock on mine as she rubs herself in small circles. "Does that feel good?"

"You feel better."

"Slip two fingers inside yourself and tell me what it feels like."

Isabel smiles, a brow quirking as she glides lower and slips two fingers inside her pussy. I'm a rock of a man on the edge of an avalanche.

"I'm warm," she starts. "So wet." *Motherfucker!* "Oh, Maddox," she moans loudly. "I'm so tight."

"Fucking tease."

She laughs and nods. "Yes. But I'm ready all the same. Please. I need you."

Taking a condom out of my wallet, I sheath myself up. Stroking my cock lazily, I watch her wet entrance as I try to picture a world where I don't blow my load instantly. The threat is real. "Baby, stand up." She does immediately, and fuck if that doesn't make me harder. "I'm going to lay down and you're going to lower yourself onto me. You're going to be in control tonight. Go at your own pace. I'm a rotten bastard, but I'd rather die than hurt you."

"Okay," she agrees softly, her nerves finally starting to show.

Climbing onto the bed, I position myself so I'm sitting up, my gaze staring up at her. I could die now and know that I lived happily. My life has been a mess. Heartbreak and death and fucking anguish.

But Isabel? This woman sets me free. Makes me feel worthy of this second chance.

"I love you," I tell her again, because before she slides down on me, she needs to know it for sure.

Her soft smile tells me everything I'll ever need to know. "I know." *Cheeky brat.* "Crazy, right? We're crazy."

"Maybe. But that doesn't make it any less real."

She leans in and plants a soft kiss on my lips, then straddles my thighs. Slowly, *so effing slowly!*, she lowers herself onto me. "Oh," she hums. "Ah!"

"Take a breath." I do the same because *holy crap.* I need to move so bad, but I force myself to stay frozen. Her expression is etched with pain and that breaks me. I reach up, cupping one of her breasts, trying to get her body to relax. "You have to breathe. Relax."

"It hurts."

I clasp her hands, intertwining our fingers. "Take your time." My lips meet hers, kissing away her pain. Whispering anything I can think of to soothe her. I feel her body start to meld to mine, her muscles releasing from their tensed position. "You okay?"

She nods jerkily before trying again. She makes it two more inches and my head rolls back, my eyes with it. It feels so good. God, she feels so good. "Isabel," I groan.

"Maddox," she cries out. "Thrust up and end this."

"I can't. It'll hurt."

"Please. I can't do it. I need you to rip off the Band-Aid."

Jesus Christ! "Isabel, look at me." She opens her eyes and stares down at me. "Tell me." She shakes her head. "Dammit, woman. Tell me."

"I love you." I thrust up just as she finishes her words, my lips smashing back into hers. I kiss her through it as she whimpers into my mouth, holding her against me as her body is finally fully seated on mine. I slide back down a little only to thrust up again, and her head flies back on a screech. My thumb finds her clit, rubbing it in circles. I hope it helps her along. She's frozen forever, and just when I start to reach my breaking point, she grinds forward against me. "Better."

"You sure?"

"Yes. Keep doing that." I do. I rub her clit like my life depends on it as her body rocks back and forth against me. "So good now."

You have no idea. I sit here like her vessel, my arms wrapped around her, and allow her body to consume mine. She grinds against me. Slides up and down with painfully slow strokes. It takes her forever to fully acclimate to my size. To having me inside her body. She's wet. Slick as hell. But it doesn't matter. I'm big for her and it hurts, but once she's ready, she starts to bounce on me, and I lose all control. My hips thrust up, meeting hers. My thumb and forefinger roll her clit. My mouth is on her nipples, and when she finally comes, she does it hard, clamping so tight around me, my vision blanks out in a flash of white light. I follow her over the edge in a mass of loud grunts and groans that likely make me sound like the savage I am with her.

She falls against me, both of us covered in sweat. Nothing has ever been so good in the history of the world. I'll swear under oath to it. I hold her, kissing her hair softly, feeling her heart beat against mine. I never want this night to end. Getting up, I dispose of the condom and return with a warm wet cloth for her. I press it against her, and she hums in delight.

"I meant it," she whispers, her head pressed against my shoulder once more. "I think I really love you."

"I know I do."

TWENTY-FIVE

ISABEL

AN ACHE TO change the direction of the tides swims through me. I'm spent. My body lacking the rigidity of bones as I lay here on my bed in a heap of sweat and skin. Maddox flips me over against my will, drawing me in against his body. His arms wrap around me, holding me so close my breaths become his breaths. I just lost my virginity in the most epic display of fireworks. It hurt in a way that reminds you God might actually hate women, but once that pain subsided, Maddox isolated every pleasure sensor I own and tweaked them just right.

"Are you okay?"

"I have no idea." It's the truth. I feel incredible, and yet I feel broken. Not sure how those two opposing forces meld together, but they seem to be inside my vagina right now.

Maddox props himself up on his elbow, staring down at me like I'm his reason. "You have to help me out more than that. What can I do? Did I hurt you really bad?" He's already replaced this warm, wet towel twice. It feels good, but I caught sight of the blood on it and it makes me not want it near me.

"Sleep here tonight."

"Done. Anything else?" I stay quiet. "Isabel. You have to tell me the truth."

"The truth?" I snort. "It's a beautiful and terrible thing and therefore should be treated with caution."

Maddox laughs. "Numbing the pain for a while will make it worse when you finally feel it."

"Holy shit," I gasp as he returns my quote with another one. "You're a Harry Potter geek."

He laughs harder, smiling down at me as he presses a kiss to my nose. "So are you. But I think everyone pretty much is, so maybe that doesn't make us so unique. That quote always resonated with me." He leans in and kisses my lips.

"How so?"

"That's a story for another night, my beautiful smart girl."

"Is that who I am to you?"

Staring at me in the darkness, considering my question, he smiles softly. "I see you as many things, Isabel. Smart. Beautiful. Mine. Yes, you are all of those things to me and more. But it doesn't matter how I see you. It matters how you see yourself. I'm not sure you fully know who you are yet."

His honest assessment of me, his words so strong and forthright, sting. He's right. Maybe that's what hurts the most. I lose myself in books. I read everything and anything I can get my hands on, much of it with no real practical use in my life. I learn languages I'll never use. Read textbooks for classes I'll never take. Lose myself in fictitious worlds. I let Anthony Conti call the shots in my life because every time I try to mix it up or do something on my own, he thwarts my attempts. Sometimes with force. I have no identity. I am a pretty face with a nice body and that's all I'm ever seen as.

"I know what I want to be."

His thumb glides across my bottom lip, his eyes tracking the movement. "And what's that?"

"Free to make my own choices. Free to go out and explore the world."

Maddox sucks in a stuttered breath. Maybe he thought I was going to say I want to be a teacher or a doctor or a stay-at-home mom who runs the PTO for her kids. Whatever it was, he certainly didn't expect that. It's a sobering thought to know you're a caged bird, with the wide-open world just on the other side. I didn't need Anthony Conti ripping up my acceptance letters in my face to know I wasn't leaving this town. I didn't need him ripping me off the stage in front of the entire club to understand that my decisions are not my own to make. I certainly didn't need him tying me to a chair for kissing a boy to know that I belong to him. And I really didn't need him telling me he loves me to know that when he's ready, he'll own me for good.

By that point, he'd already proved himself to me.

Does that make me weak? I've often wondered and gone back and forth on the answer. I don't want to be weak. Despite my age and inexperience with the world, I like to imagine I have what it takes to conquer it. But the basic truth is Justin. The ugly truth is a fundamental lack of self-worth, confidence, and trust in my decisions. All of which has been drilled into me for years. I'm working on fixing that. Inside, I hate being at anyone's mercy. I hate being their practice target, hate that my compliance is a foregone conclusion. I love Maddox, but I'll be damned if I allow another man to call the shots in my life and claim possession of me.

"You will be," he says to me with so much conviction in his tone and expression that my insides quake. "I promise you, Isabel. Whatever you want for your life, for your future, you'll have it. Whether that's with me or not. Soon enough, things are going to be very different for you."

"Do I want to know what you mean?"

Maddox shifts, staring out into the blackness of my room. His arms wrap tighter around my body, holding me so impossibly close our bodies are one. "People fear Anthony Conti because they don't understand him. He's ruthless. He's a killer. He takes what he wants, when he wants it, without asking for permission or fearing the consequences. He doesn't have limits or rules, and that strength makes others feel weak and vulnerable."

"But not you?"

I catch a glimpse of his smirk before it's gone. "He doesn't know my limits. He doesn't know who I am past what he's seen and what I've made sure to show him. But most importantly, he views me as inferior in every way."

It's true. Just sitting in that meeting earlier today, with him laughing off about how inept he is with security, I knew it was a lie. Maddox is quietly brilliant. Anyone who dares peer closely enough, dares to pay enough attention, can see that. But to the lazy or disinterested, he's a brainless thug with a high-profile job he didn't earn.

"Even after you killed Fiona's husband?"

I've been dying to ask him about it forever. Dying to know more. Believe it or not, there isn't much about it out there for public consumption. The internet doesn't always know everything.

He puffs out a heavy breath. So heavy I feel its weight settle in the air and all around me. "Can I trust you with a secret?" He finds me, holding my face in his large, warm hands. "This is a no joke secret. It impacts more than just my life. I've never told anyone, and I will take it to my grave. Can you handle something like that?"

Holy crap. How do I answer this one? I nod slowly. "Yes. But if you don't want to tell me, I understand."

"I didn't kill Fi's husband. A friend of mine did, but I took the hit for it because that's the way it had to go. I don't regret it and I wouldn't change it. And if push had come to shove, I would have pulled that trigger without a moment's hesitation."

I suck in a rush of air. I think that makes me love him even more. I think he might truly be my hero.

"But yes, even with Conti believing I killed Fi's husband, he still sees me as the fool. And that's how I'd like to keep it. At least for now."

Pushing Maddox back, I climb on to him, straddling his thighs and ignoring the growing ache in between mine.

"I see you," I tell him, running my fingers across the muscular planes of his chest and abs. "I know who you are. The real you. It's why I'm here with you now. It's why I never stood a chance."

He grips my hips, staring up at me with a form of devotion I have yet to acclimate to. His cock hardens between us. "Not everything," he says hoarsely. "You don't know everything."

"No," I agree. "But those are just details. And right now, I'm not sure how much I care. You're dark. But so am I. Maybe that's what makes us beautifully sinister together."

Maddox smirks, sliding his hand up my stomach and cupping my breast, squeezing it firmly in his large hand. "Beautifully sinister, huh?"

I nod firmly. "Maybe that's more me than you?" I scrunch my nose and tilt my head. He laughs, raising his other hand and rolling my nipple between his far too skilled fingers.

"Badass," he whispers, and I grin like the giddy girl he makes me feel like.

"I never wanted to be the one to take him down before," I admit. "But now I'm thinking it has to be me." The more I think about it, the more I know this as a truth. It has to be me. It can't be anyone else. I don't know the true nature of the fight between Anthony Conti and Maddox Sinclair or Jake Turner. I know there is more to it than I realize. Conti doesn't wage war without purpose. And I can't imagine him blindly going after these two men for shits and giggles just because he one day got a hankering for Turner Hotels. No. There is so much more going on here.

But that doesn't make this battle any less mine.

Maddox shakes his head, squeezing me harder. "Maybe," he hums. "But I don't want you involved any more than you already are."

I want to laugh at that, but the bitter taste of bile climbs up my throat despite what Maddox's body is doing to me. "Too late."

"Now isn't the time for this fight." I open my mouth to lay into him, but he sits up in a flash, putting us nose to nose. His expression has shifted. Become something else I'm not quite sure about.

"What are you doing?"

"Looking into your eyes, Miss Bogart. Checking to see just what sort of woman you are."

My lips curve up into a devilish smirk. "And what's your verdict?"

"That you're easily the strongest woman I've ever met, and coming from me, that's saying something extraordinary."

My bottom lip begins to tremble of its own volition, but I do my best to force my eyes to stay dry and clear. "Then why does it feel like I'm barely hanging on?" I manage, my voice as shaky as my stupid lip.

"Beautiful girl, that's what makes you so strong."

Damn him. I turn away, staring into nothingness. I have to blink a few times to clear my vision and thoughts. He means it. I know he does. I could see that written all over his gorgeous and sincere face. He thinks I'm strong. I'm not. Not yet at least. But I will be. If anything, his words strengthen my resolve.

"Maybe. Now flip me over and fuck me, Maddox, before I take matters into my own hands."

Maddox's smile is unstoppable. "Yes, ma'am. Whatever my woman wishes is one hundred percent my desire."

That I believe.

I start to grind against him, back and forth as I feel his cock swell between my legs. His grip on my hips tightens just as he flips us over, so he's on top and I'm beneath him. His hips dip down, pressing into me in the most perfect of ways. Those crazy magical fingers stroke my clit, playing me like I'm his perfectly tuned instrument. The one he loves and cares for most. The one he can pluck the most perfect notes from. "You like that, don't you? Or do you wish my mouth is where my fingers are?"

"Yes," I pant, taking his head and shoving it down. He laughs even as he groans, kissing a slow, hot trail of lust down my belly. His kisses are warm and wet and all I can smell is him. That intoxicating blend of sandalwood, rain, and pure Maddox. "I don't want this night to end."

I don't want tomorrow to ever come. I want to get lost. To act my age. To be reckless. To enjoy myself and the moment and not think about the consequences or the tomorrows or the reality of how Maddox and I are never meant to be. The world, with all its unfathomable beauty, has so many people who make it ugly.

"It'll only end if we let it."

I smile as I think on that. On the way he and I seem to always play the word game. Maddox rises above me, his hands pressing into my mattress, his elbows straight as he looms over me. He slides into me, slowly, knowing I'm still sore. But this time, it doesn't hurt. It feels outrageously good. So good that I wrap my long legs around his waist, changing up the angle and allowing him to sink in deeper.

"You feel that?" he half-groans as his hips plunge back and forth. "Feel how perfectly we fit together?" I nod my head, humming out a moan of my own. "I may be your first lover, but it's not always like this. This good. This is special. We're special, Isabel."

I wrap my arms around his neck, my back arching as my lips seek his kiss. "It's too much." I'm so close I can't seem to control myself. I'm chasing fire. Desperate for the burn and heat. Sensing how close I already am, Maddox pounds into me, hitting that spot inside me over and over until I'm deranged with sensation and pleasure. My nails dig into the muscular flesh of his shoulders and I let go, succumbing to the ecstasy.

Maddox topples over the edge with me, roaring out. He stills, his body shuddering, and I watch as this strong powerful man comes apart inside me.

His forehead falls to mine as we both drop back down into my mattress, panting and smiling and so sweaty we'll need a shower. "I mean it," he says after he's caught his breath. "It'll only end if we let it."

It would be so easy to believe him. My lips press to his as I whisper, "Things are always different when the sun comes up and life breathes down our necks once more."

TWENTY-SIX

MADDOX

THE PROBLEM with work is that I have to act like shit isn't complicated. It is. It's a goddamn pit of snakes masquerading around as business as usual. Since I had Isabel beneath me on her bed last week, I've barely interacted with her. Not in public. She does her job with the casual indifference of an old washing machine, doing the bare minimum. She hasn't balked at anything I've asked her to do. She responds with one- or- two-word answers and typically that second word is a *sir*. She's inexperienced, insubordinate, a general pain in my ass, a delightful distraction, and I can't fire her—though I'm pretty sure that's what she's after.

That comment about her being the one to take down Anthony Conti is haunting me.

She meant it. I saw it.

Now I have to stop her.

There is still so much she doesn't know and understand. Isabel is a wildcard and when it comes down to it, I have no idea what she's truly capable of doing. What 'being the one to take him down' actually means to her. Is she talking about sending him to prison—that'll never happen—or killing him? No way in hell would I let that be her fate.

Since I begrudgingly left her apartment in the wee hours after our first time together, I've only been able to sneak over there two other times. He's been watching her. Whether or not he knows what I've been doing with her is another question. Two nights ago, he was even there himself, sitting outside her building in his Mercedes, his eyes fixed on her door. He never got out. He never went inside. He didn't even call her.

But he was there.

Since then, I haven't dared to go near her place, let alone try to see her.

When I was able to get to her, we spent the night wrapped up in each other. Talking. Touching. Kissing. Loving. Fucking. She's become my haven. My heaven. At work, she maintains distance from me. But it's more than that. In the last three days since I was able to get to her apartment, she's been quiet. Cautious. Reserved. Edgy. *Angry*. And she won't meet my fucking eyes.

The storm is coming. The tension building. All the pieces are set up, it's just a matter of waiting for the first move.

Scrolling through the latest updated information on my monitor, my eyes feel like they're bleeding out of my head. I've already read this once, and yet here I sit, reading through it once more, just to make sure I'm getting it all. On the very last word, a knock sounds at my door. "What?" I snap, in absolutely no mood to be disturbed. Or maybe disturbed is exactly what I am.

"Mister Sinclair?" That's another fucking thing. This Mister Sinclair shit.

"What?" I don't look up when she opens the door.

"There is a situation down in the high-limit roulette area that requires your immediate attention." Now I do look up. But first I check my phone and find about sixty-thousand texts and missed calls. I guess putting my phone on silent wasn't the best idea I've ever had.

"What is it?"

She shakes her head, her eyes locked on the edge of my desk. "I'm sorry, sir, they didn't say. Just that you're needed down there immediately."

A growl gnashes past my lips as I rise, save everything, log out of my computer and grab my suit jacket, throwing it on as I walk. Isabel steps back as I approach, like she's ready to flee back to the safety of her office. *Not today, sweetheart.* I grab her upper arm with zero force, but she flinches anyway, her movements excitable and slightly unco-ordinated. "Where do you think you're going?"

She glances up to my neck. "Back to my office."

I shake my head. "Not right now. I might need you." I don't. I mean, at least not in a work capacity. I just don't want her away from me right now. Remember seconds ago when I mentioned waiting on that first move? Yeah . . .

She doesn't respond other than to gently unhook her arm from my grasp and retrieve her phones. Both of them. Hmmm. I wonder if he's contacted her again without my knowing about it. Without her mentioning it. That sets my teeth on edge.

Flipping through the last few texts, I shoot one off in response and then find one from Brian, my chief floor security guy and the bartender at the club where Starshine used to work. His mainly consists of "Get your ass down here" or some variation of that. It's clear we have yet another high-grade cheat. Awesome. What a fantastic way to end my day. Can't these guys come in the middle of the night? Why do they have to pull this crap at four-thirty on a Friday?

The nice thing about the corporate level is that we're only a couple floors above the main casino and if you take the back stairs, then you're basically dropped right there. Isabel wordlessly follows me, keeping up with my pace and not giving me reason to bark at her. But there's something almost hesitant about her movements. Like she's not entirely sure what to do with her posture and position. Or if she should even be following me through the back throngs of the hotel.

The metal stairs clink loudly beneath the polished soles of our expensive shoes. My lips hum the tune, my mind circling over everything again and again until I'm positive I have it perfected.

"When we hit the floor, stay right beside me and don't speak unless I ask you something."

"Yes, sir."

I close my tired eyes, rubbing my too-stubbled jaw. "Is it your life's mission to drive me insane?"

I catch the smallest of perceptible smirks. "No. I wouldn't say it's my life's mission. Just a fantastic perk of the job."

"You forgot to say sir."

"Is that a question? I was specifically instructed not to speak unless you ask me something."

"Infuriating little brat." She giggles, and I nearly trip over a step at the sound of it. "Have you missed me this week?"

"No, sir. I haven't. I've had an extremely busy week with no time for your shenanigans. It's been quite delightful actually."

"You're killing me, Izzy. Fucking killing me." That's not a lie. I am about ninety-eight percent positive that this woman will be the end of me. Probably in more ways than one if this plan goes to shit.

My phone buzzes and I fish it out of my pocket. Brian again. **They're up fifty grand with no signs of leaving.** Fantastic. That gives me exactly ten seconds to spare. We hit the base of the stairs, the door straight in front of us when I spin her around and pin her back to it. She gasps, her onyx eyes going wide and her body trembling. *It's just you and me here, baby. No one will catch us.*

My palms plant themselves onto the cool metal directly on either side of her head, caging her in as I grossly encroach into her personal space. "Shouldn't we be going? What are you doing? *Sir*," she adds with an edge that instantly makes my cock hard.

I'll admit it, her antagonism is a turn on.

I can practically feel her heart pounding against mine and I realize as an afterthought just how close to her I am. I hadn't meant to get this close. I just meant to force her gaze to mine. To try and get a read on her. It's the longest I've been in the same space with her since Tuesday. Something shifts in her demeanor and she finally, *fucking finally*, stares up at me. I cup her face, grazing my thumb along the soft fullness of her bottom lip that I'm dying to bite.

"Why are you suddenly afraid? What's happened since the last time I was with you?"

That bottom lip begins to tremble, and my heart stutters raggedly at all the potential unknowns. "He's been watching me."

I nod my head because I already know that.

"It's different than how it typically is. He can't see us like this, Maddox. It's too dangerous for you."

"He can't see us here. It's just us. You don't need to worry about me. I'm a big boy who knows how to cover his bets. Is that all that's upsetting you?"

She swallows, then clears her throat and averts her gaze to the wall. "Yes."

Liar.

"Now back off. We should be going."

I don't move, and she huffs out an exasperated breath.

"Haven't you had enough?"

I press my lips into hers and devour her mouth like the world is ending. I ravage her. I consume her. She moans into me, her fingers raking through my hair, dragging down my scalp like she can't hurt me enough. She wants my pain and I revel in hers. This is what we do. We push and pull. Bite and hit. Fight and kiss. It's something I'll never grow tired of. My tongue tastes hers, tastes her fear, and then I pry myself away and stare into her eyes.

"There is no such thing as enough with you."

Her hands drop from my hair to the tops of my shoulders. "We'll see. But until then, we really should be going."

"They're not going anywhere."

I kiss her again and step back, waving for her to exit first. She tosses me a wink and an impish smirk over her shoulder.

This girl . . .

Since the moment I met her, I've despised how attracted I am to her. Looking at her is an addiction. And if looking at her is an addiction, then riling her up is my drug of choice. Allowing her to slither under my skin might be up there with some of the dumbest fucking things I've ever done. She's too young. Too mixed up with the wrong people. Too much my employee.

And currently aiming to take me out at the knees.

We hit the casino floor. No matter how many times I walk through here, I never get used to the bright flashing lights and loud fake sound of coins clanking into slot machines. I hate this part of the casino. Finding the small of Isabel's back, I guide her through the maze until we reach the roulette table our marks are sitting at. Brian is there, casually observing them and another table without appearing as if he's onto them. He could have nabbed the two assholes by now with the small security force I notice bouncing around the perimeter. But this makes the third time in only a few months that these well-funded cheaters have hit us up. It's a pattern. It's a shout-out.

Typically, these guys don't continue at the same hotel chains, especially when they've been caught each time—at least I hope it's each time. Brian finds my eye and I nod to him. His gaze shifts to Isabel and then back to me with a questioning furrow of his brows. I throw him the not-the-time-or-place stare and he goes back to work. Both men have their backs to me, but I can see the action on the table well enough even if I can't see their faces.

I will be honest, before we caught the first guy, I believed magnetic balls to be an urban Vegas legend.

They're not.

And they don't actually use magnets inside the balls, otherwise they'd stick to ordinary metal objects. Instead, the ball contains a special coil with diodes—a semiconductor device with two terminals, allowing the flow of current in one direction only. That's how they're able to manipulate the ball's action. When the ball is dropped onto the wheel, the cheating motherfuckers predict where they expect the ball to land. If, as the ball bounces around, it appears like it will not land in the area they bet in, the cheating assholes can influence the loaded ball with magnetic pulses. All this happens very quickly—we're talking mere seconds, so it rarely causes a noticeable interference with our electronic systems. They also don't do this every single time, just more often than not, and load up their bets when they know they'll win. Oh, and it's a real bitch to get the ball into play in the first place.

That's usually how they're caught.

Not this time, which makes me think the dealer is in on the scam.

It's ballsy. It's bold. It's well-funded. And it's rare.

It's why we're watching them play instead of tackling them to the ground and kicking their asses.

"Are they cheating?"

"Yes. Rather elaborately." I peek down at her and then quickly back over to the two men.

"Don't they know they'll get caught? That people are watching them?"

Maybe. Probably. They're a ruse. A distraction. "Couldn't say."

They win this round and when one of them steps to the side, Isabel sucks in a noticeable breath. "What? Do you see something?"

"N-no." She not only stuttered, she hesitated.

"You're a bad liar. Where do you know him from?"

"The club, I think. I don't know. He just looks familiar, is all. I didn't expect it."

I stare at her, but I can't tell if she's lying or not. She's the type of woman who typically wears her emotions on her fists, proudly and for all to see. This last week, she's been a closed book, frustrating me with her silence at every turn.

I watch them for another minute and then I give Brian the nod. He speaks into his earpiece and immediately, six men, two dressed as regular civilians and the other four in hotel security uniforms descend on the cheaters. They're secured, wrapped up within seconds despite the decent fight they put up.

But then I get the buzz in my pocket. So does Brian and two of the other remaining security guys. I check my phone and almost laugh out loud. Almost. Though there is nothing funny about what's going on. Three more tables are being compromised. One more here and one at each of the other two Turner hotels on the Strip.

"Now what?" she asks after they're dragged away, and the residual crowd of curious onlookers returns to their gambling. She doesn't know what's happening, but Brian is already gone and so are the other two security guys. I have no idea what's happening at the other hotels, but I need to get my ass in gear and up to the security tower.

I turn to face her and catch the movement out of the corner of my eye.

The man, partially obstructed by a slot machine. The woman, staring up at the side of his face as she smiles and speaks to him. *Fuck!*

"Now we get you the hell out of here." She blinks up at me, bewildered by the harsh tone of my voice. I grab her hand, tugging her back toward the stairs, though that might be a mistake. Sending her home, alone out there on the streets, would be worse. But I can't take her with me, and I need her somewhere safe.

"What's wrong? What's going on?"

"Everything."

TWENTY-SEVEN

ISABEL

MADDOX PUNCHES IN A CODE, swipes his badge and leads me up a different set of stairs than the ones we came down. We reach a door at the top and he does the same thing, punching in a code he's careful I don't see and swiping his badge. Then the door opens and we're back somewhere on the corporate level. Only, we're alone. Everyone is gone for the day. The lights are still on, the carpets still as pristine, the desks still as organized.

But everything feels different now.

Probably because Maddox is practically ripping my arm off as he speed-walks down the hall toward his office.

"Maddox," I try, shaking my arm to try and get his attention. He ignores me. We walk around the corner and down the hall and suddenly, we're back in the main part of the corporate office. This place is a maze. I had no idea where Jake's office was, but I caught his name on the door of one we just passed. I don't have a lot of experience with corporate executives, but I don't think I've ever experienced this level of security from one space to another.

We reach our office spaces and I try to break away, back towards mine, when Maddox grips my upper arm a bit tighter, stopping me. "I'm not sure how long I'm going to be with those guys." He sounds funny. Calm now. Like he didn't just tell me that everything is wrong. I realize he mumbled it under his breath. So faintly I could hardly make it out. It still took me a couple of seconds to compute what he was saying. "I know it's late in the day, past when you typically leave, but I need you to hang out a bit. Stay in my office and wait for me. Can you do that?" He's asking this like it's a question. Like it's my choice. But it's not. I can see that on his face. I am to wait in his office for him.

"Um. Okay. Sure."

"Great." He smiles at me and it's . . . normal. It's his normal smile. Could I have misheard him when he said everything? Misread his expression? No. I didn't. Whatever he's worried about, he's trying to hide it from me.

He seemed to believe me when I told him that I didn't know those cheaters. I probably should have told him then. I probably should tell him now, but I can't seem to make the words come out. I'm too thrown off. Too put off by this new Maddox, who feels like he's suddenly lying to me.

Those men who were just caught and captured? Yeah, I know them. Both of them. Thankfully, they have no idea that I know them. Anthony Conti met with them one night in the back room of the club. He did a lot of business there. They're buttons. As in, he presses the button and the job gets done. Expendable men that he pays reasonably well to do his bidding.

I was taking a breather in the supply closet—it was the only quiet place in the whole damn club—and Conti felt the need to have his gangster pow-wow right outside the damn door. I watched the three of them through the crack and listened as he asked them to take care of a man who refused to open a restaurant in his hotel. He spoke with the same casual indifference he would have if he were asking them to take his car to get gas.

Two days later, the owner of Table 99 was found in his car, dead from carbon monoxide poisoning. It was ruled a suicide. Case closed. I don't even think the death was investigated. The new owner of Table 99 announced the following week that they'd be opening a restaurant in The Conti. That was the night I truly understood he was more than possessive or aggressive or trying to take care of me. He was a monster. Certain men are above the law. If I went to the police, I'd be dead. Justin would be dead. If I went to the FBI, same result. His pockets were lined with those men.

So what do you do when you're forced to deal with the devil?

You play his games until the timing is right.

Maddox walks into his office, ripping off his suit jacket and unbuttoning his shirt. He tosses both of those on his glass table as he digs through his closet. I stare at him, wondering what the hell he's doing until he pulls out a pair of jeans, a plain gray shirt and a dark jacket. He slips off his suit pants and changes into his new outfit. He looks like the Maddox I first met in the grocery store. The laid-back, easy-going guy. It ratchets my nerves up even further.

"I'll be back as soon as I can. You'll stay here and wait for me?" he double checks, but there's something extra in his voice.

I nod, wrapping my arms around his waist. I suddenly need to be closer to him. This feels like a goodbye. Not a 'see you later.'

"Hey, it's fine." He runs a hand down my hair, comforting me. I swallow past the lump in my throat and put on my brave face just as he tilts my chin up to look at him. "I promise, baby." He kisses my nose, staring intently into my eyes. "I need you to stay here. Promise me."

"Yes."

The smallest of perceptible smiles touches his lips just as his reach mine. He kisses me once. Twice. Three times. And then he's gone, shutting the door to his office behind him. If he could lock it without my having a kitten on him, I'm sure he would.

Suddenly, here I am. Alone and sick to my stomach.

I head toward the couch to sit and wait, but my work phone ringing stops me dead. Only Maddox calls me on this thing, but when I check it, it's an out-of-state number. A Connecticut area code and now my heart is really doing overtime. "Hello?"

"Good evening. Is this Miss Isabel Bogart?"

"Yes." My trembling hand comes up to my chest, pressing in directly above my pounding heart.

"My name is Doctor Stewart. I'm a physician in the emergency department here at UCONN Medical Center."

"Justin," I whisper. My brain shatters, high on this new jolt of adrenaline that seems to have dismantled my ability to think clearly and rationally.

"Yes. Your brother Justin is here. He's okay," he stresses. "He came in with a broken left wrist and a minor concussion as a result of a collision during lacrosse practice. The wrist will need to be set surgically and as his guardian we require your consent for the procedure."

I feel my eyebrows pinching together as I stare at the wall. "I'm sorry. Did you say you'll need *my* consent as his *guardian*?"

"Yes, ma'am."

"You have me listed as his guardian?"

He pauses, and I hear him clicking around. "That's what it says in our system. I have the information the school provided us with. They have signed documents by you that will allow for medical treatment, but with surgery of a minor, we like to get fresh consent."

Signed documents? Me as Justin's guardian? What the hell is going on?

"Is the surgery safe?" I finally manage.

"All surgery has risks associated with it. But he's young, in good physical health and has no known allergies. We have no reason to believe he'll have any issues tolerating the anesthesia or the procedure."

"Is he there? May I speak with him?"

"Of course. Hold for a moment, please."

The line goes silent and I collapse to the floor, my knees bent and my head between them as I take in slow deep breaths. My vision sways, my hand pressing onto the floor to steady me, because I'm *this* close to losing myself completely. I'm Justin's guardian? How can that be? Wouldn't I have had to go to court? Hired a lawyer? Signed those damn papers he's speaking of? All this time Conti told me there was a fictitious person as his guardian. A John Doe, so to speak. He said it was a lawyer somewhere and that Justin was in good hands. Was he lying all this time, using my ignorance as leverage?

"Is?" Justin's groggy voice comes through the line.

"Justin. Oh my god. Are you okay?"

"Yeah." He laughs, and I can tell by his wobbly tone that they gave him something for the pain. "I'm fine. But I messed up my wrist pretty good. Doc says they might have to put a pin in it or something. I don't know." He clears his throat and I hear him shifting around on the other end of the line. His voice drops to just above a whisper. "They have paperwork that says you're my guardian. Is that true?"

"I don't know," I admit.

"I gave them your work number after they told me that." Smart kid. I should never underestimate him. Fifteen or not, he knows everything.

"You did good. Go get your wrist fixed and I'll be there as soon as I can. I'm on the next flight I can get."

"You'll come?" I hate how surprised he sounds. Fuck. That just breaks my heart.

"Of course. I love you."

"I love you, too. I'm sorry to make you fly out here, but I'm really happy you're coming."

I smile, just as the first tear slips down my cheek. Poor kid is all alone, in pain, and about to have surgery. I can't imagine how scared he is right now. If I am his guardian, everything is going to change.

"Don't be sorry. Just get better. I'll see you soon."

The doctor comes back on the line a few seconds later and I consent to the surgery. I disconnect the call and then I find the number for the registrar of Justin's school. A woman picks up after the fourth ring. "Hi. My name is Isabel Bogart. My brother Justin is a student there and was just brought to the hospital. I want to make sure that all of our documentation of guardianship you have on file is correct."

I pull myself up and off the floor as she politely asks me to hold, sinking down into the soft leather of the sofa. Wiping away the residual tears, I suck in a deep breath just as she comes back on. "It looks like everything is up to date. I have the latest documents that you signed at the beginning of the year that names you as his legal guardian, as well as a copy of the court documents." *Court documents?* That motherfucker. "His consent for medical treatment is here as well. Is there anything else you need? We were sorry to hear that Justin was sent to the hospital. How is he doing?"

"He's about to have surgery on his wrist, but other than that, he seems to be in good spirits. I was wondering about his tuition. I know the final payment for the semester is due soon, but what happens if it's not paid?"

"I'm sorry?" she asks, her intonation falling to incredulous. "What final payment? Justin doesn't owe any tuition. All payments for each semester are due prior to the start of the semester. That would have been back in December. But Justin is paid up through all four years."

My hand comes up, covering my trembling mouth as I shake my head back and forth. "Are you saying he's paid up through graduation?"

"Yes. I'm sorry. I thought you knew that. Full four-year tuition with room and board was paid prior to his starting as a freshman."

I'm going to be sick.

"Thank you." I disconnect the call and race to Maddox's bathroom, reaching the toilet just as the contents of my stomach empty. I spit and heave, one hand holding my hair back, the other plastered onto the seat, holding me up. I throw up until there is nothing left and then I go for the sink, rinsing my mouth out and staring at my haunted reflection in Maddox's mirror.

All this time Justin has been mine and his school tuition has been fully paid.

I can't believe it. This is a dream come true, and though part of me is inconceivably happy, the other part of me wants to find Anthony Conti and demand answers. There is no worse feeling than being used. That's what I've been living with all these weeks. But discovering that not only are you being used, you've been duped? I don't think I've ever experienced this level of rage before. My wrath knows no limits.

I need to get on a plane. I need to get to Justin. But I'm blinded. My vision a deluge of red.

I rinse out my mouth one more time, using some of Maddox's expensive mouthwash, then I splash more cold water on my face. It doesn't help. I'm not sure anything short of seeing my brother will help. The real question is, what sort of power does Conti maintain over us? If he was able to obtain falsified court documents, he could easily have ones revoking my guardianship made. He could pull back all that tuition money.

What the hell do I do now?

Brushing my hair off my face, I pull myself together. I look like hell, but who cares. I go to exit Maddox's bathroom and practically jump out of my heels, a screech belting from my throat.

"Jesus, Morgan," I gasp, grabbing my chest. "You scared the hell out of me." Morgan is standing on the edge of Maddox's bathroom, one hand outstretched like he's trying to calm me down.

"Sorry," he says. "I didn't mean to scare you. You okay?"

"Sorta," I laugh the word, covering my chest with my hand to try and slow my heart rate down. "What are you doing here so late?"

"Looking for you."

"For me?" I tilt my head. "Why?" It's then that I notice the gun, clutched in his other hand, dangling at his side. Before I can scream or run or even duck, he raises that hand and smacks me in the head with the butt of the gun.

And everything goes black.

TWENTY-EIGHT

MADDOX

THE MOMENT my feet hit the casino floor, my phone rings.

Jake.

"What the motherfuck is going on, Maddox?" he yells. "We've got multiple high-grade cheats going on simultaneously and I just got a call from Cash that there are men trying to infiltrate the towers and roaming around my hotels."

"I just watched one of the cheats go down," I tell him, shaking my head as I scan the floor wildly. "I also know about the other cons. The men are new to me. Is Cash securing the towers?"

"Yes. No one is going in or out. If Cash feels the need, he'll shut down our systems."

Shit. That's bad. It's the sort of bad that probably requires us to call in the FBI or SWAT. But we're not just dealing with high-grade cheats or even men looking to take the house down. We're dealing with Anthony Conti and he knows we won't call anyone. He knows we'll handle this ourselves because that's what Jake and I do. Thankfully, the man believes I'm as dumb and dense as a sack of bricks and considers Jake to be a weak pushover since Jake 'let me kill Niklas Vaughn' and take the fall for it.

But I'm not dumb nor dense, and Jake is nowhere close to weak or a pushover.

"Why today, Jake?" Because it doesn't make sense unless he was on to us.

"I don't know," he replies. "This was not part of the plan, brother. All our intel has Conti making his move Friday. Not today. It's too soon. Our backup isn't close."

"Shit," I hiss into the phone, marching around with wide steps, doing my best not to run as I search for the couple I saw when I was with Isabel. Sabrina and Gavin need to get their asses back here, but they're nowhere to be found. "Where is Gavin? Have you been able to get in touch with him?"

"Not yet. He's not picking up. Where are you?"

"In The Grand, man. On the floor. Where are you?"

"On my way there now. I was off-site with Fiona. She's up in our place now and promised to stay there with it all locked up tight. But she's not happy and I'm not happy. Where's Isabel?"

"My office. She promised to stay there and wait for me."

"Good. We need to get up to the tower and check out the video. Lock everything down. Figure out our strategy for how we want this to go, because it certainly can't go the way we planned."

Probably not. Definitely not.

Which means I have to come up with something new. A plan B.

"I'll meet you there," I tell him, disconnecting the call as I head in that direction. My heart is racing so fast it's threatening to tear its way from my chest. Because Jake is right. This wasn't supposed to happen today. We were ready for everything to go down on Friday. What the hell made Conti move his plan up two fucking days? Sweat slicks the back of my neck and I wipe it away. But that sick knot in my stomach? The one that comes when nothing goes according to my plan? The one that eats me alive as everything starts to unravel, and I can't stop it? Yeah. It's here. Because Anthony Conti is a methodical bastard.

At least Isabel is safe.

I can manage everything else as long as she's safe. She will likely hate me when this is all done. I never told her what I had planned. Truth be told, I don't want her involved with this. My girl is too emotional. Too fiery. Too unpredictable. Fiona was supposed to be left out of our taking down Niklas Vaughn and then the bastard showed up early and got to her. He nearly killed her. I won't let that happen to Isabel. I won't let Conti get to her.

Even if it means I'll lose her in the end.

On Friday, Anthony Conti was planning to try and take down all of Turner Hotels' systems with the tablet Morgan Fair stole when Jake, Luke, and Ryan took him over to the tower. Only, I was going to be waiting for Conti before he could even make that first swipe of his finger across the Gorilla Glass to start up his blackmail scheme. It was going to go down one of two ways. One would end with him going to prison forever. The other in his death.

I think we all know which way it was going to end.

But now that plan is fucked. Because Morgan has a tablet, which means Conti has a tablet—one we had to make look legit enough for it to be considered legit, so there is some stuff on it that he could start messing with at any time. Those high-grade cheats were early. And now men are attempting to launch a coup of the hotels on the Strip. And we can't reach our ace up our sleeve Gavin.

And our backup isn't close.

So my plan to kill the sick, twisted bastard who has been lying, murdering, manipulating and destroying people might have to be altered.

I dial up Gavin again, but he doesn't answer. I know he's working on something else. I know our gig isn't his only gig. But still. That knot of uneasiness in my stomach grows tighter. I'm not sure how to play this. How to strike back. How to wield it all to twist it in our favor.

Just as I make it to the edge of the security tower entrance, I stop dead in my tracks. Two men dressed like they're from *Reservoir Dogs* are staking it out. Conti's men. They're not even doing anything other than standing in front of the door as if they're guarding it. *Or waiting for someone.* I don't have to wonder how they knew where this door was located, though it's far from public knowledge. And if you were to see it, you'd just think it was a random metal door with a number lock on it. There are no signs above it. No indication of what's beyond.

I have to wonder if Morgan is the reason things were moved up.

He wasn't at work today, but honestly, I didn't think much of it.

I'm betting that's another mistake to add to my list.

That kid has had his own agenda in this game since he first stepped foot in Turner Hotels. But he was dumb enough to get involved with Conti. To allow himself to be sweet talked, manipulated, and wooed with promises of money, power, and control. Don't people ever learn from movies? You never get involved with the bad guys. They're bad! Then again, so is Morgan.

Around me, the casino, the hotel, they're all operating without a hitch. You'd never have a clue what was going on behind the scenes.

My phone buzzes in my pocket and I slide it out, ensuring I'm hidden from the goons' sightline while maintaining mine. It's a text from Brian. ***All cheats secured. Waiting further instructions.***

I text him back. ***Keep them locked up. No one goes in or out unless they give you my code.***

Got it. At least that part of things is handled. It's a relief.

Another text comes in immediately, this one from Jake. ***Behind you.***

I spin to find Jake, his brown hair a disheveled mess like he's been running agitated hands through it. He juts his chin just past my shoulder in the direction of the tower door. "Looks like Mr. Pink and Mr. White are waiting for us," he says.

See, this is why I love the man like a brother. I didn't even have to throw out the *Reservoir Dogs* reference. He got that all on his own.

"What's your thinking?"

"Honestly?"

He stares me down like I'm trying the last of his patience, then folds his arms over his chest. This is not typical Jake Turner attire. The man is wearing a white tee that shows off his colorfully inked up arms and dark jeans. This is not CEO Jake Turner. This is casual husband to Fiona Jake Turner. "I'm thinking you go back upstairs to Fiona and sit it out."

"Maddox—"

"No," I quickly interrupt, leaning in and dropping my voice as I put my full weight behind it. "If it's going to go down, which it seems like it will, then I don't want you there for it. Gavin is one thing. He's a lone wolf. But you have Fiona. Don't be stupid about this. You were never supposed to be in on the action."

"And you have Isabel."

I want to laugh at that. Yes, I have Isabel. And yes, I love her. More than I love myself. She's about ninety percent of the reason I'm doing this. I'm not a killer. It's not something I seek out or take enjoyment in, but Anthony Conti deserves to die. Her words about her being the one to take him down scare me. I can't let her do it. Killing ain't easy, even when you know the person has it coming. She may say she hates him, but she's also conflicted where Conti is concerned.

I have to do this for her and when I do, I'll lose her.

"You think I'm going to let you walk into this blind?"

"Yes. It's the way it has to go. I have to be the one to take him down. That doesn't mean you have to be there for it."

"No way you get the kill shot on him today. He's pulling the strings. Not us."

I open my mouth to argue that I can still do it when a voice beside us says, "I'll kill him." Gavin steps forward, like a ghost materializing from the mist wearing all black and a murderous expression I haven't seen on him since he went after Niklas Vaughn.

"When it turns bad, I'll be the one to fire the shot." He pins Jake with his cold, emerald eyes. "Whatever happens today, Fiona will not be a widow." He shrugs, rolling his eyes. "Well, not again." I roll my eyes at that, because calling Fiona Niklas Vaughn's widow just seems whack. "Once we make sure we have everything we need on Conti recorded, it'll be easy to do, and you'll walk away. He's going to push you both. Blackmail the fuck out of you with your every weakness. He's going to promise to kill Maddox. You're going to *agree*," he says firmly to Jake. "He'll instruct his thug to do it, because that's the way Conti rolls and I already heard as much on the audio I have from his office, but I'll shoot him and his man before anyone dies."

Jake nods firmly, clearly liking that plan a lot. "Can you live with that?" he asks me.

Can I live with having Gavin do the killing? Can I live with Gavin killing Conti so I don't have to, meaning I might actually get to keep Isabel?

"Yes. When the time comes, you'll pull the trigger first. But it would be nice to have some additional backup in the room. Wherever the hell that room is," I growl. I hate not knowing what's coming our way. It's convenient that Gavin seems to know Conti's plan from our bugging his office, but something still doesn't feel right about this.

"I have a pretty good idea where it is. I'll see you later then, boys," Gavin says with a hint of a smirk on his lips. "Looks like your escort is waiting on you."

With that Gavin is gone, instantly immersed in the casino crowd.

"Are you ready for this?"

"Looks like we don't have much of a choice. Let's get it going."

Jake and I take our position, heading for the security tower because that's what we're supposed to be doing. "Hey Mr. Pink?" I call out and both men pivot in our direction. "You're not supposed to be back here." The other shifts like he's going for his gun. "I wouldn't try it, Mr. White." Then I land a punch across his face, fracturing his cheekbone with a delightful crunch.

"Motherfucker," the guy wails as he launches himself at me,

landing a few good blows to my face. We grapple for a minute or two before I allow him to secure me, especially once he shoves a gun to the back of my head. "Don't move, asshole," he spits in my face. "Conti asked for you alive. Doesn't mean I have to listen."

Jake laughs, even though Mr. Pink already has him secured with a gun pointed at his back. "Of course you have to listen, moron. You'll be dead if you don't."

Unfortunately, I can't see Mr. White's face or take pleasure in his panicked expression, but it's nice to know that Anthony Conti trusts some real geniuses with our transfer. The man really doesn't think very highly of us. And when push comes to shove, we'll play into his hands. We'll be exactly who he expects us to be. And then Gavin will kill him.

TWENTY-NINE

ISABEL

WHEN I COME TO, I find my wrists and ankles bound with duct tape, another piece over my mouth, and I'm on the floor of the backseat of a car. No, an SUV. A large one with tinted windows. Morgan is driving, listening to some bullshit country song that the asshole is singing along to. Singing. He's singing after he knocked me unconscious with a gun and tied me up. Where he's taking me is anyone's guess, but I can't see all that much out of the windows. They're too dark and it's already pretty close to dark outside.

As quietly as I can, I squirm, trying to stretch the tape at my wrists so I can break free. My head is throbbing where he hit me. Morgan. I mean, what the hell? This is why I hate people. I should have listened to Maddox when he told me to stay away from him.

Maddox.

I promised I'd wait for him. Hopefully, when he comes back for me and finds me gone, he'll come looking for me. But then again, who knows how long he'll be dealing with the cheaters?

Who knows how long I've been unconscious? We could be in Utah by now for all I know.

"I knew you were a whore the moment I met you at the club," Morgan starts.

I wonder how he knows I am awake. I hardly made a sound. He turns the volume down on the music and reaches back, stroking my face with his hand. I turn away, trying to roll out of the reach of his touch, but all he does is laugh as he pulls his hand away.

"I just didn't realize you were his whore. I mean, he told me to sit in that area of the club that night with my friends. Obviously, he wanted us to meet. I watched you all night. So tell me, how much is he paying you to fuck Maddox and get all his secrets?"

I can't respond. I can't tell him to fuck off or that he's a lowlife piece of shit, because I have a fat piece of duct tape covering my mouth. Clearly, his question is rhetorical, meant to rile me up and piss me off. Mission accomplished.

"Did you know my mother was a whore like you?" His head rolls over his right shoulder to peek down at me. He's smiling like he doesn't have a care in the world. His attention diverts back to the road. "She was. She found my father, fucked him, got pregnant with me and took him to court for a lot of money. It's why he never liked me all that much. I'm the product of the biggest mistake he ever made."

Fantastic. Not only does he have daddy issues, he has mommy issues, too. Why can't he just go to therapy and have crappy relationships like the rest of the world? If he's looking for sympathy from me for his messed-up parentage, he's barking up the wrong tree. I have more mommy issues than he could imagine. He chances another glance at me, and I make a show of rolling my eyes at him. Grow up, Morgan. Be your own man and stop chasing after your father if he wants nothing to do with you. He has money, a college education, and good looks. The world is open to him. And I've seen him with his father. Yes, Morgan Senior is hard on him, firm, but it's more in the way that he's pushing him to excel and succeed rather than holding him back and putting him down.

So yeah, grow the fuck up!

"Conti asked me to bring you to him, but he never said in what condition. Are you fucking him, too? Is that why he brought you in on this? It's the only thing I can figure. You're beautiful, but not all that smart. Not exactly special. Pussy is pussy, but yours must be magical to con both Anthony Conti and Maddox Sinclair. Why do you think I asked you out? I was hoping to find out what I was missing."

God, what a loser. "You're the dumbass with mommy and daddy issues," I garble through the tape. I have no idea if he can understand me, but I don't fucking care. He thinks *I'm* stupid. Conti will blow a gasket once he sees the condition I'm in. The car turns a sharp corner and then stops short. Morgan unbuckles his seatbelt and then rotates his body over the center console to land a punch directly to the side of my face. The same side he hit me with the gun. Bright flashes of light spark behind my eyes as flames of heat and pain radiate up my face to a pounding crescendo on my temple.

"You're just another stupid whore." He's yelling now, spitting in my face. "You're nothing. Maddox. Conti. They're just using you. That's all you're good for. Spreading your slutty legs. Getting used up and tossed aside."

I raise my cheeks in a big grin, brightening my eyes, even though it hurts like a bitch, and my vision is slightly hazy from the multiple blows. My lips are sticking to the tape, but I can move my cheeks, and my message is clear and received, judging by the fresh look of hate he's tossing me. Who knew Morgan was such a bitter misogynist?

"He'll throw you away like the trash you are and then it will be just me. Conti promised I'd run Turner Hotels, Las Vegas. I bet he didn't offer you shit."

Just threats.

Morgan's out of the car, throwing open the back door and tugging me out by my feet. My bare feet, I realize once I hit the pavement. I have no idea where my heels ended up. My ankles are bound, my equilibrium is off, and I crumple awkwardly down without the luxury of my hands to break my fall. My hip hits the ground first, followed by my shoulder and all Morgan does is laugh. Sick fucker.

"Come on, beauty. Time to take you to see the beast." He hauls me up, ripping the tape from my mouth, wrists and ankles. It hurts like hell, but I'll never give him the satisfaction of letting him see my pain. The second I'm free, I move to attack until I realize where we are.

We're at Conti's warehouse on the outskirts of Boulder City.

Why the hell are we all the way out here?

I have no idea what's going on. All I know is that Morgan is working with Conti. Conti had a high-stakes cheat going on at Turner. And now here we are. If this is a pow-wow for like-minded, hotel-stealing thugs, I want no part of it. Christ, this is bad. I have no phone. No purse. I have nothing. All I have is a man who has officially crossed over to Crazyville, and his gangster boss.

Morgan drags me into the back of the warehouse. It's dark and dusty and I really wish I was wearing my shoes because I'd bet some really good money I don't have that there are rat and mice droppings in this place. There isn't much here. Some old boxes and wooden crates, a few stray pieces of what appears to be ancient hotel furniture up against one wall. This warehouse is a front. Everyone knows it. He used to hold high-stakes poker games here while naked women danced for the men. Drugs and sex were rampant. I remember hearing some of the girls at the club talk about it. They were paid phenomenal money to come dance and fuck the men. All of that—minus the drugs—are legal in this town. Except, you don't typically get all of that in one place. And it's usually controlled, whereas here it wasn't. But judging by the state of this place, he hasn't held any of those fun nights in a while. Personally, I've only been here twice, and on both occasions, I was made to sit outside in the car.

Oddly enough, I'm not afraid. Maybe I should be. But I'm not. I want Anthony Conti to look me in the eye and explain to me how I came to be Justin's guardian and why he prepaid his tuition. And why he kept me in the dark.

"Hey, Morgan," I whisper quietly before we reach what I assume is an office as it's up a flight of metal stairs with a closed door. Just as his face shifts toward mine, I rear back and launch a punch directly in his nose. It hurts my hand something fierce, but the blood gushing from his nose along with his bellow of pain makes it worth it.

"You fucking bitch," he screams, his voice shrill. "I'll kill you for this."

I laugh, shaking my head. He clearly doesn't get it. I grab him by his stupid collared shirt, shaking him until his blue eyes meet mine. "Don't you ever fucking touch me again, you pathetic asshole. I'm not a whore. Either of theirs." I smirk menacingly. "You should have done your homework on me before you roughed me up. I'd be terrified if I were you."

Shoving him away, he stumbles back, and I turn, ascending the stairs. I hear Morgan following, but I don't give him a second glance. Honestly, I don't care if he's afraid or nervous or still hateful and arrogant. I'm tired of being hit. I'm tired of being pushed around. Morgan knowingly got himself into bed with Conti and that's on him.

There is a man standing in front of the door. A man I've seen and sort of know if only by face and not name. He's Anthony's main guy and he does not speak. Ever. Why? I have no idea, and I've always been too afraid to ask. He gives me a long once over, then frowns. He always liked me. But when his gaze casts over to Morgan, he smirks and shakes his head slowly like I've amused him by fighting back. I get a wink. I didn't think this man was capable of facial expressions, but evidently, I was wrong. I wink back, because I'm pretty proud of that punch. The man pounds on the door three times and then Conti answers, "Send them in."

He opens the door for us, and I let Morgan enter first. I need an extra second. I don't want to be here. I want to be on a plane to Connecticut. I mentally shake my head. I need to get my mind focused and back into this.

THE room is large with high ceilings and exposed duct work and piping. It's cool in here with cement floors and lacking any warmth in the form of warm-blooded humans. But it's bright and a million times cleaner than downstairs. It's also furnished with a desk, a filing cabinet, a large safe and a couple of chairs.

"It's about time," Conti snaps at Morgan, eyeing the blood on his face, hands, and shirt.

It's in this moment that I finally take a breath. If you want to understand the beauty of this world, you have to embrace the ugly. That might be where I find myself. I've finally found beauty with Maddox. At least, I think that's what that was. Ugly is not something new to me. However, embracing it might be.

"I had trouble finding her," he says, but I don't miss the tremor in his voice.

Anthony Conti growls something out to Morgan and then turns away from him, toward me. It's like it happens in slow-motion. The way it all unfolds.

"There's my darling—" Only he never makes it to the word girl. His expression solidifies, turning harder than granite. He takes in my bare feet, the red marks on my wrists and ankles from where the tape was ripped off, all the way up to my face. I have no idea what I must look like right now, but I was in rough shape before Morgan showed up and I have to believe it's much worse now.

"Who?" It's a simple question, but that one word, those three letters, hold so much meaning. So much power. And for that reason alone, I hesitate. "Tell me now, Isabel." It's a command laced in a threat. "Tell me who hurt you."

Luckily, I don't have to say anything.

"I did," Morgan says coolly. I watch as both men pivot to face one another. Morgan is practically sneering, his anger turning pointedly on me. "And the little bitch hits back."

"You hit her?"

"She's a whore!" Morgan bellows, throwing his hand out in my direction. "I told you this. She's been fucking Sinclair, and judging by the warning you gave me, I'd be willing to bet that wasn't part of your arrangement. I found her in his office tonight waiting for him. I don't know your situation with her, but she's messing with you, man."

I'd love to say that Maddox and I were always careful. That our moments were private. But I honestly don't know if that's true. Morgan could have been watching us the entire time for all I know.

"So you say, Morgan." Conti's voice is smooth butterscotch without even the smallest hint of irritation. "But you see, you know absolutely nothing about Isabel, or about my arrangement or my situation with her. I believe I explained to you the other night that your opinions regarding her are unwanted. Was my message not received?"

Morgan blanches, his gaze shifting briefly over to me before returning to Conti. "It was, sir. I'm sorry. I just don't want to see her make a fool out of you."

Oh boy. That was the complete wrong thing to say to Anthony Conti.

Conti's expression is unmoving, but his eyes flash with venom as his voice turns acerbic. "Go stand over there and do not speak again unless I ask you a direct question."

Morgan does exactly as he's told. He walks over to the corner where there is still some construction material and stands like a naughty boy in a time-out.

"Come here, Isabel."

I peer up into his cold dark eyes as I quicken my steps toward him.

"Does it hurt?"

"Yes. My heart is bleeding," I tell him. He stares at me, reaching down and taking my hand to lead me over to a chair placed in front of the desk. "Is it true? Am I really Justin's guardian? Has his tuition been paid up all this time and you never told me?"

Conti grins, the corner of his mouth turning up. I can't remember the last time I saw him smile with anything other than malice. This grin is amused. It's respect. And I don't understand any of it. It makes me want to punch him a million times harder than I punched Morgan.

"Yes. Of course, it's true. How did you discover this?"

"I got a call from the hospital. Justin was injured during lacrosse practice. Then I called the school and they confirmed everything." I'd always been afraid to call Justin's school unless absolutely necessary. Afraid they'd ask questions about his guardianship. How maddening.

He helps me into the chair, and though I don't want to sit, I do anyway. My head is pounding from the two blows it sustained and my body aches from being tied up in an awkward position and falling onto the pavement. Conti kneels down in front of me, his hands resting on my thighs as he faces me directly. The floor is cleaner in here than it is out in the main warehouse, but I wouldn't exactly call it clean. It's dusty as hell and this is a man who does not like to sully his expensive suits. It's why my mouth is closed. It's why I'm going to listen to everything he has to say because I can tell it's going to be one hell of a story.

"Is Justin all right?"

I shake my head as my eyes glass over. "He's having surgery. I need to go to him."

He nods slowly, but it's not a nod of agreement. It's a nod of understanding. "I'm sorry, my darling girl. I know you want to go to him, but that's just not possible at the moment."

The first of the tears fall, followed closely by the second. "Please," I sob, a flurry of emotions suddenly unleashing from within me. I can't take this anymore. "How could you do this to me? How could you hold his life over my head the way you have, lie to me repeatedly, and then, when he needs me most, not let me go to him? I *have* to go." I lean forward, placing us eye to eye. "I've never fought you. Not on anything real. But I will fight you on this."

He smiles at me, warmly, seductively even. It turns my blood to ice. He cups my face, his thumb brushing at my tears, rubbing them into my skin rather than wiping them away. "Your spunk and determination were why I first noticed you. You were standing outside

The Conti, speaking with Franco, the valet. He was giving you money for you to go grocery shopping for him. You couldn't have been any older than fifteen at the time, but you caught my eye. I knew who you were, of course, but it had been years since I had seen you and your beauty caught me by surprise."

"You knew who I was?"

"Haven't you figured it out yet? After all this time?"

I shake my head, because nothing is making sense to me anymore. The smile that had been flirting on the edges of his lips grows.

"Justin is my son, Isabel. I had a very brief affair with your mother, and he is the result. I wanted nothing to do with her, or him, really. Your whore mother was not about to become my wife, and I had no need of any children from a mistress. But I paid for him anyway, without following his life or hers after."

"Justin is your son?" I'm skeptical. They look nothing alike. Hell, I look more like him than Justin does. It makes sense, though. It explains how he found us in the first place and why he sent Justin off to school. I sigh out a harsh breath.

"Yes. A test was done after he was born and that's all there is to it. But that day I saw you outside The Conti, I was intrigued. I paid your mother well for Justin and couldn't fathom why you were shopping for Franco or why you would need the money at such a young age. I followed you to the grocery store and watched as you bought Franco's groceries. Then you grabbed a candy bar from the shelf and had the woman ring it up separately.

"You could have easily tacked it on to Franco's bill. He wouldn't have minded, as I'm sure you well knew, but you didn't. You paid for it out of the small tip he gave you. I followed you as you delivered the groceries to his house and handed them off to his wife, who was too ill to shop herself, and then I trailed you all the way back to the pit you were living in," he bites out the last words. "I was furious to see the place your mother was raising you and Justin. I watched as you and he sat outside on the front balcony and you gave him the candy bar with a small candle in it. I came to remember it was his birthday and when he tried to share it with you, you waved him off so he could have it all."

I remember that day. My mother had her pimp and dealer over. They were busy getting high and fucking each other while Justin and I sat outside celebrating his birthday. All that money, however much Conti had been paying her, had gone straight into her body in the form of her various poisons. And her clothes. The woman loved her designers. Whenever I'd ask her where she got them from, she'd tell me they were gifts from her lovers. How stupid and naïve I was. It makes me hate her so much more than I ever thought it was possible to hate someone.

"That's the reason you had her killed," I surmise, suddenly unafraid to speak so frankly about her death. About her murder.

"Yes. I watched you two out there for hours, well into the dark. You did homework together and talked. You took care of him," he says affectionately. "That was the day I knew you'd be mine. That I was going to stop at nothing to *make* you mine."

I swallow down the wave of nausea that confession elicits. I was fifteen. A child. And though Conti has not touched me intimately, he's no less a predator. A trafficker. That might actually describe him perfectly. "And Justin?" I finally manage.

"You love him and he's technically my blood. He'll continue on in school and you'll continue on as his legal guardian as long as it works for all parties."

Translation: as long as I cooperate.

"You turn twenty in two months, and then, we'll be married. I had planned to wait until you were twenty-one. The idea of taking a teenager never appealed to me. It's a vice for weak men, but I've grown too impatient. And one day *our* sons will be the ones to rule my empire."

His hand drops to my stomach, caressing over my empty womb and I want to die.

Conti leans in and presses his lips to mine. It's the first time he's ever done this, and it catches me completely by surprise. Do I kiss him back? Do I shove him away? I'm not exactly afforded the option for the latter as he rakes his fingers through the back of my hair, holding me to him. His kiss is forceful. Rough. Passionate and animalistic. It's a kiss that claims total possession and leaves no room for error or argument. It says, "If you thought I owned you before, you haven't seen anything yet." He pulls back, his eyes darker, matching his smile.

"Now, it's time to finish business so we can start our life together."

Conti stands up without bothering to wipe at his dust-covered knees. He types something into his phone and two seconds later, the door opens once more. I spin around in my seat and watch in stunned horror as a bruised and bloodied Maddox is led into the room by a tall, muscular man. A beautiful, blonde woman with a smile etched on her pretty face enters next and Jake Turner is last, though he's been spared the beating Maddox sustained. A man I can't focus on is pressing a gun to Jake's head. No, I'm too busy staring at Maddox, silently begging him to look at me. He meets my eyes, but only for the briefest of seconds. And in them is nothing. No warning. No comfort. No evidence that this is all part of some elaborate plan. Nothing. They're blank and lifeless and I don't know what to do.

All I know is that I have to do something.

"Excellent," Conti exclaims like he's beyond thrilled that the gang's all here. I twist back to him just as he lifts a gun I hadn't noticed from the desk, raises it in the air, aims it, fires it, and kills Morgan Fair before the scream makes it past my lips.

THIRTY

MADDOX

THAT SHOT RINGS throughout the room, refracting off the hard surfaces of the walls, ping-ponging back and forth until it finally dies out and I'm officially deaf. Why can't he use a silencer the way they do in all the mob films? It's hard and loud, and Isabel screams like the world is ending. Maybe it is. The apocalyptic theme is reminiscent to how this feels at the moment. I watch helplessly as Anthony Conti shoots Morgan Fair dead in cold blood. I'm rendered immobile by the gun in my back as Isabel falls to the floor in a heap of distress. My girl. My poor girl. She can't be here for this. She's not *supposed* to be here for this.

How Conti got her wading around in this muck is likely at the hands of the fallen in the corner, and now I can't even kill Morgan for dragging her here or kick the shit out of him before I kill him for hitting her.

My fingers are itching to grab the gun digging into my ribs and shoot Conti in the face. And maybe that plan would have worked out better than Gavin's, but Isabel is here now. She's tough, but even tough people have their limits, and I don't want to be the one to push it. At least, not until I absolutely have to. Not until the time is right.

"Stand up, Isabel," Conti demands. Isabel's slacken form is huddled against the chair she was sitting in, her face in her hands as she openly weeps, her shoulders trembling with her hiccupping sobs. And yet, Conti has no sympathy in his eyes. No, Isabel knew what she was saying when she said he fought dirty and without remorse or hesitation. But being the gunner is not his style, and I wonder if Gavin somehow miscalculated this situation.

"You didn't have to do that," she snaps at him, her face streaked in tears and black mascara. I love her all the more for her bravery. Yelling at the man in charge in front of the detainees he's trying to hold a commanding presence in front of takes guts.

"I did, darling girl. He was no longer useful, and he knew too much. Two strikes against him. Plus, he hit you." I wonder if the prick's aware of the irony of that statement. "End of story. Now come here."

She doesn't move.

"*Isabel*. Come. Here." His tone is not to be bargained with. That fucker. Him getting to hold her when I can't jacks up my heart rate another decibel. This game that I'm trying to play and feel like I'm suddenly losing? Well, it didn't include my girl being here. It didn't include Morgan Fair losing his life at Conti's hands.

She rises slowly on shaky legs and falls into him. *Goddamn*. It's a sight I didn't expect. He wraps his arms around her, holding her close to his chest as he whispers something I can't hear in her ear. She nods her head at whatever it is, and I never knew jealousy could hurt this bad. Could be this sharp and cutting and gut you while you're forced to stand on your feet with your hands casually at your sides and do nothing about it.

"Does this bother you, Mister Sinclair?"

I know for a fact I am not that transparent. I didn't even clench my jaw or ball my fists, though the desire was there. Which means he's baiting me.

Now I cross my arms. "Is what bothering me, Mister Conti? The fact that my face probably looks like it's been through a meat grinder thanks to your asshole assassin, or the fact that I have a gun aimed at my back? Oh, no wait, how about the fact that you just killed that kid and I have to see his body bleeding all over the plastic he was standing on? Or maybe it's that I'm even here in the first place?" I tilt my head and smile pleasantly at him. "You might have to be a bit more specific than that? Are you asking if I'm pissed you're holding Isabel like she's your obsession when she's actually mine?"

He chuckles. She pales. "She's always been your obsession. It's why I placed her in your path in the first place."

I knew that, so I just shrug, because clearly, I'm amusing him as I fall directly into the palm of his hand.

I catch Jake's grunt off to my right. I still don't like that he's a part of this. This was not part of our original plan. Not how anything was supposed to go down. Jake Turner should not be here, but if this moment proves anything, it's that you can't always get what you want. Cue The Rolling Stones. Fiona is going to string me up by the balls when this is all over, and I'll deserve the castration. I can only imagine how savagely fried her nerves are right now.

I don't blame her. I have no idea if I can get any of us out of here alive.

He strokes Isabel's hair tenderly, but he's doing it with the hand still holding the gun, so it doesn't quite convey the same sentiment. It's intentional, though, and I know he knows that I know. Fuck, all joking aside, this just went up another level. Why he would want her to witness his cruelty, I have no idea. That, and she's in his arms with a placid expression that might actually be throwing me off.

"Mister Fair was convinced you were having a secret relationship with your obsession."

For Christ's sake. This guy, I swear. Always fishing. "That would work in a world where she didn't hate my guts from the word go. You can keep her. I take back what I said at our last meeting. She was a shitty assistant at best and anything more than that I wouldn't know about. Besides. . ." I level my gaze on hers and wait for her to look at me. *Look at me, Starshine.* It takes her a long beat, but eventually she twists her head against his chest and our eyes lock. *Ah. There she is.* I grin smugly and let him see it as my focus returns to him. "Obsession or not, she's too young for me. Was too much my employee." I find her eyes once more. "And my thoughts are too dirty to be gentle."

She doesn't smile, but I catch the glimmer of recognition all the same. It's what we do. *I'll get you out of this somehow.* Only it's a promise I don't know that I can keep. The crazy fuck is not playing by the rules. He freaking ambushed us today.

Anthony Conti is not the type of man to growl or snarl or even raise his voice. He never shouts. He just speaks firmly as he eviscerates you. Like the way he just spoke to Isabel. But I think part of him knows that Isabel and I have been a thing from the get-go. I also think the dumb bastard believed that his warning for me not to touch her would stick and her loyalty to him would win out. He's just that type of arrogant.

But still . . .

He's going to kill me over her.

He always was.

I knew it the moment I stepped into his office and he told me how I was going to repay my debt. I knew it before I even met her, and made that initial call to him the day Niklas Vaughn died. I knew it the day Jake and I found those documents his father had stuffed away in his safe. Isabel, Fiona, they're worth it. They're worth it all. I meant it when I told Isabel she's the girl I risk everything to save. Well, here we are.

But what I don't care for is what's to come next. I can see the devious excitement lighting up his ugly, cruel eyes. He's about to annihilate any affection Isabel ever held for me, and he knows how to deliver the perfect kill shot. And why the hell did Gavin have to bring *her* here as backup? It's certainly not what I intended when I asked for it.

"I suppose all that's true," Conti drawls, walking Isabel over toward me, still tucked firmly against his chest like a prize. Her cheeks are red, and her face is downcast, and she's beyond despondent. I stare at her, losing the battle of wills. I need her to find me again. To look into my eyes and know the truth. Conti peeks over at the blonde on my right. "Your taste and judgment in women aren't what I'd call sound, Mister Sinclair. Isabel hates you and you fuck women who work for me. Wouldn't you agree, Samantha?" Conti asks Samantha—or really Sabrina, Gavin's super-secret chick. His super-secret gunless chick.

"Taste? I'd say he has excellent taste. Judgment?" She shrugs. "Maybe not so much."

I inwardly cringe. And the goddamn woman I've absolutely never had sex with, but have been seen out with, turns my head with a tight grip on my chin and kisses me full on the mouth. Isabel is suddenly standing up straight as she watches the whole thing. The entire sloppy kiss Samantha lands on me. My eyes are open, and my expression is bored, and I'm most definitely not kissing her back, but the damage is done. Isabel thinks I've been two-timing her with the blonde.

As I just experienced first-hand, hell hath no fury like jealousy. And it's already been established that my Isabel is a jealous woman. It's one of the attributes I love most about her. Crazy girl is just as possessive of me as I am of her. Isabel's eyes flare, but instantly cool as Conti peers down at her, desperate to gauge her reaction. She gives him none. Just watches with unmitigated apathy as Samantha goes to town on my mouth. Samantha pulls back and smiles at me.

"Sorry, babe. You were a great fuck and all, but I think it's safe to say our relationship is over."

Awesome. Conti might as well kill me now because I can't bear to look Isabel in the eyes and see what I know I'll find.

Conti chuckles again. Like ha, ha, isn't this moment so precious?

Why can't I wring his neck? Why can't I inflict an untold amount of pain on him? He's got my girl. Judging by the hold he has on her, I know something else is brewing. At least, that's what I have to believe. Otherwise, everything she ever told me was a lie.

I have to get Isabel out of here before it's too late, but there is absolutely no way I can before the shit hits the fan. And it's going to. It's seconds away. I can feel it. Especially when Conti turns to Jake and my brother smirks at him.

"Could you have picked a more cliché place to hold this little pow-wow? It's like Batman meets Two-Face." He pauses here and then pivots toward Isabel. "Oh wait, that's you. Isn't it?"

Isabel pales, swallows impossibly loud and hard, but finds the will to stare Jake in the eyes as she says, "Yes. It is."

"And you played my boy here like a fiddle."

"I might have."

"Nicely done. I'd shake your hand and congratulate you properly, but I don't like touching snakes." Ouch. I think that one hurt both of us.

"Jake," I admonish, because that's what I'm supposed to say. Even if his words are so true it stings.

"Fuck that. We're here because of her."

"No. We're not and you know it."

"What happens to your wife if you die?" Conti asks, ignoring our small banter.

Jake, for all his charm and brilliance, laughs. "She inherits double her billions. That includes all of Turner Hotels. And in case you missed it, Fiona Foss-Turner is a very pretty *public* face. So, you can try and mess with her, but you won't get very far."

"You've done well with her."

Jake grins like a mastermind. "That's all her. I've done nothing but be the lucky bastard by her side."

"But if I kill you, I can easily get to her. I'm sure you're very aware of that."

"Leave my wife out of this. You can threaten me all you want, but

I saw you coming the moment you talked my friend here into hiring Isabel. Threatening my life and my wife's won't coerce me into turning over Turner Hotels to you. The way my stupid coked-out father was planning to."

Conti beams at him like a proud papa. "So, you know about our arrangement?"

Jake nods. "Yes. I found the unsigned documents. He was going to sign everything over to you and retire. The purchase price was very nice, I'll admit. And since Turner Hotels isn't a publicly traded company, there wasn't much to stand in your way."

"Except his heart."

Jake laughs. "Except that. He never had much of one in the first place, so it's no wonder it eventually gave out on him." The truth of the matter is, Jake's father would have never turned over Turner Hotels to Anthony Conti. Not willingly, at least. But if we've proved anything here today, it's that Anthony Conti doesn't need much in the way of coercion other than his threats.

"And what if I threaten your friend's life?"

Jake stands up taller, but he doesn't dare glance in my direction. "You mean the way you're threatening mine and my wife's?"

"I'd rather not kill you, Mister Turner. Believe it or not, I respect you. And your wife has been through enough. I'm sure you'd agree with me on that. Depending on how you allow this to play out, the only other person who has to die is your friend. I don't take kindly to men who covet what's mine."

"How nice for you," Jake deadpans. "And I don't take kindly to men who tell me they're going to kill my friends. And I really don't fucking take kindly to men who threaten my wife. Isn't that how we got into this mess with you in the first place?"

Conti does that stupid chuckling thing again. Like he's just that sinister and scary.

"I have a tablet from your security tower. It has access to everything on Turner Hotel's, servers. All your security. All your clients' protected information, including credit card numbers, phone numbers, and addresses. Gaming cameras. Your advanced recognition software. The list goes on and on and on. Absolutely everything is in my possession. I also have men in your three hotels on the Strip. You know this because I placed them there, so you'd catch them gambling, but what you don't know is that they were a distraction for your security teams. My men are all over your casinos and they're in place, waiting for my word to take over your security towers. So, I'll make a deal with you, Mister Turner. You sign over your three Las Vegas hotels and I'll let you keep the rest."

Jake's eyes widen, and he steps forward almost involuntarily.

"Yes, you heard me correctly. Give me those three hotels and you and your wife will be rid of me forever. I won't kill you and I won't kill her. I'll call off my men and return your tablet. None of the information I have or will gain from my men goes public, which will ruin you and your company's credibility. Millions of people will be compromised. I can promise you that. If you don't, you'll watch your wife die and your company go down before you die."

Jake hesitates, his reluctant gaze straining on me for a very long while before turning back to Conti. "And Maddox?"

"I think we've already covered that. I can't allow him to live at this point, regardless of the deal you and I strike. But how your friend's life ends is up to you. If you give me those hotels, I'll end it quickly. If you don't, I'll make sure he suffers like no man ever has."

Jake stiffens, his hand reaching out for my arm as if he's going to do something when we both know he can't. It's too late for that now. But Jake still keeps his mouth shut.

Dammit, Jake!

"He'll do it," I say, gritting my teeth. "He'll sign over the hotels."

"No. I won't."

"Yes, you fucking will!" I turn and yell at my friend, my eyes blazing, my fists a clenched ball of bloodless tissue. "You will, Jake. You're not dying for me, and neither is Fiona. *Especially* not Fiona. I spent way too much damn time making sure you two got together. I killed Niklas Vaughn, so she'd be safe. You've spent too much time rebuilding and reworking Turner Hotels to watch it go down. I'm dead anyway. It's non-negotiable, asshole. Sign his bullshit and go."

"You had to get involved with him," Jake hisses out, the malice in his tone unmistakable.

"What was I supposed to do? I killed a man, self-defense or not. But hey, it's been a good few years. Name one of your sons after me and get the fuck out of here!" I shove him. Hard. Because if he could leave before this goes down and take Isabel with him, all the better. He takes a few steps back. "You knew this was how it was going down for me. This is how I *want* it to go down for me."

Jake shakes his head at me, the color in his cheeks rising. "She wasn't your fault, man."

Now it's my turn to take a step back because that just blindsided me. Sure, I might have said too much. Might have gone just a bit too far. Gotten too wrapped up in the moment. But that? "Don't," I warn, because I cannot hear him tell me that driving drunk and high and crashing my car and killing Kim wasn't my fault. It was. Yes, her father had a part in that. A large part, and I own and accept that. But my actions that night are a fact. My tox screen and blood alcohol level are facts. Kim is dead. Another fact.

He throws his hands up, but his expression breaks, and I know, *I know,* how hard this is for him. Every single step along the way has led us here. We pause, both catching our breath. Our eyes are locked, his brown ones to my blue ones, and after an eternity of unspoken words, I nod my head.

He blows out the heaviest breath I've ever heard and then says in a strangled tone, "I'll do it."

That's when the gun fires and I go down.

THIRTY-ONE

ISABEL

NOTHING HAPPENS IN SLOW MOTION. That's what you always read about in books and see in movies. A montage of events that slowly unravel while your senses are at the top of their game and you're able to take it all in frame by frame. Yeah, that's not how this goes. At least not for me.

This is chaos. My senses are frazzled. My mind is a jumbled-up mess of freaked-out and terrified and adrenaline and haze. The scent of blood and death and gunpowder still linger in the air from Conti killing Morgan. *Jesus.* Morgan is dead and I'm sweating in a twisted panic.

Because I'm standing at Anthony Conti's side, listening to the exchange between him, Jake, and Maddox. I watch as that woman kisses Maddox's mouth like a deranged animal after she admits she's been fucking him. And that's sorta where I get stuck. At least for a while. Seconds? Minutes? I'm not sure. I'm too keyed-up for a proper frame of reference. Because my first inclination is to hate Maddox for being a lying two-timing piece of shit asshole male. I want to reach out and slap his already beaten-up face. I might even want to do the same to the woman for screwing someone I consider to be mine. That jealousy? Yeah, it eats me up pretty good.

But then I realize something.

Maddox wouldn't cheat on me.

Maddox, who took my virginity with love, tenderness, and patience. Maddox, who stared deep into my eyes and told me he loved me. Maddox, who has risked everything for me. *"You're the girl I risk everything to save."* Those were his words to me that night at the club as I sat on his lap and told him I was going to be the girl he regrets. That seems to be who I am in this moment, because I feel like I got us here. Maybe, maybe not, but it's how it feels.

I don't trust people.

Never have.

A junkie mother who doesn't tend to the basic needs of her children sort of sets the stage for that. Anthony Conti being a lying, deceitful monster reinforces that. And being surrounded by drunk, gropey, horny men who talk a good game but are only after you for one thing seals the deal. You learn that the only person you can rely on is yourself. You learn that being vulnerable in front of another human being is a costly mistake. You learn that love masquerades as a bright, shiny apple, when in truth, it's fleeting, conditional, and dangerously poisonous.

Only . . . with Maddox, it wasn't like that.

I would climb onto his lap, stare him in the eyes, and see his honesty and sincerity shining back at me. His love has been unconditional. He knows my ugly and dark and has met it head-on without a falter in his steps. He proved time and time again that I can trust him. *"I can't always tell you everything. There are things I'm holding back. But my ultimate goal is to keep you safe and protected and alive."* Those were his words to me the night I lost my virginity. In fact, I'm pretty sure that's what he was trying to hint at when he told Conti that I'm too young, too much his employee, and that his thoughts are too dirty.

So, this woman who kissed him? Yeah, that hurts. Did he truly fuck her? I don't know. But my gut is telling me he didn't. Maddox wouldn't do that. I know it. I know *him*.

Which means something isn't right.

Maddox and Jake are yelling now, fighting back and forth about Conti's demands. Maddox is trying to force Jake to take the deal to save himself and Fiona and Turner Hotels. Even though it means Maddox . . . dies? Did I hear that correctly? Maddox is going to die? Sacrificing himself is something he would do without hesitation. But suddenly, I can't watch them fight. I probably should. This situation, this conversation, is without a doubt the most intense I've ever heard. The implications behind it has tears coursing down my face, dripping onto my shirt. It has my insides reeling and roiling. I'm listening. I'm overwhelmed. So much so that I think I've stopped breathing. I can't lose Maddox. The mere thought has bile repeatedly climbing up the back of my throat and I have to keep swallowing it down or I will throw up everywhere. But if something isn't right here, then there is no way Maddox will die. Someone will stop it. They have to.

And it's that someone I'm currently staring at. Not Jake or Maddox or even Conti.

No. I'm watching the man who had the gun pointed at Jake this entire time.

And he's watching me back.

I've finally figured out where I know him from.

He's the man with the dark hair and piercing green eyes. The one I saw with Maddox, who Fiona hugged, that day in the atrium when I was walking with Morgan so long ago. He's the man staring back at me. He communicates nothing. There is no smirk or wink. No signs of recognition. But he's staring at me in the midst of this showdown for the ages. But then . . .

"I'll do it," breaks through and without the benefit of foresight or reaction time, Anthony Conti, the man on my left, lifts his hand and shoots Maddox directly in the chest.

Just like that.

Maddox falls back. Just falls, twisting to the floor and landing hard on his stomach, his arms splayed. My mouth drops open, but no sound comes out. Nothing like when Morgan was shot in front of me. I watch him fall and all I can think is, I was wrong. This dark-haired, green-eyed man stood by and let his friend get shot. Jake stood by and allowed it. Hell, he gave the go-ahead. Not everything Maddox does is planned and well thought out because I'm standing here, watching him on the ground and there is blood seeping out from beneath his body.

Blood.

Dark, red blood and there is so much of it.

"There's so much blood," I whisper.

Jake hasn't moved. I don't know if he's also staring at Maddox's body the way I am, because I can't look at him. I hate him. I hate him for letting Maddox die. I hate the dark-haired, green-eyed man for letting Maddox die. I hate the woman who claims she was having sex with him when I know it's a lie. But I absolutely despise Anthony Conti for killing him. He killed Morgan and now Maddox and I can't. Oh god, I just can't.

I take a step forward, closer to Maddox's lifeless body. Why is no one speaking? Why is no one moving? Or are they and all I can see is Maddox? He's not breathing. At least not obviously. And the blood. God, it just keeps coming. I'm standing in it now, that's how much there is and how close to Maddox I've gotten.

Maddox. You can't be dead.

Crouching down I press my hand to his back, directly between his shoulder blades. He's not breathing. *Oh my god. No. Please, Maddox, breathe. Don't leave me. I need you.*

But he's gone. Maddox is gone.

Standing up, I turn around, away from Maddox because I can't look or touch him anymore, and it's then that I realize that Jake is standing with his hands clutching the back of the chair I was once sitting in. His breathing is labored, and his head is down like he's losing his mind. Conti is . . . flawless. Fucking buoyant. He's actually fishing around, searching for the right papers. Is he for real? All this over a few hotels? Over the idea that Maddox coveted me?

And now Maddox is dead.

Conti is talking, but I can't hear anything he's saying. My ears are ringing, and blood is rushing through them and it's so loud. Like a helicopter is taking off inside my skull. Conti is staring at me expectantly.

"Isabel?" he questions, waiting for a response, but I have no idea what he wants from me.

It's like I'm outside my body. Like my mind is somewhere else and I'm stranded, stuck in this alternate reality. Because this can't be real. "Take her out of here," he says to someone, but I shrug off the hand that grabs me. My gaze drops to my hands, searching for Maddox's blood because that's all I'll have left of him. And before I can even comprehend how sick that concept is, I realize they're not trembling. Not even shaking a little. And this makes me smile so goddamn hard.

Because Jake is a mess. Morgan and Maddox are dead. The blonde is who the fuck cares where and the dark-haired, green-eyed man is suddenly right next to me. Maybe he's the one who tried to lead me out of here, but he doesn't touch me. It's like he knows exactly what I'm about to do and is giving me the option because I grab the gun from his hand, and he doesn't stop me. And suddenly, all that sound comes rushing back. The blood in my body is no longer deafening to me. I'm aware of everything. I see it all.

Conti's gun is on the desk, discarded because the arrogant fool doesn't fathom that anyone here would dare go against him. But I have nothing to lose at this point. My fucks to give are all used up. Maddox is dead, and I fell in love with the stupid lug. And Justin's education is all paid for. But most importantly, I don't want Anthony Conti to live. He deserves to die, and I have to kill him.

"Put down the gun, Isabel," Conti orders, like his orders mean anything to me at this point. "Now, or you'll regret it." He points to someone behind me, probably the guy who had the gun on Maddox and yells, "Grab her." But no one touches me. I hear a scuffle behind me and grunts of pain, but I don't dare turn away from my target.

I fire the gun before I can think twice about my actions. Jake jumps back, out of the way, though I wasn't anywhere close to hitting him. No, I may have never fired a gun before, but I wasn't that far off for my first time. The bullet hit the cement wall beside Conti's head.

"Isabel," he bellows, shock and maybe even a touch of fear flashing across his face. Let him believe it was a warning shot. He ducks, practically hitting the floor, but recovers quickly, scrambling for his own gun, which is now in Jake's hand. Smart man. Jake turns and fires the gun behind me. I have no idea if someone dies and I don't care. I have so much I want to say to Anthony Conti. Years and years' worth of stuff. War and Peace caliber stuff. But I can't find where to begin. I can't figure out exactly how I want to say it. And really, what does it matter at this point? His life is over, and maybe one day, if I live through this, I'll tell his grave everything.

I stare into his eyes, his cold, black eyes, and I see my hatred reflected back at me. He's surprised, which is almost comical. How could one man be so arrogant? I hear him shout out my name one last time and then he yells for his man on the other side of the door. I don't care, and I don't waste time, I fire the gun before Jake can get another shot off. He will not get the pleasure of killing the man who has essentially enslaved me to him for the last three years, who perpetually held the life of my brother over my head, who threatened me at every possible turn. The man who hit me and killed my mother and Morgan and Maddox. He killed Maddox. I fire the gun again and again and again, the kick on the thing is fierce, nearly knocking me down. The gun is large, too large for my small hands, and it's difficult to fire. My fingers cramp with the effort, but I don't stop.

The gun finally lets off a satisfying click, indicating it's out of bullets and I can't even tell who or what I hit. My eyes are too heavy with my tears to see through them because I just killed Justin's biological father. The man who paid for his entire education and gave me guardianship of him. The man who, for better or worse, claimed to love me for the last three years. Got me out of a bad situation with my mother. Gave me a job. Introduced me to Maddox.

The gun slips through my fingers but before I can fall to the floor with it and let go completely, strong arms wrap around my waist. I don't want the dark-haired, green-eyed man to touch me. I don't want Jake Turner or the blonde or Conti's man to touch me. The only man I want to touch me is dead, so I push them away, slapping wildly at the determined hands holding me up.

"No," I scream, but it's too late to stop them. It's not Jake or the blonde or the dark-haired, green-eyed man or even Conti's man. It's a man with brown hair and brown eyes, dressed in all black.

"Luke Walker?" I utter, and he smiles at the fact that I remembered his name. I don't return the sentiment.

I'm secure in his grip as he says to a group of . . .*agents* who are now crawling about, "I don't care about the scene. I just want the tech. As far as I'm concerned, Conti's death saved us a whole fuck nugget of time and paperwork. The shooting of Anthony Conti and his man was self-defense. Done only after Anthony Conti shot and killed that kid in the corner and then shot Maddox. Is there anyone in this room who disagrees with that or how this ended? Anyone who feels we should take this to the next level?"

His voice is direct. His tone pointed. Dozens of people stop whatever the hell they're doing in synchrony and pivot to us. It's in this moment that I realize that the blonde and the dark-haired, green-eyed man are gone. It's just Jake and me as the sole survivors.

"All good."

"Nope."

"Let's get this done and go."

I blink at all of them in stunned bewilderment.

One of the agents who is dressed like someone from *Men in Black* walks up to me and stares me dead in the eyes. "He killed my cousin," he says to me. "Had him murdered over where he'd open his next restaurant. Made it look like suicide, but there were defensive wounds on his body. I couldn't prove it, and I couldn't push it with local agencies."

I swallow hard and nod. He looks so similar to his deceased cousin that I don't mistake him for a minute.

"The man who carried out that order was detained as part of a high-stakes gambling cheat at The Turner Grand today. I'm sure Mister Turner can direct you further on that."

The man in the suit with an FBI badge around his neck reaches out his hand to me. "Thank you."

We shake hands. "You as well."

"He killed the kid in the corner," Jake explains, now on the ground beside Maddox's body. "His name is Morgan Fair. Isabel and I saw him do it. He also threatened my life, the life of my wife, as well as Maddox's. We can testify to that if need be."

"We'll do ballistics and run the scene because we have to, but Luke is right. I think it's pretty clear what happened in here today," one of them says, her eyes scanning about the room. "Yep," she drawls. "I think we'll have this all cleared up within a few hours." She smiles and winks at me like we share a dark secret. Maybe we do.

Jake turns to Luke, his brown eyes dark and angry. "You're late."

"I know. I'm sorry. But you didn't give me much time. We got here as quickly as we could. From the looks of it, you all handled it even if it wasn't how you wanted it to go."

Jake shakes his head at Luke like he can't figure it. "No one was supposed to die today other than Conti. Whether they deserved it or not." Jake drops to his knees beside Maddox's body. "Come on, man," Jake coaxes, his hand lightly slapping Maddox's cheek. "You gotta take a breath. I know it hurts, but your girl is freaking the fuck out and just—" Jake pauses, glances around the room at all the agents.

"Killed Anthony Conti for you," Luke Walker finishes with an air of disbelief to his voice. "It's fine. It won't change our report on what happened here."

I shake my head, my body trembling violently now that the last of the adrenaline has abandoned me. I just killed a man. Anthony Conti. *My* Anthony Conti. Shot him I have no idea how many times, but the agents are placing him in a bag like they're not even going to do an investigation. I've seen enough crime dramas to know that they don't typically do that so quickly. Just what the absolute fuck is going on here? Who the hell is Luke Walker? Clearly, he's a hell of a lot more than an executive for Grant Technologies.

Luke finally releases me, and I stumble forward on newborn colt-like legs, my eyes glued to Maddox. I can hardly hold my weight up as I stare down at his body. He's still on his stomach. There is still a ton of blood everywhere. His face is still ashen white.

But he's breathing.

"Fuck," he hisses quietly and a sob I didn't know I was capable of emitting flies past my lips. I drop to my knees, my face in my hands as I start to lose it. Big, ugly, hiccupping, I can't breathe crying.

"This hurts more than I thought it would." I hear him exhale a loud coarse breath. "Isabel?"

I can't respond. I'm too busy losing my mind because he was dead. *He was dead!* I felt his back and confirmed he wasn't breathing. I stepped in his sticky, red blood. If he really is alive, I want to kill him all over again for putting me through this.

"You were dead!"

"Baby," he puffs like it really does hurt him as he slowly rolls onto his back. His beautiful blue eyes blink open slowly and he scans the scene around him before settling on me. Screw the scene. There are people everywhere doing whatever it is they do. But Jake is still on his knees, directly beside Maddox, and I can't move. I can't move.

"You son of a bitch. I hate you!" I seethe, swatting the air when the stupid ass reaches for me. "How could you do this to me? How could you not tell me? How could you let me believe it was real?"

"Come here."

I shake my head, but my resolve is faltering. Part of me wants to go to him. To have him hold me, feel his beating heart. He's alive. As in, not dead. "He shot you. I saw him shoot you. I stepped in your blood. You weren't breathing."

"I'm sorry," he hums, his voice strained. "He did shoot me. That's not how he typically does things. He was supposed to order his goon to do it and then we were going to kill Conti. That didn't happen the way it was supposed to. Nothing did. Regardless, I took precautions way before we got here when I changed in my office. I'm wearing a jacket made from Kevlar and these are fake blood packets. But it wasn't supposed to go down like this. You weren't supposed to be here." He reaches for me again, resting his hand on my knee. "I am so sorry, Isabel. So very sorry."

I shake my head some more, my tears undeterred. "I thought you were dead. I *believed* you were dead. I shot him. I killed him because he killed you."

"Isabel." His voice is gravel dipped in acid. "There is so much you don't know."

"No," I yell, shoving his hand from my body. I don't want him to touch me. "There is so much *you* don't know. You stupid bastard. Imagine what that felt like for me. Imagine if the roles had been reversed." He blinks, his expression anguished, cloaked in regret. His eyes glass over, and I don't care, because he may think he has a clue, but he doesn't. That was the worst moment of my life—and that's saying a whole lot.

"I know exactly what that feels like." His hand finds mine. I let him hold it and he squeezes me. "To believe the person you love is dead. I know. And it's not something I ever wanted you to experience. Christ," he blows out. "Izzy, baby." He squeezes my hand again. A tear glides down his cheek as he stares into my eyes. "I love you and I'm so fucking sorry. Forever, I'll be sorry for that."

"I killed a man. He's dead and I trusted you."

"Isabel—"

"No! I trusted you. And you just shattered that. You let me down. I'm a murderer. I'm no better than he was."

It wasn't supposed to go down like this.

But it did and now I have to live with that. "I never want to see you again."

I stand up slowly and drag my focus away from Maddox, who is suddenly rendered silent. Good. I can't handle his stupid words. I turn around and watch as they zip up Anthony Conti. It's the last I'll ever see of him, so I watch until he's completely covered. I'm hit with the worst, most painful pang of guilt. Justin. I just killed Justin's father. Conti was evil and brutal and dark, and yes, he did deserve to die. I don't regret that he's dead. I regret that I pulled the trigger. Now I have to go and tell my brother that I killed his father.

THIRTY-TWO

ISABEL

I WALKED out of that warehouse alone. Maddox was sitting up by that point, wiping at his face and body. He continued to beg me with his eyes, but I couldn't stand the sight of him.

Maybe if I hadn't just learned how badly I had already been duped by Conti I would have felt differently about what Maddox did. Maybe I would have had a stronger appreciation for all he went through and tried to do. I get Jake Turner's role in this. It's his company. His wife. And to some extent, I get Maddox's role, too. But god, I'm so tired of people lying to me. Of people hiding the truth. Jake followed me out, but I told him what I told Maddox.

I never want to see either of them again.

I went home and waited patiently for the police or the FBI to knock on my door.

To come and arrest me.

They never did, and I didn't have the stomach to go online and look up whatever was being reported. Not having a television with cable occasionally has its benefits.

I land at Bradley Airport just outside of Hartford, Connecticut on a bright sunny day not even twenty-four hours after I shot a man. The hospital Justin had surgery at is about forty minutes from the airport. I rent a shitty little car—the cheapest one they have—and then somehow find my way there without causing a huge accident. I don't drive. I mean, I have driven. My mother had a car and I used to run errands using it, long before I even got my license. But I haven't driven in a very long time and to say it scares the crap out of me is an understatement.

Yet, I'm grateful for the focus driving requires.

Last night, being home alone with my thoughts was brutal. Maddox didn't come to me. I was relieved for the most part, but still, there was that small piece of me that waited. That hoped. That thought if he really loved me, he'd come and fight for me. He didn't. So, this morning, I got up, packed up every stitch of clothing I own, got in a cab and went to the airport with no real intention of return-ing. I mean, what is there for me in that town now? Nothing. I no longer have a mob boss holding me hostage. I have no job. No boyfriend.

I'm free.

It's as liberating as it is debilitating, because what the hell am I going to do now?

Checking in at the main desk, I'm given a visitor's sticker and directed where to go. Justin spent the night here, but when I spoke to the doctor prior to my connecting flight, he informed me they'd wait for me, but they were planning on discharging him today. Justin can go back to his school, to his dorm, but he just had surgery. The doctor assured me Justin was already on the mend and would do fine back in his dorm. "Teenagers are resilient and heal quickly," he had said.

And when I enter Justin's hospital room, I see he is correct. Justin is walking around his room, his cell phone to his ear. His wrist isn't in a cast the way I thought it would be. It's in a splint of sorts. He's also not in one of those hospital gowns. My brother is wearing gray track pants that say Hollister Prep Lacrosse and a matching t-shirt. His light brown hair is all over the place, and wow, my baby brother got *tall*. And handsome. I smile at that, noticing for the first time that he's turning into a man.

Justin catches me hovering in the doorway to his hospital room and a smile erupts across his face. I see nothing of Anthony Conti in him, and that alone has me crossing the room and wrapping my arms around his neck despite the phone still pressed to his ear. "I gotta go, man. My sister just got here. Yeah. Later."

He tosses his phone on the hospital bed and hugs me back with equal ardor. "What the hell happened?" he finally asks, stepping back and cupping my face with his uninjured hand. I have a bruise on my temple from where Morgan hit me. Justin scans toward the door and when he feels comfortable enough that we're alone, he follows that up with, "It's been all over the news and since there isn't much else on the televisions here, I've been watching."

I puff out a breath and step back, my eyes growing watery before I can stop them. "I'm so sorry." I drop to the edge of his bed and he follows me, standing before me expectantly.

"Your boss killed him?"

"What?" My head whips up to his. Justin has pretty green eyes. Something I've always wished I shared with him even if they match our mother's. "What the hell do you mean?" I shake my head. "No." I swallow and take a breath to steady my racing heartbeat. "*I* killed him."

He hisses out a low whistle, glancing once more toward the door. "No. You didn't." His eyes meet mine and the meaning behind his words is unmistakable. "NBC and CNN just informed me that a Maddox Sinclair of Turner Hotels killed Anthony Conti in self-defense after Conti killed an intern and shot him."

"Morgan Fair," I supply because his death, his part in all of this, has been difficult to swallow.

"Right. He's the intern." He bobs his head.

"Justin . . ." I trail off, unsure how to start. So, I chicken out with, "Are you okay?" I motion toward his wrist. "Why are you standing. You just had surgery."

"On my wrist, Is. Not my feet. I'm fine. My wrist hurts, but they give me stuff for it and I'm all good. My season is over, which sucks, but I'll be back for junior year. You're not getting around talking about this."

"Stupid little brothers," I grumble, and he laughs. Falling back on his bed, I bring my arms up to rest above my head. I stare up at the drop ceiling, noting the various stains and trying not to think about what those could possibly be from in a hospital.

"He was your father." I'm greeted with silence. Not even an exaggerated intake of breath or shift of movement. No, this is the type of silence that acts like a pause. Like he's waiting for me to follow that up. I chance a peek at him and he's staring down at me.

"Did he tell you that?"

I nod.

"And you didn't know before? Never figured it out?"

I shake my head against the white linen of the uncomfortably firm hospital bed. He half-grins, but there is no humor in that smile. It's pained and angry.

"I did. Know, I mean."

"You did?" I sit back up.

"Yeah. Mom told me shortly before she died. I saw him tailing us. Tailing you, and I told her about it. I was afraid to worry you. We had no shortage of creeps in our neighborhood or hanging around our place, but this guy was different. She told me he was my father and once Mom died and he held on to you like a prized doll, I kept my mouth shut."

"So, you just never told me?"

His gaze shifts as does his posture. "I . . . He was an evil man. Even at twelve I knew that. I was embarrassed that he was my father and I knew how you felt about him. How much you hated him and the things he made you do. The things he did to you that you never told me about. I was afraid you'd think less of me if you knew."

Shit. Now I'm crying. I stand up and snake my arms around him once more, burying my face in his chest.

"When did you get so big?" I muse, a half-laugh gurgling around my tears.

He squeezes me back and I think this might just be one of the most perfect moments ever.

"I could never ever think less of you. *Ever.* I've never been anything but proud of you, Justin."

"Good. Because I feel the same way about you. I know all that you've been through. All that you've sacrificed for me. One day, I'll make it up to you. I promise."

"I did all that because I didn't have much of a choice with Anthony Conti. None of that stuff was because of you. And everything I did because of you, I don't regret, and I don't need you to make it up to me. I'd do it all again a million times over."

"He's not yours. Your father, that is. In case you were wondering."

I step back and wipe at my face. "I know he's not. The man had plans for me that did not mesh with a father-daughter relationship." I scrunch up my nose. It's still beyond my comprehension that he wanted to marry me. Maddox put it correctly when he referred to me as his obsession. That's what it was. An odd, sick obsession forged when I was only a teenager. I guess the one thing I can be grateful about is that the man had one limit, and child molestation was clearly it. I shudder to think of the alternative.

"I'm glad he's gone." His whispered confession eases some of the tension from my shoulders. Loosens the knot in my stomach.

"Me, too," I admit.

"What are you going to do now?"

Justin sits on the edge of his bed, taking me with him. Tossing his arm over my shoulder, he pulls my head to his. We sit like that for a moment. Me thinking. Him waiting.

"I want to go to college. I think I want to be a teacher."

"Then go to college. Become a teacher."

"I'm in love with my boss. The one taking the fall for me." That's what Maddox is doing, I realize. Taking the fall. He didn't have to say he was the one who killed Anthony Conti. Those agents in that room under Luke Walker's command didn't seem to care about how it went down, just that it was over, and that Conti was dead. But the public was going to find out. A story like that couldn't stay hidden long. Especially with Morgan's death. Maddox stepped up so I wouldn't have to. So it wouldn't be me in the public eye, having questions thrown at me.

"Does that mean you're going back to Vegas?"

I let out a breathy laugh. "I told him I never wanted to see him again."

"Why?"

"Things got pretty intense in that room, and I thought Maddox—that's his name—was dead. I thought Conti had killed him. It broke me," I concede. "I couldn't stand the thought of him being dead, and I shot Conti because of it. I'm not sure I would have otherwise. I didn't want to marry him. I didn't want to be part of his sick world and depraved plan. But killing him wasn't exactly what I had in mind as part of my exit strategy."

"And you resent this guy Maddox for that?"

"Yes. I did, I mean. I don't know how I feel about any of it anymore, in truth. But he didn't fight for me, either. He let me go."

"Or maybe he's giving you time to cool down." Justin meets my eyes, a hint of a smile curling up the edge of his lips. "You've got a temper, Is."

I bristle at that, even though I know he's right.

"Don't give me that look. I know you know it's true. You're quick to burn and slow to cool sometimes. Maybe he knows that about you. Maybe he's just waiting it out."

"Aren't I worth getting burned for?"

He chuckles. "Yes. But there is a difference between getting burned and being incinerated."

Touché.

"Regardless, I think I'll stay for a little. Just to make sure you're back on the mend. I'm sure March in Connecticut is lovely. Cold as fuck, but lovely."

"March is actually one of the shittiest months here," he laughs the words. "But I'd still like you to stay. Even if it's just for a little."

THIRTY-THREE

MADDOX

JAKE and I sat in the living room of Morgan Fair Senior's house for over an hour. We explained how his son died. Except, about ninety-five percent of what we told him was a lie. He didn't need to know the truth. He didn't need to know what his son was really up to all the months he had been working for Turner Hotels. That his son repeatedly went behind his back and plotted with a known head of an organized crime ring.

Certain truths are just not meant for a parent's ears.

Morgan Fair Senior believes that his son died bravely and with honor, and that's all there is to it. It's what the parent of every soldier who doesn't return home alive is told. Only in their case it's true. Jake and I have done this before. Gone to the homes of fallen brothers. Spoken with grieving family members. It's not something one ever grows accustomed to. In part, I blame myself for Morgan's death. Conti had never in his life been the one to do the dirty work. He had men for that. He made the calls and gave the orders and they carried them out. Never him.

That's where I fucked up. Where we all fucked up.

It never occurred to me that he'd kill Morgan. Never. Me? Yeah, I knew he'd want to shoot me. I was baiting him with the one thing he had zero cool for. Isabel. That man's obsession ran deep. So much deeper than I bet she's even aware of. Every lock. Every combination. The numbers are always her birthday. He had pictures of her lining the drawers of his desk. Mostly candid ones, taken as she was being watched. Some are posed. Some are of her as a child. Some are of her from the club. We're talking hundreds of pictures. And that's not even close to everything.

In a way, she's lucky he obsessed over her so much. It probably kept her alive and safer than she would have been otherwise.

The News caught wind of this story before the warehouse was even cleaned up, gobbling it up like a fat man on Thanksgiving. We fed them every single line with care and precision. You'd think after two men dying at my hand in 'self-defense' there'd be more negative press my way. Questions raised by different local and government bodies. But no. The world was not sad to be rid of Niklas Vaughn once they learned he was a horrible wife beater, and Las Vegas was certainly not sad about losing their most menacing figure. Hell, the mayor called me to thank me personally. Off the record, of course, but still. I've practically been given a key to the damn city.

The word on the street is that Conti's men were staging a coup against Turner Hotels. They had done a series of simultaneous high-level cheats in order to distract all our security forces with the ultimate goal of taking over the security tower and infiltrating our networks and servers. That's true, and we have plenty of proof to back that up in the form of video and attempted back-door access to our systems.

What's not true is what the world believes happened in the warehouse.

Morgan, Jake, and I were kidnapped. I was beaten as part of that endeavor. The three of us were threatened at gunpoint by Conti's thugs. Jake was being blackmailed into signing over Turner Hotels. Morgan was shot and killed to reinforce that threat with the promise that my life was next if Jake didn't comply. He shot at me and I fired back, killing him. That's when the Feds walked in, since Jake and I had called them right when we found out there were multiple security infringements going on at the hotels.

Only. . . they're not really FBI. Luke Walker does work for the government, but it's some super-secret black ops faction of some unknown organization that no one talks about.

The FBI certainly aren't about to say that it wasn't them who took down one of the most notorious mob bosses this country has ever seen. That's just bad PR for them. They gratefully accepted the evidence they were handed and went from there.

Isabel's name was never mentioned. I made sure of that. There was no way I was ever going to let her take the fall. That's all there is folks. Game's over. Show's done.

And I'm miserable.

I know I don't deserve Isabel, but damn, did I want to. *Want her.* I know I hurt her. I deserve this pain, this penance and misery. I deserve it all, but that doesn't make it any more palatable. Any easier to swallow. I miss her. I can't stop thinking about her.

"How long are we going to let him continue to be a sulky bastard?" Jake asks off to my right as he and Fiona obnoxiously share a lounger, all cuddled up together like the annoyingly adorable couple they make.

"Leave him alone," she says. "His heart is broken."

"I get that, baby. But it doesn't have to stay that way."

I roll my eyes, sinking back further and taking a sip of whatever wine we're drinking. I'd tell them to shut up or mention the fact that I'm sitting right here and can hear them perfectly, but there really is no point. It wouldn't stop them.

"Didn't she tell him she never wants to see him again?"

"Thanks for the reminder, Fi," I grumble like the surly bastard I am.

"That's probably my fault," Gavin jumps in with zero intonation to his tone. "I let her take the gun from me and shoot him instead of doing it myself." He's been standing at the edge of the balcony, staring straight out at nothing. I mean, yeah, the Strip is there and the mountains beyond that, but he's not looking at any of the natural and not-so-natural scenery. He's working on something in that mind of his. A job that nearly cost him everything. One he won't talk about more than what we already know went down.

Gavin isn't really a man of many words once you get to know him. When he was working Fiona, he was this charming, flirty guy. All smiles and asking her out on dates and pushing the line. But that's not who he is. He'll play whatever role he has to play for work, but at his heart, this guy has way more demons than we know about. Than we've even come close to scratching the surface on.

Oddly enough, despite his chosen profession, he's a good man. An honorable man, I guess. At least to some extent. I trust him. Not sure I thought I'd ever trust a contract killer, but there you have it. He's the one who really got us what we needed with this Conti thing. And we've slowly been leaking all the information he got on that bastard. It's my insurance policy and it's working like a charm.

"Why did you do that? Let her take the gun?" Fiona asks, and part of me feels like she shouldn't be sitting here for this. But try telling her that. The truth is, she's as much a part of our team now as any of us. I just don't like her being involved more than she has to be.

"Because she was staring into my eyes and I saw it. The recognition. The anger. The hatred. The fear. I saw it all, and I respected how she let me see it. And when Maddox was shot, and she believed him dead, I watched her. I watched her heart break, and then I watched as her resolve for revenge solidified. She's a force, that girl of yours," he says with something close to admiration. "Anthony Conti needed to die. But more importantly, he deserved it. And the only one of us who earned the right to end his life was her. Did you know that monster once tied her to a chair in his office when she was sixteen because she let a boy in her class kiss her and accepted a date to a dance with him?" Gavin doesn't turn around to watch our expressions, because his question is rhetorical.

Obviously, none of us knew that. Jake, Fi and I all exchange disgusted, tormented glances.

"Yeah. The prick made her sit there like that throughout the entire dance and wouldn't untie her until it was over. Then he slapped her around just to drive the point home that she belonged to him and no one else."

I take a deep breath, scrubbing my hands up and down my face. I would have shot him in the face had I known that. Maybe beaten him to death instead. Ripped him apart with my bare hands. I wouldn't have cared about the potential consequences. About the plan we had to take him down the "legal" way. I would have killed that mother-fucker first chance and Gavin knew that. It's why he waited until now to tell us. To tell me.

"She may have claimed she didn't want him dead," he continues, "but it didn't take her long or much of a push to get her to pull that trigger. And it's not like she pulled it once, saw that she killed him, and broke down into a fit of regretful tears. She emptied my entire magazine. That was pure rage. So, I'm not sure how much that 'I never want to see you again' stuff is true. I think she just didn't like facing that side of herself. The side that reminded her of him, and she blamed you for that."

"Yeah," Jake agrees. "She was angry. She was emotional. It takes time to process that." Jake looks directly at Fiona. "I seem to recall a time when you needed some space to figure your own shit out. And I also remember someone flying all the way to Dallas to get you."

Yeah. I did that for him. But that was different. "That was different," I say, vocalizing my thought because it feels like a really valid point for some reason.

"No. It really wasn't. Shit went down. Shit went wrong and completely unlike the way we planned it. I went nuts for two weeks while Fiona was getting her head on straight and then you brought her to me."

"Is this my 'kick Maddox's ass into action' intervention? Are you expecting I'll jump up all rejuvenated and run off into the sunset and win her back? Because I'm thinking that's not how my situation with her will go."

"She's still in Connecticut with her brother," Gavin says. I already knew that, but I wonder why he's still tracking her. "She's going to have to come back soon. Conti's estate is a deal she's a part of."

"What sort of deal? And how the hell do you know all this?"

"It's my job to know all this. And the deal won't hurt her or her brother."

"Do you love her?" Fiona asks, and I can't roll my eyes at her because she's Fiona.

"Yes, I love her. Of course, I love her. You already know that because you're the type of woman who knows things like that long before the rest of us do. It's why you were all hot to meet her."

"Does she love you back?"

I sigh, because I think she does. I really do. I think I just fucked up in the worst possible way. Isabel is a hothead and highly excitable and dramatic in the way most teenagers are. "She's a teenager," I say, once again giving voice to my idiotic thought process.

Fiona laughs hard. "I was eighteen when I married Niklas."

"That's different. And that was sick, so you're not really selling me on the age-difference thing."

She rolls her eyes at me, and I wonder why she can do that to me, but I can't do that to her. She shifts deeper into Jake's chest. "I was twenty-two when I met and fell in love with Jake. Barely twenty-three when I married him. He's older than me and none of that crap matters. Stop looking for stupid excuses."

I chuckle. "For once, Fi, couldn't you say shit? That none of that *shit* matters?"

"My point is, your arguments are irrelevant. You love her. She loves you. That's it."

"He doesn't think he deserves her."

I shift in my seat and take a long pull of the wine because it really is very good and worth finishing off before I smash the glass on Jake's head.

"God, why are men so stupid?"

"It's in our DNA," Gavin explains. "And I think this is my cue to leave." He gives me the bro shake, does the same with Jake, and then kisses Fiona on the forehead. "Later, beautiful. I'll be in touch soon." Gavin walks out, and my eyes trail him for a beat.

I know he's not going far. After all Gavin went through this past week here in Vegas, he'll be staying for a little.

The second Gavin is gone, Fiona stands up and walks the two steps over to my lounger. She's a tall woman. Probably close to six feet, so even though I'm a big man, I'm slouched down, and I have to raise my head up to find her. Fiona shoves my legs aside so she can sit on the edge of my chair and stare into my eyes. Her intensity has me squirming. It's almost laughable that this pretty, blonde, Southern belle could make me twitch. Hell, I didn't so much as break a sweat when dealing with Anthony Conti, but Fiona Foss-Turner? Yeah, this woman is a force to be reckoned with.

"I never thanked you, Maddox."

I swallow, and she smiles, reaching out her hand and grasping mine. She doesn't intertwine our fingers. No, that's what lovers do. Instead she holds me, grips me tight and lets me know she means business.

"You found me lost, homeless, totally and completely broken. I was at my bottom. Mentally at my end, and you helped me find my way back. Find my way to Jake. Find my way to learning how to fight for myself. To having a sense of self-worth and self-respect when I had next to none before. You risked your life for me without hesitation or question, and I know that you'd do it again for me without even batting an eye. You are honest and loyal and smart and funny. But most of all, you're a good man."

I swallow past the lump forming in my throat. This woman is stripping me bare. Fiona inches closer to me, her other hand dropping to my chest, directly above my pounding heart. She smiles when she feels it, her eyes welling up. My instinct is to get up and leave. To push her away. I'd never do that to her, but I do not want to hear whatever she's about to say.

"Fi—"

She shakes her head, instantly stopping my objection. "No. I'm your friend. This is what friends do for each other. We help each other when we need helping the most. And we kick some sense into each other when we need it the most."

I glance over at Jake, looking for some help, but he doesn't give me the I-can't-stop-her helpless husband shrug. No. He's right in line with her and that takes this to a whole other level.

Fiona cups my cheek and drags me back, so my full attention is on her. "We make mistakes, Maddox. We are human. It's what we do. God." She laughs half-heartedly, a sad smile etched on her pretty face. "I've made so many mistakes in my life. There are a million things I wish I could take back or undo or change. But we can't. All we can do is move forward, learn, and adapt, and grow, and *accept*. You have to accept that there are things in this world you cannot change. Giving up doesn't make them go away or reverse time. And making a mistake does not make you unworthy of good things." Fiona leans forward, her forehead dropping to mine as she closes her eyes. I close mine, too, sucking in a deep breath and holding it still in my chest as I allow her words to eviscerate and rebuild me. "You deserve Isabel, Maddox. But more importantly, *she* deserves *you*."

"Fi—" I try again.

"No, Maddox. It's time you start fighting for yourself instead of everyone else."

She gently presses her lips to mine before standing up and wiping at her wet eyes. She lets out a small laugh, but it's not the self-conscious sort. It's the sort that makes you feel fearless. Whole. I chance a glance back over to my friend. He's beaming up at his woman with unflappable adoration. Jake reaches a hand out for her and she happily slinks back to the comfort and love of his embrace.

We're quiet. Lost. That is, until Jake asks, "Is he still here?"

"Fucker," I bark, but laugh all the same. So do Jake and Fiona, because someone had to cut the intensity before it ate all of us alive. "She's gone," I tell them. "She left town over a week ago and hasn't come back. I'm not sure I should go after her," I admit. "How do I ask her to come back to Vegas? This town has never done anything right by her."

I'd give Isabel the world. Everything she's ever wanted and dreamed of. College. Travel. Using those languages she pushed herself to learn. I'd never hold her back. I'd never restrain her. I'd let her set her wings free and follow her wherever they took us.

"Maybe not," Jake answers. "But don't you think that should be her decision and not yours?"

THIRTY-FOUR

ISABEL

MADDOX HAS CALLED me a total of five times since that day in the warehouse. I wouldn't say I'm avoiding him. He just always happens to call at a time when I either miss his call or can't pick up my phone. And I haven't called him back because I'm not sure I'm ready to. I miss him, of course. Like mad. Like the sea when it's angry and turbulent and a storm is about to break.

But this time with Justin? This time on my own? This time with no rules to follow or anxious tingling up my spine or fear twisting up my gut? It's sorta priceless. I know I have to do something soon. I'm going to have to make a decision because I'm going to need money. That old necessity.

This interlude won't last much longer, especially since I've been dodging Conti's lawyers as well.

What they want from me is anyone's guess, but I'm afraid to speak to them. Maybe more than I'm afraid to speak to Maddox. I just left Justin at his school. He's got a full day of classes today, so I'm officially left to my own devices. The campus is beautiful here. It snowed a little last night, coating the ground in a few inches of pristine white powder. I'll admit it, the snow made me giddy. The sky is still overcast and gray, and the air is cool but not unbearable. I had to buy a winter coat. The coat I had for Vegas was most definitely not cutting it in Connecticut.

Strolling along the mostly clear path that leads back toward the parking lot, I hit play on the voicemail and listen. "Miss Bogart. This is Jerome Flores from Flores, Locke, and Chase. It is urgent that I speak with you regarding Anthony Conti's estate. Please call me back as soon as you receive this message. Thank you."

"Crap," I mutter, staring down at my phone like it will magically have all the answers I need written on it.

"You, too?" a voice says, startling me out of my reverie. I whip my head up at light speed to find Maddox standing in front of a Jeep—of course, it's a Jeep—all bundled up in a light gray wool jacket and a black beanie. His pale blue eyes appear even bluer against the dingy sky. He hasn't shaved in what looks like a few days, and that layer of stubble is doing things to me that I wish it wasn't. Wow. Rough and rugged Maddox is a work of art. "Why do girls always say crap instead of shit?"

I shake my head at him but refuse to smile. "Probably because I'm standing on the grounds of a high school."

He considers this. "I suppose that makes sense, and I suppose it means I should curtail my foul language."

"What are you doing here? How did you know this is where Justin went to school?" I can't decide which question I want him to answer first. I don't like the idea of him still stalking my phone. But I love the idea of him finding me anyway.

He pushes off from the front of the Jeep and steps toward me, still maintaining a wide berth of space between us. "That first night I snuck over, and you let me in, when your hair was up and you were wearing flannel pants and a black Misfits t-shirt?"

I stare at him, wondering if he's real. Debating if I should walk over to him and smack his face or kiss his lips. I'm not mad at him anymore. Just how aggravating is that?

"Those flannel pants had the name of this school on them." He takes a step toward me, swallowing up the distance I had been clinging to, hoping it would keep me sane. "And I'm here because I miss you." Another step. "Because I love you." Last step. "And I can't accept your terms of never seeing me again. That's crap." He smirks at the word. He cups my face, holding me like I'm made of glass and staring at me like I'm a diamond. Like I'm strong and unbreakable. Like I'm the most beautiful, dazzling thing he's ever seen. "I messed up, Izzy. I know I did. I should have told you the truth, but I was trying to protect you. To keep you safe and protected and alive. That was all I cared about, and then everything went wrong. But I need another chance, because where you end, I begin. There is no me without you."

"I'm not going back to work for you."

He smiles and it's like the sun bursting through the clouds. "Nope. You're not. I get no work done when you're there. I'm too busy staring at your ass and trying to figure out a way to kiss you without anyone catching us."

"And no more secrets. Or lies," I tack on, raising an eyebrow.

"Promise. From now on we're open and honest with each other about everything."

"Okay then."

"Yeah?"

I laugh at his slightly incredulous tone. Maybe I should have put up more of a fight, but the truth is, I don't want to. I want him back. "Yeah. Were you nervous?"

He laughs, wrapping me up in his arms and lifting me off the ground as he does. I squeal, snaking my arms around his shoulders so I can look into his eyes. "Like crazy. You've got a temper and I wasn't sure you'd cooled down yet."

I roll my eyes. "My brother said the same damn thing to me. My temper isn't *that* bad." I narrow my eyes at him.

"You're right. Let's not fight."

He cringes dramatically, and I giggle, shaking my head. "Okay, point made. Maybe I do have a bit of a *tiny* temper. And I'm seriously stubborn. And impetuous."

"I wouldn't change any of it. Or you." He closes the final gap between us, pressing his lips to mine. His mouth devours me, and our tongues dance in a kiss that is far too passionate for the parking lot of a high school. He nips the soft tissue of my earlobe, kissing the sensitive skin just beneath before sliding to the side of my mouth. My fingers comb through his hair, struggling to grip the too-short ends. The second our lips meet again; I know this is it. There is no going back for me. This kiss brands me to him. Makes his soul part of mine. His tongue skates over mine and my hips roll involuntarily against him. It's only now that I realize I've wrapped my legs around his waist.

Crap. We're on a high school campus. I pull back, both of us panting.

"This is what we've been waiting for," he says. "*This.*" His lips press to mine again as if proving a point. "No more hiding. We're free now."

That truth is something else entirely. I knew it before. Felt some of that power. But hearing him say it detonates a million happy fluttering butterflies inside my stomach.

"Say it back," he breathes against my lips, his eyes searing into mine.

"No more hiding. We're free now." I give him a cheeky grin, because I know for a fact that's not what he wants me to say. He reaches down and smacks my ass, confirming my thoughts.

"Brat."

"I love you, too." I lean in and smile against him, rubbing our noses together. "Where you end, I begin. Now take me somewhere and shag me rotten."

He chuckles, giving me one final kiss before setting me down. "Shag you rotten?"

"High school, remember? The NC-17, X-rated version comes once you get me in your car."

"Jeep. It's a Jeep, Izzy. Wait." He pauses just before opening the passenger side door for me. "Can I call you Starshine again?"

I smirk. "Hoping to get a lap dance and a strip show?"

"Does it make me a pig if I say yes?"

"Yes."

He shrugs. "I'm not sure I care if it gets me the lap dance and strip show." He winks, opening the door for me and helping me in. He leans toward me and kisses my lips before shutting the door and climbing in behind the wheel, then he starts the Jeep and drives off like he knows this town by heart. His hand reaches across the console and finds mine, and we hold hands like everything is the way it should be. The way it will be from now on.

I wait for it to come. The fear. The uncertainty. The desire to be on my own.

But it never does.

I take a deep breath, and everything feels . . . right.

"Why are you smiling?" he asks, peeking over at me and then quickly back at the road.

"Am I smiling?" I guess I am. "I want you to meet Justin."

Maddox nods like that was already part of his plan.

"I'm supposed to pick him up for dinner tonight. Will you come?"

"Without a doubt. But until then, you're all mine." Maddox pulls off the road, taking us up a winding, partially paved street, heading toward a reservoir. The lake springs up on the right, large and oddly shaped and still as it's partially frozen. It's beautiful, as are the tall trees—some bare, some evergreen or a variation of it with a name I don't know.

"I bet it's incredible here during Christmas. Cold and dark with twinkling lights and white snow."

He squeezes my hand as we continue to wind through, heading I don't know where and not caring in the least. "Then we'll come back. Take Justin and go to Vermont or something. Learn how to ski."

I laugh at that image. Maddox Sinclair. All huge six feet six of him on skis. "Or maybe just snow-tubing. Justin's done that before and said it was a lot of fun."

"Baby, if I can surf, I can snowboard."

"We'll see. We have a long way to go before next winter."

Maddox pulls the Jeep off the road, twisting us between a few trees and hiding us somewhere we won't be found. It's deserted out here anyway. Too cold and gray and snowy for hikers or bikers. "Come here," he says, sliding his seat all the way back and reclining it some. I make quick work of my seatbelt and scurry over onto his lap, straddling him. He brushes my long hair back off my face and over my shoulders, staring up into my eyes.

"We do have a long way to go before next winter. I still owe you that Grand Canyon date. And I'm thinking May is a really nice time of year to go to Southern California and hit up the Pacific. And even though the summers are a beast in Georgia with the heat and humidity, the breeze off the Atlantic helps some, and I'd like you to meet my mom and sisters. And I bet the fall is a beautiful time of year to visit England, France, Italy, and Spain. And by then, we're practically at winter. So, maybe not so far off."

This man . . . I smile down at him. "Maybe not so far off." I dip my face to his and kiss him. "Maybe not," I hum into him. He cups my butt and I groan as he slides me closer to him. Onto the large, very hard bulge poking me through his jeans. My head falls back, his hand gliding up and down the column of my neck. He squeezes me. Not hard, but possessively, and it makes a rush of wetness pool between my parted thighs.

"Kiss me," he says, and I drop my head as our eyes lock. Our mood suddenly shifts, becoming heavier as we strip each other bare and shed away the last of our baggage, allowing what this is to take over. "Kiss me, Isabel."

So I do. I kiss him, snaking my tongue with his. Fighting a battle of dominance and letting him win because I want him to. I want him to own me. I savor the way he tastes. Love the way his rough stubble scratches the sensitive skin on my face. I inhale his scent that will likely forever cause my chest to clench in just the right way. He's my home, I realize. And no matter the choices I make or don't make for myself, that won't change.

I can still be the woman I want to be while being *his* woman.

And wow, that's just quite possibly the best revelation ever.

I rip off my new coat and my black thermal beneath. I go to town on his outerwear next and he helps me along, removing his coat and shirt. His chest and abs call to me, and I wish the confines of the Jeep weren't restricting me because I'd really like to explore them with my tongue. But I can't, so I settle for gently caressing them while he watches me touch him. "I want to suck you off," I tell him, my mouth watering at the idea.

He groans, thrusting up into my spread thighs. "Take these off." He unhooks the button of my jeans. His hands cup my breasts over my bra, squeezing me with enough pressure to make me moan in return. I climb back into the passenger seat and take off my pants, panties and bra, all the while watching him watch me. It's no strip tease. It's far from a lap dance. But he likes the show I'm giving him and starts to get himself naked as well, stroking his cock once it's free of his pants. I don't even care that we're in a rented Jeep in the middle of a public park. This is easily the most erotic moment of my life.

"Climb back on me."

I do. But I do it slowly because I don't want this to end as quickly as it should. I mean, we could get caught. But hell if that isn't adding to this moment. His warm breath. My cold body as I shiver against him. I sink down on him and that's when I feel it. How perfect this is. How *good* this is.

"Baby," he groans. "Isabel." It's a plea this time.

"You're not wearing anything, are you?" His eyes are pinched closed as he shakes his head.

"Fuck." It's a hiss and a prayer. "You're so tight." He pants out twice. "Christ." Now he's groaning, his head falling back because I've started to move. "I have to pull out or I'm going to come and we're going to make a baby. Although, I actually like that idea. Maybe that's insane, but I do. So, if you want me to give you a baby, keep going. If not, get off me and I'll cover up."

"Hate to break it to you, but I'm not ovulating. But my real question is, are you clean?"

"Like a vestal virgin."

I laugh, throwing my head back and riding him like I have plans for the two of us. No, not pregnancy. I know when I'm ovulating, and it's not now. But I want him inside of me without something between us. "No more barriers."

My hips rock forward. My body grinding in that most perfect of ways. Maddox takes over, his hands gripping my hips as he lifts me, slamming me back down on him and, "Oh god!"

"Yes. Feel me. Feel this." He does it again and I lose my mind. I lose my sanity.

"Maddox."

"I'm going to screw you crazy. You feel that?" I nod my head up and down as he does just that. Up and down. Up and down. *So good.* "Am I hitting your spot?"

"Yes!"

"You want more?"

"So much more. Don't stop."

"This is me, baby. Us. There is no stopping. There is only more."

"Give me more."

And he does. He pounds into me. Harder. Faster. *Deeper.* And it's everything. So amazing, I have no words. Only sounds I didn't know I could make. And suddenly, I'm coming, hard and fast. He follows me, growling out my name as his face falls into my chest and he swears out hard and long. He sucks my nipple into his mouth and chuckles. "That was . . ."

"Yeah."

"It's never . . ."

"I know."

His head falls back, and his eyes find mine, a lazy, dopey grin on his face. "How is it possible that it keeps getting better? That's not possible, is it? Because if it is, eventually my brain will short-circuit for good and I'll be a victim of sex-crazed madness."

"Sounds like that epidemic has already struck the majority of the male population."

"Har, har." He leans in and kisses me. "Can we stay like this for the rest of the day? With me inside you?"

I open my mouth to respond with something cheeky when my phone rings. I scramble off of him, in case it's Justin, but it's Anthony Conti's attorney again. I swipe my finger across the screen to answer and then listen to what the man has to say. The conversation doesn't last that long, though looking at Maddox's expression you'd think he was aging by the second.

"Okay. Thank you," I say as I disconnect the call and slip my phone back into my purse.

"What? Who was that?"

"Conti's lawyer."

"And?"

"And tomorrow morning we need to go back to Vegas."

EPILOGUE

Three years later

MADDOX

ONCE UPON A TIME, there was a beautiful girl who was unfortunately born into an ugly world. For years, she struggled, cast down at
the hands of her cruel mother who cared nothing for her. But the
beautiful girl, Isabel, saw beyond the ugly of her world. She was loyal.
She was loving. She was a bright light in the darkness. And it's that
radiance that eventually caught the eye of an evil, hideous monster.

A monster who ruled his kingdom with an iron fist.

A monster who stole the beautiful Isabel from her mother and
made her his own.

Time passed as the darkness grew heavier, engulfing the girl's—
who was now a woman—life. This evil, hideous monster with all his
vicious ways, forced the beautiful Isabel to do his nefarious bidding.
To sacrifice and toil, forever under his thumb without hope of escape.

Despite his ruthlessness and depravity, he was unable to extinguish Isabel's light, her resiliency, or her determination. Nor could he extinguish her desire to one day destroy the evil, hideous monster.

You see, the monster had one weakness. He coveted his beautiful Isabel above all else. Above common sense and reason. And it was with that knowledge that the woman began to plot. Isabel was smart. She was brave. She was patient. But best of all, she met the gorgeous, strong, cunning, and oh-so-sexy prince who swept in and saved the beautiful damsel.

Oh wait, that's not how this goes.

No, Isabel took matters into her own hands, fighting the monster head-on. And as with all monsters who fall in love with smart, beautiful women, she became his demise.

Peace was finally restored to the land. The monster had been defeated. And the beautiful Isabel married the gorgeous, strong, cunning, and oh-so-sexy prince.

Except, that last part hasn't happened yet.

After Isabel and I returned to Vegas from Connecticut, everything changed for her. Anthony Conti had named Isabel Bogart as his sole heir. It was a nightmare. First off, the Feds were crawling all through his books and businesses. Second, every person Conti had ever wronged—which was a list longer than my dick—was looking for a piece of that action. Third, once news spread around that she was his heir, the world wanted a piece of her.

Society glorifies the mob's villainy when the reality is something else entirely.

That's pretty much what Isabel came out and said. She was tired of being hounded. She was tired of having to repeatedly explain herself and her relationship with the deceased Anthony Conti. And I think it's already been established that my girl has a temper when challenged.

She held a press conference where she told her side of things. Once that part was done, she answered each and every question thrown her way, including her plans for Conti's estate. Conti, for all his shit, actually kept very detailed accounts of his business transactions, even his non-legitimate ones. It wasn't exactly difficult to figure out how everything should be divvied up.

She sold off his house and used that money to pay back people he had wronged financially. She gave Infinity to Carla and distributed his other clubs and various businesses to the parties she felt were owed them. As for The Conti Hotel and Casino, well, that was slightly more difficult. Jake didn't want it. Three Turner Hotels on the Strip was enough. Isabel entertained offers and eventually sold it for an insane amount of money.

Over the years, she's done a lot with that money.

She used it to go to college, to travel, to get Justin whatever he needed, and she's donated to more charities than I ever knew existed. Justin is finishing up his freshman year at Stanford. He and Izzy talk on the phone a few times a week and are closer than ever. Justin's name was never mentioned in relation to Conti's. Both decided to keep him as far removed from that as possible.

As for Isabel, she is just about ready to graduate college—the smart little overachiever did it in three years instead of four—and then her plan is to start her Master's in the education program this fall. She still wants to be a teacher, which I think is awesome. We've been living together pretty much from the moment we returned three years ago, and though the woman continues to challenge me at every turn, I wouldn't change our life together.

Well, I'd change one thing.

I've been patiently biding my time until Starshine got just a little older and things fully settled down. Until it was the absolute perfect moment. And in case you're not quick on the uptake, that's now. Because for Isabel's spring break, I flew us out to Savannah. We came to visit my mom and my sisters. Isabel has gotten very close with all of them, and as such, so have I.

After I lost Kim, I stayed away. Not just from Savannah, but from my family. I joined the Army and then I got myself going in Vegas. I just couldn't face this place or my family. Whether that was wrong or right, it was how I coped. How I made it through.

But now, I'm ready to rewrite my memories of this place.

Of this beach.

The rising sun casts off the most outrageous kaleidoscope of colors. Shades of blue, pink, orange, and purple reflect off the few stray clouds and the choppy dark waters of the Atlantic. The air is mild, and the wind is cool, coating us in a salty brine as it whips past us. Isabel is holding my hand, staring out at the show as we walk the beach. While I've been planning to get down on one knee and finally make her mine forever, she's been off. Not just today, but since before we arrived in Georgia.

She's quieter than usual. Distant. And whenever I ask her about it, she just blows me off. Claims she's tired or stressed out with end-of-year projects in school. But I don't think that's it. So instead of getting down on one knee, I ask, "Are you still happy being with me?"

"What?" She stops walking and I step in front of her, facing her. The wind is starting to pick up off the water, blowing her hair into her face. Releasing my hand, she wraps it up, tucking it behind her ear and around her back. But after she's done that, she doesn't retake my hand. "Why would you ask that?"

That's not a yes.

"Because you've been pulling away from me."

"I have not."

"You have, too."

She puffs out a breath, turning back to the sunrise and away from me. My heart starts to pound as she falls silent. I can't take my eyes off her. Off the way her dark hair flies back behind her. Off the way the explosion of light dances across her creamy skin. She's so beautiful it hurts, and I can't help but feel like I'm losing her.

"I'm sorry," she starts after a long moment. "This is not how I wanted to do this. Not here anyway. Not while visiting your family."

Isabel pivots back to me, her expression grave. Nervous.

I reach out and take her hand again, because I have to touch her.

But it's not enough, so I pull her toward me and into my arms. She comes freely, falls into me, but not fully. There's hesitation in the way her body melds to mine.

"Just tell me," I whisper, kissing her hair, breathing in her scent. If she's ending this, I'm going to change her mind. We're happy. At least, I thought we were. I'm happy. Fuck, I've never been so goddamn happy. And I do everything I can think of to make her as happy, so what the hell is going on?

"Maddox," she sighs my name like it hurts her to say it. "I don't know how—"

"No," I interrupt before she can continue. "You're not ending this, Izzy. Whatever you're upset or unhappy with, we can fix. I'll do whatever I have to do." I cup her face and draw her gaze up to mine, staring beseechingly into her eyes. "Don't do this. Don't end it."

She rolls her eyes at me, shaking her head. "I'm not ending this you big, dumb ox. I'm pregnant."

"Pregnant?"

She nods like I'm a moron for not figuring this out sooner. *Pregnant?*

"We're careful."

She stares at me as if I have two heads. "No, we're not." Then she laughs. Why is she laughing? "We have tons of sex. And about forty percent of that is without anything around that big dick of yours."

She's right. We have lots of sex without the glove, and I do have a big dick.

"Most of the time we're too impatient to stop and find one, or we're having a naughty quickie in a place where there are no condoms."

I sigh. And I kinda smile, too, but I'm trying to hold it in, because she's not smiling, and she'll kick my ass for being so excited when she's not. A baby. My baby. That's . . .

"I think I have to marry you."

She shakes her head adamantly, stepping back out of my grip and crossing her arms over her chest. There are people walking the beach all around us, taking in the natural symphony of light, but Isabel doesn't seem to notice them. She's gearing up to fight with me, and wow, just how stunning is she when she's mad at me while carrying my child?

"Absolutely not," she yells. "That's so damn lame. I am not marrying a man because he knocked me up. There is no obligation here, Maddox. I don't need your money or your time. I don't need anything from you. You've already donated one tiny sperm. Thanks. I'll be sure to send you a tax deduction form for your efforts."

This is why this woman drives me nuts. It's why I want to both kill her and fuck her. It's why I'm absolutely fucking insanely in love with her. "It's my baby, too, Izzy. *Our* baby," I remind her because I think she might have forgotten. It's the hormones. We'll blame the hormones. But really, I think she just needs me to be a man. *Her* man. So, I take a step toward her. I drop to my knees and press my lips to her flat belly. Then I look up into those dark depths and say, "I love you. I want you. And I want our baby."

"You're such an asshole. I'm supposed to start my Master's program this fall."

Right. Now it all makes sense. "Baby, we'll do whatever we have to do to get you to finish your Master's. I promise. Whatever I have to do for you and the baby, I'll do. Happily. Joyously. With a big, stupid, sleep-deprived smile on my face."

Those big, beautiful dark eyes that hardly ever cry despite the hard and heavy shit her world once brought shine with tears. They shed tear after tear as she stares incredulously down at me. "You will?"

I nod.

"And as for marrying you, well, you can fight me all you want, but . . ." I pull out the ring I've had tucked away in my pocket for the last few weeks, just waiting for the right moment. "I'm still gonna ask."

Her mouth pops open in the most adorable display of surprise.

"Isabel, I had this whole thing planned out. All kinds of romantic, flowery words. But the simple truth is, I love you. You're my heart and my soul." I press my hand to her chest, right over her pounding heart, and then I drag it lower, over her belly with my baby growing inside it. "My home. I don't have a forever without you in it. Without our baby and our future babies in it. Marry me?"

She blinks down at me. "Yes. I'll marry you." She laughs as more of those pretty tears fall. "Of course, I'll marry you."

"Hell yeah!" I stand, scooping her up into my arms and kissing the hell out of her just as the last of the sun fully rises from the ocean.

This woman . . . She's the best thing ever. The high. The ride. The deep dive.

And I get to have a baby with her.

Marry her.

"Say it," I whisper against her lips, making her grin as her eyes open, staring straight into mine.

"No."

"Such a stubborn brat." I spank her ass in front of God and everyone. "Tell me."

She laughs, smiling so big. This is the smile. The one I love on her the most. The one that tells me absolutely everything I'll ever need to know. "I love you, Maddox Sinclair. Where you end, I begin. There is no me without you."

"Us," I correct. "Now we're an us."

***THE End

Thank you so much for reading Catching Sin! If you liked Maddox and Isabel, you'll love Gavin's story Darkest Sin!

Love billionaire romance? Check out my Start Again series! You can read chapter 1 of that book after the end of book note!

Please, if you enjoyed it, leave me a review! Sign up for my newsletter to get all of my latest book updates!

ALSO BY J. SAMAN

Wild Minds Duet:

Love to Hate Her

Hate to Love Him

Crazy to Love You

Love to Tempt You

The Edge Series:

The Edge of Temptation

The Edge of Forever

The Edge of Reason

Start Again Series:

Start Again

Start Over

Start With Me

Las Vegas Sin Series:

Touching Sin

Catching Sin

Darkest Sin

Standalones:

Just One Kiss

Love Rewritten

Beautiful Potential

Reckless Love

Forward - FREE

END OF BOOK NOTE

For those of you who have read my books before, you know this is the part where I sort of unleash my inner crazy and babble on about the book. This story... It fucking broke me to write.

It started out completely different. I had this whole, pop star whose secret father was this mob boss and Maddox owed him a favor and he cashed it in to find the guy who was stalking her. Yawn. It bored me to tears. And I felt like it had been done. This might have been done too, but Isabel felt different to me. Maddox too I guess.

Once I got going in this story, I couldn't stop writing it. Like, I kept writing scene after scene and then had to cut it back because otherwise, this book would have been like 500 pages. I couldn't get enough of Maddox and Isabel together. They might (and that's a super strong might) be my favorite couple to date.

I'm slowly working on Gavin's story. I think I know who he is, but since he's a man of many faces I need to figure out his angle perfectly before I fully do his thing. I'm also working on a few other stories because I'll be honest, writing suspense stuff is not my strong suit and I usually need a mental break after it and write something more me.

Thank you to everyone who helped me with this story. All the betas I use and my editors and the gorgeous people in my fan room who kept encouraging me. My family most of all who had to deal with my moody ass when I labored over a scene or how things were going down or the first draft that I wanted to throw across the house.

Okay, enough babbling. If you liked this book, I'd appreciate a review. Those are tremendous and I covet each one. Thank you again for reading my books. You have no idea what it means to me to be able to do this - it's truly a dream come true. One I cannot live without you!

Come stalk me. Join my fan room, J. Saman's Radtastic Readers on Facebook. We have a lot of fun in there. Also, check out me out on Facebook and Instagram. Thanks so much! Keep reading for 1st chapters of The Edge of Temptation and Touching Sin. LOVE YOU ALL! XO

START AGAIN

Chapter 1

Kate

Freshly baked zucchini bread fills the air with the scent of cinnamon and chocolate. It should be comforting, but it's not. Partially because comfort and I haven't been on speaking terms for quite a while, and partially because I have the unhappy task of trying to speak to my mother about something important this morning.

Never a pleasant thing.

The couch cushion sinks beneath me as I shift my position to cross my legs, taking my can of Diet Coke with me. I haven't slept much this week. Not that I've been sleeping all that great over the last two years, but it had been better until now. My fingers go up to the pendant hanging off my neck, touching it gently, a reflex when I think about them.

I should be in a better place than I am.

At least that's what my therapist says. She hasn't been too pleased with my progress to date. Every time she mentions something along those lines in her perfectly crafted, psychobabble way, I remind her—

far less subtly—that I lost my reason for living, so she should just back the fuck off. I think the fact that I haven't offed myself should be considered a major accomplishment.

Apparently it's not.

I'm done with therapy.

I made the changes I had to, and the rest is just a matter of getting through each day.

But now those changes are no longer enough. I don't see them in my car or my tiny studio apartment, because they were never in either of those places. I don't even see them at work, because I switched hospitals too.

But I see them everywhere else.

I see them in the grocery store, at the movies, in the coffee shop, and walking around town. Everywhere. And it's killing me. Little by little. Day by day.

It's killing me.

And even though I make that daily promise that today won't be the day I kill myself and end my misery, it's happening anyway.

I can feel it, and I need to do something. I need to get out of here. Away from the place that I spent my entire life with Eric, and then the last few years with Maggie.

So I'm sitting on my mother's couch, nursing my Diet Coke and avoiding the guilt zucchini bread in front of me. Her small frame is sitting across from me in her hideous floral chair, patiently waiting for me to say something. Here goes.

"I'm leaving, Mom."

"Leaving?" she asks, her dark blonde eyebrows raising up to her hairline. "But you just got here."

I sigh. This isn't going to be fun. "No, Mom. I mean, I'm moving away. Leaving town."

She leans forward with a scowl etched on her wrinkle-free surgically enhanced face. "Where do you intend to move to? You know your problems will follow you wherever you go."

Right. And *that's* why I hate talking to my mother.

Couldn't she have just wished me well? Given me some modicum of encouragement?

"I don't know where I'm going," I say, ignoring her jab. "I haven't decided yet."

"Well," she leans back, crossing her arms and legs, essentially dismissing the idea. "Be sure to let me know when you figure it out."

Now it's my turn to lean forward. "Actually, I plan to just get in the car and drive around the country until I find a place that speaks to me."

"That's absurd," she shakes her head, her lips pursing off to the side. "You can't just drive across the country—" Her arm sweeps out in front of her toward the window, before folding it across her chest again. "—by yourself, until something *speaks* to you." Her head is shaking back and forth, her blonde bob swinging around her shoulders. "It's not safe for a young woman to go off on her own with no plan or agenda. No, Kate. No." She points her finger at me as if that makes it final.

"Mom, I'm twenty-seven years old. I am perfectly capable of not only making my own decisions, but I don't need your permission."

Yeah, I'm trying to hold firm, but this woman has always had a way of reducing me to a weak puddle of coward.

"I'm going," I huff out, setting my can on the coaster and rubbing my hands up and down my face. "I need this, Mom," I confess, my hands still covering my eyes. I hate speaking to my mother this way. She's never been loving or nurturing, which makes emotional confessions that much harder. "I'm drowning here, and I can't find my way back."

She scoffs. Actually freaking scoffs at me. "That's ridiculous. You'll be fine. You just need to get yourself back out there."

I suck in a deep breath, holding it tight in my lungs before I let it out and explode at her. Because I'm *this* close.

Instead, I sit back, squaring my shoulders and looking her dead in the eyes. The same blue as mine.

"I'm going, Mom. In two days. I've given up my apartment,

packed my things, and that's it." I stand up, glaring back at her narrowed eyes, wishing I had her love and support because I desperately need both right now. "I was just letting you know."

I take two steps toward the front door before she calls out to me. "Wait," she sighs, sounding just a little defeated and a lot annoyed. "Fine."

I turn back to her, but don't bother to sit again.

"I get it. You're a grown woman and you're leaving." She waves a dismissive hand. "I can't stop you." She stands now, walking toward me and placing her hands on my shoulders. "If I suggest something, will you listen?"

"Maybe," I say hesitantly. I can see the wheels spinning in her eyes, and that's hardly ever a good thing.

"Well," and then she laughs lightly. "This is just too darling for words." She giggles like she's just had the most brilliant idea. "So I was talking to Jessica Grant this morning. You remember her." I shake my head to her statement, but she just continues. "You met her when you were six, at their house outside of Philadelphia. She was my sorority sister in college." Another head shake. "Whatever." She waves me off like it's not important. "She was telling me how her son is moving across the country to Seattle for a new job that he starts next month."

"And your point is?" I tilt my head at her because I have a bad feeling about where this is headed.

"My point is," she's smiling huge now, "that he doesn't like to fly and was debating renting a car to drive out there. Jessica was against this, naturally, but now that I know you're going off into the wind," she points at me, "*you* can take him."

"Um. No."

"Katherine, he's a nice young man, and since you don't have a destination picked out, this is perfect."

"Mom, I'm not driving a stranger across the country." I'm trying to be firm here, but she's not listening. She's already decided on this, and I can feel her itching to run over to the phone to tell this Jessica woman—whom I'm certain I've never met—about the ride I'm giving her son.

"You know him. I just told you," she huffs, annoyed that she has to repeat herself. "You met him when you were six."

"Right. Let me amend that then. I'm not driving across the country with a man I don't *remember*," I widen my eyes for emphasis.

"You are. It's the friendly thing to do, and if you're going to be traveling in a car across this godforsaken country, it's much safer if you do it with a man. I won't take no for an answer, young lady."

"Mom. No," I stomp my foot like a small child because that's how she makes me feel.

"It's done." She's smiling like she just won. "I'm calling Jessica now and telling her that you'll pick him up in three days. His name is Ryan and he's a very nice young man. A computer whiz or something."

Have I mentioned that my mother is mad old-school? Like she thinks that this is the 1950s or something. Even her furnishings are reminiscent of that era, and not in a cool mid-century modern way, but in a very floral, ugly, grandmotherly way.

"Mom. I don't feel comfortable driving with a man I don't know for several weeks." It's my last ditch effort. "Please understand that I can't take him."

"Katherine," she grabs my shoulders again, leveling me with her most serious motherly expression. "If you don't travel with him, then I will be calling you eight times a day *at least* to make sure you're safe." She means it. *Shit.* She just got me, and judging by her smug expression, she knows it.

"Fine," I huff out, feeling like such an epic failure. If this were a few years ago, she never would have won. Losing Eric and Maggie has taken all the fight out of me.

Now I'm a spineless zombie.

"I have to go finish packing. Text me his info." I lean forward to kiss her cheek, which she accepts stiffly. Maybe this guy won't want to drive with me any more than I want to drive with him.

"I'm going to call Jessica now." She's bubbly sunshine, and now all I want to do is go home and crawl back into bed for the rest of the day.

And that's exactly what I do. I go home, shut off all the lights and close the curtains, making the small apartment as dark as it's going to get for this time of day. I hate this bed. I hate this apartment. I hate this life. So I sleep, ignoring the phone calls and chimes to indicate voicemails and text messages.

I wake an untold amount of time later to the familiar feeling of a vise wrapped around my chest. I dreamt of them again. Of the time that Eric and I took Maggie to the playground and she went down the slide by herself for the first time. The look of pride and triumph in her eyes is something I will never forget.

I drive by that park every day on my way to work. Followed by the ice cream store that we went to after the park. It's the same place that Eric took me for our first date when we were twelve and then proposed to me nine years later.

It's the same place they were on their way to the night of the car accident.

That's why I need to get out of here.

I will never be able to move forward if my grief is constantly holding me back—at least that's what my therapist says. In my gut, I know I'm running away. I know this, but I have to.

I miss them too much. I can't take it anymore.

Instead of getting easier, it's getting harder, and I find I have to remind myself of my morning promise more and more throughout the day.

I don't want to die. I just don't want to live without them.

I don't know *how* to live without them.

Eric and I met when we were twelve; when he moved into the neighborhood with his parents and older sister. And even though we were impossibly young, I think I fell in love with him instantly. He married me ten years later on the anniversary of our first date, and then a year later, we had Maggie.

Life was perfect.

We were happy.

Rolling over, I grab my phone and see that I have two text messages and one missed call, with a voicemail from an unknown number. I check the texts first and see that one is from Maya and one is from Ellie.

Ellie and I used to be best friends, and then the accident happened. She couldn't handle my grief. I think it made her uncomfortable. And I get that. Grief makes people uncomfortable.

Deal with it!

It's not exactly like I am having the fucking time of my life.

She completely bailed on me without a word, and any time I run into her, I get the pity eyes.

Let me tell you, there isn't much worse than those, because no one wants pity. Someone to listen? Sure. A shoulder to cry on? Absolutely. But pity is the worst, and that's all I get from her. That and her talking about me behind my back. So when her text says, *Heard you're moving away. I think that's a smart idea. Good luck with your life,* I don't respond. I mean, what can I say to that anyway? Thanks? Yeah, no.

Maya, on the other hand, is a good friend. One of the few who can tolerate being around me. Even my nursing friends can't handle it. People talk shit about you when you're happy, but they cannot stand you when you're miserable. They treat you like it's contagious.

I need out of this place, like yesterday.

Maya wrote that she's bringing over wine tonight. I knew I liked that girl for a reason.

Finally, I get to the missed call. I hit the button to listen to the voice message and put the phone on speaker so I don't have to move my position to hear it. An unknown male voice comes out of the speaker.

"Hi, I hope this is Katie Taylor—" No one has called me Katie since I was a child. Which suddenly gets me thinking. "My mother, Jessica Grant, gave me your number. She said that according to your mother, you offered to drive me out to Seattle. I have no idea if my mother was fucking with me or not—she can be a bitch like that—but if she wasn't, please give me a ring back. If she was, then I'm sorry to have bother you. Later."

And then he hangs up, and I have to just laugh at that.

This guy actually called his mother a bitch. Who says that on a voice message to a complete stranger? Then there's the fact that he wants me to call him back if I'm willing to drive him. That means he's interested in riding with me.

I don't exactly know what to do with that.

I was sorta banking on him not being into it.

The way I see it, I have two choices.

Choice one: Call this guy back, offer him a ride, and give it a shot.

Choice two: Don't call him back and deal with my mother incessantly calling me all the time—which she will.

My fingers drag up to the pendant resting flat against my sternum. I really don't have a choice, do I? I'll go insane with my mother calling me, and maybe I can just drop this guy off in Seattle and then be off on my own way. Or maybe I'll make him crazy after a day and he'll run for the hills.

Crap.

I hit his number before I can talk myself out of it, and the phone rings exactly three times before his voice fills my ear. "Katie," he says like we're old friends.

"Yeah, um. Is this Ryan?"

He chuckles softly into the phone. "Obviously it is, since you called me and I picked up using your name."

"Right." I close my eyes feeling just a little stupid and annoyed. *So* not digging the sarcasm. "And it's just Kate. I haven't been Katie since I was a child."

"Sure. So was my mother fucking with me or what?"

"Can I ask you something?" I throw my arm over my eyes because this has to be the oddest conversation of my life, and we're only a minute into it.

"Shoot." His tone is light and casual.

"Is driving across the country with a complete stranger something you're actually interested in doing?"

Another chuckle rumbles through the phone. "You're not a stranger, Katie. We met once before. I was ten, and you were six."

I sigh. "It's Kate, and I realize that, according to my mother, we've met before, but that was twenty-one years ago, and I have no memory of you."

"Well, I remember you, so to me that doesn't make you a stranger."

Okay, we're going around in circles here. This guy is already pissing me off; no way I could tolerate being in a car with him for several days on end.

"Is that your way of saying yes?"

"Sure," he says this like it's the easiest thing in the world. "Why the hell not? Beats the shit out of renting a car and going solo."

"But you don't even know me," I'm practically pleading now. Why am I the only one who thinks that this idea is insanity?

"My mother told me a little about you, but she got that from your mother, so I'm going to reserve judgment since my mother is batshit crazy, and I'm assuming yours is as well." I have no response for that. "Listen. I don't have to be in Seattle for another four weeks. I'm up for a road trip if you are. Come to Philadelphia and meet me. If you can't stand me, then no hard feelings and we'll go our own way. Sound like a plan?"

I sigh. He makes some sense.

"I can do that. Text me your address, and I'll be there in three days."

"Awesome. Later." He hangs up, and I toss my phone on the bed beside me, wondering what the hell I just got myself into.

Want to find out what happens with Kate and Ryan? Get your copy of START AGAIN now to get lost in the world of billionaires and second chance romance!

CHAPTER 1 OF THE EDGE OF TEMPTATION

BLURB:

It starts out as a bet.

A way to forget about my latest in a string of bad relationships and move on. I know it's a mistake. My head and heart are just not into the game. Especially when I have a terrible knack for picking the wrong men.

Then I see him.

The gorgeous man in the dark suit, drowning his sorrows in a glass of scotch is only supposed to be one night of fun. No strings. Zero expectations. No one gets hurts. Sounds perfect, right?

And when I wake up alone the next morning, it appears I've gotten everything I was after. That is until I find the shiny gold cuff-links he left behind. Oh, and discover that he's my new boss.

With our ugly pasts still heavy on our shoulders, it should be easy to stay away from each other. To be one hundred percent professional. To ignore the way his heated glances set my skin ablaze, even from across the room. Yep. Impervious is my new middle name.

Even if tempting is his...

Grab your copy of The Edge of Temptation today and keep reading to meet the sexy doctor who turns Halle's world upside down!

Halle

"No," I reply emphatically, hoping my tone is stronger than my disposition. "I'm not doing it. Absolutely not. Just no." I point my finger for emphasis, but I don't think the gesture is getting me anywhere. Rina just stares at me, the tip of her finger gliding along the lip of her martini glass.

"You're smiling. If you don't want to do this, then why are you smiling?"

I sigh. She's right. I am smiling. But only because it's so ridiculous. In all the years she's known me, I've never hit on a total stranger. I don't think I'd have any idea how to even do that. And honestly, I'm just not in the right frame of mind to put in the effort. "It's funny, that's all." I shrug, playing it off. It's really not funny. The word terrifying comes closer. "But my answer is still no."

"It's been, what?" Margot chimes in, her gaze flicking between Rina, Aria, and me like she's actually trying to figure this out. She's not. I know where she's going with this and it's fucking rhetorical. "A month?"

See? I told you.

"You broke up with Matt a month ago. And you can't play it off like you're all upset over it, because we know you're not."

"Who says I'm not upset?" I furrow my eyebrows, feigning incredulous, but I can't quite meet their eyes. "I was with him for two years."

But she's right. I'm not upset about Matt. I just don't have the desire to hit on some random dude at some random bar in the South End of Boston.

"Two *useless* years," Rina persists with a roll of her blue eyes before taking a sip of her appletini. She sets her glass down, leaning her small frame back in her chair as she crosses her arms over her chest and purses her lips like she's pissed off on my behalf. "The guy was a freaking asshole."

"And a criminal," Aria adds, tipping back her fancy glass and finishing off the last of her dirty martini, complete with olive. She chews on it slowly, quirking a pointed eyebrow at me. "The cocksucker repeatedly ignored you so he could defraud people."

"All true." I can't even deny it. My ex was a black-hat hacker. And while that might sound all hot and sexy in a mysterious, dangerous way, it isn't. The piece of shit stole credit card numbers, and not only used them for himself but sold them on the dark web. He was also one of those hacktivists who got his rocks off by working with other degenerate assholes to try and bring down various companies and websites.

In my defense, I didn't know what he was up to until the FBI came into my place of work, hauled me downtown, and interviewed me for hours. I was so embarrassed, I could hardly show my face at work again. Not only that, but everyone was talking about me. Either with pity or suspicion in their eyes, like I was a criminal right along with him.

Matt had a regular job as a red-team specialist—legit hackers who are paid by companies to go in and try to penetrate their systems. I assumed all that time he spent on his computer at night was him working hard to get ahead. At least that was his perpetual excuse when challenged.

Nothing makes you feel more naïve than discovering the man you had been engaged to is actually a criminal who was stealing from people. And committing said thefts while living with you.

I looked up one of the people the FBI had mentioned in relation to Matt's criminal activities. The woman had a weird name that stuck out to me for me some reason, and when I found her, I learned she was a widow with three grandchildren, a son in the military, and was a recently retired nurse. It made me sick to my stomach. Still does when I think about it.

I told the FBI everything I knew, which was nothing. I explained that I had ended things with Matt three days prior to them arresting him. Pure coincidence. I was fed up with the monotony of our relationship. Of being engaged and never discussing or planning our wedding. Of living with someone I never saw because he was always locked away in his office, too preoccupied with his computer to pay me even an ounce of attention. But really, deep down, I knew I wasn't in love with him anymore.

I didn't even shed a tear over our breakup. In fact, I was more relieved than anything. I knew I had dodged a bullet getting out when I did.

And then the FBI showed up.

"I ended it with him. *Before* I knew he was a total and complete loser," I tack on, feeling more defensive about the situation than I care to admit. Shifting my weight on my uncomfortable wooden chair, I cross my legs at the knee and stare sightlessly out into the bar.

"And we applaud you for that," Rina says, nudging Margot and then Aria in the shoulders, forcing them to concur. "It was the absolute right thing to do. But you've been miserable and mopey and very . . ."

"Anti-men," Margot finishes for her, tossing back her lemon drop shot with disturbing exuberance. I think that's number three for her already, which means it could be a long night. Margot has yet to learn the art of moderation.

"Right." Aria nods exaggeratedly at Margot like she just hit the nail on the head, tossing her messy dark curls over her shoulders before twisting them up into something that resembles a bun. "Anti-men. I'm not saying you need to date anyone here. You don't even have to go home with them. Just let them buy you a drink. Have a normal conversation with a normal guy."

I scoff. "And you think I'll find one of those in here?" I splay my arms out wide, waving them around. All these men look like players.

They're in groups with other men, smacking at each other and pointing at the various women who walk in. They're clearly rating them. And if a woman just so happens to pass by, they blatantly turn and stare at her ass.

This is a hookup bar. All dark mood lighting, annoying, trendy house music in the background and uncomfortable seating. The kind designed to have you standing all night before you take someone home. And now I understand why my very attentive friends brought me here. It's not our usual go-to place.

"It's like high school or a frat house in here. And definitely not in a good way. I bet all these guys bathed in Axe body spray, gelled up their hair and left their mother's basement to come here and find a 'chick to bang.'" I put air quotes around those words. I have zero interest in being part of that scheme.

"Well . . ." Rina's voice drifts off, scanning the room desperately. "I know I can find you someone worthy."

"Don't waste your brain function. I'm still not interested." I roll my eyes dramatically and finish off my drink, slamming the glass down on the table with a bit more force than I intend. *Oops.* Whatever. I'm extremely satisfied with my anti-men status. Because that's exactly what I am—anti-men—and I'm discovering I'm unrepentant about it. In fact, I think it's a fantastic way to be when you rack up one loser after another the way I have. Like a form of self-preservation.

I've never had a good track record. Even before Matt, I had a knack for picking the wrong guys. My high school boyfriend ended up being gay. I handed him my V-card shortly before he dropped that bomb on me, though he swore I didn't turn him gay. He promised he was like that prior to the sex. In college, I dated two guys somewhat seriously. The first one cheated on me for months before I found out, and the second one was way more into his video games than he was me. I think he also had a secret cocaine problem because he'd stay up all night gaming like a fiend. I had given up on men for a while—are you seeing a trend here?—and then in my final year of graduate school, Matt came along. Need I say more? So as far as I'm concerned, men can all go screw themselves. Because they sure as hell aren't gonna screw me!

"You can stop searching now, Rina." This is getting pathetic. "I have a vibrator. What else does a girl need?" All three pause their search to examine me and I realize I said that out loud. I blush at that, but it's true, so I just shrug a shoulder and fold my arms defiantly across my chest. "I don't need a sextervention. If anything, I need to avoid the male species like the plague they are."

They dismiss me immediately, their cause to find me a "normal" male to talk to outweighing my antagonism. And really, if it's taking this long to find someone then the pickings must really be slim here. I move to flag down the waitress to order another round when Margot points to the far corner.

"There." The tenacious little bug is gleaming like she just struck oil in her backyard. "That guy. He's freaking hot as holy sin and he's alone. He even looks sad, which means he needs a friend."

"Or he wants to be left alone to his drinking," I mumble, wishing I had another drink in my hand so I could focus on something other than my friends obsessively staring at some random creep. *Where the hell is that waitress?*

"Maybe," Aria muses thoughtfully as she observes the man across the bar, tapping her bottom lip with her finger. Her hands are covered in splotches of multicolored paint. As is her black shirt, now that I look closer. "Or maybe he's just had a crappy day. He looks so sad, Halle." She nods like it's all coming together for her as she makes frowny puppy dog eyes at me. "So very sad. Go over and see if he wants company. Cheer him up."

"You'd be doing a public service," Rina agrees. "Men that good-looking should never be sad."

I roll my eyes at that. "You think a blowjob would do it, or should I offer him crazy, kinky sex to cheer him up? I still have that domination-for-beginners playset I picked up at Angela's bachelorette party. Hasn't even been cracked open."

Aria tilts her head like she's actually considering this. "That level of kink might scare him off for the first time. And I wouldn't give him head unless he goes down on you first."

Jesus, I'm not drunk enough for this. "Or he's a total asshole who just fucked his girlfriend's best friend," I protest, my voice rising an octave with my objection. I sit up straight, desperate to make my point clear. "Or he's about to go to prison because he hacks women into tiny bits with a machete before he eats them. Either way, I'm. Not. Interested."

"God," Margot snorts, twirling her chestnut hair as she leans back in her chair and levels me with an unimpressed gaze. "Dramatic much? He wouldn't be out on bail if that were the case. But seriously, that's like crazy psycho shit, and that guy does not say crazy psycho. He says crave-worthy and yummy and 'I hand out orgasms like candy on Halloween.'"

"Methinks the lady doth protest too much," Aria says with a knowing smile and a wink.

She swivels her head to check him out again and licks her lips reflexively. I haven't bothered to peek yet because my back is to him and I hate that I'm curious. All three ladies are eyeing him with unfettered appreciation and obvious lust. Their tastes in men differ tremendously, which indicates this guy probably is hot. I shouldn't be tempted. I really shouldn't be. I'm asking for a world of trouble or hurt or legal fees. So why am I finding the idea of a one-nighter with a total stranger growing on me?

I've never been that girl before. But maybe they're right? Maybe a one-nighter with a random guy is just the ticket to wipe out my past of bad choices in men and make a fresh start? I don't even know if that makes sense since a one-nighter is the antithesis of a smart choice. But my libido is taking over for my brain and now I'm starting to rationalize, possibly even encourage. I need to stop this now.

"He's gay. Hot men are always gay. Or assholes. Or criminals. Or cheaters. Or just generally suck at life."

"You've had some bad luck, is all. Look at Oliver. He's good-looking, sweet, loving, and not an asshole. Or a criminal. And he likes you. You could date him."

Reaching over, I steal Rina's cocktail. She doesn't stop me or even seem to register the action. I stare at her with narrowed eyes over the rim of her glass as I slurp down about half of it in one gulp. "I'm not dating your brother, Rina. That's weird and begging for drama. You and I are best friends."

She sighs and then I sigh because I'm being a bitch and I don't mean to be. I like her brother. He is all of those things she just mentioned, minus the liking me part. But if things went bad between us, which they inherently would, it would cost me one of my most important friendships. And that's not a risk I'm willing to take. Plus, unbeknownst to Rina, Oliver is one of the biggest players in the greater Boston area.

"I'm just saying not all men are bad," Rina continues, and I shake my head. "We'll buy your drinks for a month if you go talk to this guy," she offers hastily, trying to close the deal.

Margot glances over at her with furrowed eyebrows, a bit surprised by that declaration, but she quickly comes around with an indifferent shrug. Aria smiles, liking that idea. Then again, money is not Aria's problem. "Most definitely," she agrees. "Go. Let a stranger touch your lady parts. You're waxed and shaved and looking hot. Let someone take advantage of that."

"And if he shoots me down?"

"You don't have to sleep with him," Rina reminds me. "Or even give him your real name. In fact, tell him nothing real about yourself. It could be like a sexual experiment." I shake my head in exaspera-tion. "We won't bother you about it again," she promises solemnly. "But he won't shoot you down. You look movie star hot tonight."

I can only roll my eyes at that. While I appreciate the sentiment from my loving and supportive friends, being shot down by a total stranger when I'm already feeling emotionally strung out might just do me in. Even if I have no interest in him. But free drinks . . .

Twisting around in my chair, I stare across the crowded bar, probing for a few seconds until I spot the man in the corner. Holy Christmas in Florida, he *is* hot. There is no mistaking that. His hair is light blond, short along the sides and just a bit longer on top. Just long enough that you could grab it and hold on tight while he kisses you. His profile speaks to his straight nose and strong, chiseled, cleanly shaven jaw. I must admit, I do enjoy a bit of stubble on my men, but he makes the lack of beard look so enticing that I don't miss the roughness. He's wearing a suit. A dark suit. More than likely expensive judging by the way it contours to his broad shoulders and the flash of gold on his wrist that I catch in the form of cufflinks.

But the thing that's giving me pause is his anguish. It's radiating off him. His beautiful face is downcast, staring sightlessly into his full glass of something amber. Maybe scotch. Maybe bourbon. It doesn't matter. That expression has purpose. Those eyes have meaning behind them and I doubt he's seeking any sort of company. In fact, I'm positive he'd have no trouble finding any if he were so inclined.

That thought alone makes me stand up without further comment. He's the perfect man to get my friends off my back. He's going to shoot me down in an instant and I won't even take it personally. Well, not too much. I can feel the girls exchanging gleeful smiles, but I figure I'll be back with them in under five minutes, so their misguided enthusiasm is inconsequential. I watch him the entire way across the bar. He doesn't sip at his drink. He just stares blankly into it. That sort of heartbreak makes my stomach churn. This miserable stranger isn't just your typical Saturday night bar dweller looking for a quick hookup.

He's drowning his sorrows.

Miserable Stranger doesn't notice my approach. He doesn't even notice me as I wedge myself in between him and the person seated beside him. And he definitely doesn't notice me as I order myself a dirty martini. I'm close enough to smell him. And damn, it's so freaking good I catch myself wanting to close my eyes and breathe in deeper. Sandalwood? Citrus? Freaking godly man? Who knows. I have no idea what to say to him. In fact, I'm half-tempted to grab my drink and scurry off, but I catch Rina, Margot, and Aria watching vigilantly from across the bar with excited, encouraging smiles. There's no way I can get out of this without at least saying hello.

Especially if I want those bitches to buy me drinks for the next month.

But damn, I'm so stupidly nervous. "Hello," I start, but my voice is weak and shaky, and I have to clear it to get rid of the nervous lilt. Shit. My hands are trembling. Pathetic.

He doesn't look up. Awesome start.

I play it off, staring around the dimly lit bar and taking in all the people enjoying their Saturday night cocktails. It's busy here. Filled with the heat of the city in the summer and lust-infused air. I open my mouth to speak again, when the person seated next to my Miserable Stranger and directly behind me, gets up, shoving their chair inadvertently into my back and launching me forward. Straight into him.

I fly without restraint, practically knocking him over. Not enough to fully push him off his chair—he's too big and strong for that—but it's enough to catch his attention. I see him blink like he's coming back from some distant place. His head tilts up to mine as I right myself, just as my attention is diverted by the man who hit me with his chair.

"I'm so sorry," the man says with a note of panic in his voice, reaching out and grasping my upper arm as if to steady me. "I didn't see you there. Are you okay?"

"Yes, I'm fine." I'm beet red, I know it.

"Did I hurt you?"

Just my pride. "No. Really. I'm good. It was my fault for wedging myself in like this." The stranger who bumped me smiles warmly, before turning back to his girlfriend and leaving the scene of the crime as quickly as possible.

Adjusting my dress and schooling my features, I turn back to my Miserable Stranger, clearing my throat once more as my eyes meet his. "I'm sorry I banged into you . . ." My freaking breath catches in my lungs, making my voice trail off at the end.

Goddamn.

If I thought his profile was something, it's nothing compared to the rest of him. He blinks at me, his eyes widening fractionally as he sits back, crossing his arms over his suit-clad chest and taking me in from head to toe. He hasn't even removed his dark jacket, which seems odd. It's more than warm in here and summer outside.

He sucks in a deep breath as his eyes reach mine again. They're green. But not just any green. Full-on megawatt green. Like thick summer grass green. I can tell that even in the dim lighting of the bar, that's how vivid they are. They're without a doubt the most beautiful eyes I've ever seen.

"That's all right," he says and his thick baritone, with a hint of some sort of accent, is just as impressive as the rest of him. It wraps its way around me like a warm blanket on a cold night. Jesus, has a voice ever affected me like this? Maybe I do need to get out more if I'm reacting to a total stranger like this. "I love it when beautiful women fall all over me."

I like him instantly. Cheesy line and all.

"That happen to you a lot?"

He smirks and the way that crooked grin looks on his face has my heart rate jacking up yet another degree. "Not really. Are you okay? That was quite the tumble."

I nod. I don't want to talk about my less than graceful entrance anymore. "Would you mind if I sit down?" And he thinks about it. Actually freaking hesitates. Just perfect. This is not helping my already frail ego.

I stare at him for a beat, and just as I'm about to raise the white flag and retreat with my dignity in my feet, he swallows hard and shakes his head slowly. Is he saying no I shouldn't sit, or no he doesn't mind? Crap, I can't tell, because his expression is . . . a mess. Like a bizarre concoction of indecision and curiosity and temptation and disgust.

He must note my confusion because in a slow measured tone he clarifies with, "I guess you should probably sit so you don't fall on me again." He blinks, something catching his attention. Glancing past me for the briefest of moments, that smirk returning to his full lips. "I think your friends love the idea."

"Huh?" I sputter before my head whips over my shoulder and I catch Rina, Aria, and Margot standing, watching us with equally exuberant smiles. Margot even freaking waves. Well, that's embarrassing. Now what do I say? "Yeah . . . um." Words fail me, and I sink back into myself. "I'm sorry. I just . . . well, I recently broke up with someone, and my friends won't let me return to the table until I've re-entered the human female race and had a real conversation with a man."

God, this sounds so stupidly pathetic. Even to my own ears. And why did I just admit all of that to him? My face is easily the shade of the dress I'm wearing—and it's bright motherfucking red. He's smirking at me again, which only proves my point. I hate feeling like this. Insecure and inadequate. At least it's better than stupid and clueless. Yeah, that's what I had going on with Matt and this is not who I am. I'm typically far more self-assured.

"I'll just grab my drink and return to my friends."

I pull some cash out of my purse and drop it on the wooden bar. I pause, and he doesn't stop me. My fingers slip around the smooth, long stem of my glass. I want to get the hell out of here, but before I can slide my drink safely toward me and make my hasty, not so glamorous escape, he covers my hand with his and whispers, "No. Stay."

Want to find out what happens next with Jonah and Halle? Grab your copy of The Edge of Temptation Today!

Made in the USA
Coppell, TX
20 April 2022

76817622R00193